Don't Laugh at Fools

DON'T LAUGH AT FOOLS

Mary Minton

CENTURY

LONDON MELBOURNE AUCKLAND JOHANNESBURG

First published in Great Britain in 1988 by
Century Hutchinson Ltd
Brookmount House, 62–65 Chandos Place
London WC2N 4NW

Century Hutchinson South Africa (Pty) Ltd
PO Box 337, Bergvlei, 2012 South Africa

Century Hutchinson Australia Pty Ltd
PO Box 496, 16–22 Church Street, Hawthorn
Victoria 3122, Australia

Century Hutchinson New Zealand Ltd
PO Box 40–086, Glenfield, Auckland 10
New Zealand

ISBN 0 7126 2208 X

Phototypeset by Input Typesetting Ltd, London
Printed and bound in Great Britain by
Anchor Brendon Ltd, Tiptree, Essex

To dear Marjorie Bridge, whose friendship has meant so much to me over the years.

1

'Close the window, Sarah dear,' her father said. 'Your mother is going to have hysterics.'

Isabelle did have hysterics; she often had them. Sarah was never quite sure whether it was all the clocks that ticked and chimed in the house that got on her mother's nerves, or whether it was her father's inventions – or whether she would have been neurotic, anyway.

'Neurotic' was a word often used by Grandmother Frome in connection with her eldest daughter.

'Isabelle was never neurotic until she married Jonathan Torent,' she would say, tight-lipped. Then add if the person had not met Jonathan, 'He's a foreigner – comes from some outlandish country called Finland. Their ways are not ours.'

At these times Sarah fumed, hearing her adored father spoken of in this way.

At first, Sarah had blamed her grandmother for the trouble this evening, but later had to admit that the responsibility was wholly her own.

Her mother had asked her to get some potatoes when she came out of school and take them to her grandmother. But Sarah had called in at her father's shop on the way, and that was fatal. Once she was among the clocks she forgot everything else. She stayed until her father closed the shop and came home with him, and it was not until her mother enquired, 'And what did Gran have to say?' that Sarah remembered her errand. Her hand flew to her mouth.

'Oh, I'm sorry, I forgot to go. I called at the shop, it was the clocks you see, I –'

'Clocks!' Isabelle exclaimed. 'The shop! Inventions! That's all I ever hear. You're to stay away from the shop in future, is that clear?'

Jonathan said in his quiet way, 'No, Isabelle, Sarah will

1

not stay away from the shop. She has a great love of clocks and has a right to know about the working of them.'

Isabelle, looking distraught, insisted that the shop should be out of bounds to their daughter and Jonathan, equally insistent but calm, stated she would come whenever she wanted to, adding, 'I know Sarah did wrong in not going to her grandmother's, but she will not suffer such a drastic punishment for this small misdemeanour.'

That was when Isabelle became hysterical. And Jonathan, as always, was gentle with her. He took her in his arms and stroked her hair.

'Why do you let yourself get so worked up, Isabelle? It's not worth it. Everything can be discussed calmly.'

She laid her head against his shoulder, the hysteria subsiding. Sarah felt a lump come into her throat. She loved her mother almost as much as she loved her father and hated to see her upset. She knew that her parents had a deep love for one another even though her grandmother was fond of telling anyone who would listen how 'incompatible' they were.

'*Wholly* incompatible,' she would declare, her eyes as cold as those of a dead fish. 'Jonathan, *believe it or not*, loves Charlie Chaplin films, barrel organs and the music hall, while Isabelle is steeped in classical music. She comes, of course, from a highly musical family. *My* grandfather was conductor of the biggest opera company of his day!' This was said with a proud lift of the head.

Jonathan said, 'I'll make you a cup of tea, Isabelle,' as he wiped the tears gently from her cheeks. 'I won't be a minute.'

When he had gone from the room Isabelle held out a hand to Sarah. 'I'm sorry I was so cross with you love, but you know what Gran is, so fussy. She knew you were coming and would be looking out for you.'

Sarah flung her arms around her mother. 'I'm sorry, I really am! I can take the potatoes now if you like.'

Isabelle said no, tomorrow morning would do, Gran was not waiting for them.

Tears still lingered in Isabelle's eyes, giving them a lumi-

2

nous look. She had dark, expressive eyes. Her skin was creamy, her hair jet black – from her Spanish ancestors, she once said. Sarah thought her beautiful, and so did many people.

In contrast, Jonathan, who was over six feet tall, was blue-eyed and fair-haired with high cheekbones. He had his admirers, too. Sarah had seen the coy looks some of the women gave him.

Sarah was glad she had taken after her father in her colouring but she would have liked to have been taller. At eleven years old she was quite small. Her brother Victor, on the other hand, was tall at nine years and had inherited his mother's dark looks and her love of music. He was learning to play the piano and, according to his teacher Miss Hedley, was showing great promise. He was out this moment at his music lesson and Sarah was glad of this, too. Victor always went pale when his mother was upset.

In bed that night Sarah lay listening to the four clocks ticking in her room and wondered why her mother had no liking for clocks. She loved them all – the small ones with their busy ticking that seemed to be saying, 'Hurry up, hurry up, there's work to be done', and the larger ones, like the grandfather clock in the hall with its slow ponderous tick that said, 'Take your time . . . take your time.'

She thought of her grandmother sitting in her high-backed chair, all prim and proper, waiting for her to arrive, and suddenly she felt she hated the old lady. Never once had her grandmother told anyone how her parents had adjusted to one another, especially as far as entertainments were concerned. 'Compromising', her father called it. Isabelle would go with him to the music hall once a week and he would accompany her to a classical concert or the opera. Even though Jonathan would take one of his scientific books to read during the performance, Isabelle refrained from making any comment.

Nor did her grandmother tell anyone how gifted her son-in-law was, how he had built a big telescope in the attic that showed the mountains on the moon. And what about the metal tips he had fitted to nearly every teapot in the

Avenue, to stop the spouts dripping? There were dozens of other small inventions as well as the bigger ones which Isabelle called, 'Jonathan's contraptions'.

True, her mother did get annoyed when some big structure that half-filled the front room had to be dismantled when company was coming on a Sunday. Sarah remembered the one where tiny metal balls careered around curves and up and down slopes to discover something called 'perpetual motion'.

The first excitement came when her father called gleefully up the stairs at two o'clock one morning, 'Come down all of you, the miracle has happened!'

Even her mother tumbled out of bed but no sooner were they in the room than the hurtling balls stopped and her father said cheerfully, 'Oh dear, not this time! Tomorrow perhaps.'

Isabelle never tumbled out of bed again to her husband's rallying call of 'Eureka!' Victor stopped too after a while but Sarah never failed to come down, and would always put her arms around her father's waist and say softly, 'You'll do it, Poppa. I know you will.'

The perpetual motion structure was eventually dismantled and relegated to the attic, to be replaced by the massive parts of a clock which had once adorned a church tower. These parts ended up in the attic, too, and now a model autogyro was the latest thing. According to Jonathan, this, once completed, would rise, hover, and come down in its own space. His closest friends, who spoke of him affectionately as a 'crank', teasingly asked how a plane with propeller blades on the top could possibly fly. Jonathan replied with his gentle smile, 'If you give me time I'll show you.'

Sarah drifted off to sleep with the hope that her father would prove to be right.

She was up early the next morning, knowing that her mother always had one of her migraines after a hysterical bout. Her father was already up and not only had the fire blazing and bacon cooked, but had been out to get the bag

4

of potatoes so that Sarah could go straight to her grandmother's.

He cracked an egg into the pan and said, 'I took your mother a cup of tea, Sarah, but she's fallen asleep again. I don't think we'll disturb her. She wrote a list for you of a few things you can collect from the grocer's on your way back. There's not much. Maggie says she'll come and cook the dinner for us – I saw her coming from the Fletchers' earlier.'

Maggie was the woman who came on Mondays to do the washing and clean the house from top to bottom every Friday. She had gypsy blood in her, wore heavy gold earrings and her black hair braided round her head. Her features were coarse, she had a raucous laugh and whistled through her teeth while she worked, but all the family loved her. She had second sight and had prophesied many things, good and bad, which had come true.

Sarah was glad it was Saturday so she would see more of Maggie than on the schooldays when she usually came. She went upstairs to call Victor who was a sleepyhead, then sat down to the bacon and egg and fried bread that her father put before her.

'You're a good cook, Poppa,' she said appreciatively. 'You never break the yolk.'

He smiled. 'I would not like to make a living at cooking, but I could make a meal for the family if an emergency arose.'

'You could do anything, *anything* at all if you had to.'

'Let me say I can do a lot of things, Sarah, but am not really expert at any of them.' Jonathan speared a piece of bacon on his fork then looked up. 'Sarah, will you do something for me? Will you be nice to Grandmother Frome today? She seems to have the impression that you don't like her.'

'I don't. Who does? There are times when I hate her. She's always saying nasty things behind people's backs. She's a terrible woman.'

'She's a very lonely old lady,' Jonathan said gently. 'And at times an unhappy one. She's had a difficult life.'

5

'So have a lot of people,' Sarah retorted, 'but they don't go on the way Gran does. I don't know how Bertha sticks it living with her. Gran's always on at her.'

'Yet Bertha has nothing but good to say of your grandmother. You must learn to be more tolerant, Sarah. We all have faults. Bertha would have gone to an orphanage had it not been for Gran giving her a home. All I ask is that you try to be nice to her. Surely that is not too much to ask?'

'No,' Sarah admitted. 'I'll try.' Then in a slightly aggressive way she added, 'But I'm not promising anything, Poppa.'

Jonathan's lips trembled in a smile. 'Do you know something, Sarah? I think you have a little of your grandmother in *you*.' Which shocked his daughter and left her for once without a reply.

After Jonathan left for the shop Sarah went upstairs, pulled the bedcovers from Victor, waited until he was out of bed then told him she was leaving him in charge. When she had washed the dishes she was going out, so he must listen to hear if their mother called.

Victor came down into the kitchen, yawning, just as Sarah was leaving.

'Your breakfast is in the oven,' she announced. 'Dried up.' And with that she left.

The September morning was crisp and sunny and in spite of hating her errand Sarah felt happy. Saturday meant no school and seeing Eddie that afternoon. Eddie worked for the shoemaker who had the shop next to her father's. He had ginger hair and freckles but she liked him because he treated her as an adult. He was gentle, like her father and, in common with Jonathan, was interested in scientific things and read a lot. Sarah read a lot, too.

Seeing a piece of stick on the pavement, Sarah picked it up and drew it, rattlety-tat, along the railings that fronted the small gardens of Berkeley Avenue. The terraced houses, considered to be in one of the better-class neighbourhoods, were bay-windowed and three-storeyed with seven rooms:

6

three bedrooms, sitting room, kitchen, scullery, bathroom and attic. The bathroom was her mother's pride and joy.

When her parents started married life they had lived in a one-up, one-down house and had to use a big tin bath in front of the fire. But there was, said Isabelle, a big garden at the back. In their present home they had a backyard with wash-house, WC and coal-shed. Her mother had added tubs of flowers and shrubs to brighten it up.

In Berkeley Avenue every house except one had crisp white curtains at the windows; the front steps were sand-stoned and the brass doorknobs gleaming. The exception was Mrs Cotton's house at the top of the Avenue. Most of the neighbours refused to speak to her, not because of the dirty curtains but because her six children all had different fathers. Sarah had learned this through all the whispering that went on between gossiping women. She had thought it interesting about the six fathers and wondered why none of them lived at the house.

When she asked her mother, she was told she would know the reason why when she was older. Sarah was used to getting this answer whenever she wanted to know something special, and sometimes wondered how old she would have to be before she found the answers.

She liked Mrs Cotton. The woman always smiled when they met and spoke to her in her soft, ladylike voice. Sarah had never been inside the house though, for it was forbidden by her mother, who said she would come back with fleas and things in her hair. Yet Mrs Cotton was always neatly dressed and wore a veil with her hat. One of the gossiping women had sneered and said the veil was to 'hide the muck on her face'.

Sarah was nearing the top of the street when she noticed Mrs Cotton standing at her door. This morning she was wearing a faded kimono and her hair was loose. She was pale and there were dark circles under her eyes. She looked fatter without her outdoor clothes.

Mrs Cotton called and beckoned to her and after a moment Sarah went up the short path to the door. 'Yes, Mrs Cotton?'

7

'If you're going to the shops would you be a dear and get me a packet of Woodbines? I'll have ten. Here's the five-pence and a penny for yourself.'

Sarah refused the penny, having had it drilled into her by her mother that she must not accept money for doing an errand for a neighbour. 'I'll get the cigarettes for you,' she said, 'but I must go to my grandmother's first. I have to take these potatoes.'

'Oh, that's all right, Sarah. I still have one cigarette left, it's just that I don't want to be without any.'

Smoking cigarettes was another black mark for Mrs Cotton as far as the neighbours were concerned. She was a brazen hussy.

None of the six Cotton children went to Sarah's school. In fact, they were never seen out playing. According to one report the children were with Mrs Cotton's mother for most of the time.

Sarah put Mrs Cotton from her mind for the time being and concentrated on thoughts of her grandmother. It was not going to be easy to be pleasant to her. From stepping into the hall there would be orders. 'Wipe your feet . . . Don't slouch . . . Stop throwing your hair back.' Sarah wore it out of pigtails at the weekends. If she was given a piece of cake she would be ordered not to drop any crumbs on the floor, this in spite of the fact that Sarah would pick up the minutest crumb from the plate with a dampened fore-finger and pop it into her mouth.

Oak Crescent where her grandmother lived consisted of nine houses in a cul-de-sac, once described by someone as having an air of genteel poverty. The tenants were a mixture of retired businessmen and their wives or widows of busi-nessmen. Grandpa Frome had worked in a bank.

If rust showed through the paint on the railings fronting the gardens it would be touched up immediately. Small darns could be seen here and there in spotless lace curtains; no woman stood gossiping, nor was a dog allowed out to roam on its own.

Sarah lifted the gleaming brass knocker and let it fall, resisting an urge as always to give it a quick rat-tat. Bertha answered the door and immediately a voice called sharply from within, 'Wipe your feet, Sarah.'

Bertha, who at thirty was round-shouldered, scrawny and sallow-skinned, gave Sarah a conspiratorial wink and whispered, '*Madam* is in a bad mood today.' Sarah whispered back to ask when her grandmother was in a good one, which had Bertha covering her mouth to stifle laughter. She motioned to Sarah to go ahead.

It was a gloomy house, with dark wallpaper and sombre paintings. Although every square inch of parquet flooring and every piece of furniture were polished daily, this did nothing to lift the gloom. Rugs, carpets and curtains had all faded to an indiscriminate merging of greys and browns.

'Well, come in,' the old lady ordered, as Sarah tapped at the door of the living room.

Henrietta Frome sat in her high-backed chair beside a fire in which a single flame was trying valiantly to penetrate the shovelful of coal-dust with which it must recently have been fed.

Sarah had never seen her grandmother in anything else but black; her dress or shirt-blouse always having a high neck. Her iron-grey hair had a natural curl but only once had Sarah seen it loose. It was worn parted in the middle and drawn severely back and pinned in a bun. Sarah had fastened her own hair back today with a ribbon.

'Sit down, girl,' her grandmother commanded. 'I hope you remembered to bring the potatoes. You do know you were expected here with them yesterday afternoon?'

Sarah said yes, apologised for forgetting and added that she had given the potatoes to Bertha.

This brought the rejoinder that she would forget her head if it was loose. It was lack of discipline, that was the trouble. She should have been made to bring the potatoes, no matter what time it was. Henrietta had fancied one baked for her supper and no shop hereabouts sold potatoes with this particular flavour.

Sarah felt furious. How could one be kind to this – this dragon of a woman?

'Is your mother calling this morning?' Henrietta asked. 'I

9

haven't seen her since last Monday. I could be dead for all anyone cares about me.'

Sarah closed her eyes, knowing that this remark was the prelude to one of the four monologues her grandmother went through at frequent intervals. Today she guessed it was the 'alienation' one – and she was right.

'You have no idea, being a child, how your father has alienated my dear daughter Isabelle from me. She used to be such a lovely, happy girl, now she's a bundle of nerves ... And there's Lucy, why does she not come and see me more often? She has plenty of time on her hands with that sailor husband of hers away at sea. I'll tell you why. It's because her husband has poisoned her mind against me. He never did like me, not from the first day we met ... And there's my dear son Harold – why did he emigrate with his family to Australia?'

Bertha, who had come in at that moment, mouthed at Sarah, 'Because his awful wife Charlotte forced him to go.'

Sarah pressed her lips tightly together and looked down at the floor, terrified she might burst out laughing.

Bertha said aloud, 'I've brought in some gingerbread for Sarah. Do you want a piece, ma'am?'

'No, no,' the old lady waved the plate aside. 'You know I don't eat between meals. And mind you don't make any crumbs, Sarah. Bertha has enough to do without sweeping up after you.'

'I'll be careful, Grandma,' Sarah said meekly.

Bertha had successfully ended the monologue, which Sarah had to admit was not spoken in a whining way as some people did when complaining, but rather stated as facts. While Sarah nibbled at her cake Henrietta asked how Victor was getting on with his piano lessons, how her mother was, whether she had had any more migraines, at which point Sarah refrained from mentioning that her mother was suffering from one that very morning, and finally, how business was with her father. Without waiting for a reply, she told Sarah that her boots needed cleaning. There was nothing more slovenly in a child than having dirty boots.

Sarah looked down at them. Her father cleaned all the

boots in their house with an electrical gadget – his own invention – and the only mark to be seen was a small smudge on the toe of the left boot where she had kicked a stone in the road. She rubbed the mark off with her finger and was immediately told it was a filthy trick and she must go and wash her hands at once.

Sarah stifled a sigh and went out into the scullery. Bertha grinned at her. 'I heard that.'

'How do you put up with it, day in and day out? Why do you stay?'

'I close my ears most of the time. I couldn't leave her, she's been good to me, still is. She's a lonely old woman, drives everyone away but she can't see it. Your grandmother does have her good points, after all. She's fiercely independent and will insist on paying your mother for the potatoes you brought next time she comes.'

'What are you doing in there, Sarah? Having a bath?' came the tart voice of the old lady. Sarah pulled a face and went back to her grandmother.

She stayed another ten minutes then said she would have to go, as she had some shopping to do for Isabelle. She left with the unhappy news that the family were invited for tea the following Sunday. 'Not tomorrow, remember,' Henrietta warned her. 'The next Sunday. Close the door quietly when you go out, *and* the gate.'

'Yes, Grandma.' Sarah, remembering her father's words to be kind to the old lady, leaned over and dropped a kiss on the sallow cheek. Not being a demonstrative woman, Grandmother Frome seemed surprised. Sarah left, feeling she had done her duty.

She did the shopping for her mother, bought Mrs Cotton's cigarettes and called with them on her way home. The front door was ajar but no one came when Sarah knocked. There was a strange smell in the hall, like the smell in the house of one of her schoolfriends. Her mother had described it as the smell of poverty.

To Sarah's cry of, 'Mrs Cotton, are you there?' came groans, from the direction of the living room. When she called again, there was a brief, sharp moan then Mrs Cotton

11

was calling out, 'Come in, Sarah, *please*.' Her voice had an anguished sound.

Sarah stepped inside, left her shopping bags in the hall, then went into the room. There she stopped, nonplussed. Mrs Cotton was lying on the floor, her legs spreadeagled, and there was a big hump under her nightdress.

'Sarah – ' Mrs Cotton's face was suddenly contorted with pain and for a moment she couldn't speak. 'Will you get the midwife for me? She lives at – ' Her face screwed up again then Mrs Cotton screamed. 'Oh, Sarah, the baby's coming – right now!'

Sarah looked around, expecting someone to bring a baby in. But there was no one. Then she looked back at Mrs Cotton and stared both fascinated and scared as she saw a tiny head appear between the woman's outstretched legs.

'A towel, Sarah,' Mrs Cotton gasped. 'A towel quick, to put under me . . . in the scullery.'

Sarah ran into the scullery and pulled a towel from a hook on the back of the door. It did not look too clean but there was no other. With a feeling of dire emergency she hastily put the towel under Mrs Cotton then, as the woman thrust down grunting, Sarah instinctively put her hands gently round the baby's head, and helped it into the world.

It gave a lusty cry and Mrs Cotton gasped, 'It sounds like a boy.'

'Yes, it is,' Sarah said softly, deeply moved by her experience. 'Oh, he's lovely, Mrs Cotton, he's got a lot of dark hair.' Then she looked up suddenly with a feeling of panic. 'What do I do now?'

'Wrap him in the towel then put a newspaper under me, because the afterbirth has to come away. Then go and get the midwife – she lives at number two, West Street.'

Sarah saw the afterbirth come away before she left the house and felt bewildered, yet at the same time she marvelled at having seen a baby born. But how had it got there?

Fortunately, the midwife was in and came at once with Sarah. 'You say you saw the baby born, she said. 'Well, you'd better not tell your mother or she'll be upset.'

12

Sarah thought no, she would not tell her mother, but she would tell her father. It wasn't something she could keep to herself.

The midwife did allow Sarah to see the cord being cut but after that she hustled her out. 'You've seen enough for one day and don't go telling all your schoolfriends about it. And I want you to promise me that.' Sarah promised.

The girl went on marvelling at all she had seen. How could a baby get born from such a place? And why didn't baby and mother bleed to death when the cord was cut? That lovely, tiny little baby – she must see it again, she *must*.

When Sarah got home she found Victor standing on the doorstep, his cap on, his music case in his hand. 'Where've you been?' he demanded. 'Miss Hedley sent a message to say I could play some of my pieces on a friend's grand piano. A grand piano – imagine! I must go. Mother's all right, she's still asleep. Ta-ta!' He was away, racing up the street.

Grand piano! Sarah went inside, took the shopping into the scullery then went up to see her mother. Isabelle was awake but looking pale. She drew herself up in the bed. 'Was Gran cross with you about yesterday, Sarah?'

'No. She wants us all to go to tea a week tomorrow.'

'Oh.' Isabelle gave a small groan and slid down in the bed again. 'It's a good job it's not tomorrow, I don't think I could have gone. That sounds unkind but your grandmother can be a bit of a trial.'

'Yes, I know.' There was the sound of the back gate slamming, brisk footsteps crossing the yard, then a moment later Maggie was calling from the kitchen. 'Sarah – are you up there?'

'Yes.' The steps were quieter as Maggie came up. She tiptoed into the bedroom.

'Feeling better, Mrs T? I saw Mr T this morning and he told me you were poorly. Eh—I hear Mrs Cotton's got her new baby,' she turned to Sarah, 'and I'm told you went for the midwife. Good girl.'

'What's this?' Isabelle drew herself hastily up in the bed again.

Colour had rushed to Sarah's face and she sought frantically in her mind for a suitable answer. 'She asked me if I would, it was on my way back home. She was poorly.' That at least was true.

'This one'll make seven,' Maggie mused. 'Poor soul, and her with not a husband among all the fathers.'

Isabelle gave her a warning sign not to say any more then told Sarah to go downstairs and start peeling the potatoes. Sarah was only too thankful to escape from any further questioning.

When Maggie came down she took off her coat, put on her big white apron and went into the pantry, talking as she went. 'Your ma says there's some steak and kidney cooked – I'll just make a crust.' She brought in flour, fat, the board and the rolling pin.

Sarah said, 'Maggie, what did you mean when you said that Mrs Cotton hadn't a husband among all the fathers of the children? Isn't she married to any of them?'

'No, lovey, she isn't. But you'd better ask your ma about it. She doesn't want me to say anything.'

Sarah made up her mind to ask her father that very afternoon, that is, if her mother let her go to the shop. After all the upset of the night before, Isabelle might decide to make Sarah stay in.

She picked up the flour-shaker and floured the board. 'Tell me about the time you saw the Angel, Maggie.'

2

Isabelle came down for the midday meal, still looking pale but saying she felt much better. Maggie had gone after cooking the dinner and Sarah told her mother excitedly about some of her prophecies.

'Do you know what she said? She told me there would be an unexpected visitor who would call just after dinner with some good news and she also said we would have *another* unexpected visitor at breakfast-time tomorrow morning!'

Isabelle put a hand to her head. 'Heaven forbid! Visitors are the last things I want, even though one of them *is* supposed to be bringing good news.'

But when the first visitor did materialise, Isabelle was as excited as Sarah had been. It was Miss Hedley, Victor's music teacher, and she had brought good tidings. A spinster in her mid-thirties, Miss Hedley was normally a drab little person, but today bright spots of colour burned on her cheeks and her eyes were shining.

'Oh, Mr and Mrs Torent, I just had to come and tell you my news. I had talked to Professor Mascagni about Victor's potential with his music and he suggested I bring the boy to his house, sit him at the grand piano and leave him to play what he wished. The professor and I listened from another room. I had expected Victor to play the pieces he's been practising for weeks but instead – ' Miss Hedley pulled at the tips of her well-darned grey gloves and a look of rapture came over her face, '– he began to play a Chopin sonata.'

'A Chopin sonata?' Isabelle exclaimed. 'I've never heard him play one.'

'Neither had I, Mrs Torent. I just sat there utterly astonished and I can tell you this, the Professor was astonished, too. After a while he flung up his hands and said, "Such

15

talent! The boy has the making of a concert pianist. He must be trained. I, myself, shall train him." '

Isabelle, tears in her eyes, said, 'Oh, I can hardly believe it! How wonderful, my mother will be overjoyed. Where is Victor, he must be told.' Sarah said he had gone to play conkers with his friend Joey and Isabelle exclaimed, 'Conkers? And his future is in the balance! Go and find him, Sarah.'

Sarah found him just outside the front door, alone. 'What's Miss Hedley come for?' he asked with a worried frown. 'It is to complain about my playing?'

'No.' Sarah gabbled out the good news and the colour began to drain from Victor's face. He asked if it meant he would have to leave home and Sarah said she didn't know, he'd best come in and find out.

Victor was the only one who showed no outward excitement, but Sarah knew by the way he rubbed the palms of his hands together that he was excited inside.

They talked for some time, with Miss Hedley saying that Professor Mascagni would visit Jonathan and Isabelle to discuss their son's future. When she got up to leave there were tears in her eyes, too. She said it was worth having been born just to have had the honour of teaching a pupil with genius.

'Dear Miss Hedley,' Jonathan said when she had gone. 'She's had such a drab life. I can understand how she feels, though. I am delighted for Victor, delighted for your sake, Isabelle, and for your mother, too. It will mean so much to her, brighten her whole life.'

Sarah could imagine her grandmother boasting to her neighbours. 'My grandson Victor, so talented, you know. His Professor says . . .' Sarah looked at her father who was standing with his hand on his son's shoulder, his face full of warmth and she felt suddenly mean. Victor would have been pleased for her if the positions had been reversed.

One good thing did come for Sarah out of Miss Hedley's visit. Her mother raised no objections when she asked if she could spend the afternoon at the shop.

While Sarah walked with her father through the streets

she slipped her hand into his. 'Poppa, I was jealous of Victor.'

He squeezed her hand. 'I know how you feel, Sarah. You remember I told you how I was apprenticed to a shoemaker when I lived in Finland? Well, another boy who was apprenticed at the same time began to make beautiful fine leather boots for special customers while I was still making the heavier ones for everyday wear. I was jealous of all the praise he got and took my complaint to my father. He said, 'Jonathan, every person is gifted in some way. Olaf has a talent for making fine footwear; he loves the work, takes a pride in it, while to you the work is just a means of making money.' And you know, Sarah, he was right. But my father did point out that I had a creative mind and was interested in all things mechanical. He also reminded me that through my reading I had a knowledge of the moon, sun, stars and planets, and that someday I might have the opportunity of developing my talents.'

'And you came to England.'

'Yes, I did, and by an odd coincidence I met a clock-maker on the very first day I arrived. He offered me a job and by another strange coincidence he, too, was interested in astronomy. He was a wonderful man, who taught me so much. You love clocks don't you Sarah.' Jonathan laughed softly. 'I don't know of a lady clockmaker but who can tell – you could be the first.'

'Oh, I would like that, Poppa, I would like that *very* much.'

They had come to the main road and Jonathan made Sarah wait for the traffic to ease. Being a Saturday there was a constant stream of trams, big drays, bicycles, milk-carts, muck-carts and men with barrows. Normally she would take her life in her hands and dart across or weave her way between them.

When they did cross they passed Leaven's Emporium, the draper's, the Penny Bazaar and the bread shop with its lovely smell of hot loaves and buns, then turned right into George Street where her father had his shop, which announced in gilt letters, J.Torent, Clocks and Watches.

Next to it was Mr MacTavish the shoemaker, where Eddie worked. At one time the shops had been one big one, run as a furniture emporium. Now they were separated by a partition, with the front doors set in an inverted V. Before they reached the shops Sarah could hear the thud of the hammer as Mr MacTavish or Eddie nailed on soles or heels. She peeped in at the door and both Eddie and the Scotsman gave her a wave. 'See you later,' Sarah called.

Jonathan unlocked the door of his shop and as they went in a bird popped out of a clock on the left-hand wall and gave a 'Cuckoo . . . Cuckoo!' Sarah laughed. 'Oh, Poppa, you've mended it. I'm so glad, I missed it.'

There was a small fireplace with the fire left banked up while Jonathan had been out. He stirred it and flames rose from the red embers. The shop was actually quite warm. Sarah took off her hat and coat and hung them on the door that led to the upper floor. Then she looked around the shop, feeling a stir of satisfaction: it was like a second home to her.

One part of the shop was given over to the sale of watches and clocks and the other, larger section to the repairing side. In this was a lathe and several tall but narrow chests of drawers, which held watches awaiting repair, watch parts and Jonathan's tools.

His reputation extended beyond the locality of the shop to other districts, even to small market towns. People of all classes came to him, from market stallholders to gentry.

On the shelves around the shop were clocks of every description: lantern-clocks, bracket, chamfer, marble, inverted belltops and many others.

Sarah liked going through the drawers and studying the watches. She also liked tidying up the numerous clock parts which lay in boxes beneath the shelves. Jonathan, so meticulous in his actual work, had had no system of storing stock until Sarah took the matter in hand. He would search for a certain item among a jumble of bits and pieces, saying he just knew he had one – somewhere.

The little bell above the door jangled and a customer came in. Judging by the conversation between the two men, a watch exchanged hands. When the customer had gone Jonathan brought it over to Sarah and said softly, 'Look what I've bought for your mother. Its tick is so quiet, she couldn't possibly object to it. She can wear it on a chain, or as a fob-watch.'

Jonathan flicked open the heart-shaped silver case. Inside was a tiny watch surrounded by chased silver. On the back of the watch was an inscription *To My Dear Wife, with Love*.

Sarah looked up at her father, her eyes shining. 'Oh, Poppa, Mother will love it, it's just so beautiful. Are you going to keep it for her birthday?'

'No, I shall give it to her this evening. I cannot wait to see her pleasure.'

Sarah, suddenly serious, asked if the watch had belonged to the man's wife. Jonathan said yes it had, she had died recently. Her husband had not wanted to part with it but he had two small boys to bring up and needed every penny. Then Jonathan added, 'The poor man was only grateful that the watch would go to someone like your mother, who would appreciate it.' He wrapped the watch in its piece of chamois then smiled. 'Well, Sarah, shall we get on with some work? What is it you want to study today?'

Sarah was interested in every clock but felt she must remind her father that he had a clock to repair and he had promised his customer it would be ready at tea-time. Yes, he said, perhaps he had better do that first.

Isabelle once said that one of her husband's biggest faults was chatting to people who dropped in, instead of getting on with his work. That afternoon several of his friends stopped by and earnest discussions took place. At four o'clock Sarah said, an urgent tone to her voice, 'Poppa, your customer will be in soon for his clock! You're wasting time.'

Jonathan, who had been working in between chatting, took the small magnifying glass from his eye and said, 'Talking to friends, Sarah, is never a waste of time. The gentleman I bought the watch from earlier was recommended to me by one of my friends. I was able to

19

help him and your mother will be getting a watch I feel sure she will treasure.'

Sarah thought he was probably right, but hoped the customer would get his clock on time. He did, but he was one of the more fortunate ones. Jonathan, who dreamed a lot as well as enjoying a discussion, was a 'tomorrow's man'. 'Sorry, I just couldn't manage to get it done today but I promise you shall have it tomorrow.' Most times the promises were kept.

Jonathan always worked late on a Saturday evening so Sarah prepared to go home without him at four o'clock. She and Victor always went with their mother on a Saturday evening to order the groceries and Mr Donaldson invariably gave them a bag of sweets. It was something not to be missed.

'Bye then, Poppa,' Sarah called. 'I'll just nip in and see Mr MacTavish and Eddie.'

'Mind when you cross the main road, Sarah, no darting across.' She promised and went next door.

Mr MacTavish, big, brawny and bearded, greeted her with, 'Hello there, lassie, thought we were not to be honoured with a visit from ye today. Just heard the news about your brother. That's a grand thing, isn't it? A genius, I'm told.'

Eddie hammered a stud into the heel of a boot and smiled. 'News travels fast. Your brother's music teacher came in for her shoes. She was full of sunshine.'

Sarah loved Eddie's odd sayings. But that was just how Miss Hedley had been. Radiant.

'And are you no' learning to play the instrument as well, Sarah?' Mr MacTavish asked. 'You could be playing duets, the pair of you.'

'I did fancy learning to play the violin,' Sarah said, musing. 'I might ask if I can take some lessons.'

'I would, now. You might turn out to be a genius, too.' When Sarah said she had better be going the Scotsman suggested that Eddie deliver a pair of boots to a customer then he could see Sarah across the main road. Eddie took off his leather apron at once and hung it up. As they were

20

leaving Mr MacTavish called, 'And make sure you get the money for the repairs, Eddie lad, or the wife will be telling me there'll be no Sunday roast.'

Eddie said as they walked along the street, 'Mr Dodds will pay. He'll want them for church tomorrow and he knows I won't leave them without the money. A great churchgoer is Mr Dodds and the meanest man I know.'

Eddie had a quiet, pleasant voice. He came from a large family which lived in Badger's Row, a very poor part of the city, but he was always neat and clean. He asked Sarah what she had been doing this past week and she shrugged.

'Nothing in particular. I got into trouble for not going to my grandmother's when I should have done. I went this morning and felt like hitting her. She's a terrible woman.'

'Sarah.' Eddie's tone was gently rebuking. 'You're lucky to have a grandmother. Both sets of my grandparents are dead.'

'I've tried to love Gran,' Sarah pleaded. 'I really have, but she's always saying nasty things about people, especially about Poppa, such as him being a foreigner, and that his ways are not ours. Now Mother says the same things, but – well, not in such a hurtful way. She loves Poppa you see, and that makes a difference.'

'Oh, it definitely does.' Sarah thought that Eddie was making fun of her but when she looked up at him he was quite serious. Curious now, she asked him if he liked repairing boots and shoes.

He thought about it then said, 'Yes, I do. It gives me time to think.' Sarah asked what about and he told her the Universe, then enlarged on the subject. 'I think about the millions of stars, the billions of them, and wonder how they got there. And then I wonder if there are other worlds like ours, and if so what language the beings there speak.'

Sarah had lost a great deal of interest in the heavens when she realised that the dark contours of the moon were not the features of a man, but only mountains. She said, 'Poppa is always saying that men will go to the moon in the future – not in his lifetime, but in ours. His friends smile and tell him he's crazy.'

21

'I don't think he's crazy.' Eddie was solemn-eyed. 'Not when I read some of the books he lends me. He gave me a number of his *Popular Science Siftings* magazines to read and I found them so interesting I burned a whole candle down the other night reading them in bed.'

They came to the house where Eddie had to deliver the boots and Mr Dodds paid him for them, scratting out the money from a leather purse and paying in pennies and halfpennies. When Eddie came over he was laughing 'A regular old Scrooge,' he declared. 'I bet he would lose a night's sleep if he dropped a ha'penny down a drain. I hope I can always listen to the music of money rattling in my pocket, even if it's just a few pence.

He saw Sarah across the main road then said softly, 'You look real bonny this afternoon, with that blue dress matching your eyes. Take care of yourself, lass. I'll see you next Saturday, if not sooner.' And before Sarah had time to recover from her astonishment at the compliment Eddie was away, dodging the traffic. He paused to give her a wave from the opposite pavement then disappeared with his long stride.

Sarah stood for a moment, watching him. What a lovely person Eddie was, always making her feel grown-up.

When Sarah reached Berkeley Avenue she stood hesitant outside Mrs Cotton's front gate, wondering if she dare visit the woman. If she did, she mustn't stay long. The front door was unlocked so Sarah peeped in and called, 'Are you there, Mrs Cotton?'

'Yes, Sarah, I'm in the front room. Come on in.'

The only furniture in the room was a double bed and a cot. The floor was bare, without even a rug. But Mrs Cotton, sitting propped up against some pillows, was wearing a pretty pink nightie, trimmed with lace. Her hair was tied back with a piece of pink ribbon. Her cheeks had the flush of fever, and her eyes were bright. 'Hello, Sarah, how nice of you to call. I want to thank you for what you did this morning. You were marvellous.'

Sarah went forward. 'How are you? How is the baby?'

22

'I feel fine and the baby's lovely. He's slept since he arrived. Take a look at him.'

Sarah walked round the bed. The cot was just a box on four legs, but it contained a white knitted cover in a fancy pattern and the baby was wearing a new matinée jacket. Sarah gently touched the dark curly hair. 'He's beautiful,' she said, 'What a lot of hair.' The baby stirred, gave a snuffle and brought a fist up to his mouth. She laughed. 'They pull such funny faces, don't they?'

'You like babies, Sarah, don't you? I used to watch you when you were younger pushing the babies of various neighbours out in their prams. A regular little mother, one woman said about you.'

'Yes, I do like them. I want a big family when I marry. My mother said I'll probably change my mind when I have two.' Sarah, remembering Mrs Cotton's big family, felt colour rush into her face. She eased away from the cot.

'I must go, Mrs Cotton, I promised to be home at half-past four for tea. Is there anything you need, anything I can get you – food?'

'No, I'm all right Sarah, thank you. My mother and sister have been and will be coming back soon. Thanks again for what you did. A lot of girls would have panicked. Come and see me again, if you can.'

Sarah promised and after a last peep at the baby, left. She puzzled over Mrs Cotton. Her house was so sparsely furnished yet she looked pretty in her pink nightie, and the pillowcases, she remembered, had crotcheted lace around them. Then Sarah, seeing her brother go rushing into their house, quickened her footsteps.

Her mother was still excited over the earlier good news about Victor, but once they sat down to their tea she started on practicalities. She pointed out to Sarah that there would be higher fees for her brother's tuition now and she stressed that Sarah must not keep her father from his paid work by constantly asking about clocks. It was sometimes a struggle to make ends meet.

Victor said, his expression earnest, 'I don't have to be

taught by this Professor. I can easily keep on with Miss Hedley, if it's going to run you and Dad short.'

'No, no,' Isabelle said hastily. They would manage – it was just that she wanted Sarah to understand that time could not be wasted. This was an important step in Victor's future career; they would find the money somehow.

Sarah felt a sudden spurt of resentment. Her head went up. 'I had thought I would like to learn to play the violin but I don't suppose there'll be money for that!'

Isabelle, who had picked up a knife to cut into the ginger-bread loaf, put it down again and looked at Sarah with mild astonishment. 'You want to learn to play the violin? Why, that's splendid! Your grandfather was a wonderful player. I never thought that you had any musical bent in you. You do sing a *little* out of tune, Sarah. But there, you might prove to have talent. I shall certainly encourage it. I'll discuss it with your father this evening.'

When they went out later for their evening trip to the grocer's Isabelle stopped to talk to so many people on the way about their good news that Sarah and Victor asked permission to go on ahead. It was granted and the two of them raced down the Avenue towards the shops, with Victor saying he was fed up with all the talk about the Professor and for two pins he'd chuck playing the piano altogether.

Sarah's footsteps slowed, then she stopped. Victor stopped, too. 'You can't mean it!' she gasped. 'You couldn't stop playing the piano. It's – it's in your blood.' This was Isabelle's expression.

Victor, hands thrust into pockets, kicked at the kerbstone. 'No, I know, but Mother's making too much fuss. I might turn out not to have the talent the Professor expects, then she'll make herself ill. You know what she is – highly strung and all that.'

'It's because she's so musical,' Sarah said gravely, echoing her father's explanation. 'It makes her very sensitive. You must go on playing! Just think, we might all be coming to hear you play in London or Edinburgh, or even Vienna. Isn't that where some of the great pianists play?'

A dreamy look came into her brother's eyes for a moment.

'It would be great, wouldn't it? Everyone standing up and applauding.' Then his expression became melancholy. 'But just think of all the people Mother will be telling. *Everybody*. Even Mr Donaldson, I bet. I don't think I could stand it.'

Although Sarah had inherited her father's dreamy nature, she had also inherited a practical side from Isabelle. With hands on hips she eyed her brother with disapproval.

'Well – you'll have to make up your mind, won't you? You'll either become a great pianist and put up with all the fuss, or throw the whole thing up – *now*. Rember this, it'll cost a mint of money to have you trained, hard-earned money, so don't let Mother and Poppa pay all that money out then decide that *you* are neurotic, too.'

Victor looked at his sister with a new respect. 'I wish I could think like you do, sort of clearly. I have music going round and round in my head all the time.'

'It wouldn't do if we were all alike, would it? Otherwise we'd all be cabbages.' Sarah quoted Maggie.

Victor suddenly grinned. 'I'm all for Vienna. Come on, or we might not get our bags of sweets.'

They raced the rest of the way.

3

Mr Donaldson, the grocer, was a big jolly man. He greeted the children with a, 'Hello, there!' then he looked beyond them. 'Where's your ma?'

Sarah told him she was on her way then walked happily round the shop, breathing in the smells of spices, cheese, smoked bacon and the creosote firelighters. All the goods that were weighed out into packets were stored in sacks; white sugar and Demerara, currants, sultanas, raisins and dried peas. Sarah thought sometimes that she would like to work in a grocer's and be able to packet up sugar and the other goods in the deft way that Mr Donaldson had. He would weigh out the sugar, put it on an oblong piece of stiff blue paper, take both sides to the middle, fold them over twice, tuck one end in, stand the packet up, shake down the sugar, tuck in the top end and that was that. For smaller items, he would make a small cone of paper and tuck the end in.

Isabelle arrived a few minutes later and Sarah thought how attractive her mother looked, even in her everyday dark green hat and coat. The grocer drew up a chair for her and Isabelle sat down, thanked him and said with a smile: 'Oh, Mr Donaldson, we've had some splendid news today about Victor.'

Victor gave his sister a pained look then motioned outside with his eyes. Sarah retorted, 'I warned you what would happen.'

Once outside, he grinned. 'I know, but it takes time to get used to fame. Come on, let's go to the paper shop.'

They looked in the window for a while at the comics – *Comic Cuts*, *Jack and Jill* and *Puck*, and eyed the few toys on display. On their return to the grocer's, Mr Donaldson gave them the long-awaited sweets in a coned packet. There were liquorice allsorts, fruit gums, dolly mixtures, jelly

26

babies and two extra bootlace-strips of liquorice. Sarah always thought they got these extras because the grocer liked her mother – not that she ever flirted with him.

When they reached home her father was back and Sarah hoped she would get a chance later on to tell Jonathan about seeing Mrs Cotton's baby born. He would understand – and perhaps explain some of the things she wanted so badly to know. Her mother would never get over it if she were to tell her.

Some of Isabelle's hysteria was brought on by Jonathan's habit of 'calling a spade a spade', One evening, they had been out for a walk and a stranger had asked the way to the nearest chemist. Jonathan had directed him, then added that the shop was opposite the gentlemen's urinal. Isabelle had been horrified: one did *not* use such words. Mystified, Jonathan had asked why. It was the given name in the dictionary, after all.

Once, he also described a woman who had asked after the family, as being big-bosomed and wearing a red hat. This, too, had Isabelle angry – it was being deliberately rude.

The worst time was when Jonathan described his home in Finland to visitors at the house in Berkeley Avenue. He told the assembled company how they all lived in one room and how they had sauna baths together, slapping one another's backs with branched leaves to stimulate the circulation. After that, Isabelle had taken to her bed. Although Jonathan could not understand what he called the 'Victorian mock modesty', he did promise to think before he spoke, in future.

On a Saturday evening Sarah was allowed to help her father wind all the clocks in the house. Some were permanent fixtures and others were ones that had been repaired and that Jonathan wanted to check before returning them to their owners. There were six in the front room, four in her bedroom, only one in her parents' room, none at all in Victor's room, for he couldn't stand the ticking and five in the hall, including their own lovely grandfather clock, which Jonathan always wound himself. Sarah loved this clock the best. It not only had a sea scene painted on the face but it told the days of the year, when the moon quarters would rise and the position of the sun.

After Jonathan had adjusted the heavy brass weights he would close the door then rub his hand lovingly over the beautiful patina of the wood. Recently, Sarah had found herself doing the same.

She hated Sundays if they were not entertaining or visiting people she liked. Then it would be church, morning and evening and Sunday School in the afternoon. Isabelle, who was a staunch Protestant, went to church with the children. Jonathan was an agnostic, which grieved Isabelle who said that people would think him a heathen. Sarah wasn't sure what an agnostic was, but she knew that her father did more good turns for people than some of the 'pillars of the church'. Isabelle admitted this and said she was pleased that Jonathan had not objected to his children being brought up as 'Christians'. Victor liked going to church just to hear the organ. He hoped to be able to play it some day.

On the Sunday morning at breakfast, Sarah, whose throat was sore, was busy wondering if she could make this an excuse for missing church when there was a rat-tat at the front door. Isabelle glanced at the clock. 'Who on earth can be calling so early?'

It was Frederick, Isabelle's brother-in-law, who went to sea.

'Why, Fred,' Isabelle exclaimed, giving him a quick hug. 'What a surprise! Lucy said you wouldn't be home until tomorrow. When did you dock?'

'Five o'clock this morning, earlier than we expected.' Jonathan pumped his hand and told him to sit down and have some breakfast.

'Thought I'd give you a call,' Fred went on, 'tell you I was home. You must all come up for the day. Lucy'll be delighted to have you. Sarah girl!' He picked her up and gave her a smacking kiss. 'How you're growing! Where's Victor? Oh, there you are, come and say hello to your Uncle Fred.'

28

Isabelle ordered them all to sit down and dished out the bacon, scrambled eggs and tomatoes. Fred gave a sigh of pleasure. 'Ay, it's good to be home.' He grinned. 'This is home to me too, you know.'

He was tubby, had a moustache, twinkling brown eyes and oozed friendliness. He was steward on a cargo boat, and having been all over the world had some marvellous stories to tell.

This time he informed them that he'd brought a little monkey back with him, but he'd left it on the boat for the moment and would fetch it in a couple of days. He laughed. 'Can't have my homecoming spoilt by a monkey. He's a funny little devil, all the women want to cuddle him. I want the cuddles, don't I?'

Isabelle laughed. 'Oh, Fred, you never change.'

Sarah loved going to her aunt and uncle's house. She enjoyed her talks with her cousin Jenny, who was two years older and knew a lot more things than Sarah did. Her young cousin Eric was the same age as Victor, and as Eric also played the piano and both boys were adventurous, they got on well.

Uncle Fred pretended to play the piano, strumming in as tuneless a way as Sarah sang, and making up the verses as he went along. It was always fun when Uncle Fred was home.

Fred often broke his journey to call and see Jonathan and Isabelle. They were just a tram-ride away from the docks, whereas he lived near the coast. He left after breakfast with Jonathan's and Isabelle's promise to come and visit them that afternoon.

They caught the three o'clock electric train and when they arrived at North Shields Sarah and Victor ran on ahead, with Victor arriving first and having the privilege of banging on the door with the heavy knocker. Sarah peeped through the letterbox. A flight of stairs led straight from the front door to a landing, with her Aunt Lucy's flat on one side and old Mrs Wilkinson's on the other. It always intrigued Sarah, the way someone would come out on to the landing, pull on a wire and the front door would open.

29

It was her cousin Jenny who came out this time and once the door was opened Sarah raced on up the stairs and gave a breathless, 'Hello'.

Jenny said, 'Why didn't you come earlier? I've been waiting for you.'

Sarah began unbuttoning her coat. 'I wanted to but Poppa said you would all want some time with your father before we came.'

By this time Jonathan and Isabelle had arrived and there were greetings all round. Then Lucy, whose face was flushed, her eyes shining said, 'What a lovely surprise to have Fred arrive this morning. I wasn't expecting him until tomorrow.'

She was Isabelle's younger sister and a redhead. Jenny, auburn-haired, was like her mother, while young Eric took after his father, and was just as jolly.

The flat had only three rooms – a living room, front room and one bedroom, which was only big enough to hold a double bed and a chair. A cupboard held all their clothes. Eric slept on a bedchair in the front room and Jenny slept in the living room on a bed that pulled out when the sideboard doors were opened.

Whenever Sarah stayed overnight she slept with Jenny and enjoyed the novelty of snuggling down in a room where the dying embers of the fire cast a warm red glow on the ceiling.

All the cooking had to be done in this room, where there was a gas stove as well as an oven in the black-leaded range. Water had to be carried up from a tap in the backyard, and the family washed in a bowl on the landing at the top of the back stairs.

Sarah even thought this fun, too, but Isabelle was always on at her sister to look for a house. Lucy said she would, but she was happy-go-lucky and never tried. Not that she was untidy, for the flat was spotless and she always dressed nicely.

The adults went into the front room to talk and the boys disappeared.

Jenny said to Sarah, 'You can help me lay the table for

tea and tell me what you've been doing.' Sarah longed to confide in her cousin about Mrs Cotton but hesitated, thinking of her promise to the midwife. Then she thought, Jenny is not a schoolfriend, so she told the story in a low voice.

Jenny, who had been laying out the side plates, stopped dead when Sarah began on her story and when she had finished, stood staring at her cousin in disbelief. 'You mean the baby came out of that little place? I can't believe it. I just *can't*.'

'It's true, I swear it. I'll swear it on a stack of Bibles! But what I want to know is, how did it get there in the first place? Did God put it there? Is it only married people who have babies?'

'No, it isn't. Betty Weston across the road had one and she wasn't married. It was black. Her mother said she had got it through eating oranges. African ones.'

Sarah was fascinated by this piece of news. 'I'd love a black baby, but how will I know which oranges are the right ones?'

'The man in the shop would know.'

Sarah made up her mind that when her mother bought the fruit next weekend, she would ask her to make sure the oranges came from Africa.

Lucy always had a reserve of cakes in case any of the family turned up unexpectedly and she had made several kinds of tarts since her husband's return. 'Oh, I just knocked them up,' she said now. 'I hope they'll be all right.'

'A feast,' Isabelle declared later.

There was a lovely party atmosphere, especially when Fred did his turn then Victor and Eric played a duet. The front room was crowded, with its sofa and chairs of black horsehair, the piano, the bedchair and three china cabinets which were full of lovely things Fred had brought home from abroad.

Sarah's favourite piece was a Japanese tea set for twelve people. The china was so fragile that a small child had once bitten a piece out of a cup. The most delicate blue, the china had a translucent look and you could almost see

31

through it when you held it up to the light. Each piece was painted with Japanese ladies and gentlemen in kimonos.

By half-past six, Sarah's throat was beginning to be really sore and she knew she was in for one of her attacks of swollen glands. She would have said so, but her mother began to get a headache and went to lie down. Lucy said to let Isabelle stay the night – she could sleep with Jenny in the sideboard bed. Isabelle felt too poorly to protest

Jonathan started to make preparations to leave with the children and when they were in the train he put his arm around Sarah and said gently, 'I think you are suffering from a sore throat.'

She nodded, feeling miserable that she too was responsible for curtailing their lovely afternoon.

When they got home Jonathan painted her throat with iodine and saw she was tucked up in bed with two hot water bottles. He brought a jug of water and told Sarah he would look in on her through the night to see if she needed anything.

Sarah spent a restless night but each time her father came in quietly to see if she was all right, she made a pretence of sleep, not wanting him to worry.

Monday morning was a general washday for housewives and at six o'clock she heard Jonathan get up and go out to the washhouse to light a fire under the boiler, ready for when Maggie came.

Half an hour later, the back gate opened with a crash and Sarah sleepily knew that Maggie had arrived. Before she was at the kitchen door she was shouting, 'It's me, Mr T!'

It was Maggie who brought her up a cup of milky tea. 'Poorly again, are you, me love? Your da'll bring you some porridge up in a few minutes. Let's have a look at your throat. Yes,' (with some prodding) 'they're up, all right, them glands. Now that your ma isn't here I'll cure them for you, but I'll have to wait till old Joe comes by.'

Sarah presumed that 'old Joe' was one of the people from whom Maggie obtained her herbs. Maggie had great faith in herbs. Sarah tried to sip the tea but it hurt so much to swallow she gave up. Nor did she want the porridge when her father brought it. He smoothed her hair away from her brow and said kindly, 'Poor Sarah. Perhaps you'll feel better a little later on, it's still early. Try and sleep.'

It was impossible to sleep for all the activity going on in the Avenue. Wooden-rollered, iron-framed mangles were dragged from washhouse to yard with the sound of a team of traction engines. Then came the thump of poss-tubs being brought out, followed by the clatter of tin baths – two as a rule, one to blue the whites and one for starching.

Later, there were all the other sounds. Although Berkeley Avenue was considered to be a cut above the other local streets, there were all the usual cries of vendors in the back lane as elsewhere. The fishwife proclaimed with her sing-song cry, 'Herrings, fresh herrings! Thirteen a penny. Get your herrings!'

This could be followed by the rag and bone man, who would give a balloon to a child in exchange for some old clothes, jars, bottles or bones

The 'rubbing stone' woman had a shrill voice as she offered a piece of yellow sandstone to colour the front door step in exchange for old clothes, or one could buy a piece for a halfpenny.

But the voice the housewives dreaded to hear was that of the coalman. He had a deep, booming voice that carried and, on his first call of 'Co-al'! Shillin' a bag!' women would rush out, as they did now, lower props which pushed up the clothes lines, remove pegs and hastily bundle the clean washing into big wicker baskets.

When he was safely gone and the clothes were being re-pegged the gossip would start. That morning, Mrs Cotton was the main topic. 'Just had her seventh . . . what a disgrace bringing another into the world and her with not enough money to feed the other six . . .' As no one seemed to know who the father of this baby was, there were wild guesses. 'Bet it was that rollicking sailor who was buying bread at the corner shop,' . . . Or the butcher's son who had been seen going into the house one night. Then a

33

woman shouted with a laugh, 'But she'd have us believe it was the Holy Ghost who was responsible!'

There was some laughter at this, but it was uneasy laughter. The women in Berkeley Avenue were all regular churchgoers.

Sarah was glad that Maggie was not one of those gossiping. She could hear her in the yard, whistling through her teeth over the slurp of water and the thump of the poss-stick as Maggie pounded the clothes in the tub.

It was about an hour after this that Maggie came busily up the stairs and into the bedroom, bringing with her an odd sour smell. 'Just seen old Joe,' she said, 'and he's given me one of his socks. Nothing like a sweaty sock for curing throat troubles.'

'No, no,' Sarah croaked weakly, but she might just as well have saved her voice.

As she said to Victor when he came home from school, 'Before I could say Jack Robinson the awful thing was pinned round my neck, with Maggie warning me if I took it off I wouldn't be well enough to go to Doris Wilson's party on Thursday.'

Victor, his nose pressed between forefinger and thumb said, 'I don't know who old Joe is but that sock of his is a real humdinger!'

Sarah agreed wholeheartedly, but to her surprise by early evening she could swallow more easily, and by the time Jonathan came home Maggie had her downstairs, wrapped in a blanket by the fire.

'There, now.' Maggie put on her old black coat. 'I'll be going now, Mr T. I've toasted some muffins and made some scones, and there's the rice cake Mrs T made and some fruit cake if you want it. I don't suppose you'll starve.' She gave Jonathan a broad grin. 'Not when *you* are around, Mr T. As handy a man as I ever did see.'

Maggie had the greatest admiration for Jonathan, declaring him to be a 'proper gent'. She said she had never known a man who would raise his hat to his children playing in the street, or stand up when she came into the room.

She put the muffins on the table and ordered the family

34

to eat up while they were still hot. 'Maggie, whatever would we do without you?' Jonathan asked. 'You're a tower of strength to this family.'

'And glad to be so. Ta-ra now, I'll see you all in the morning, in case Mrs T's not back home.'

Sarah enjoyed her tea and Jonathan laughed when she told him of Maggie's cure. 'Quite a woman,' he said. 'One of the wonderful rough diamonds of this world.'

After tea Victor went into the front room to practise scales. Jonathan drew a chair up to the table in the kitchen to repair a watch and said, 'Well now, Sarah, what questions do you want to ask?'

After a moment's hesitation she admitted, 'Actually, Poppa, I want to tell you something first. It's about Mrs Cotton.' Sarah explained about being present when the baby was born and Jonathan pushed the small magnifying glass up on to his forehead and eyed his daughter in a thoughtful way.

'That was quite an experience for a girl of your age, Sarah. Does your mother know?'

Sarah shook her head. 'I thought it best not to tell her. She doesn't seem to like Mrs Cotton and neither do any of the other women. One woman said she was a slut. Poppa, how does a baby get into your stomach?'

Jonathan tugged at his earlobe. 'Well now, I could tell you but I think it is something your mother would rather do. Only I do think she would want you to wait until you're a little older. Will you accept that decision, Sarah?'

'Yes, but there's something else I want to know. Why do Mrs Cotton's children all have different fathers and why don't any of them live there?'

For a second Sarah thought she saw her father's lips trembling in a smile, but the next moment he was solemn as he said, 'This connects with the other question you asked, Sarah. But this is something that only happens to a certain type of woman. I feel sure that all the children of the families you know have only one father. And that's the way society expects it to be. You can take my word on this.'

'So what is a slut? What does the word mean?'

35

'A woman who is untidy in her home and in herself, but that same woman can love her children dearly and would die for them if necessary.'

'Like Mrs Cotton?'

'Yes, like Mrs Cotton. She does love and care for her children, no matter what you might hear to the contrary. There is a great deal you'll learn about people as you grow up, Sarah, but you must never condemn any person for what seems wrong unless you know the full circumstances. Now, shall we have a talk about clocks?'

Sarah said there was just one more thing she wanted to know: was it possible to have a black baby by eating oranges, African ones?

Jonathan had a fit of coughing and got up to get a drink of water. 'Sorry about that,' he said when he came back, he'd had a tickle in his throat. 'No, Sarah, it's not possible to have a baby by eating oranges, African ones or otherwise.'

He then explained carefully how it was considered by many people to be a shameful thing for a girl to have a baby if she was not married. He went on to say that many girls in this position were disowned by their parents and had to go to the workhouse.

'Mrs Weston in North Shields didn't send Betty to the workhouse,' Sarah said. 'But why did she say it was because of oranges that Betty – '

'Sarah.' Jonathan spoke gently. 'I know Mrs Weston. She's a very simple woman, a very kind soul, and I know that her daughter and her small grandchild will be well taken care of, but she would be embarrassed about the baby arriving and perhaps said the first thing that came into her head. I don't know, but I do think we ought to talk now about clocks, don't you?'

Sarah nodded but wished she could grow up quickly and learn the answers to so many questions that bothered her. For a long time now she had wondered where babies really came from. Uncle Fred had once sent her a beautiful card from abroad, on which a husband and wife were choosing a baby from dozens inside cabbages. Someone else had told her they were found under rose bushes, but then there was

36

the book she had read in which the stork brought the baby. And the doctor's black bag was supposed to carry a baby to certain women. She had seen Dr Forster go into Mrs Johnstone's and later Peggy Johnstone had come out and said she had a baby brother. The doctor had brought it.

Well, she knew now that all these things were wrong, but she still had no idea how the baby got into its mother's stomach in the first place. And why mustn't she ever sit on the knee of a strange man, or take sweets from him? Her mother had kept stressing this point over and over again, especially when Sarah was going to the park. But to all her questioning she had the same answer – you'll know when you're older.

Sarah sighed. How much older? A year, two years? Perhaps Maggie would tell her. But even as she thought this Sarah knew she would never get the answers from that source. If she even asked for a biscuit Maggie would say, 'You'd better ask your ma – or your da.'

Isabelle arrived home on Tuesday morning, apologising for her absence and full of concern when she knew that Sarah had been poorly. 'Oh, Sarah love, I'm sorry – I should have been here. I was so concerned with myself and my headache, I never dreamt that you would be ill.'

Sarah told her about Maggie's cure and then Isabelle was horrified. 'A sweaty sock! Think of the germs that could have been on it.' Jonathan laughed. 'Germs or not, it did the trick.'

Victor pulled a face, said the sock stank to high heaven. He suddenly giggled then they were all laughing and Sarah thought how good it was to have her mother home and cheerful. Isabelle said she felt completely recovered and was sure that the change, albeit short, had done her a power of good. Fred was such excellent company. Jonathan had teased her once, saying that men liked her company and she had replied, a twinkle in her eye, that she liked theirs.

Sarah thought it was nice to be popular. At the last party she had been to, six boys had asked for her number in the game of Postman's Knock. One of the girls had said with a sneer, 'Thinks she's Belle of the flippin' Ball,' but Sarah had not minded. It had been a lovely evening.

4

Although Sarah hated going to her grandmother's for tea on the following Sunday, she did like the family being all together. Her mother was wearing a dark grey costume with a velvet collar, a brimmed hat with a feather that curled around her face and a shell-pink blouse with a fichu. Sarah thought she looked both elegant and saucy.

There had been a heavy downpour of rain but now the sun was out. Isabelle, who was walking in front with Victor, raised her skirt to avoid a puddle and Jonathan teased her, saying she was showing the lace on her petticoat. Isabelle gave an 'Oh' of alarm and lowered her skirt then glanced back over her shoulder and said, a twinkle in her eye, 'So, the lace is showing. Why not? Let's give the gentlemen a treat!'

Jonathan chuckled. 'Why not, indeed? It was just a tempting peep.'

Isabelle laughed and raised her skirt again when she came to the next puddle. She had a warm, infectious laugh and Sarah was glad she had this bit of devilry in her, although she could get so upset if her husband said anything out of place.

When they arrived at Grandmother Frome's house, Henrietta made a fuss of Victor, as usual, and ignored Sarah.

'My clever grandson, a genius.' She patted his shoulder. 'I knew it would come out in you – I said from the day you were born that you were destined for great things. Now, take off your coat and give it to Bertha.' Henrietta then turned to Sarah and snapped, 'And get your coat off too, girl. Don't stand there like a statue.'

Isabelle flushed, while Jonathan silently helped Sarah off with her coat. The old lady said sharply, 'For goodness'

38

sake, Jonathan, the girl is old enough to take off her own coat!'

Isabelle spoke up and her voice was sharp, too. 'Yes she is, Mother, but my husband extends all the courtesies to his children that he gives to adults, and this pleases me.'

Henrietta gave a sniff. 'There's a difference between common courtesy and mollycoddling. Come along, Victor, tell me all about your new music master and what he has taught you.'

Victor liked talking to his grandmother because she did have a great knowledge of music. Sarah sat between her parents on the black horsehair sofa, the skirt of her dress folded under her so that the horsehair did not prickle her skin. She was glad when, a few minutes later, Bertha came in to announce that tea was ready.

Henrietta struggled to her feet, her rheumatism making her stiff, but she was so fiercely independent that no one dared offer to help.

The table was spread with a white linen cloth with a deep edge of fine, hand-crocheted lace. Henrietta was not a lavish entertainer but Bertha was a good cook and the children especially liked her coconut snowballs and maids of honour. When Isabelle complimented Bertha on the cakes Henrietta retorted, 'That is what she is paid for.'

Isabelle, who never usually criticised her mother, did so for the second time since arriving. 'You could pay a lot of women, Mother, to be your housekeeper, but you might find it difficult to get someone like Bertha, who is excellent at all jobs, especially cooking. And who is always so pleasant.'

Henrietta retorted that if Bertha was otherwise she would not be here, it was as simple as that! Isabelle said no more.

Jonathan did the talking. He told Henrietta about Fred coming home and how they had gone there for tea in the afternoon. He had the reply that when Jonathan saw her daughter Lucy again he could tell her if she couldn't be bothered to come and see her mother more often, she could stay away – for ever! Sarah thought, end of conversation, but Jonathan went on to talk about some new inventions

39

that aided shipbuilding. Henrietta snapped that she was not interested in such things. And after this a longish silence ensued . . .

After tea they went back to the sitting room, where Victor played some pieces from memory at his grandmother's request. Sarah, bored, wished he would play a really lively tune, but Henrietta was delighted. 'Excellent, Victor! You really do show great promise. Forget about kicking a ball around and going off to the park; concentrate on your music instead.'

'Victor must have recreation and mix with other boys, otherwise his work will become mechanical,' Jonathan said quietly.

'Rubbish! I know how much hard work is needed to become a concert pianist. It means *dedication*. Deny your son this right and you will live to regret it.'

'My son's health must come before everything else. He's in school all day so he needs fresh air, needs to kick a ball about.'

'You are a foreigner and don't understand the British guts to succeed,' Henrietta's tone was vicious. 'You play around with astronomy, with silly inventions, neither of which earn you any money. Do not deny your son the right to succeed.'

Isabelle had gone pale, so had Victor, as they always did when anything unpleasant happened. Sarah sat fuming. Jonathan, however, seemed unmoved by the old lady's remarks.

'I appreciate that you take an interest in Victor's music, Mother-in-law, but I must stress that his future career is the sole concern of Isabelle and myself. We must be the judges of how much of his time is spent in practising.' Jonathan smiled as though to soften his rebuke. 'I hope, of course, that with your knowledge of music you will continue to discuss his work with him.'

Henrietta's head went up in an arrogant tilt. 'You belittle me if you think I would withdraw my expertise because my grandson's parents are so misguided. Isabelle, of course, is dominated by you.'

Isabelle appeared to be about to protest at this but Jonathan laid a hand on hers. He said to Henrietta, 'Your neighbour, Mr Duncan, asked if I would call and look at a clock he has that needs repairing. Mrs Duncan also asked that Isabelle come with me. This might be a good opportunity to make the call.' He stood up and drew Isabelle to her feet.

Sarah asked eagerly if she could come too, but her mother told her to stay and keep her grandmother company. Sarah felt furious. Her grandmother did not need the company of anyone, except perhaps Victor. There was an old green plush armchair in the room and she moved over to it, dropped into it and sat slumped.

Immediately her grandmother rapped out, 'Sit up, girl! And straighten your face. You're thoroughly spoiled. You are in my house now and you'll show some manners. I'm thinking of asking your mother to let you stay here with me for a month so I can teach you some discipline.'

Sarah felt like exploding but remembering how calm her father always was in such situations said quietly, 'Poppa is boss in our house, and I don't think he would let me come. In fact, I'm sure he wouldn't.'

Henrietta thumped her stick on the floor. 'Don't you dare speak to me in that tone of voice.'

Sarah sat looking at her grandmother, curious now. 'What makes you hate me, hate my father?' she asked. 'Why are you always calling him a foreigner as though he were nothing?' Sarah was aware of her brother looking from one to the other and getting more and more agitated but she continued. 'There's nothing but good inside my father. He thinks well of everyone, even of you. He asked me to be kind to you.'

'Will you stop this talk, girl?'

Sarah stood up. 'No. I might get the biggest hiding of my life from Mother, but I'm going to have my say. You're mean, bad-tempered, people are afraid of you, all except Poppa and – well, I'm not afraid of you, either.'

Victor, who had slid off the piano stool said, 'Hey, Sarah, I say - you can't talk to Gran like that.'

'I can and I will.' Sarah was trembling and tears were not far away but she was determined not to give in to this tyrant of a woman.

'Come here, girl.' Sarah made no move and her grandmother repeated it, no longer shouting but her voice deadly quiet. 'At once!' Sarah moved towards her then stopped.

'Now listen to me, and listen carefully. You're just starting out in life – you know nothing about it, nothing about the troubles people have. You've been spoon-fed. Well, there might come a time when you'll know what poverty is, know a time when people will be cruel to you, then you'll become bitter and you'll lash back because it's the only way to live a life of your own, not in someone else's pockets. Now get out of my sight. Go into the dining room, and don't start whining to Bertha or I'll throw her out. Go on!'

Sarah ran into the dining room and dropped to her knees in front of the dying fire, tears rolling unchecked down her face. She was sorry now, not for what she had said but because her mother and father would be upset by her behaviour.

It seemed a long time before she heard her parents return. There were voices and then her father came in to her. He drew Sarah to her feet, sat her on a chair then pulled one up opposite.

'Sarah dear, I know how you feel. Your grandmother can be very irritating, but you must remember she's an old lady and she has had a rather awful life. Some day, your mother or I will tell you about it.'

'She says awful things about you and I won't have it,' Sarah sobbed.

Jonathan drew out a handkerchief and dried her eyes gently. 'Yes, yes, you must,' he said when Sarah shook her head. 'Not only for your own sake but for your mother's sake. She's upset. And so is Victor – you know how sensitive they both are.'

Sarah nodded miserably. 'Yes, I know.' She looked up. 'All right, I'll tell Gran I'm sorry, but I won't ever like her, not ever.'

Jonathan held Sarah's hand tightly while she made her

apology. Henrietta, frozen-faced, said she would accept it but she would not tolerate or forgive such behaviour again. Then she remarked to Isabelle in quite normal tones, 'How is Mrs Duncan?' and the awful moment passed, but Sarah could not wait for the visit to be over.

They did leave earlier than usual and very little was said on the way home. When they arrived back Isabelle said to Sarah, 'Go on up and get into bed. I'll bring your cocoa, I want to talk to you.'

Sarah was prepared for a thrashing. Her father had never laid a hand on her, ever, but her mother was a great believer in the maxim 'Spare the rod and spoil the child'.

When Isabelle came up she put the mug of cocoa on the bedside table and drew up a chair. 'Now then, Sarah. You do know you behaved badly towards your grandmother and I won't accept any excuses. Yes, I know you were protesting against the way Gran spoke about your father, but you've always been taught not to speak back to your elders, and you were unforgivably rude. Your grandmother is an old lady and must be respected, no matter how she behaves.'

'But that's not fair!'

'It's considered to be fair in our society. I'm a married woman but it was not until today that I dared make some small protest to my mother.' Isabelle suddenly straightened. 'So, Sarah, you must be punished for your behaviour. There will be no party on your birthday next week.'

Sarah, who had been lying with the sheet pulled up to her chin, shot up in bed. 'No party? You can't do this to me! All my friends have been invited.'

'You must tell them the party is off. I'm sorry, Sarah, but it has to be done.'

'Oh, Mother, no, no,' Sarah wailed. 'Give me a good hiding, beat me all night but don't make me cancel my party.'

'It's the only way.' Isabelle now spoke gently. 'If I thrashed you it would be forgotten by tomorrow or the next day, but this way you'll remember.'

'Oh yes, I'll remember,' Sarah said, bitterness in her voice. How could she tell all her friends the party was off?

43

As it turned out, she got a lot of sympathy from her friends. 'Rotten, miserable relatives. Always making trouble.'

Sarah, who was not expecting much in the way of presents was astonished when a bicycle was brought in, with her parents smiling and wishing her a happy birthday.

'A bicycle? Oh, Mother, Poppa. I can't believe it!' She hugged and thanked them, overwhelmed. 'What a surprise. I still can't believe it.' Victor informed her that the bike was secondhand but presented her with some comics and sweets.

'Oh, Victor, they're lovely,' Sarah declared. 'I can sit and read and eat my sweets. Here, have one now.'

Isabelle said, 'There is one more surprise for you, Sarah. It's from your father. He's going to give you threepence a week. He said it's to do with as you wish, but I suggest you save most of it and put it in the post office. In fact, I would like you to save it all.'

'*Threepence?*' Sarah said, full of awe.

'I will still give you your halfpenny for sweets on a Saturday and your father will continue to give you a penny for the Picture Palace matinée. I personally think that three-pence is too much for a girl of your age, but there, your father wants you to have it. However, as I said before, I do hope you will save it all.'

Jonathan protested at this. 'No, Isabelle, I want Sarah to do with the money as she wishes. She's twelve years old now, getting to be a young lady. I want to give her a feeling of independence and also to learn responsibility where money is concerned.'

To Sarah he added, 'To encourage you to save some of it I shall give you twopence for every tenpence you save. You will get a form from the post office to stick the penny stamps on. When you have twelve they will issue you with a savings' book.'

Sarah felt overwhelmed at such generosity. At first, she did save the whole threepence and was like a dog with two tails when she had her first shilling entered into a post office savings book. But eventually, the devil, in the guise of Victor, persuaded her to save only one penny and to spend the rest on sweets. He pointed out that if she bought some lucky sweet potatoes she might win a silver threepenny piece!

Sarah studied the notice in the sweetshop window. It said: '*Lucky Sweet Potatoes, Containing Charms and Mottoes*'. And underneath in bold letters, 'ONE IN EVERY BOX CONTAINS A SILVER THREEPENNY PIECE.' It sounded to Sarah like all the treasure of Ali Baba's cave. She went into the shop and bought two. The 'potatoes' were made of marzipan and were dusted with chocolate powder.

Inside the first one she found a small metal charm in the shape of a horse that said, '*Be of Good Cheer*'. The second one produced a ring studded with a piece of red glass and a motto promising, '*Tomorrow is Another Day*'.

Despite Sarah's disappointment over the contents of the potatoes she continued to buy them – sometimes four, sometimes six, until at last, her fingers overloaded with glass-studded rings and her neck scratched to pieces with her necklace of tinny horses and other animals, she took her complaint tearfully to her father. 'All those potatoes I bought,' she wailed, 'and not one silver Joey!'

Jonathan said, 'Well now, Sarah, a little gamble is a stimulation, but to gamble your all is foolish. Why not buy one potato and then, if you are disappointed, you have the rest of the threepence to console you.'

Sarah took his advice and when the silver 'treasure' still eluded her she stopped buying them altogether.

Maggie, when told said, 'You're a very lucky girl, me old love. Although you may not realise it your Da's teaching you a lot of valuable lessons about life.'

Sarah stifled a sigh. She was having all these so-called lessons, but a fat lot of good they were doing her as she still didn't know how babies were made.

At the turn of the year Maggie read the tea-leaves, and predicted a change in the household: someone was leaving and someone else coming. And she was right. Three days later the girl who usually sat in with Sarah and Victor when their parents went to the music hall or a concert told Isabelle she was getting married and going to live in Scotland. She recommended someone else and on the following Wednesday they met Daisy, a big buxom girl with rosy cheeks and laughing blue eyes.

'She's a lovely, warm-hearted girl,' Isabelle told Jonathan. 'I'll have no worry leaving the children in her care.'

Sarah and Victor were always in bed before their parents left and more often than not, already asleep. But on the first night that Daisy came Sarah was still awake when Daisy popped her head round the door and asked if she and her brother would like to hear a story. Victor who was in the next room called, 'I would', and was there before Sarah had time to throw back the bedclothes.

Within minutes the children were curled up in chairs in front of the living room fire with Daisy sitting on a stool between them. She told them the old stories of Cinderella, Jack and the Beanstalk and the Three Bears, but these were Daisy's personal versions and contained either a dragon, a beast with three heads or a donkey with a hump. Sarah and Victor were fascinated and begged for more. She told them two more then said they must go to bed. She brought them up some cocoa. Although Daisy didn't say they were not to tell their parents they both had enough sense to know there would be no more stories if they did.

The snow was thick on the ground when Daisy came round the next Wednesday evening, and to the children's astonishment, once their parents had gone she asked them to get up and get dressed.

'Dressed?' Sarah said, wide-eyed. 'Where are we going?'

'On an adventure. I thought I'd take you tobogganing in the Dene.'

In the Dene? This was adventure indeed. Daisy, her eyes alight with laughter, helped them into their outdoor clothes, wrapping scarves around their throats and buttoning up leather gaiters. Minutes later, the wind was stinging their cheeks as Daisy ran down the street, pulling the toboggan, the steel runners zipping on the crisp snow.

The outing was especially exciting as the Dene was a forbidden place to the children, unless they were accompanied by an adult. They could hear shouts and laughter long before they reached the Dene. It was a fairy-land to Sarah, with the gas-lamps on the bridge above casting a warm cosy glow over the expanse of snow, which was dotted by adults and children on toboggans.

Daisy instructed them to join the other people on the slopes as she had someone to meet, but she wouldn't be away for long. Sarah was moving off with Victor when she heard a man's voice say, 'So you managed to make it, Daisy.' Sarah turned and saw a sailor take Daisy in his arms and kiss her. She stopped, and was watching fascinatedly when Victor gave her a nudge and said gruffly: 'Come on, it's none of our business.' He began to pull the toboggan up the slope and Daisy and the sailor were forgotten as the two children joined in the fun.

It seemed no time at all before Daisy was back, and hurrying them to get home before their parents returned. They were glowing by the time they reached Berkeley Avenue and Daisy told them to get undressed while she made them a hot drink. It was cocoa but had a strange flavour. Sarah, sniffing at it, said it smelled like the rum and butter that her mother made for Grandmother Frome. Daisy replied that the drink was the kind *her* grandmother made to ward off chills but it must be a secret between them. Sarah agreed happily, liking the taste of the rum.

Daisy then promised that if the snow held she would take them to the Dene again on the following Wednesday.

The snow held for two more weeks. On their second visit to the Dene, Daisy met a soldier and on the third a man in a cap, with a white muffler round his throat. Sarah said to Victor, 'Daisy has a lot of friends, hasn't she?' and once more got a dig in the ribs from her young brother and was urged by him to mind her own business.

On the third occasion they left the Dene later than usual, and as Isabelle and Jonathan had left the theatre early because of Isabelle's headache, both parties met practically on the doorstep. Daisy only had time to tell Sarah and Victor to leave the talking to her when Isabelle exclaimed, 'What on *earth* are you doing out here?'

With her gift for story-telling, Daisy related how someone

had called to say that her poor granny was at death's door and would Daisy please come at once. Then Daisy went on to say that as she could not leave the children alone, she had taken them with her. She described this dying grandmother so vividly that Sarah felt tears come to her eyes. Even Isabelle was convinced and agreed that Daisy could not have done anything else under the circumstances. She added, however, that the children must be got to bed at once.

To Sarah's undying regret she was responsible for Daisy's undoing by wailing, as her mother hustled her to bed, that she had not had her rum and cocoa.

Daisy disappeared from their lives and when Sarah handed her teacup to Maggie the next day and asked if she would ever see Daisy again, Maggie said all she could see were men at war. There were soldiers and guns.

'Well,' announced Sarah, 'that's interesting.'

'No, it isn't,' Maggie replied. 'It's sad.' And there was a bleak look in her eyes.

A cold little shiver ran down Sarah's spine. She asked Maggie what else she could see, but for answer Maggie took the cup to the sink and rinsed out the leaves.

5

Back in October, Sarah had not received anything from her grandmother for her birthday, and she had presumed it was because of her bad behaviour. But ten days later a violin in a case was delivered with a note that said: *'If you wish to learn to play the violin I shall pay for your lessons. In return I shall expect dedication. If you find you do not have the talent then I shall expect you to pass the instrument on to some other child who has enthusiasm and talent.'* It was signed simply, *Grandmother Frome.'*

'Well, Sarah – what do you think of that? A violin,' Isabelle enthused. 'We must see about finding a good teacher for you, as your grandmother would want the best. You do still want to learn to play, don't you?'

Sarah would rather that the gift had come from anyone else, but knowing she must try to seem pleased for her mother's sake at least, she said, 'Yes, of course. I only hope I have the talent to play.'

She started her lessons with grit and dedication, determined to prove to her grandmother that she could become a musician, too. She practised every dinnertime and evening, either up in the attic or out in the washhouse – because of Victor's protests that it was impossible for *him* to practise with such screechings going on. Despite all this, her music teacher was in despair over her.

'I'm afraid you're tone deaf, Sarah. It happens sometimes to just one member of a musical family.'

To this she replied with some spirit, 'Mr Beethoven was deaf from childhood but he wrote musical scores – my mother told me. I should like to go on trying.'

The teacher gave in, even though there were times when there was a wild look in his eyes, and his hair stood on end where he had pushed his fingers through it while Sarah fiddled on.

Victor, as it turned out, was the one who unintentionally brought the violin-playing to an end. Sarah was practising scales in the kitchen on a Saturday morning and was 'sawing' away determinedly when her brother who had just come back from his piano lesson said, a note of glee in his voice: 'Hey, our Sarah, do you know what the fishmonger said about your playing? He said it was like a dog shitting cinders.'

Isabelle, horrified at such language exclaimed, '*Vic-tor*! How dare you come out with such words?' She made to give him a box on the ear but he ducked, grinning.

'It wasn't me that said it, it was the fishmonger. I only repeated it.'

Sarah laid down the violin and that was the end of her playing.

Victor apologised to Sarah later when they were on their own and, as he seemed genuinely sorry, Sarah said, 'It's all right. I wasn't any good, I would never have made a violinist. I knew it, my teacher did too, but I just had to go on trying. What I'm really mad about is having to admit it to Gran. She'll gloat over it, she hates me so much.'

'I don't think she does. She just has to grumble about something. I think she would have been pleased if you'd been able to play.' Victor paused, fidgeted for a moment with a catapult he had taken from his pocket then said, 'I know something about Gran that you don't know, and if you did you would be sorry for her. I am, but I can't tell you. Jimmy Fairbairn told me but made me promise on Scout's honour that I wouldn't tell anyone else.'

Sarah stared at him. 'How could Jimmy Fairbairn know something about Gran that we don't?'

'Well . . .' Victor put a pellet of paper in the catapult and aimed it at the window. 'It was something he heard his aunt tell his mother. His aunt used to live next door to Gran's family.' He released the pellet which hit the window pane with a plop, then he went to pick it up.

'Never mind that,' Sarah said impatiently. 'What else did he tell you?'

'Only that it was something – *awful*.' Victor lowered his

50

voice to the necessary pitch to create drama. 'It wasn't only *one* thing, it was lots of things. But I just *can't* tell you.'

'Yes, yes, I know.' Sarah was furious at being thwarted, at being denied this secret from her grandmother's past. Yet she knew that Scout's honour had to be respected. An ordinary promise had to be respected. This had been drummed into her by her mother and in a more gentle way by her father. She agreed reluctantly, to try and be kinder to Henrietta.

It was hard to do this when her grandmother called her a miserable shirker. Sarah had just returned the violin, explaining that she apparently had no ear for music. It was just an excuse, the old lady declared. Any lazy fool could come up with an excuse like that.

Sarah determinedly kept her temper. 'When I *stopped* playing, the neighbours all said thank goodness, I had nearly driven them mad with my practising. The fishmonger described my playing as being like a –' Sarah found it impossible to repeat the words. She substituted, 'like the caterwauling of an army of cats.'

Her grandmother sniffed. 'Well, if it was as bad as that then perhaps it's just as well you stopped. It wouldn't do your mother's nerves any good. I thought she looked poorly when she called the other day. I hope she's getting enough to eat. Your father can't make all that much money repairing old clocks. Your mother was always well when she lived at home with me.'

Sarah stood up, ready to go, her hands clenched tightly at her sides. 'We eat very well, Grandma, very well indeed. Father *makes* clocks and watches, as well as repairing them. He's a craftsman, everyone says so. He repaired a clock for a wealthy gentleman and was given two golden sovereigns, even though Poppa was only going to charge him ten shillings. He gave the sovereigns to Mother. I must go now, Grandma, I have an errand to do. Thank you for paying for my violin lessons and I'm sorry I let you down.'

Sarah bolted then before she could say anything more that would get her into trouble. Bertha, who was standing

51

in the hall, mouthed 'Good for you!' and patted her on the shoulder. They exchanged conspiratorial smiles.

On the way home Sarah called in at Mrs Cotton's house. She had got into the habit of calling every Saturday morning for a few minutes and at odd times on her way home from school. Although the house still had its 'poverty' smell the baby, who had been christened James, was always sweet and clean. He was small, but thriving. She took him from his mother and held him close.

'And whose little pet are you?' she crooned. The baby nuzzled into her neck and Sarah stroked his back. 'And a lovely new matinée jacket! Who knitted that, then?'

'Your mother did,' Mrs Cotton said, smiling.

'My mother?' Sarah eyed her in astonishment. 'I didn't know, she didn't say anything.'

'Your mother has been very good to me, Sarah. She brought me calves-foot jelly earlier on and some groceries. She also gave me all the baby clothes she had, saying she would not be needing them again, not after her operation.'

Sarah knew about the operation – it was something to do with her mother's insides. This had been a year after Victor was born. But although her mother had once told her she could not have any more babies, which would be explained to her 'when she was older', Sarah had not connected it with the operation. She said now, 'Oh,' and left it at that.

The fact that her mother had visited Mrs Cotton and taken baby clothes gave Sarah the courage to ask if she could take baby James to the park one Saturday morning, after she had finished her household chores.

'Yes,' Isabelle granted, 'but only if you are going with some other girls and you promise not to speak to any strange man or take sweets.'

Wondering how many times she was going to be told the same thing, Sarah promised in a weary voice. At this, Isabelle spoke sharply.

'I know you get fed up being told the same thing, Sarah, but what I'm telling you is important. *Very* important. If any man speaks to you, a stranger that is, you are to come home right away. Is that understood?' Sarah said it was, in a firm voice.

There were two or three other girls who took baby brothers or sisters out for an airing at the weekend, and on this particular Saturday morning Sarah went to the park with Evelyn Dobson and Betty Medhurst. They all discussed the warnings given them by their mothers.

'Honestly!' Evelyn Dobson said. 'It gets you right fed up with all the hoo-ha – don't do this, don't do that. What would happen if you did take a sweet from a man?'

'You might have him put his hand up your clothes,' declared Betty Medhurst. 'Or even up your knicker-leg. That's what my Dad told me and he ought to know, being a policeman. He says there's a queer lot of folks about.'

Sarah eyed her friend with interest. 'Why should a man want to put his hand up your knicker-leg?'

Evelyn Dobson giggled. 'If he put his hand up mine I would say he was after my biscuits. I pinched two out of the pantry before I left. Here, do you want a piece?' She extracted the biscuits, broke them up and handed out portions.

They were all laughing by then, with Evelyn saying cheekily, 'I wouldn't mind a few sweets, if that's all a fellow wanted to do.'

Sarah sobered. 'No, you mustn't. It's sort of – well, dirty.'

'Oh, go on with you. Anyway, chance is a fine thing! Come on, I'll race you to the park gates.' They charged along with their prams and arrived breathless. Automatically they made for the bowling green, which was their favourite spot. The morning was cold and there was a shelter they could sit in and watch the old men bowling at the same time. But this morning the green was bare. They went and sat in the shelter, discussed all that had been happening to them during the past week, then fell silent as a young man in a raincoat came in.

'A bit nippy this morning, isn't it?' he greeted them with a smile. 'Mind if I sit down and join the party?'

Betty, a small plump girl with frizzy fair hair and a bold look in her eyes said, 'The shelter's free.' She shuffled up so she could make room in the corner beside her. Sarah envied the way her friend could chat to any boy or young man, and this young man was certainly good-looking, with his dark curly hair and very blue eyes.

He told them his name was Harry. He admired the babies, wanted to know who they belonged to then said merrily that he had a baby nephew and would bring him along one morning to make up the party. The girls laughed at this, with Sarah feeling sorry that he was not sitting next to her. He really was attractive, with a lovely voice, soft and a bit classy.

But when he brought out a bag of sweets and offered them around, she sat up straight. Evelyn hesitated before accepting, but Betty accepted at once, saying, 'Lovely.' Sarah longed to take one but refused. And continued to refuse when he kept trying to persuade her.

'Why?' he asked in his soft voice. 'Do you think I'm one of those awful men who go about trying to tempt young girls with a sweet? I've been ill, unable to work. The doctor told me I must get some fresh air to build up my strength. I've been more or less alone for a month, so I just want to talk to people, be friendly.'

There was such a wistful note in his voice that Sarah found herself weakening. Then she looked at him and he was looking away, his gaze on Betty Medhurst's breasts. Betty was well-developed for her age and had once boasted of having a lovely bosom. Her mother, who had overheard her, slapped her face and warned her that talk like that could get her into trouble.

Sarah jumped up. 'I must go. Are you two coming?'

Evelyn eyed the bag that the young man was holding out, then looked at Sarah, who was shaking her head at her in a desperate way. Evelyn got up. Betty laughed and said, 'You won't get me to move, not while I have the chance of sweets.' She moved closer to the man. He put his arm across her shoulder, smiled and told her she was being very sensible.

Sarah nodded towards Evelyn and hurried away with the pram. Evelyn walked quickly after her and said, sounding a little panicky, 'There's something funny about that Harry. I think we should go and tell Betty's mam.'

Once they were out of the park they began to run. At the end of the Avenue they could see PC Medhurst, in uniform, talking to Jonathan. The girls garbled out their story. Betty's father started running in the direction of the park, and Jonathan, after instructing both girls to go straight home, went sprinting after him. Sarah delivered the baby back to his mother, told Mrs Cotton briefly what had happened then went home.

Isabelle, when told the story, scolded Sarah for having left Betty alone. Sarah protested that her friend had refused to leave.

'She knows about things like that from her father,' Sarah insisted. 'She should have come away without being asked.'

Isabelle nodded. 'Yes, you're right, but we can only pray that Betty has come to no harm.'

When Jonathan returned he told them that the man had been caught, and that he, Jonathan, had brought Betty home. Her father had taken the man to the police station to be charged.

'Is Betty all right?' Isabelle asked. 'Has she – come to any harm?'

'No *real* harm,' he said, and when Isabelle tried to probe further he gave her a warning glance then asked if the meal was ready.

Sarah was kept in for the rest of that day. She went with her mother and Victor to church on Sunday morning and evening, and only Victor was allowed to go to Sunday School.

'Why Victor and not me?' she wailed. 'I haven't done anything wrong, so why do I have to be kept in?'

'Because I say so,' replied her mother firmly.

She tried to get out of her father what had happened, but he said quietly, 'Just leave it for the time being, Sarah.' And so she did not get any further information until the Monday morning, when she went to school. There were all sorts of wild rumours flying around, as the whole school was agog with the incident.

One girl was imparting in an authoritative way to a group of her companions, the fact that Betty Medhurst had been 'interfered with'. Another girl holding court declared that a man had made a hole in the wall of the park lavatories and had put his hand through and touched Betty's bottom. There was a gasp at this from the listening audience and a vow that none of them would go in the lavatories again. Underlying all this was excitement at the drama.

Sarah had expected to be questioned but it seemed that none of the other girls knew that she and Evelyn had been present with Betty at the park. Betty did not come to school that day and Evelyn was late. She whispered to Sarah as they went into their classroom that she would tell her *all* at playtime.

There was a lot of whispering going on at first until the teacher rapped the desk and declared if there was not quiet the culprits whispering would be brought out and caned severely. They settled down.

When the break came Evelyn took Sarah to a corner of the yard and said, 'I know what happened to Betty, but you must promise not to tell another soul. I overheard Mrs Medhurst telling Mam about it.'

Sarah crossed her heart. 'I promise.'

'Well . . .' Evelyn ran her tongue over her lower lip, paused then said in a dramatic whisper, 'You know what that Harry did to her? You'll never believe it but –'

'Go on,' Sarah urged. 'Spit it out.'

'Well, he *wet* on her, that's what he did – all over her!'

Sarah's eyes went wide with astonishment. 'You mean he –?'

Evelyn nodded. 'Yes, he peed on her. Soaked her.'

'Whatever for? Why should he do that?'

'I don't know, I suppose he was just a dirty pig. I expect it's the same thing as men exposing themselves.'

'Exposing? What do you mean?'

'You know, men opening their raincoats. They always wear raincoats and show their – you know what. Their John Willies. I haven't seen one but PC Medhurst was telling my

56

Dad about them once.' Evelyn grinned. 'I overheard that, too.'

It was all bewildering to Sarah. 'I just can't understand it. Why should they do that? It seems daft to me.'

'To me as well. PC Medhurst said they all come into the category of sex maniacs, whatever that is. My mam won't ever tell me anything.'

'Nor mine,' Sarah commiserated with her. 'They just won't tell you a single thing. It must have been rotten for Betty, I could understand why they don't want anyone to know. Is she very upset?'

'Her father gave her a good hiding and told her she should have come away when you and I did. He said she asked for all she got, taking sweets from a stranger. He warned her if ever she did such a thing again he would take his belt to her. I heard Mam telling Dad that PC Medhurst was very upset that it was his daughter, him being a policeman and all that.'

When Sarah went home for dinner she told her mother that Betty had been absent from school, hoping she might get some more news.

Isabelle said, 'No, and she won't be there all this week. Her parents are hoping that the whole unpleasant incident will have died down by then. I didn't say this to you on Saturday, Sarah, but I'm saying it to you now. Let what happened to Betty be a lesson to you.'

'Mother – I did come home when the man offered me a sweet and so did Evelyn.'

'Yes, yes, you did, but I still hope you'll think of it as a lesson as to what could happen speaking to a stranger. Sarah,' Isabelle's voice softened, 'it's very worrying for parents. I want you to understand this and to accept it's not that I want to keep on at you all the time, telling you of all the things you mustn't do.'

Sarah appealed to her mother then. 'So why won't you tell me what *would* happen if I took sweets from a stranger, or even talked to one? If I don't know the danger –'

Isabelle hesitated then shook her head. 'I think perhaps

57

in another year's time.' She straightened a knife and fork on the table. Here's your father, I must dish up the dinner.'

What had happened to her friend worried Sarah so much that she began viewing every boy, every man, as someone who might unexpectedly do to her what the man called Harry had done to Betty. She wondered if Eddie would do such a thing and when she went to the shop on the next Saturday afternoon she walked straight past Mr MacTavish's window without calling in on her friends.

She busied herself for a while tidying the watch drawers while her father was dealing with a customer then, as the man went out, Eddie came in.

'Hello, Sarah,' he said quietly. 'Mr Mac and I wondered what was wrong, if we had said something to upset you. There was nothing amiss with the chocolate that we gave you for your birthday, was there? If so we can complain to the shop where we bought it.'

'No, no,' she said, 'it was lovely, I did ask Dad to thank you. And I'll thank you again. I haven't eaten it all, I have to save some. It was very kind of you both, very kind indeed.' Sarah forced a smile. 'I'll look in on you later. I must have been thinking about something and just – well, walked past.'

Eddie smiled. 'Well then, that's all right. As long as our favourite girl isn't upset with us. See you.'

When Eddie had gone Jonathan turned Sarah to face him. 'So what is worrying you, Sarah dear? Something is, I've noticed it these past few days. Are you worrying about what happened to Betty? If so, you must put it from your mind.'

'Poppa – what's a sex maniac? Why do men open their raincoats and – and – and expose themselves?'

'So that's it. Come and sit down, love. I'll see if I can explain this big problem. Or at least a part of it, for it's too big a subject, too complex, to discuss fully with you at your age.'

It was a dark, damp day and Jonathan stirred the fire into a blaze before they sat down. Sarah sat on the little stool.

'Well now, Sarah.' Jonathan spoke slowly as though weighing up each word, 'I don't know where you heard the description "sex maniac", but I want to stress that this type of person is in the minority.'

Sarah gave a small sigh of relief and Jonathan glanced at her before going on. 'It's a strange quirk in their nature, a weakness, often brought about by something unpleasant that happened in their childhood. At least, so I was told by a medical man. I don't know, I'm not an authority on the subject. I'm only trying to explain this to you, Sarah, so that you won't worry and view every stranger you meet with suspicion or distaste.'

Sarah said in a low voice, 'It wasn't strangers. I was wondering if – well, if someone nice like Eddie could do this awful thing. The young man called Harry was very good-looking and – sort of friendly, nice.–'

Jonathan turned to her. 'And yet there was something about him that made you and Evelyn come running home to tell Betty's parents what was happening.'

Hot colour rushed to Sarah's face and Jonathan laid his hand gently over hers. 'You don't have to tell me what it was, it's sufficient that an instinct or commonsense made you realise the man was strange. Our instinct is a good guide and if commonsense *and* knowledge are added you ought not to come to much harm. You are learning all the time as you are growing up.'

'But you and Mother won't tell me the things I really want to know.'

Jonathan pulled at his earlobe. 'I know how you feel, Sarah. I'll have a talk with your mother this evening and see what she says.'

The result of the talk was the raised voice of her mother when Sarah was in bed saying, 'No, no, no, Jonathan! I won't have Sarah told, not yet. Let her enjoy what childhood she has left. There's time enough to know all about the filth of life when she's an adult.'

Filth? Sarah gave a little shudder and felt at that moment she did not want to become an adult.

6

It was during the following summer that Sarah learned how babies were made. She also acquired a new knowledge of bodily functions. This furthering of her education came about during the school holidays, when Isabelle, Lucy and the four children shared a furnished house in the country.

They had done this for the past few years; and every year Henrietta complained at the extravagance, pointing out that the money could have been put to a better use, such as the buying of essentials, like footwear or clothes.

In the past Isabelle had offered no protest in reply to her mother's complaints, but this time she made a spirited attack on her.

'I see no reason why you should consider the holiday an extravagance, Mother. We benefit from the lovely fresh country air, especially the children, and also we get dairy produce *and* at a much cheaper price than in the town.'

'But there's the rent of the house and the train fare,' declared Henrietta. 'That doesn't come out of thin air.'

'No, it doesn't. Both Lucy and I work for it. We get no more than coppers for our work but we put them in a jar – from one year to the next – and when the holidays come around we have enough to pay the seven shillings and sixpence a week rent for the house, the train fares and have enough left over to provide the children with a few extras, like sweets and comics.'

'Work for it?' Henrietta's horrified tone was overheard by Sarah and Bertha in the kitchen, where they had been silently listening to the conversation.

'Yes. Lucy and I make lace edgings for a small firm who specialise in putting hand-crocheted lace on sheets, pillowcases and tablecloths. Both Jonathan and Fred know about it and being sensible men do not think it demeaning that their wives should be paid for – let us say a pastime, which we both enjoy. And Mother, I do not want to hear any more on this subject, is that understood?'

There was silence. Bertha, clapping silently, gave Sarah a broad grin and whispered, 'Good for her. It's time she stood up to her ma.'

Sarah was intrigued. She was aware that her mother and aunt crocheted while they were talking but she had never thought about them being paid for it, because all her best underwear was edged with lace and so were her mother's camisoles and petticoats.

Isabelle called to Sarah then to say they were leaving and when Sarah got up, Bertha wagged a finger at her, warning her not to say that they had been eavesdropping. Sarah, avid to discuss this piece of news with Jenny, was glad to be saved from making any promises by her mother calling again, this time on a sharper note. She scuttled out, said a quiet goodbye to her grandmother and hurried after her mother who was opening the front door.

Once outside, Isabelle began talking about one of Henrietta's neighbours, gabbling in an almost feverish way and about nothing in particular. Bright spots of colour burned on her cheeks and Sarah, realising her mother was terribly upset and on the verge of a migraine, wondered what she could say to calm her. Then she suddenly remembered her father once saying, 'Isabelle, stop bottling things up. It does you no good,' and she decided to bring up the subject of the lace-making.

'Bertha and I overheard you, Mother. We couldn't help it, as both doors were open.'

Isabelle seemed startled for a moment, then a look of relief came over her face. 'Thanks for telling me, Sarah, it does help. I didn't want to tell your father that I had had words with your grandmother, he has enough to worry about.' She half-smiled. 'But I must point out that you or Bertha could have closed the door.'

'We never thought about it,' Sarah said earnestly. 'But I'm glad I do know about the lace. I think it's marvellous of you and Aunt Lucy to do what you do. We all enjoy the holidays *so* much.'

61

Isabelle gave a quick nod. 'And we do too, Sarah.'

During these holidays Jonathan came for weekends, cycling the journey and if Fred happened to be home from sea, he came too. Fred was an extra treat, he was such good fun.

The house at Corbridge was the largest they had ever rented, having five bedrooms, a sitting room and a large kitchen. There was also a big garden at the back and they were allowed to dig up the vegetables in it and pick the fruit. The farmer and his wife had a large family, but in spite of this, Mrs Curson, who was a big, happy woman, told the children they were welcome to visit at any time they wished. She extended the invitation to Isabelle and Lucy.

The children, of course, were in their element. What could be more exciting than having the run of a farm? Although they were never asked to do any jobs they happily mucked out byres, swept the yard, fed the hens, drew water from the well and, in fact, tackled any of the jobs within their capability that running a farm entails.

It was hay-making time, and one of their greatest pleasures was having rides on the hay-wagon. This brought the girls in contact with two of the Curson sons who were in charge of the wagon. By the end of three days Jenny had a crush on Joe, who was sixteen and Sarah was drawn to Chris, two years younger. Both were sturdy boys with dark curly hair but whereas Joe teased them and was always laughing, Chris was more shy and had less to say.

Beth Curson, who was the same age as Jenny, warned her not to get too soppy about their Joe, for he was a great one for the girls.

At midday the four children would eat with the men in the fields, big 'doorstep' sandwiches packed with roast beef, pork or cheese; sometimes there would be chunks of meat pie. Cake followed, and the whole lot was washed down with home-brewed ale for the men and lemonade for the younger ones. The weather was glorious and they would race back, suntanned and dishevelled, with straw in their clothes and hair.

Sarah enjoyed the evenings at Corbridge almost as much

as the days. There was something rather special about them, a certain stillness when the only sounds seemed to be the chittering of the birds as they settled to roost and the constant gentle rippling of the river as it wended its way among the water meadows.

It was during the evening walks, with promptings from Sarah and Jenny, that their mothers would reminisce about their childhood and growing-up days. Sometimes incidents would be repeated, but mostly there was something new they had not heard before. On one particular evening, the reminiscing was started by Eric grumbling because Lucy had scolded him for swinging on the branches of a tree and snapping off a branch.

'It's only an old branch,' he retorted as he picked it up. He pulled a face and flung it away from him. 'You make such a fuss about nothing, Mother!'

'It's part of a growing tree,' Lucy said, 'and don't you dare speak to me like that. If I had spoken to my mother in that tone I would have been given a good hiding, locked in my room and put on bread and water for a couple of days.'

Victor stared at her. 'Bread and water – for *two* days?'

'Oh yes,' Isabelle said. 'We all suffered the same fate at different times.'

Jenny looked at her mother, puzzled. 'You're always telling us how strict Gran and Grandfather were but you and Aunt Isabelle went to parties, to soirées and to balls.'

Lucy nodded. 'Yes, we did, but that was before Father lost all his money. He had a position to keep up and he wanted husbands for his eligible daughters.'

'And didn't care what age the men were as long as they had money,' Isabelle added grimly.

'But you did meet *young* men, Aunt Isabelle, Mother told me.'

'Yes, Jenny, we did.' Isabelle smiled. 'There were always plenty lined up to sign our dance cards. We had fun.'

No matter where their walks took them they always came back by the woods which brought them out near the house. Because it was nearly always dusk when they returned from their evening stroll, a lamp would be lit and left on the table in front of the window so that its glow could be seen from the dimness of the trees. Sarah thought this a lovely welcome and she and Jenny would race the boys to get into the house first.

After they had had cocoa and biscuits, candles were lit to see them up to bed and although they were all healthily tired after their day in the fresh air, Sarah and Jenny never went to sleep without discussing the events of the day.

On this particular evening, once they were settled in bed Jenny confided, 'I know that Joe runs after the girls and they run after him, but he's the kind of person I would like to marry. He's fun and he never ever gets bad-tempered.' After a pause she added, 'Chris seemed to have more to say for himself today.'

'Yes, he did. He said he didn't want to be a farmer, but train to be a teacher. He studies hard when he can get the chance. He's quite clever, and knows an awful lot about history and geography, two subjects I hate, ugh! He told me he might not be on the hay-wagon in the morning.' Sarah leaned up on her elbow. 'He said that he and Joe were taking the cow to be served. What does that mean, Jenny? Served with what?'

'I don't know, we'll have to ask Beth. Whatever it is I hope it won't take too long. I can't wait to see Joe again. I think I'm in love with him, Sarah, really in love I mean, forever and ever. I can't bear the thought of having to go home and leave him.'

Sarah stifled a yawn and lay back on the pillow. 'Well, that's not for another three weeks.' She closed her eyes. 'And by then you might have fallen out of love with him.'

'Never,' Jenny declared fervently. 'You'll understand what I mean when *you* fall in love. It's a sort of torment.' She went on talking but Sarah was asleep, leaving Jenny to suffer on her own.

The children were all up early in the mornings and would spend an hour at the farm before coming back for breakfast. Every morning had been the same so far, bright and with a pleasant breeze and a mist over the fields that prefaced another hot day. The girls took off their plimsolls and ran over the field to the farm, revelling in the coolness of the dew-soaked grass. Sounds filled the air, the lowing of cattle, the clattering of pails, the clucking of hens and the shouts of the men.

Beth came out of the dairy, gave them a wave and waited. She was plump, like her mother, but despite her deep dimples, was much more solemn. When Sarah asked if Victor and Eric had arrived she pointed over the fields to a farmstead and told her they had gone with Joe and Chris who had taken a cow to be served.

'What exactly does that mean?' Jenny asked.

Beth eyed them in surprise. 'Don't you even know that? But I suppose you wouldn't, you being townies an' all that. It's so the cow can have calves, silly.'

Observing the mystified looks exchanged between Sarah and Jenny she said, 'Eee, you really don't know nothing, do you? Haven't you ever seen a bull mount a cow?'

'Mount a cow?' Sarah echoed, looking more puzzled than ever.

'Oh, honestly, you really want educating, don't you? Well, you have a bull . . . it climbs on to the cow's back . . . then it sticks its John Willie into the cow's hole, right? Do you know what I'm talking about? You *must* know what a John Willie is . . . you've got little brothers.'

Sarah swallowed hard. 'Yes, yes, we do know.'

'So that's it,' Beth said, wiping her hands down her coarse sacking apron. 'They do what all animals do to get their young *and*, what all people do.'

Mrs Curson called then to Sarah and Jenny from the kitchen door, wanting to know if they needed anything to eat. They both thanked her but refused. Then Beth told them if they wanted a job to do they could swill out the dairy for her.

Jenny drew a bucket of water from the well, threw it over the floor and Sarah brushed it into the gully to drain away, all without a word having been exchanged. They took turns at this job and as Sarah handed the brush to Jenny and picked up the bucket she paused.

'Beth said that people do it, too. It sounds awful. I can hardly believe it.'

'But it's nature, isn't it?' There was a defensive note in Jenny's voice. 'After all, it was God who made us that way, so it can't be wrong, can it?'

'I don't know. It just seems dirty to me, that's all.' Sarah took the bucket out to the well and dropped it into the water. When she returned she said, 'Jenny, tell me something: can you imagine *your* father climbing on to your mother's back to do that thing, because I can't imagine *my* father doing it.'

Jenny grinned. 'It does sound daft when you put it like that. But is it any dafter than a baby coming out of the place you say it did?'

Sarah picked up the bucket and threw the water over the floor. 'That's different, somehow. There was something beautiful about it, a sort of miracle.'

Jenny laughed. 'I'd say miracle is about right!' The next moment she exclaimed, 'That's our Eric and your Victor laughing. Joe and Chris must be back. Come on!'

Sarah, who was reluctant to meet the boys now because of where they had been, mumbled, 'I'll finish off here. You go, I'll follow.'

But before she had finished brushing the floor Jenny was back, saying, 'It wasn't the boys. Beth said they won't be back until after breakfast.'

When they did eventually see them, Victor and Eric were running around doing chores. Chris bade them a shy good morning and Joe teased them, saying it was going to be a scorcher and if they were missing from the hay field he would know they had gone for a dip in the river.

Jenny gave him a pert smile. 'So we might at that. See you there, perhaps?'

Sarah said worriedly to Jenny afterwards, 'I think you'd better be careful what you say to Joe or you might find yourself getting into trouble.'

Jenny began to giggle. 'Do you know what, I've had such a job to stop myself from looking at Joe's – you know what.'

'Oh, honestly, Jenny, you're terrible,' Sarah said, but her

lips were twitching because she had been having the same problem.

Jonathan's weekend visits always started early on a Friday evening. The girls were out in the road waiting on the next Friday evening when Jenny suddenly pointed ahead. 'Who's that coming? It looks like—'

Sarah laughed. 'It's my father *and* yours on a tandem!'

There was a reunion between fathers and daughters as if they had not met for months. Fred explained that his ship had to come into dry dock for repairs, so he had called in to see Jonathan and well – here they were! By this time, Isabelle and Lucy had come out and there was an equally joyful reunion.

Sarah thought it impossible to be happier. Her mother and aunt seemed to be glowing with love, with her father teasing them, looking so handsome in his grey Norfolk tweed jacket and knee-breeches and Uncle Fred, with his strong, sturdy figure and his eyes full of merriment.

Later that evening, when they all went for their stroll they called in at the farm, as Mrs Curson had issued an invitation should either of the husbands arrive. She greeted them, beaming. '*Both* husbands, now isn't that nice? Come along in and I'll make you a cup of tea.'

While the adults were talking, Jenny, who was sitting near the window, nudged Sarah and glancing over her shoulder indicated Joe and Chris out in the yard. Chris was toying with a piece of rope and Joe was chewing on a straw. Jenny suddenly jumped up and announced that she and Sarah were going out into the yard for a 'bit of fresh air'. When no one took any notice Jenny grabbed Sarah's arm and hurried her outside.

Chris gave the girls a shy smile as they walked across to them. Joe nodded towards the house and grinned. 'I see you brought company.'

'Yes, Sarah's father and mine.'

After a pause Joe said, his tone casual, 'By the way there's a village fête at Hexham next Saturday. Some of the family will be going. You can both come if you like. There'll be stalls, some coconut shies and other things.'

'And afterwards there'll be a dance in the Wainwrights' barn.' This from Chris, who had momentarily lost his shyness. 'It doesn't matter if you can't do all the dances, we'll teach you. It's fun.'

'We don't need to be taught dances,' Jenny retorted. 'We can match anything that you lot can do.'

Chris looked so crestfallen that Sarah said quickly, 'I think it will be lovely. We'll go if our mothers will let us, won't we, Jenny?'

Later, when their parents came out into the yard Sarah ran to tell them about the fête. Their gaze on the boys, both Isabelle and Lucy looked a little doubtful until Mrs Curson explained that some of her family would be going, too.

Then that was all right. Sarah was excited. Victor and Eric had come up while the fête was being discussed and as parents and children set off for home all the boys could talk about was the fête and perhaps winning a coconut.

All Jenny could talk about was Joe. He was in love with her – had Sarah seen how he looked at her in a special way? Sarah said yes to please her, but didn't think Joe had looked at Jenny any differently from how he had looked at her.

The boys, who were ahead, ran backwards and forwards over the stepping stones spanning the river then, racing across a small field, they clambered over the stile. And because their parents were not in sight the girls too, clambered laughingly over the stile.

Five minutes later Jenny stopped. 'Something's happened.' She indicated the blood running down the inside of her right leg. 'You must have caught your leg on a piece of rough wood, or a nail when you were climbing over the stile,' Sarah said. 'I'd better tell your mother.' Jenny tried to stop her, saying she would get told off for behaving like a tomboy, but Sarah was away and, breathless, explained to the parents what had happened.

Lucy, with a quick glance at Isabelle, left. Sarah would have followed but her mother caught her by the hand. 'You stay here, Sarah.'

Jonathan then said quietly to Isabelle, 'You had better go

and see if Lucy needs any help. Sarah can stay here with us.'

Sarah was bewildered by what she thought was a lot of secrecy over a cut leg and was further mystified when they arrived back at the house to find that Jenny was in bed and was not to be disturbed, nor was Sarah to ask any questions.

Her father seemed to be extra gentle with her when she said good night. He gave her a hug and told her that Jenny would be all right.

The candle had been left burning in the bedroom. Jenny's eyes were closed; shadows wavered on the walls. Sarah shivered as she undressed. Had Jenny got blood poisoning from a rusty nail? She crept into bed and lay still and was wondering whether she should nip the candle flame when Jenny spoke. 'You needn't worry, I'm not dying.'

Relief flooded over Sarah. 'What's wrong? No one will tell me anything. What happened?'

Jenny drew herself up in the bed. 'Something that happens to all girls. I was told not to tell you, but I think you should know. I didn't know anything, did I, and I got a shock when it happened.' After a pause she added, 'It's to do with babies . . . and things.'

Sarah exclaimed, 'Babies?' and was told by Jenny to keep her voice down or she would have the mothers in and then there would be trouble. Jenny then proceeded to explain about the monthly cycle in a dramatic whisper, which had Sarah staring at her in astonishment.

To her query of every month Jenny said, 'As regular as clockwork apparently, and you can suffer a lot of pain but I haven't felt any yet.'

As a thought struck Sarah she sat up. 'The fête! Will you still be able to go?'

'Oh, yes, this thing only lasts a few days.' The next moment, Jenny was urging Sarah to blow out the candle as someone was coming. Sarah nipped out the flame between finger and thumb and lay back as the bedroom door opened. It closed quietly again and both girls heaved a sigh of relief. Jenny made Sarah promise she would not tell what she knew then they settled for sleep.

69

Although there was no day of rest for farming families the children were not allowed to go to the farm and disturb the Cursons. Although they were excused going to church morning and evening they were expected to go to Sunday School.

When they came back they found Joe and Chris having an experimental ride on the tandem. They were having a lot of fun. The bike was wobbling, they were laughing and so were Jonathan and Fred. Then the boys seemed to have mastered the technique of riding tandem and brought the bike back safely. Joe and Chris acknowledged the girls then Joe said to the men, 'Our Chris has two left feet.'

Chuckling, Chris protested, and Sarah was sorry when the boys told them they must go. After thanking Jonathan and Fred for letting them have a go on the bike they told Sarah and Jenny they would see them the next day.

When the church bells began to peal, calling the people to the evening service, Jonathan and Fred prepared to return to Newcastle.

'You will be careful, both of you,' Isabelle urged. Lucy echoed her. At this Fred made a protest. They were responsible men, not kids.

'You might be,' Isabelle said, 'but it's other people, in cars.'

Fred chuckled. 'And travelling madly at twenty miles an hour.' He teased them, saying that if the women started nagging they would find themselves two pleasant new companions, and take them dancing.'

'Just you dare!' Lucy exclaimed.

They left, laughing and promising to be there the following week.

The next few days were heavenly to Sarah, the mornings bright with the promise of heat, fulfilled by midday and red-hot in the afternoon. Mrs Curson had given the girls sun bonnets to wear to save their skin peeling. On the third day they started on a new field where the grass had already been scythed and had to be turned. The children worked hard with the rest of the labourers, now fairly expert at using a fork.

70

There was fun, too. As the lines of hay were drawn into piles Joe and Chris, with some of the other men, took to tumbling the girls in the soft, fragrant heaps. But this play was cut short by Mr Curson if he thought that things were getting out of hand.

When Chris tumbled Sarah, he laid his lips gently to her cheek; when Joe did it she felt his hand on her thigh, which scared her, but she tried not to show it, wanting to be thought grown up.

Jenny laughingly mentioned the fun later, telling Sarah that Joe had been a bit naughty, putting his hand where it wasn't allowed. Then she added that thank goodness she was finished with all this monthly business, for the time being anyway.

As next Saturday drew near there was a lot of talk about the fête. On the Friday, during their midday break, one of the men began teasing Joe about his big appetite. 'Never saw anyone put away as much grub as you do, Joseph . . . Well, there's one thing, lad – you'll be all right at the fête tomorrow.'

Joe's sister Beth explained to Sarah and Jenny that you could eat as much as you liked for sixpence a head.

A girl called to Joe, 'You're a good shot on the rifle range Joe, win me one of those kewpie dolls, will you?'

'Why don't you ask your Tom?' Joe replied, in a good-humoured way. 'He's a better shot than me.'

'But it wouldn't be the same getting it from him, would it now?' the girl replied pertly, and the others all laughed.

Sarah and Jenny and their brothers could hardly contain their excitement at the thought of the coming adventure. The boys were ready first and went to the farm while the girls decided what to wear. Sarah settled for a pale blue cotton dress with red piping while Jenny chose a small checked green and white gingham. They had blancoed their plimsolls the night before and now they were snowy-white. At last, with many instructions from their mothers to calm down and behave themselves, they were away. Isabelle and Lucy were to follow later with Mrs Curson in the pony trap.

When they arrived at the farm they found two wagons

waiting, one for the older folks and one for the young people. Chris and Joe appeared to be doing the organising. They were both wearing crisp white shirts which emphasised their deep suntans. Sarah noticed that Joe received the most attention from the girls who were clambering into the wagon and realised then that although she liked Chris very much, it was Joe who had the stronger attraction for her. She had no idea why.

It had already been arranged that Victor and Eric would travel with two farm workers and their wives and sons, leaving Sarah and Jenny feeling free from responsibility.

Chris and Joe caught sight of the girls and waved them to come over. Joe said, 'Come on, then, up with you!' and lifted them into the wagon. Beth and her sister Maisie made room for them on the makeshift seat, with Beth saying, 'It's rough but it's all part of the fun.' And it was fun, the girls as well as the boys making Sarah and Jenny feel as if they belonged. The morning was full of sounds, both animal and human, the clucking of hens, the grunting of pigs rooting and the bright chatter of the people. Isabelle and Lucy had come to see them off and were standing in a group with Mrs Curson and other members of the family.

Joe and Chris took their respective places on the wagons and cracked their whips. Mrs Curson warned the boys there was to be no tomfoolery on the journey, then they were away to cheers and laughter. It was a bumpy ride, but as Beth said, it all added to the fun.

By the time they reached the field where the fête was to be held Sarah was in a rapturous state of excitement with the brilliant sunshine, the colour, noise and movement. Members of a brass band were tuning up and when they began to play a Souza march a number of small boys marched up and down and others, older ones too, were moving to the rhythm.

Joe and Chris went to see to the horses and wagons, saying they would catch up with the girls soon, and while they were away the four girls walked round the stalls.

One, spread with a big white cloth, held jars of homemade jam and preserves, red cabbage, beetroot and pickles. The sun shining through the jars made a kaleidoscope of patterns on the cloth. They looked at a handicraft stall, paid a penny at a cake stall to guess the weight of a huge fruit cake, and then the boys came up – and for Sarah, the fête really started . . .

7

Joe led them to where a man was calling, 'Come along, gents! Test your strength! Have a go, tuppence a try!'

The machine consisted of a tall piece of wood, marked off in inches; the test was to hit a knob at the foot of it as hard as you possibly could, with a wooden mallet. This sent a piece of metal racing up the wood, the aim being to ring a bell at the top.

Several men had a go, some of them well-muscled – but they groaned when they failed to ring the bell. Joe boasted, 'Watch me, I'll do it!' But he didn't, not even afer five attempts. 'I can't believe it,' he exclaimed disgustedly.

Beth pushed Chris forward. 'Let our Chris have a go. I think it's the knack of doing it, not the blow.'

Chris refused at first but was urged on by the crowd. 'Go on, lad, I'll pay for you,' one man offered and handed over tuppence to the man in charge. With a sheepish grin, Chris gave in. He felt the weight of the mallet, studied the marked wood, spat on his hands, took a tight grip of the mallet and swung. The resounding clang of the bell brought a loud cheer from the onlookers and, slapping Chris on the back they urged him to have another go. Ever modest, Chris declared his sister to be right. There *was* a knack to it.

They went next to the rifle range where one had to shoot so many clay pipes to win a kewpie doll. Sarah longed to have one. If a boy won one for a girl it was assumed she was special to him. The dolls, pot-bellied, had a wisp of gauze for a skirt. Their hair was painted on and each had a kiss curl on the forehead. Their eyes had a saucy look. At this stall Joe excelled himself. He won two dolls, giving one to Sarah and one to Jenny, saying he would no doubt win one each for his sisters at an autumn fair.

When Sarah thanked him for the doll and said how much she would treasure it he ran a finger lightly down her nose and murmured, 'You're a funny girl, Sarah.' Then he added with a smile, '*Nice* funny,' which to Sarah was as big a compliment as any she had ever had.

Jenny glanced from one to the other. Although she passed no remark she did keep close to Joe when they moved away.

They wandered from stall to stall, went in and out of tents, licked toffee apples, sucked sherbet dabs, chewed on bootlace strings of liquorice and drank a glass each of homemade lemonade. By then Maisie remarked that none of them would want anything to eat at midday. But when they paid their sixpences and went into the barn where all the food was laid out it was not only the boys who said they felt ravenous.

'The trouble is,' said Jenny, 'there's so much to choose from. I don't know where to start.' There were long trestle tables all around the barn and not a space anywhere to put another plate or dish. Sarah stood looking around her, fascinated not only by the quantity and variety of food but by the way it had been arranged. A large oval dish piled high with slices of pale pink succulent-looking ham was decorated around the edges with small sprigs of parsley; around a plate of beef were small pickled onions and gherkins; slices of tomato decorated a pyramid of slivers of tongue . . .

At the end of the meal, the girls unanimously declared that they would not want anything else to eat for the rest of the day, if not the week, but Joe just laughed and told them to wait until the dance, when there would be another feast.

It was not long after this that Mrs Curson, Isabelle and Lucy arrived by pony trap. The girls told them all they had been doing; they showed them the kewpie dolls, pointed out the handicraft stall and then asked to be excused. They had promised to meet up again with the Curson brothers and sisters.

Mrs Curson laughed. 'What it is to be young!'

To Sarah there had been many highlights of the fête, but she decided that the very best part was the dance in the Wainwrights' barn. Everyone mixed, and young children too joined in the dancing. Sarah had dances with Chris, with Joe, some other boys, and even some of the older men. She polkaed, was swung off her feet in the Lancers, dipped and pointed her toe in the Roger de Coverley, and waltzed. She and Jenny could have danced every dance, had their mothers not restrained them. They must calm down, they were flushed and overexcited. Both Lucy and Isabelle had dances too, but most of the time they sat talking to the other women.

Although Sarah and Jenny did not sit with Joe and Chris in the wagon on the way home the boys did say how much they had enjoyed their day and that they would see the girls the next morning, which was enough for Sarah to fall asleep that night with a smile on her lips.

The two girls were up bright and early, even beating their younger brothers in getting to the farm, but then they had their first disappointment of the holiday. Chris and Joe were not there. They had gone to help a neighbour with his haymaking.

And even when the haymaking had to stop because of heavy rain and high winds they still didn't see them. Mrs Curson said the boys had gone to their grandparents' farm to repair a shed roof and mend some fences.

With the deluge continuing Lucy and Isabelle talked of returning home. The girls begged them to stay a little longer and they agreed, for after all, the weather could change. But then Victor and Eric developed barking coughs which kept them all awake at night and so the decision was taken. They would leave on the Saturday.

On the Friday evening they went to say goodbye to the Cursons. Some of the family were there but Joe and Chris did not come in until they were ready to leave. Chris was quiet, but Joe teased Sarah and Jenny. 'We'll miss you – best workers we've ever had! Be sure and come next summer.'

Isabelle and Lucy said they hoped to and Isabelle extended an invitation to the Curson family to give them a call if ever any of them came to Newcastle. Mrs Curson promised.

Chris said to Sarah in an undertone, 'Would you write to me, Sarah?' She told him with a smile that she would and he promised to write back.

'And that's it,' Jenny said flatly when they left. 'End of holiday, end of romance. They won't come to see us and don't you expect Chris to write. I heard him asking you about it. It'll be a question of out of sight, out of mind.'

'I think Chris will write,' Sarah said quietly. 'He's that type of person, more serious than Joe.'

'Yes,' Jenny said, and Sarah, detecting a note of pain in her voice, felt sorry for her cousin, knowing how it hurt if you had a crush on a boy and he didn't feel the same way about you.

They had a lovely warm welcome from Jonathan when they arrived home, and high tea was waiting, prepared by Maggie. But although the adults talked non-stop Sarah was quiet and so was Jenny, until Jonathan announced that he had found a job for her, when she left school in the autumn.

'Oh, where, where, Uncle Jonathan?' Jenny asked excitedly. 'At the jewellery shop down the road from you?'

'Yes. Mr Turner has agreed to take you on as an apprentice and has generously offered to pay you five shillings a week.'

Isabelle arranged there and then that she would give Jenny her midday meal every day and Sarah was especially pleased that she would be seeing her cousin every day to have a chat.

Jenny had made up her mind a year before that she wanted to work in a jeweller's shop. When Sarah asked her why, she told her that she wanted to learn how jewellery was made because she knew she could eventually make some herself and sell it to friends and neighbours. That way, she could earn much more money than by working in an office or a haberdasher's. She had added, 'I'll teach you, Sarah, then when you leave school we can make the pieces together and one day start our own business.'

Although this had sounded interesting to Sarah her first love was clocks, and she could hardly wait to leave school and work with her father in his shop.

As it turned out, Jenny's news of a job was not the only excitement of the homecoming. On the Sunday morning Sarah answered a knock on the front door to find a strange woman standing there. The woman was well-dressed and would have been really beautiful had it not been for a fiery birthmark down the lower part of her right cheek, extending to her neck. The woman said in a slightly shaky voice, 'You must be Sarah. I'm your Aunt Mary.'

'Aunt Mary?' Sarah was staring at her in bafflement when Isabelle and Lucy came hurrying up; after tearful greetings had been exchanged with the visitor, they hustled her into the front room and closed the door firmly. Jenny, who had come into the hall on tiptoe, listened unashamedly outside the door and put a finger to her lips, a gleeful expression on her face.

Although Sarah knew that Mary was the sister of her mother and Aunt Lucy, she had never met her, and her name was hardly ever mentioned. According to Jenny, who was an inveterate eavesdropper, Mary was the Frome family's 'skeleton in the cupboard'; the story went that Mary had run away to Gretna Green to marry a commerical traveller named Roger Dale and she had been disowned thereafter by Henrietta.

Sarah was intrigued by the story and thought it all very romantic. She couldn't help but feel a little tremor of excitement as she heard the low secretive murmur of voices from behind the door. Why should Mary pay a visit now?

A few minutes later Jenny was able to impart the answer. Mary's husband had left her and was living 'in sin' with a young girl!

'Poor Aunt Mary,' Sarah said. 'What a shame. What's her husband like?'

'I've never seen him but I overheard Mother telling your mother once that he was very good-looking and a real charmer. She also said that when Roger changed his job for a better one with a car thrown in, the car went to his head. He started taking young girls out in it when he was away on his journeys.'

Sarah was silent for a moment then she said, 'I didn't

know that Aunt Mary had a birthmark on her cheek.' Jenny told her that she didn't, either. Isabelle and Lucy then came to ask the girls to get ready for church and warned them they were not to mention Mary's visit to anyone. Victor and Eric had gone to spend the day with one of Lucy's in-laws, so they were conveniently out of the way.

While Sarah and Jenny walked to church Jenny scoffed, 'Isn't it daft, making such a mystery of it. I hope we get to meet Aunt Mary.'

But they didn't. She spent the rest of that Sunday in bed and left for London, where she lived, the following morning before the girls were up.

When Sarah and Jenny started to ask questions they were silenced by Isabelle and Lucy. There would be no discussion. It was none of their business, and the firm note in both their voices told the girls they would be in trouble if they persisted.

But Sarah, determined not to let it end there, spoke to her father that evening when Lucy and the children had gone home and Isabelle had retired early with a headache.

At first Jonathan declined to discuss it; Aunt Mary was a part of Isabelle's and Lucy's family, and it was not up to him to go against their wishes. But when Sarah asked him to answer only one thing – was Mary's birthmark responsible for driving her husband away – Jonathan said, 'No, Sarah, definitely not. Roger was very much in love with Mary and love sees no disfigurement. Mary is a sweet person, so caring, so generous. There are deep issues involved in what has happened recently, issues that I am not willing to discuss. Please leave it at that.'

'But Poppa, if you would only tell me –'

'Sarah, please listen to me and listen carefully, because what I am going to say to you is important. I agree that children should be curious, for that is the way they learn. But when there is a problem with someone outside our own closely-knit family, and your mother and I tell you it is something we don't want to discuss, then you must accept that.'

Sarah sighed and said all right, but it didn't stop her from

79

wishing she knew why Roger Dale, who was supposed to love her aunt, had deserted her so suddenly after seven years of marriage. And Sarah might never have known the reason, had it not been for a series of coincidences.

If she had not gone to her grandmother's one Saturday morning earlier than usual, the kitchen fire would have been well-alight. If Henrietta had not called Bertha away at the very moment when she was hastily pushing a small newspaper cutting into the heart of the still-smouldering coal, the paper would have eventually burned up and Sarah would never have known the real sin of Roger Dale.

But as it was, perhaps because nothing very much happened in Bertha's life and because she had looked guilty when trying to get rid of the paper, Sarah pulled the cutting out and quickly thrust it into her pocket.

Although she felt shame at what she had done, it did not stop her from unfolding the sooty piece of paper once she had left her grandmother's house and was out of sight of Oak Crescent. She was totally unprepared for the news the cutting contained. Staring at it aghast, she read for the second time that one Roger Dale, with addresses in both London and Newcastle, had been apprehended for having indecent photographs in his possession. Sarah looked hastily around her, feeling that eyes from every window were watching.

Indecent photographs? She thrust the cutting into her pocket and hurried away. Although she was not quite sure what indecent meant, she knew it must be something awful for Roger to have been arrested. She began to run, wanting to get all the shopping out of the way before meeting Jenny at midday from the jeweller's.

When Jenny did emerge, grumbling that she was no more than a skivvy, Sarah thrust the cutting at her. After Jenny had read it twice she looked up and her face was one broad grin. 'Well, what do you know! Our dear uncle is a criminal.'

Sarah scolded her. It was nothing to laugh about – it was deadly serious. Then she added, 'What exactly does it mean by indecent photographs?'

'Photographs of women with nothing on, of course.'

Sarah looked at her wide-eyed. 'What on earth does he want things like that for? Poor Aunt Mary, no wonder she didn't want to talk to anyone. She must feel awful. It's horrible.'

Jenny didn't agree; she thought it quite exciting to have an uncle who was a criminal. 'Gives a bit of a lift to our dreary lives. Here, do you think he'll go to prison? Will there be a court case? I'd like to attend.'

When Sarah protested that she ought not to talk like that, Jenny laughed and gave her a nudge. 'Go on, I bet you're just as interested as everyone else. Do you think our mothers know? If they do mine will be here by now and all the secret whispering will be going on.'

Lucy *had* arrived and when Sarah heard her aunt and mother talking in low urgent voices in the front room she felt no excitement, just a sudden urge to know more about the life of her Aunt Mary, a woman who had been married for seven years to a man who had photographs of naked women in his possession. Would her aunt come to stay for the court case?

Mary did, and this time she did not shut herself away. In fact, it was Sarah who went for long walks with her after school and began to love her aunt who was so gentle, so softly spoken.

Roger's name had not been mentioned between them until one day, Mary told Sarah that she would like to visit Jesmond Dene. It was a beauty spot, much frequented by families on Sunday evenings in the summer. Sarah had been barred from going unless she was accompanied by an adult, simply because the dust from the red gravelled paths would rise and cover clothes as well as shoes if one raced along the paths. The Sunday walks were very sedate.

Sarah was telling Mary how many hidings she had had in the past for going to the Dene with other friends. She had been so careful to wipe her shoes, but discovered later that the dust was all over her clothes. She laughed. 'A dead give-away.'

Mary smiled. 'I know. I had to be terribly careful too, when I used to meet Roger secretly. It was so beautiful,

Sarah, so romantic. We were terribly in love. My mother presumed I was at a friend's house. When she found out I was meeting Roger she went crazy. I was locked in my room and fed on bread and water for three days.'

'How awful. That wasn't fair, not when you were so much in love.'

'Oh, Mother doesn't believe in romance. Roger and I ran away and were married at Gretna Green and she's never forgiven me. Sometimes I wish we could make it up – I have tried, but she won't have it. Let's go down to the Grotto.'

The Grotto was a tiny place at the bottom of moss-covered steps where trickles of water ran down the walls. When Sarah used to go there when she was younger, it had seemed a magic place. Now it was chilly and damp and Sarah wanted to be up and out in the sunshine. But Mary lingered. When she came up she said softly, 'It brings back such lovely memories. Thanks for coming with me, Sarah.'

Roger's name was never mentioned again. Mary stayed until the end of the court case, when Sarah learned from Jenny's eavesdropping that their uncle had been sent to prison for six months. Dry-eyed but pale, Mary left the following day, with a promise to keep in touch.

Sarah felt unhappy. Not for Roger but for Mary, who still seemed to love her husband so much. She couldn't snap out of her depressive mood and eventually her father spoke to her about it. 'What's worrying you, Sarah? Please tell me, perhaps I can help.'

'It's Aunt Mary having that awful husband,' she blurted out. 'I hate him, having all those photographs. She's trying to be brave but I know she's aching inside.'

'Sarah, who told you about your uncle?'

'I heard Mother and Aunt Lucy whispering. And he's *not* my uncle! He's dirty. How could Aunt Mary love him?'

'Sarah dear, there are certain things I must explain. When we are young we live in a dream world, a fantasy world, where only nice things happen. But in the real world many unpleasant incidents take place, and some we are unable to understand, such as Roger having these photographs. Some men carry them as a joke, to share with other men. We may not understand this but we must try and accept that the world is made up of all kinds of people, and that we must make allowances when these people do not behave as we do. Try to understand, Sarah.'

When she made no reply Jonathan went on, 'You are young, my love, and have a lot to learn, but remember this: love between a man and woman is a beautiful thing if it is not abused. Never forget that. And remember this, too: Roger is paying for what he has done.'

'So he should!'

'Sarah, your uncle is not a bad man, more a misguided one. He's always been warm and loving and generous to Mary. He will lose his job, which is a terrible thing because without a reference he will have great difficulty in finding another one.'

Isabelle called upstairs then to say the meal was ready and smiling, Jonathan stood up and held out his hand. 'Come along, pet. Mustn't let good food spoil.'

Although Sarah felt better after talking to her father, as she always did, she could not help but feel that the world was not a very good place to live in.

8

During the following year Sarah came to think that it was perhaps the bad things that happened, rather than the good ones, that helped to shape one's life and lead to an understanding of the vagaries of human beings.

In the case of Roger, she learned that sending a man to prison for a misdemeanour did not necessarily make him turn to the straight and narrow path. Within three weeks of his release Roger was re-arrested for selling in a market what appeared to be bottles of wine, but which later turned out to be coloured water.

Jenny thought it a scream. 'You've got to hand it to him, haven't you? He really must have the gift of the gab.'

Sarah said, 'I don't think it's funny. In fact, I feel sorry for him now. Although I despise Roger for what he has done to Aunt Mary, he did lose his job and he still has to live.'

Mary did not come North this time for the court case. She had taken Roger back after his first prison sentence, but not even Jenny could find out now what their aunt had decided to do this time.

Then Roger was temporarily forgotten when Mrs Cotton suddenly married and disappeared. One day she was there and the next, the house was empty. Sarah was terribly hurt. She had become quite close to Mrs Cotton and loved the toddler, James. Now she felt as though a friend had cold-shouldered her. Mrs Cotton had not even hinted that she might be leaving the district.

The next thing to upset Sarah was trouble between her parents. Poor Mr MacTavish collapsed suddenly and was taken to hospital. Jonathan told the old man he was not to worry, he would help Eddie with the shoe repairs. But when Isabelle found out about this she flew into a rage.

She was sorry for Mr MacTavish, she really was, but

wasn't it time that Jonathan began to think of his own family for a change? They had to be fed – and the only way to do that was to get money from his *own* business. Someone else would have to fill in with the shoemaking. Jonathan pointed out that there was no one else and added, 'I *have* to help Mr MacTavish. He's a good friend and his wife is frail.'

'And *I* feel frail. You either stick to your own work or I'm leaving, Jonathan.'

'Where will you go, dear? To Lucy's, of course. I'll send you some money there. Take care of yourself, we'll all miss you.'

Sarah was appalled that her father should let her mother go so easily, then she saw a twinkle in his eyes. Her mother, who had got as far as the door stopped, then turned. 'Oh, Jonathan, you really are the limit!' A smile hovered about her lips. 'But I warn you, I will leave if you take on anyone else's work.'

Although Sarah was greatly relieved that all had worked out well she still had an uneasy feeling. Supposing her mother were to meet someone else and decide to leave? She dismissed the thought . It was pointless to start worrying about something that was unlikely to come about.

Nice things happened, too. Chris wrote the occasional letter, giving family news and in the last one, he said his father had finally agreed to let him train as a teacher: '*Who knows*,' he added, '*I might do my year's training at Newcastle University, then I would be able to come and see you all.*'

Joe always scribbled as a postscript: '*Regards to the family and especially to you, Sarah* and *Jenny.*'

Jenny dismissed this greeting as not meaning a thing. If it did, she said, he would write to her.

An exciting occasion for Sarah was when her father completed his invention, the autogyro. He planned to go to Newcastle Town Moor one Sunday morning to fly it. His friend Mr Jackson had arranged to accompany him. Sarah begged to be allowed to go, too, but Isabelle refused. It was man's work and anyway, the weather was chilly and damp. She would catch her death of cold.

When the men returned they were quietly pleased with

the result, but Jonathan said there was still some more work to be done. He explained to Sarah that the autogyro had risen vertically, as he had hoped, and it had hovered, but then it began to spin. 'The tail was at fault, Sarah, but I know how to rectify it.'

The next time the two men took the machine for a trial-run they returned jubilant. It had worked. Mr Jackson said, 'Now listen, Jonathan, take out a patent at once on this. Then send your plans to the Aeronautical Society. Our Justin will draw them up for you.'

Jonathan sent the plans to the Society, but they were returned as being impracticable. And Jonathan brought on himself the wrath of not only Mr Jackson, but all his other friends when they learned that he had not taken out a patent on his invention.

'They'll steal your ideas, Jonathan, you're a fool.'

Jonathan just smiled. If they did use his idea, the autogyro would at least come into being. The following evening he was busy on some new project to improve the turbine engine.

A few days after this Isabelle and Lucy began another whispering session. Was it something new about Roger, Sarah asked Jenny, but for once her cousin looked serious.

'No, it's – well, it's something to do with your mother.'

Sarah immediately jumped to the conclusion that her mother had met someone else but when she mentioned her suspicions to Jenny, her cousin looked at her in astonishment. 'What ever made you think such a daft thing? Of course it's not that! From what I could gather, she's ill and has to go away for a time, to the country. I don't know the whole story. You'd better ask her, or your father.'

Sarah went to Jonathan and asked if it was true. He looked at her for a moment, his expression grave then said quietly, 'Yes, Sarah, it is. Sit down and I'll try to explain. Your mother and I had intended to tell you and Victor this evening. Her lungs are affected.'

'Consumption,' Sarah began, her heart beating in slow, painful thuds. 'People die of it.'

'Only if it's neglected, pet. The doctor said she could be

fit and well again if she had six months in the country in clean, fresh air.' Six months? It seemed a lifetime. Jonathan added, a slight catch in his voice, 'Your mother is making the greatest sacrifice, Sarah. She loves us all and is having to leave us to live among strangers. But I know she will cope as she has with other upsets in her life.' He smiled at his daughter. 'And we will manage.'

'Of course, Poppa. Victor and I will help, and I can do the cooking.'

At a family conference that evening, it was decided that Sarah and Victor should go to live with their Aunt Lucy and she would see that Victor came home for his music lessons. At the weekends, they would all come back here to be with Jonathan. Maggie would come in meanwhile, and do the housework and cooking.

At first Victor was pale with anxiety but after a while he began to regard it all as an adventure. In the summer he and Eric could go to the quayside and watch the ships coming in. And even Sarah, assuming that her mother would be spending the six months at the Curson farm, felt excited at the thought of seeing Chris and Joe again.

But then she learned that her mother was going to stay on a small farm not far from Blanchland, where the air blew clean and sharp from the moors. Another disappointment followed swiftly, when Victor and Sarah found they would not be able to stay with Aunt Lucy after all. Their Uncle Fred's widowed sister had died suddenly, leaving three young children orphaned. Until other arrangements could be made Lucy had brought them home with her to the flat.

Isabelle concluded, 'Well, that's that. I'm not going away.'

'Oh yes, you are.' There was a firm note in Jonathan's voice. 'We'll just have to think again. I shall clear out the big room above the shop and put two beds in there so the children can come from school to me and sleep there at night.'

Despite strong opposition from his wife, Jonathan remained adamant. It was all settled. They would start sorting out the junk the next day. Isabelle did manage to insist that the room would be scrubbed out, some rugs laid and curtains put up at the window.

The task was duly begun on the following day. The majority of Jonathan's junk was pushed to one end of the big room, and he made a thin wooden partition to divide the rest of it. He and Victor would sleep in the larger part, and Sarah in the smaller.

Everyone helped in some way and by the time the transformation was complete even Sarah had to admit that the room looked quite homely.

Although the night before her departure, Isabelle was still issuing orders and appeared agitated, by the following morning she had calmed down and had acquired a serenity. Sarah thought she had never seen her mother look more beautiful; her skin had the creamy texture of a rose petal and her cheeks were delicately tinged with pink.

There was an emotional parting, with Sarah and Victor promising to behave themselves and to go and visit their grandmother. Then Isabelle said, in a bright forced tone, 'And you are *not* to worry about me. I will be back soon and I will get better. That is a promise from me! Bye, my darlings.'

The novelty of sleeping above the shop took the edge off Isabelle's leaving. Victor usually went to bed earlier than Sarah but on that first night she went up with him. They hadn't even settled for sleep when Jonathan's friends came into the shop and then, partly from curiosity and the novelty value, both Sarah and Victor got up and sat at the top of the stairs to listen.

One man began to talk about airships and because Victor was not interested in the subject, he went back to bed. Sarah stayed on.

'I'm telling you there *will* be a war,' the man continued. 'Count von Zeppelin is responsible for all those rigid airships being built – and *why* are they being built? To drop bombs, of course. And what fools our people are to let the Kaiser and his son visit our dockyards. They were making copious notes all the time. Harold Baxter told me.'

They discussed the question of war for some time until

Sarah's eyelids began to droop, then the men moved on to astronomy. Sarah was just about to get up and go back to bed when one of the other men said, 'Jonathan, you are a crank! A beloved crank, but a crank all the same. Of course men will never get to the moon.'

'When the scientists split the atom, Justin, they will. It may not be in my lifetime but I'm sure they will in my children's lifetime.'

A heated discussion on this had Sarah creeping back to bed, where she lay for a few moments looking up at the stars and thinking of her mother, wondering if she was looking at the same stars from the window of her farmhouse on the moors. She shed a few tears for her mother who might be terribly lonely and for herself, knowing she was going to feel lost without Isabelle.

Every night the men discussed different subjects. World politics – very dry to Sarah, religions, which she followed for a while, and on another night they spoke of evolution. Although Sarah had heard her father talk about evolution before, this discussion was over her head. How could anyone say there was no God? Of course there was, He was up in Heaven. Where else would He be? And there were Adam and Eve and the Garden of Eden. She was hearing about God all the time, at church, at Sunday School, at weekday school and from her mother.

Letters came regularly from Isabelle. Most of them were addressed to her father but Sarah and Victor had separate ones. In the first letters that came Isabelle said that although she was missing them all she was doing her best to settle down, and was helped very much by the family who were kindness itself. Although Mr Hadley was a gruff man he was well-read and interesting to talk to. His wife was a dear little soul with a nut-brown face and bright eyes like a squirrel. They had six children, all married except Catherine, who was quiet but enjoyed hearing about town life.

In Isabelle's letters to Sarah and Victor she talked of the people she met and about country life, saying that the children there had anything from two to four miles to walk to school. She had been invited to the home of the local headmaster and his wife. The couple had travelled widely and had some interesting stories to tell, especially the head-master, who had been out East for several years.

On the surface it seemed that her mother was really settling down but Sarah sensed she was homesick by her request to be told every little thing that was happening at home – what they had done, where they had been. To Sarah it was a cry from the wilderness, a need to have close contact with her family, to feel their warmth and love. Perhaps unfortunately, it had been agreed that Jonathan would wait a while before paying a visit. So Sarah wrote long letters telling Isabelle all that transpired on her duty visits to her grandmother.

Sarah had hoped that with her mother away, she could persuade her father into letting her miss these visits, but Jonathan was adamant.

'Your grandmother is old and leads a rather dull life and I feel she looks forward to your visits.' To Sarah's protests at this Jonathan smiled. 'I think she enjoys sparring with you – it's a game with her, it livens things up a bit. Try to accept her ways, play her game.' After a pause Jonathan added, his tone casual, 'You could vary the game a little by not answering her back every time. That would have her puzzled – try it.'

Sarah said she would but had not been successful in self-control until one Saturday morning, when Henrietta was being particularly vicious. The tirade and sneers had begun the moment Sarah arrived.

'And what is your father doing this morning? I suppose he's sitting reading his science books or fiddling about with his stupid inventions instead of getting on with his work! If he paid more attention to his work your mother would not be stuck in some wild, God-forsaken spot on the moors. The lack of decent food, that's what has sent her into a decline. And when I think of poor little Victor having to sleep in that awful room above the shop, a place fit only for animals! But was he allowed to come and stay with *me*, in comfort? Oh, no, I wasn't good enough for your foreign father who, I'm sure, once lived like an animal with *his* family.'

Sarah, who had made so many angry protests in the past at the vilification of her beloved father, now found herself sitting quiet, eyeing her grandmother in a thoughtful way. Was her father right? *Was* it a game to her grandmother? Henrietta was in full spate, dragging up everything about Jonathan that she could think of when, realising there was a change in the usual procedure, she stopped suddenly and glared at her granddaughter.

'So! And what is the matter with you this morning? Cat got your tongue?'

Sarah was a long time in replying. 'No, Grandma. It's just that I can't seem to think of anything more to say than I've already said when you are calling Father names.'

For once, Henrietta seemed nonplussed. She said something that sounded like 'Humph' then ordered Sarah to go and tell Bertha she wanted her.

Bertha, who was in the kitchen and had obviously heard everything, judging by the broad grin on her face, whispered. 'You flummoxed her, Sarah, you flummoxed her! Good for you.' Bertha was always on her side.

At one time Sarah would have been jubilant about scoring a small victory over her grandmother, but although she smiled she felt no pleasure. And, in fact, the world at that moment seemed the unhappiest place to be, with her mother possibly fretting herself sick living with strangers on the wild moors; her father and Victor and herself longing to have her with them and be a loving family again, and her grandmother living a life with so much viciousness in her.

Sarah came to think that the months of her mother's absence must surely become one of the most dragged-out times she would ever know in her life. What made it worse was the fact that she had no Aunt Lucy to come for visits, or Jenny to confide in. The orphaned children that Lucy was caring for had eventually been adopted by relatives, but no sooner had the children gone than Lucy had to go and look after her mother-in-law, who was ill. As she was likely to be away from home for some time she had taken Jenny and Eric with her.

In her letters to Sarah, Jenny did nothing but grumble. She was bored, there was nothing to do, she missed being at the jewellers. Not that the job was all that wonderful, but a new young man had started and had been showing an interest in her. He was good-looking, with laughing blue eyes and they could have had a lot of fun together . . .

Sarah longed to see her mother but although her father made regular visits Isabelle refused to let Sarah and Victor come with him.

'It's because she loves you both so much,' Jonathan explained. 'She says if she saw you just once she would have to come home to be with you, and that would be disastrous. She is making such excellent progress and if she left the country now it could undo all the good that's been done.'

And so Sarah spent her time after school in her father's shop learning more about clocks and watches and going in to see Mr MacTavish, who was back on his feet, and Eddie. Mr MacTavish would invariably say, 'Sarah lassie, you get bonnier and bonnier every time I see you. Doesn't she, Eddie?'

And Eddie would smile and say, 'She certainly does.'

Eddie became Sarah's confidant and she told him all her grievances. Although he could be a comfort at times, there were others when he was firm with her, especially over her mother. He pointed out that Isabelle was with kindly people and how her mother was fortunate to have the chance to regain her health. There were plenty of folk who, for various reasons, were doomed to die of lung trouble. When Sarah protested and said she missed her mother so much, Eddie replied gently, 'And I miss my own dad, who died through poverty and because nobody who could have helped him bothered to do anything about it.'

Then Sarah was all apologies. 'Oh, Eddie, I am sorry. I'm selfish, but I won't grumble any more.'

Eddie teased her, saying, 'It's not easy to be a saint,

92

Sarah. Just stay the way you are, you're all right. We must all have a little grumble to get us over the humps.'

One day he told her that his mother was marrying again and how pleased he was about it. 'George is a hard-working, kindly man and Mum needs someone to take care of her for a change. It will also remove some of the responsibility from my shoulders; if war comes I will at least feel free to join up.'

Sarah eyed him in dismay. 'That means you would have to go away. Oh, Eddie, is there going to be a war? I know that Father and his friends talk about it, but –'

Eddie, who was busy repairing a man's shoe, adjusted the leather strap over the last and looked up. 'It will come, I'm sure. But I won't be going for the excitement of it, Sarah, but because it will be my duty. Every man should do his bit.'

Sarah found herself thinking of Chris and Joe. Would they have to go to war, too? Surely they would be needed on the farm. She consoled herself with the thought that not everyone was talking war. She herself was secretly hoping that when her mother came home they could plan their yearly summer holiday, rent a furnished house, perhaps go to Corbridge again. Mrs Curson had mentioned it in one of her letters to Jonathan, saying how welcome they would all be.

Sarah had intended to ask her father about the war but when she went into the shop he waved a letter at her. 'Guess what, Sarah? Maggie has just brought me this letter from your mother. She'll be home this weekend.'

'Oh, Poppa!' Sarah screamed, and flung her arms around him. 'I can't believe it.'

He laughed. 'There's something more to believe! Your Aunt Lucy and Jenny and Eric will be home tomorrow! How's that for good news?'

Sarah felt so happy, so emotional she was unable to speak for a moment, then she said, 'I must go and tell Maggie, we'll need to do some baking. I'll have to miss my lesson, Poppa.' And she was away after nipping in to tell Mr MacTavish and Eddie the news.

The return of Lucy, Eric and Jenny was something to be celebrated but her mother's arrival was the homecoming of all homecomings. Everyone was laughing and crying and talking together.

Isabelle talked as much as anyone, describing the farm, the family and their kindness. She also spoke of the headmaster and his wife and how often they had invited her to their home, adding, 'But of course there is nothing to beat one's own home and family,' and she looked around at them, tears in her eyes.

The family settled down again in Berkeley Avenue and although Sarah felt close to her mother once more, she was aware of a dreaminess in her at times. She knew Isabelle did not want to go back to the country, but felt her mother was missing something . . . or *someone?* She had talked a lot about the headmaster and his wife – no, it was more Mr Telford she spoke of, saying what a lovely man he was and so very interesting. Surely her mother had not fallen in love with him? Sarah tried to dismiss it but it became a worry to her. That is, until the possibility of war loomed up.

One morning big headlines in the newspaper stated that the Archduke Franz-Ferdinand of Austria had been assassinated. His wife had also been killed.

Jonathan said, 'Now there *will* be a war,' and the gravity in his voice sent shivers up and down Sarah's spine.

Although she knew nothing about the Archduke and had no idea where Sarajevo was she could not help but get caught up in the drama. Newsboys were running about the streets shouting the news and people who in the normal way could not afford a daily paper, were using precious pennies to see the front-page photographs of the assassination.

Everywhere one went there was talk of conflict, especially after Austria declared war on Serbia, for they held the Serbians responsible for the assassination. After that, wherever people gathered there was speculation: other countries would be brought into the conflict. Russia was Serbia's ally, Germany Austria's. Sarah caught snatches of conversation in which Belgium was often mentioned. And always someone would add, 'Poor little Belgium, she could cop it' . . . or . . . 'She'll get the slaughter.'

Jonathan tried to explain why so many countries could be involved. Belgium's neutrality was guaranteed by Britain, who was also France's ally. For Germany to attack Russia she would have to go to France and march through Belgium to reach Paris. Britain would not allow this . . .

The Foreign Secretary said in the House of Commons that the world must prepare for the greatest catastrophe that had ever befallen the continent of Europe. Placards began to appear, saying, *The horrid spectre of War . . . Europe drifting to disaster . . . All Europe arming . . .*

This feverish atmosphere had the price of groceries rising, and those who could afford it rushed to buy and put things in store. Yet despite all this, at the beginning of the August Bank Holiday weekend on 31 July, 1914 there was an air of gaiety among the holidaymakers. On railway stations women in brightly-coloured cotton dresses mixed with men in uniform, soldiers and sailors with kitbags on their backs.

Then on 2 August, Germany marched into Belgium and a British ultimatum called on Germany to withdraw. It expired at midnight on 4 August, at 11pm, British time.

Over the weekend the British Fleet, anticipating the Declaration, prepared to go to sea. On 3 August, the British Regular Army was mobilised.

Lucy and the children were staying in Berkeley Avenue that weekend. As Jonathan had said this was an historic occasion, they all planned to stay up until after eleven o'clock, but Victor and Eric, overexcited at all the talk of war, found it impossible to keep their eyes open.

The weather had been brilliant and the night was warm. Almost every person in the street was out of doors and there was a constant buzz of chatter. With the air being so clear it was easy to hear the chimes of the town-hall clock. The son of a neighbour who worked in the newspaper office had promised to bring word when an announcement was made.

At eleven o'clock when the first stroke chimed, people

began to sing *God Save the King*, and Sarah, feeling all emotional, was unable to sing for the lump in her throat.

About ten minutes later a man came riding into the street on his bicycle shouting, 'Britain has declared war on Germany!'

The young people cheered; the older ones went silently back into their houses.

Isabelle said, a stricken look in her eyes, 'Jonathan, you are now an alien.'

'I became one, Isabelle, the moment I set foot in England. Fortunately I am not an enemy alien.'

'But people will take you for one, with your accent, and you'll be like one generally. You'll have to report to the police every week and you'll be restricted where travel is concerned. Oh why, oh why, didn't you get naturalised?'

At first Jonathan tried to tease her, saying, 'If I had, I would still have my accent.' But when Isabelle began to cry he added quietly, 'I know it's difficult for you to understand, but although I love England and am willing to do all I can to help the people around me, I don't want to relinquish the land of my birth. It's something deep inside me.'

Isabelle began to sob. 'I know, I know, Jonathan, but it's not fair to the children, or to me. We'll be taunted.'

'No, no.' He put his arm around her, and then Sarah felt like crying, not quite understanding all this about aliens, but wishing now, after all the excitement, that there would not be a war.

Within a week of war being declared, however, Sarah was caught up once more in the hysteria. Street-traders were doing a roaring business selling Union Jacks. Jonathan's friend Jimmy Barnes was selling flags instead of fruit at his kerbside stall; grocers were swamped with people buying and hoarding. The small but efficient British Expeditionary Force of seven divisions of regular soldiers had been sent to France to help the French hold off the German invasion; so had the tiny Royal Air Corps.

Hundreds of young foreigners, mostly German, had left their jobs and gone back to their own countries. Some families, too, afraid of reprisals, had left their homes and fled.

There were queues of men five and six deep waiting to enlist, men from every walk of life – in cloth caps, trilby hats, bowlers and some in straw boaters. Sarah had been told that there were men in tall hats and tailcoats waiting to enlist but she had never seen any. Bands played patriotic songs.

Posters began to appear on hoardings, in shop windows, on buses and trams. One had Lord Kitchener pointing a huge, stern finger with the words, *Your Country Needs* You. Men said that after they had looked at it they felt the eyes following them wherever they went. Other posters exhorted *Rally Round the Flag . . . Every Fit Man Forward . . . Forward the Victory . . . Enlist Now . . .*

Eddie enlisted and came back beaming. 'I've done it and Mum doesn't mind. She said Dad would have been proud of me.' Although Sarah knew she was going to miss Eddie terribly she felt proud of him too, and told him so.

Then a letter came from Chris Curson, saying that he and Joe were going to enlist. They thought they would have to come to Newcastle Barracks to train, so if they did, they would call.

Jenny said, 'Great! We'll write to them when they're away, then we can say we have a boyfriend at the Front. You *must* let me know if they do call.'

The volunteers meanwhile drilled in parks, in squares, and on beaches, but all were in civilian clothes and used broom handles for guns.

Chris and Joe did come to Newcastle to train and when they called in one Sunday afternoon Lucy and Jenny were there and the meeting took on a bit of a festive air. Everyone was talking at once, Isabelle and Lucy wanting to know how the families were, Victor and Eric asking as usual about the animals on the farm and Sarah and Jenny were agog to know when the boys would be likely to be sent to the Front.

'Soon, I hope,' said Joe, 'but I don't think they have enough uniforms made at the moment.'

97

Chris smiled. 'We might not even need them. A lot of people are saying the war could be over by Christmas.'

Jonathan replied quietly, 'I think these people are being a little too optimistic.'

Lucy agreed and quoted a chilling remark made by Sir Edward Gray in Parliament . . . 'The lamps are going out all over Europe; we shall not see them lit in our lifetime.'

'Oh, he's an old misery guts,' declared Jenny. 'He should have been telling men to get up and fight, that we're going to win this war!'

'Hear, hear,' applauded Joe.

They went on talking and Sarah sat back watching first Joe and then Chris. They both looked so attractive with their tanned skin and dark curly hair. Joe had not lost his cheeky grin and confident manner but although there was still a shyness about Chris's smile he spoke with more authority now, possibly because of his teaching job.

Joe began talking about the route the Germans were taking and Jonathan got out his map and traced it, pointing out the places where he thought they should be attacked. Joe, admiration in his voice said, 'You speak with authority, Mr Torent. You should be over there instead of some of those crackpot generals who don't seem to know what they're doing.'

Isabelle said quietly, 'My husband is an alien, and as such, not allowed to fight for this country.'

To Sarah it sounded terrible, as though her mother was ashamed of this fact, yet she could not help feeling a little ashamed herself because she knew, deep down, that she would have liked to tell her schoolfriends proudly, 'My father has gone to the Front.'

Sarah had not thought of this remark affecting Victor but after Joe and Chris had gone, with the promise to call again if they could, her brother returned to the subject. With a worried frown creasing his brow he asked Jonathan if being an alien meant that he could never ever become a soldier.

Jonathan said, 'I would not be allowed to take up arms, nor would I want to kill anyone, but if it were possible I would work with the ambulance service.'

Victor's frown deepened. 'But if the Germans came here and tried to kill Mother and Sarah and me, wouldn't you try and stop them?'

Jonathan gave a nod. 'Yes, I would, Victor. I have given this a great deal of thought and I do know I could kill to protect you all. You are my family and much loved.' He turned away and Sarah knew it was to hide his emotion; she also knew that her father was no coward.

9

It was not until news began to filter through of the atrocities inflicted on the Belgians by the Germans that people began to realise war was not all flag-waving, brass bands playing and crowds happily cheering soldiers marching to the trains, on their way to the Front.

Isabelle went around with a worried frown. Prices would go up, the clock and watch parts would cost more and might become unobtainable, as most of the parts came from abroad. And people would not want clocks.

'Of course they will, Isabelle,' Jonathan reassured her. 'The better class people will always have money to buy what they want. You must stop worrying or you will make yourself ill.'

'Someone has to worry,' Isabelle retorted, 'or we wouldn't eat. You must ask your customers to pay their debts. You're too soft-hearted and a lot of them take advantage of it, and they're mostly the ones who could well afford to pay.'

It was Isabelle who had insisted that Jonathan keep a book of money owned him but Sarah had not seen it until the following Saturday, when she was tidying out the drawers. Then she was appalled at just how many outstanding debts there were. Some of them were as low as threepence, and the highest was five shillings. All of the debts were longstanding and Sarah made up her mind to start debt-collecting that very afternoon. Her father might not think it was a job for a girl, but he would surely be pleased when she handed over the money.

Some of the women who came to their door in answer to Sarah's knock were apologetic; they had no money – could her father wait a little longer? Others were affronted. Did her father know what she was doing? Sarah said no, but if the debts were not paid her family would not eat the next day.

'And then my father would be upset,' she said. 'He's a kindly, caring man and you know it, otherwise he would not have allowed you to owe the money for so long.'

It was possibly the combination of two things that brought results; being without food – which many of them had experienced – and the fact of Jonathan being a caring man. In some cases only a penny was offered off a threepenny debt, a few paid twopence, but only one paid the full amount – sixpence – and this was a man who laughed at Sarah for her 'cheek' in coming to collect.

'You'd be all right in business, love,' he said, 'but you'd need to start up in a more posh district to make anything. By the time the folk around here have paid the rent man and the insurance man and bought a bit of grub they have nowt left. But good luck to you for trying.'

The five shillings that had been outstanding for six months was owed by a man in Dunlasette Crescent, which was certainly considered to be a 'posh' district. In this part staff would be employed in the house – a maid, cook and perhaps a gardener. The window-panes in every house shone and curtains were of velvet, brocade or satin. Not a soul was about as Sarah looked for Bentham House. When she found it her heart began to beat a little faster. Perhaps she did have a bit of a cheek to come begging at a house like this for money.

Then her head went up. No, she was not begging, she was asking what was due to her father. She went up the long gravel path, which swept in a half-curve towards a coach-house. The house was three-storeyed with wide bay windows in the two lower floors. There was not even a footmark on the sandstoned steps.

After taking a deep breath, Sarah lifted the heavy brass knocker and let it fall. When no one came in answer to its summons she had a small feeling of relief, and was about to turn away when the door opened and a young man, immaculate in a light grey suit and white silk shirt stood there, an arrogant tilt to his head. 'Yes?' he said. 'What do *you* want?'

101

Sarah's mouth felt suddenly dry. She gave a little cough. 'I would like to speak to Mr Bentham, please.'

'My father is out, so is my mother. Do you want to leave a message?'

Sarah hesitated, feeling a little out of her depth. She had never actually spoken to anyone from this kind of background before and she wasn't exactly awed, but tongue-tied. Then, remembering her father once saying that all people were equal, her head went up again.

'Yes, would you remind your father that he owes my father five shillings for repairing a clock.'

To Sarah, the young man's astonishment was comical as he replied, 'You mean you actually came here to collect the money?'

'Yes, why not? It's a debt. And what is more it's been owing for six months.'

'But this will be paid – in time. You had no right to come here demanding money.'

It was this attitude that made Sarah's blood boil. 'No right! I have every right. My father is a kind, generous man, but people take advantage of his kindness. He allows some people to pay just when they feel they can afford it. Well, that is all right when the debt is only coppers, but this is *five shillings*.' She paused for breath then rushed on, 'Every man should be paid for his labour. My father works long hours and he and his family have a right to eat. *I* want my Sunday dinner, so do my parents and my brother.'

Sarah felt she could have gone on now that she was wound up, but it was the look of amusement in Mr Bentham's son's eyes that made her stop. He clapped his hands slowly. 'Bravo, that was quite a speech.'

All the fire had gone out of Sarah. She said, 'It was not a speech, it was a request to you, to pass a message to your father to let him know there are some families who don't even have money for meat on a Sunday. Perhaps *some time* your father might settle his debt.' With that she turned away, but she was called to wait.

'I'm sorry, I can't help you in regard to the money.'

'Mr Bentham, if you can't pay the five shillings then

102

perhaps you can give me something off the debt? Some people have agreed to pay a penny a week, which does help.'

A slight flush touched his cheeks. 'I'm afraid I just don't have any money on me at the moment. Incidentally, my name is Warren Hendrix, Mr Bentham is my stepfather.'

Sarah stared at him, struck by how much he resembled Joe. He had the same kind of dark curly hair and brown velvety eyes, but this young man although well-built like Joe, was taller.

'It's no use waiting.' There was irritation now in Warren Hendrix's voice. 'The money will be paid to you, my step-father will see to it.' He paused then added, 'I don't carry money on me because I don't need to.'

'How lucky you are, how privileged.' Sarah was delighted that the right word had popped into her head. 'Yes, privi-leged,' she repeated. 'I imagine that you and your family will enjoy roast beef and all the trimmings tomorrow. My family will be lucky if we can afford to have potatoes and cabbage!'

With that she turned and walked away, and although her legs felt trembly she had a gleeful feeling that she had held her own with one of the 'toffs'. When she took a quick glance over the neatly-cut box hedge she saw that Warren Hendrix was still standing at the door. She began to run and did not stop until she was near the shop, when she paused to check again the amount she had collected. There were thirty-two pennies and the one silver sixpence. Three shillings and twopence! Wouldn't her father be delighted.

But Jonathan showed no delight when Sarah burst into the shop and announced where she had been. On the contrary, his expression was solemn as he asked her to sit down, they must have a talk.

Sarah, who had tied the money in her handkerchief, undid the knot, tipped the money on to the counter then sat down on the three-legged stool. She had hoped for praise for her effort but sensed she was not going to get it.

Although Jonathan had not relaxed his solemn expression his voice was gentle as he explained to her why it was wrong of her to have tried to collect his debts. 'As owner of this business, Sarah, and head of the household, it is my responsibility.'

'But, Poppa, you're too kind to your customers, they take advantage of you, they –'

'Sarah, only seldom has my kindness been taken as weakness. The majority of my customers have paid up in their own good time. Mr Bentham is a businessman and has recommended many of his colleagues to me. Although he is inclined to keep me waiting for my money he has never failed to pay his debts.'

'But it was six months ago when he had his clock repaired!'

'Yes, I know, and it might have been another few weeks before he paid me, but as I stressed, I do get the money. And I should say now that you must never go debt-collecting for me again. It's a little humiliating to have one's daughter asking for money from people, especially those who are poor but honest and hard-working and whose only fault is their inability to make one shilling stretch into four.'

Sarah's mouth set in a stubborn line. 'I'll accept that the people around here have a struggle to make ends meet but I can't believe that people like Mr Bentham have to struggle to live. His son, or should I say his stepson, was wearing a silk shirt and you don't pick those up for pennies.'

Jonathan was silent for a moment. He took his timepiece from his pocket, wound it then replaced it. 'Sarah dear, none of us know the struggles of other people whom we presume to be better off than ourselves. Mr Bentham has two stepsons, two stepdaughters and two children of his own. They all have to be clothed and fed and educated appropriately for their way of life. Perhaps the boys go to a public school, I don't know. Mr Bentham himself has to live up to a certain standard, he has to entertain. I only know that the people who Mr Bentham has recommended to me have helped our family to live decently. We've never ever gone hungry, as some people have.'

Sarah, who was still peeved that her 'collection' had not been greeted with cries of joy from her father sat, her mouth mutinous. Then Jonathan concluded, 'I do want to thank you for what you did, Sarah, because I know it was done only in a desire to help me and your mother. But at the same time I had to explain my feelings in the matter and to help you to understand people in similar circumstances in the future.'

Sarah, somewhat appeased at this said, 'I did tell most of them that you had *not* sent me. But I didn't tell Warren Hendrix because he was so – so snooty.' Her face relaxed into a self-conscious smile. 'I was too busy trying to think up clever things to say.'

'And did you succeed?' There was a teasing note now in Jonathan's voice.

'I – think so.'

A customer came in and the discussion ended.

A viciousness began to grow towards German shop-keepers, people who had served their customers well and who had once been liked and respected. Now they were attacked by mobs, screaming for revenge. Shop windows were smashed, the shops looted and in many cases the man and his family were attacked. One Saturday morning when Sarah was on her way to the shop, she was caught up in just such a mob and knew fear as she was jostled and pushed among people brandishing sticks.

Knowing that the mob in this enraged mood would simply trample over anyone who lost their balance and fell, Sarah began to try and push her way out of the crowd, but her efforts were in vain. She was being crushed against burly men, and then found herself being carried along backwards. This was when she began to use her elbows, her feet and her head, butting one man in the stomach. At any minute, she expected to feel a heavy blow, but she managed with a superhuman effort to reach the fringe of the crowd, where, suddenly released from heaving bodies she went sprawling on to the pavement.

Immediately someone swept her up and she screamed, 'Let me go!'

A voice, quiet but authoritative, said, 'It's all right, I have you.' She was set on her feet and found herself looking, with some astonishment, into the face of Warren Hendrix.

Still breathless after her efforts she stood staring at him. He was in uniform and bearing the rank of Second Lieutenant. A group of policemen came running up and Warren put an arm about her waist.

'I think we had better leave here before things get really ugly. Were you on you way to your father's shop?' When Sarah nodded he guided her across the main road.

Walking side by side with him she realised what an imposing figure he made, tall, straight-backed, and although he still had that slightly arrogant air he was certainly madly attractive. She looked about her, praying a friend would see her with Warren but they met no one she knew.

'Are you all right?' he asked suddenly. 'Not hurt?'

Sarah shook her head. 'No, just a little bruised perhaps. Those awful people! Some of the women were as vicious as the men. I was afraid I would fall down and be trampled on.'

Warren smiled then. 'I couldn't imagine *you* being afraid of anything.' After a pause he added, 'I kept thinking about you that day you came to–'

'Collect the debt? When did you join up?'

'I'm sorry? Oh, a few weeks ago. We felt that war was inevitable.'

When Sarah opened the door of her father's shop Jonathan, who was busy at the lathe, looked up then switched off the motor.

'Hello, Sarah.' He looked enquiringly at her companion and Sarah introduced Warren. The two men acknowledged one another then Sarah explained how they had met. Jonathan shook his head. 'War does terrible things to people. It breeds brutality.' To Warren he added, 'Thanks for rescuing my daughter, Lieutenant Hendrix, it was a nasty incident.'

'Poor Mr Muller,' Sarah lamented. 'Why should he suffer for what his countrymen did to the Belgian people? He's such a kind man.'

'That is life, Sarah, and people are an unknown quantity. I doubt whether some of them would have believed they could ever behave in such a way.'

Warren then mentioned an antique clock he had that had suddenly gone wrong. 'It was running sweetly at first then it developed a hiccup. It can go all right for days then the hiccuping starts again. Would a change in the weather have anything to do with it, Mr Torent? It is very old and could, like some elderly people, have become a little crotchety.' The corners of Warren's eyes creased as he smiled, making him more attractive than ever. Then Jonathan was laughing and Sarah knew that her father was drawn to this young Lieutenant, who spoke his kind of language. And because of this Sarah felt more drawn towards Warren Hendrix than ever.

When the two men began to discuss clock parts Jonathan brought Sarah into the conversation. 'My daughter is interested and, in fact, is becoming quite proficient on the lathe. Recently she has been working to a very close limit.'

Warren turned to Sarah. 'A promising clock and watchmaker and repairer. Would you like to fulfil that role?'

'Yes, I would, but I think my mother might have different ideas.'

'Well, Miss Torent, judging by the fighting spirit in you that I have witnessed, I feel sure you will get your way.'

Sarah was not quite sure whether she should take this as a compliment or whether there was not a touch of amusement in his tone. He said to Jonathan that he would bring the antique clock in for him to look at, then left.

Sarah, feeling a little peeved, sure now that it was not a compliment he had offered said, 'I don't think much of his manners – he didn't even raise his hat!'

'Because,' Jonathan said, 'soldiers are not allowed to. I like him, he's a pleasant young man. Are you going to have a lesson, Sarah? It will be a short one today, I have a lot of work in.'

When she met Jenny coming out of the jeweller's at midday Sarah was surprised to learn that she had been seen with Warren Hendrix.

'Several people saw you,' said Jenny. 'Going up in the world aren't you, from shop assistant, to farm workers to the gentry! A Lieutenant, they said. My, what a feather in

107

your cap. Had his arm around you, Anne Weatherburn said.'

Sarah's head went up. 'Jealous?'

Jenny grinned. 'Of course I am, who wouldn't be? Come on then, tell me all about him.'

Sarah, who had not told Jenny about the debt-collecting episode, simply said he was a customer of her father who, during her involvement with the mob, had lifted her to her feet. At this Jenny exclaimed, 'Well, what do you know! Cinderella rescued by Prince Charming. When are you meeting him again?'

'Oh, stop it, Jenny, I'm not meeting him. For one thing he's much older than I am. He must be twenty or twenty-one, at least.'

'What does that matter? Your father is ten years older than your mother and my dad is eight years older than my mother. And, as far as I'm concerned the older the better. I don't like my boyfriends young.'

'What about Joe?' Sarah asked. 'You like *him*, you know you do.'

'Well, he is three years older than me, nearly four, but he took as much notice of you as he did of me the last time we saw him.'

Jenny spoke quietly, as she usually did when speaking of Joe. Sarah said, 'He's not interested in me, and remember this, as far as my mother is concerned, I'm still a child.'

Jenny turned her head and eyed Sarah up and down. 'You're a woman and don't let anyone tell you otherwise. You have the curse every month, don't you, you've got a good bust, a good figure, and you're pretty, much prettier than I am. You're growing taller as well, Mam mentioned it the other day. I'm plump and –'

'And full of fun. You make people laugh and boys like you, so stop grumbling.'

Jenny was all smiles again. 'Anyway, let me tell you about my boss!' Recently she had talked a lot about her boss and Sarah hoped her cousin didn't have a crush on Mr Turner because he was married.

During the next few days Sarah found Warren Hendrix

coming into her mind at unexpected moments. It puzzled her because thinking of him aroused strange emotions in her, strange because the only other time she had experienced these sensations was when Joe touched her, not in any intimate way – it could be when his hand brushed against her arm, or when he once playfully touched her nose.

Jenny had once said that Joe had an animal magnetism which drew girls to him, and Sarah wondered if it was the same with Warren Hendrix. It must be, because although she was very fond of Eddie and of Chris she had not felt any of these strange stirrings with either of them.

It was not until later that Sarah remembered how, on her first meeting with him, Warren had reminded her of Joe, and oddly enough on her first meeting with Chris he had reminded her of Eddie.

A week after this Jonathan told Sarah that Eddie was going to the Front and would be in to say goodbye. She dreaded the parting but when her friend arrived he was as excited as if he were going on holiday to some exotic place. 'It'll be France, I know it, I'll be doing my bit. I can't wait to get there.' His eyes were shining. 'Write to me, Sarah. I'll write to you when I can, but don't expect a letter too soon, we'll have to get on with killing these Germans.'

Sarah longed to give him a hug and a kiss but felt it would not be right. 'Look after yourself, Eddie.' A lump came into her throat and she was unable to say any more.

That afternoon when the soldiers left to march to the station she was there cheering, with tears streaming down her cheeks.

Three days after this Chris and Joe came to say goodbye. They too were full of excitement. 'Once we're there,' Joe joked, 'the war'll be over in a week. Have the flags ready to wave.'

Chris said later, 'I never imagined myself going to war, killing people, but I want to, I really do, I can't wait. When I think of what those Germans have done to whole villages – wiped them out, tortured the people, bayoneted babies . . .'

Jonathan said it might not all be true; it could be propaganda put out to create a hatred for the enemy in the soldiers, but Joe assured him it was true, he had seen photographs of some of the incidents which had been sneaked out of France. Later there were to be a lot of rumours about spies being everywhere.

When Sarah went with Jenny to wave the boys off she found herself looking out for Warren Hendrix, but he was not in that contingent. Or, if he was, she had missed him.

Although she had not come in contact much with Joe and Chris in Newcastle, and had seen little of Eddie recently, she felt bereft. Would she ever see any of them again?

She tried to coax Maggie into foretelling what would happen to them but Maggie refused. She did, however, say that a letter would be coming to the house from a relative to report a move that a person had made.

The letter was from Mary, to say she had taken a job at the Woolwich Arsenal munitions factory. Not only were the wages good, but she felt she was doing something for her country. She had decided not to take Roger back when he came out of prison, and added she hoped he would join up and do his bit. She said she longed to see some of the family and asked if Isabelle or Lucy could come to see her for a few days. She was terribly homesick.

Lucy said she did not want to be away from home as Fred was in constant danger on the high seas and she wanted to be there in case anything happened. When she suggested that Isabelle try and go Isabelle said, a bitter note in her voice; '*I* am free to go, I have no husband in any danger, but money would be the stumbling block.'

Although Isabelle would get on her high horse from time to time she had never said anything disparaging before about Jonathan. He was silent, Lucy looked embarrassed, and Sarah was fuming. She said, 'It's not Father's fault that he can't go to France and get himself killed!' Isabelle stared at her, shocked, then burst into tears and ran from the room. Jonathan followed her.

Lucy sighed, 'Oh dear, I've stirred up a hornet's nest.' Jenny blamed Sarah – it was a daft thing to say as she knew

110

perfectly will that her Aunt Isabelle didn't want her uncle dead.

Sarah was in no way repentant. She felt that her mother needed a reminder that her father would have served at the Front doing ambulance duties, if he had been allowed.

Her parents were not upstairs for long. When they came down Isabelle was apologetic. It was an unkind thing she had said – it was just she felt that other women were talking about Jonathan for not having gone to join up.

Sarah said, 'I think you are wrong, Mother. I've noticed a lot of women talking, but I've never heard anyone say bad things about Father. He's still respected around here.'

'That's good to know, Sarah – now shall we have some tea?'

As the days went by Isabelle became depressed and Sarah guessed it was because of Jonathan being unable to take part in war activities. This was confirmed when Maggie arrived one morning and announced that her husband Ted had joined up. 'Not that I am pleased about it!' she exclaimed.

'Oh, Maggie, you should be proud that he can help his country.'

Maggie began to roll up the fireside rug. 'Well, it's like this, Mrs T. My Ted has never been a big wage-earner, that's why I started charring. Now with the pittance he gets as a soldier we won't even be able to help our parents, as we have been doing. Both his dad and mine can't work. And that, Mrs T, is because they were both wounded in the Boer War. Crippled, both of them, and my mam and Ted's mam have gone out charring, for a few shillings a week. No, you can keep your heroes.' Maggie took the rug out into the backyard, shook it vigorously and hung it over the line.

Isabelle said no more about her husband being unable to join up. Victor was always wanting to know about the war – were we winning? Did his father think the war would still be on when he grew up, he did so much want to enlist. Jonathan replied, 'I hope the war is over long before then,

Victor. It would be a sorry state of affairs if it went on all that length of time.'

'But are we winning?' Victor persisted. 'How many Germans have we killed?'

Jonathan explained that the public were not told, owing to the government having put a censorship on the newspapers.

'So if we're not told that means we're losing, doesn't it?'

Victor went on spooning up his porridge and Jonathan said quietly to Sarah, 'War is putting old heads on young shoulders. It's sad, very sad.'

Reports came in thick and fast from people who had fled from Belgium. The word 'Howitzers' was bandied about; the super forts of Liège and Namur had fallen to these giant German guns. British and German pilots were fighting battles in the sky, shooting at one another with rifles and pistols.

'It is pathetic,' said a man from Belgium who had fled with his family. 'I could die of shame that we were so ill-equipped.'

He told of atrocities, of whole towns being set alight, and anger built up as more and more of the Belgium refugees came flooding into England and were taken in to people's homes. One of Sarah's schoolfriends told of a mother and two children living in their house. Hundreds of these refugees were given homes at Jarrow on the Tyne. Troop trains of wounded were constantly arriving and men had dreadful tales to tell. There were so many stories no one knew how much was exaggeration, but certainly there were men maimed, blinded, limbless, gassed.

A few lines written on a scrap of paper came from Chris. He and Joe were settling down, had made a lot of pals. But, of course, they were missing home and their folks. *'And missing you, Sarah,'* he wrote. *'We talk of you all often. Think of us, write when you can. In friendship, Chris.'*

Sarah, who sensed there were so many hardships left out, felt like crying. Then, a week later she heard from Eddie. He had palled up with a lad he used to go to school with when they were eight years old. *'Small world, isn't it? How is old Mr MacTavish and your dad? I do miss our talks. Has*

112

he thought up any more inventions yet? I wish he could find one to end wars and we could all get back home. P.S. War is no fun.' It was signed, *'Eddie.'*

Trade was bad for Jonathan and for Mr MacTavish. With the wage-earners gone to war, in many cases women had no spare money to have clocks repaired nor shoes mended. Jonathan spent some time helping the old shoemaker to put patches on children's shoes and made no charge. Isabelle voiced no complaint about this.

One day, Jonathan said that with men wearing uniforms and being without a waistcoat they had nowhere to put their pocket-watches. He announced that he would try to make some wrist-watches, and Sarah, interested, offered to help.

Jenny passed on information from the jeweller who predicted that there would soon be plenty of employment for everybody; women would go out and get good money doing war work. They would soon be spending it on jewellery, wanting fancy fob-watches, and with enough money to have shoes handmade to suit them.

Neither Jonathan nor Mr MacTavish made any comment on this.

Then came dark days in which rumour after rumour told of the British forces having been annihilated. It was said that five German armies had swept through Luxembourg, Belgium and Northern France; one wounded soldier spoke of German soldiers coming in waves, yet in spite of hundreds of them being killed, the waves still kept on coming. Another wounded man described the burning of towns and villages the people fleeing – some of them with no more belongings left than a small bundle – and the sick and the aged being carried on handcarts.

Sarah grieved for these refugees, and worried about Eddie, the Curson brothers and Warren Hendrix. Were her friends still alive? She also knew that Lucy worried about Fred, with ships having been sunk by submarines. Maggie never mentioned her husband, and still whistled through her teeth as she worked, but Sarah noticed that when someone spoke about the war she would be still for a few moments, then resume what she was doing.

113

There was talk, and this from men who worked on the railway, about the many trains of wounded still arriving daily. People became increasingly despondent.

But then came news of a mighty battle, the Battle of the Marne, in which the Allied Forces had pushed back the enemy. The casualties were heavy, but it could not completely dim the jubilation of the victory; and, in fact, it sent thousands more men rushing to enlist.

But that one victory did not stop the slaughter. The daily number of casualties kept rising, lists were pinned up in public places and there was always a crowd round them. Now and again a grey-faced woman would turn away, her hand to her mouth, determined not to break down. And Sarah would search the lists, her heart thumping painfully. To her relief there were no men she knew on them.

One morning Maggie arrived later than usual, in her black coat as always, but this time wearing a hat. Maggie only wore a hat for christenings, marriages and deaths, and Isabelle said hopefully, 'One of the family getting married, Maggie?'

Maggie shook her head. 'No, Mrs T. My Ted is dead.'

Isabelle whispered, shocked, 'Dead? You've heard from the War Office?'

'No, my Ted came to me through the night to say his goodbyes. I don't need no telegram to tell me he's been killed.'

Sarah felt icy fingers run down her spine. Maggie's expression was impassive, but Sarah noticed the corners of her mouth trembling.

Isabelle said gently, 'Sit down, Maggie, I'll make you a cup of tea.' To Sarah she added, 'You'd better be off to school, dear, or you'll be late.'

Sarah, shaken by Maggie's statement, was reluctant to leave, wanting to know if it really was possible for a dead man to visit his wife through the night, but her mother was gesturing to her urgently to go and so at last she left.

A week later, coming home at midday for dinner, she found her father alone in the house and knew that something had happened. Breathless she asked, 'Is Maggie's

114

husband, has he –?' Jonathan nodded and there was sorrow in his eyes.

'Your mother visited Maggie today and half an hour after she arrived a telegram came from the War Office to say that Ted had been killed in action last Tuesday. It's so tragic, he was a nice person, kind and generous.'

'Maggie told us last week that her husband had come through the night to say goodbye. She saw him – but how?'

Jonathan was a while before replying. 'There is a lot of things that we don't understand, Sarah, and I think it is perhaps wise not to dwell too deeply on them, nor to delve into the reason for these phenomena. But I will say this, in stressful times our senses are more acutely attuned to those we care about. Some people will have a strong premonition that certain awful things are going to happen. In many cases something awful *does* happen. Although Maggie seldom talked about Ted they were very close. Her husband, naturally, would be very much on her mind in the quiet of the night. Her feelings would be strong, she would be worrying – was he all right, was he in the midst of the fighting . . . There is something known as telepathy which is a transference of thought. And may I suggest that we leave it at that.'

Although there were a lot more questions Sarah would have liked to ask she accepted her father's decision.

The following day, Maggie was back at work and whistling through her teeth as always as she worked, but her olive gypsy skin had taken on a greyish pallor, and at times her eyes held a great sadness.

In September 1914 Mary wrote to say that a blackout system had been introduced in London. There were now curtains in buses and trams, street lights had been dimmed with blue paint and cars and wagons had to drive with shutters over their headlights, allowing only a slit of light to be thrown on to the road.

'I don't know whether they're expecting aeroplanes or airships to come over and drop bombs on us, but I feel the army is on the alert and will shoot down any aeroplanes or airships that approach.'

115

She made no mention of Roger, but talked about her work in the munitions factory; they worked long hours, but it was rewarding to know they were all helping to defeat the enemy.

10

When war did come to the civilian population it was not by air but from the sea. At first the news that German destroyers had daringly crossed the North Sea and shelled the East Coast resorts of Hartlepool, Whitby and Scarborough was taken to be just one more rumour floating around, but soon news came by letter from people living there of the disaster, and then there was horror and panic. Over a hundred people had been killed and hundreds more were injured. Houses had been hit leaving many people homeless, and the big amusement places on the front had been battered by shell-fire.

Everyone was asking: was this the beginning, would they all be vulnerable? But when nothing more happened the panic died down.

Sarah's mind was presently occupied on how to persuade her mother to let her work with Jonathan. Isabelle said no, she must try and get a job as junior assistant in one of the better-class shops. When Sarah pointed out that there *were* no vacancies Isabelle said then she could wait until there were. So, Sarah, whose mind had always been set on working with clocks, could only pray for a miracle to happen, to make her mother change her mind.

The 'miracle' occurred two weeks later. Victor, who had called at the shop to deliver a message from his mother, came home to say that the door had been locked. 'Father did unlock it,' he said, 'and took the message but he didn't let me in.' Then in an offhand way he added, 'There was a woman with him. When will tea be ready? Can I go and play for ten minutes?'

Isabelle said yes in an abstracted way and stood staring into space. 'A woman? Why should Jonathan lock the door?' Then realising she was not alone she added in a sharp tone,

'Sarah, set the table – you're getting lazy since you left school.'

Sarah opened her mouth to protest at this then closed it again knowing her mother was in a temper.

Nothing was mentioned about the shop door being locked when Jonathan came home and, in fact, it was not until late that evening that Sarah was aroused from sleep by her mother's voice, shrill with anger, accusing him of having an affair with another woman. There was the low murmur of her father's voice, then her mother shouting: 'How could you do this to me, Jonathan? How could you shame me? Everyone who came to the shop would know you were locked in there with a woman. Yes, they would! Victor knew, although he told me in all innocence.'

'Isabelle!' Now Jonathan's voice was raised, but not angrily. 'Will you please listen to me?' His voice dropped and Sarah got out of bed to listen at her open door. 'I locked the shop door for one reason only: I was cutting Miss Meredith's corn!'

'Cutting Miss Meredith's –!' There was shock in Isabelle's voice. 'It's bad enough for you to do such a thing, but to have an unmarried woman bearing her leg to you –'

'Her *foot*, Isabelle. Miss Meredith is very conscious of her position but she suffers great pains from her corns. Mr MacTavish, who makes her boots, has been in the habit of attending to them, but since his illness he says his hand is not quite steady.'

'And you offered to do it. Oh, yes, I'm sure you would be delighted to offer. Cicely Meredith is a *very* attractive woman.'

'It was not Cicely but Janet, and Janet, as you know, has a crippled foot.'

'Crippled foot or not, you have your reputation to think of,' Isabelle retorted. 'And I also think that I should be considered.'

'Isabelle . . .' Jonathan's voice was stern. 'Stop this tirade at once. I'm appalled that you should show jealousy of a crippled woman.'

Isabelle protested she was not jealous, then after a pause added in a lower tone, 'Yes, I was and, well, I'm sorry.'

No more was said then and Sarah thought of poor Janet Meredith who had one leg shorter than the other and clumped along in a surgical boot with a three-inch sole, and a heel to balance; and Sarah did wonder then how her mother could be so ungenerous about a woman with this awful disability.

The next morning when she took a cup of tea up to her mother Isabelle, after thanking her, said in a thoughtful way, 'I think it might be a good idea, Sarah, if you did help your father in the shop. It doesn't do for young people to be idle.'

Although Sarah was delighted to know she would be working with her father she could not help wishing that her mother's change of heart had not come about after the locked door episode. She did not want her mother to question her about what went on in the shop.

But Isabelle never did and Sarah felt happier – at least, she did about that side of it, but it worried her that her father was spending so much of his time helping Mr MacTavish, who was getting more frail. Soon, she knew, her mother would start complaining about the lack of money coming in.

Yet all the same she began to love the time spent with her father and Mr MacTavish in the cobbler's shop. She had always liked the tangy smell of the leather but now she became aware of the fragrance of the wax, of the stain and of the heel-ball, used to polish the edges of the soles and heels after repair.

But the evenings she liked best were when Mr MacTavish would be working on a pair of handmade boots or shoes for a special customer and would talk about his childhood in the Scottish Highlands. He spoke of the sun chasing shadows across the heather-covered hills, of rushing torrents, of dark fathomless tarns that sprang to life for him when pitted with raindrops; he described the magnificence of the deer that roamed the glens and his delight at the play of rabbits. And Sarah listened, fascinated and felt soothed by the leisurely way in which the shoemaker worked, waxing threads and rolling them over and over on his apron, their quaint sighs as he drew them through the leather.

Then one evening he said he must put some patches on a pair of boots for a man who needed them for work the next morning. They were the biggest boots Sarah had ever seen and she said to the shoemaker, 'What clumsy old things! I bet the man who wears them has to clump along.'

Mr MacTavish shook his head. 'You're wrong, lassie. I've never met the man, a neighbour brought them in, but I would say on reading the soles of these boots that this man has a great zest for life – he steps out with a song in his heart.'

Sarah stared at him. 'You mean you can tell this about a person from his boots?'

'I can that. My grandfather taught me, he was an expert. He used to say that the feet of a man are the heart of the man.'

'Can you tell if this man is young?'

'I would say so, for he sets his feet firmly, not with the plodding steps of the aged. The sole of the shoe is worn in the centre, telling me he is generous. The toes turn up slightly, denoting a passionate nature, but one capable of deep love. When this man loves it will be for life.'

'Well!' said Sarah, bemused. 'Fancy being able to tell all those things about a man by the way he walks.' She picked up a pair of shoes, and another pair of boots, both belonging to men, and asked the shoemaker to describe the nature of the owners. Mr MacTavish laughed and said to Jonathan, 'I can see she'll be coming to me for advice when she meets a young man she wants to marry.' Then he added after a pause, 'But that would be wrong. You don't go into marriage because of the way a man walks.'

He picked up the pair of brown shoes and said that the owner, who tended to wear down the right sides of the soles, was outgoing, and full of confidence, for if the left sides were worn down the man would be introspective, inclined to brood and worry.

The boots, he said, when he had examined them,

120

belonged to a man who was full of uncertainties. The heel of one was worn down on the right and the other, on the left. It was the same with the soles, the toes were much more worn down than the rest, which meant he would stride forward to tackle a new project, then would withdraw.

'Well,' said Sarah again, smiling, 'that is really something to know,' and she thought how interesting it would be to examine the shoes of Eddie, Chris and Joe and, yes, of course, of Warren Hendrix. *Very* interesting.

Now that Sarah was working all day with her father she discovered new aspects to his character. She found that he liked a little gamble, that he spent quite a lot of time studying the racing form and also slipped out to put on his bet with the bookmaker.

When she asked him if he ever won any money backing the horses he said, 'Sometimes I win and sometimes I lose, but I never put more than sixpence on and then it's for a straight win.' He smiled. 'It's just a little something that creates an interest.'

Another thing she discovered was how much time her father spent on his inventions in the room above the shop. 'Just give me a shout,' he would say, 'if anyone comes in. I have an idea I want to work on.'

Then there was the amount of time he spent talking to the women who came in, not with a watch or clock to be repaired, but just for a chat. More often than not it would be a long tale of woe – a husband was on the booze again, or it was impossible to get a son out of bed in the morning to go to work, what could Jonathan advise? He would talk quietly, but never really offer a solution and yet the women would say to her, 'What a help your father's been to me, Sarah, he's so understanding. I don't know what I would do if Mr Torent wasn't here to talk to.'

Sarah privately thought that this was all very well, but it was holding up her father's work. She began to make out a list of what he had to do and stick pieces of cardboard up on his workbench to remind him that Mr so and so or Mrs so and so would be calling for the clock, or watch, at such and such a time.

If her father said that a certain bedside clock or an alarm needed only to be cleaned, she would do it. She would get a tin, put in some paraffin, take the back off the clock and lay it works-side down over the tin and cover the whole with a piece of cloth. Then it was left for four or five days for the fumes to loosen the dirt. Sarah had never known this method to fail.

Grandfather clocks or mantel-clocks would have to be taken to pieces. Some would need to be repaired because of bad workmanship on someone else's part, or it could be simply wear. Then new parts would have to be made – or bought. Sarah enjoyed going to the warehouse where parts for watches and clocks were sold, some of them so tiny it seemed impossible to believe they could be manipulated by a human hand. Most of these came from Switzerland.

Sometimes her father would have a really expensive watch to attend to and then he would use a tiny glass brush and minute instruments. She always felt that these timepieces were a special challenge to him.

A week before Christmas Sarah, much to her astonishment, received a beautifully embroidered Christmas card from Warren Hendrix, which said; *'Wishing you and your family a happy Christmas.* It was signed *Regards, Warren Hendrix.'*

Isabelle said, 'Well, he *must* like you, Sarah, to send a card!'

Sarah, her colour high, replied, 'I don't see why.' But she was delighted all the same.

The following morning there were two letters for her, one from Chris and one from Joe. Chris said they had been hoping to be home for Christmas – a vain hope as it turned out, but perhaps they might see them on leave in the New Year. Joe made no mention of Christmas. He said it was just a few lines to keep in touch. He added that he had heard from Chris that Sarah had grown three inches and wrote: *'See you don't grow any more, we like you the way you are. Not that anything can take away your bonny looks. Remember me to your family and to Jenny and her family . . . '*

Sarah felt worried that Joe had not written to Jenny; she

122

was bound to be upset. Perhaps she would just mention that Chris and Eddie had written and also show her the card from Warren Hendrix. That alone should capture Jenny's interest.

In the privacy of her room, Sarah took another look at the card. A country scene was embroidered on silk, the stitches so fine one wondered how anyone had managed to do them on such flimsy material. The only words on the card were, *Peace In Our Time*.

As it happened, the letters and cards were passed over by Jenny in her excitement at having been promised a sixpence a week rise after Christmas, plus the fact that the boss had given her a fine gold chain as a present.

'It's because he's so pleased with my progress,' she said smugly.

Sarah hoped it was nothing more than that because every time she met Jenny lately she was on about her boss. She thought they might have more of a chance to talk over these things when Lucy and Jenny and Eric came to stay with them over Christmas.

Although thousands of people had rushed to stock up with food when war was declared there was no shortage yet, and the shops were full of gifts, with war toys being the most popular among children.

Sarah liked the rituals of Christmas, dressing the tree with the baubles and tinsel that they kept from one year to another. Jonathan's friend who had the kerbside stall had got them a Christmas tree cheap and made them a present of some pomegranates and tangerine oranges.

Although all the children were old enough to know there was no Father Christmas, it did not detract from their excitement on Christmas morning when they looked to see what presents were in the pillowcases they had hung up.

The boys had extra lead soldiers for the forts that Jonathan had made them the previous year, chess sets, new games, knitted gloves and scarves and the usual orange, apple, nuts and a new penny each.

The girls had white petticoats trimmed with broderie Anglaise with blue ribbon slotted through them; there were

Fair Isle gloves with scarves to match, and as well as the fruit and nuts they had three new pennies each, because they were older.

The thrill of opening their presents had hardly died down when a new and rather frightening excitement was added to the morning. A neighbour had come to tell them that the first enemy aeroplane had crossed the Channel and dropped a single bomb on Dover. Within ten minutes Berkeley Avenue was agog with the news. Then people began to ask if it were true, or just a rumour put out by some enemy spy. 'It's true all right,' declared a woman. 'My daughter works at the doctor's house, and his brother telephoned him this morning at five o'clock. The bomb was dropped last night.'

There were angry comments about the evil Germans dropping bombs on innocent people and on Christmas Eve, too. Heaven help them all if a fleet of planes came over and managed to get further inland. The more reasonable people among them tried to calm their neighbours' fears and Jonathan might have joined in, had Isabelle not begged him to stay silent. They went indoors and before long the crowd had dispersed.

Isabelle, still agitated, explained, 'You are so vulnerable with your accent, Jonathan and although they are people we know I'm so afraid they'll turn on you at some stage and accuse you of being a spy.'

Lucy said sharply, 'Stop it, Isabelle! I can tell you now that bomb or no bomb, no one is going to stop me from enjoying my Christmas dinner.'

Isabelle made no further comment and Sarah heaved a sigh of relief. She wanted nothing to spoil their Christmas Day.

They had roast pork and rabbit with sage and onion stuffing, followed by Christmas pudding. There were silver threepenny pieces in the pudding and to the joy of the children they had one each. Sarah wondered how her mother and Aunt Lucy had managed to arrange this.

Henrietta had stated that she wanted a quiet Christmas Day but said they could all come on Boxing Day morning;

she also added that she would not be inviting them to stay for a meal this year.

'Three cheers!' Jenny said. 'She's doing us a good turn but I bet she doesn't realise it.' Both girls were scolded by their mothers, with Isabelle pointing out that their grandmother was getting older and becoming more frail. Which had Jenny saying afterwards to Sarah, 'Frail, my foot! The only thing wrong with our *dear* Gran is the fact that she's getting meaner over the years.'

And this certainly proved to be the case when they all visited the following morning. Henrietta's greeting to them was: 'Oh, you've come then, I thought you might have more important things to do. I haven't bought any presents this year. With a war on there's need for austerity.'

A tiny flame was struggling to come to life through the mass of slack coal in the grate, there were draughts from the window and although ginger wine had been poured into glasses they were only half-full and the pieces of cake that were handed round were no more than one-bite pieces.

Bertha raised her shoulders as though to say she was not responsible.

Lucy and Isabelle gave their mother handmade gifts, a black shawl knitted in soft wool, mitts to match, bedsocks and a crocheted rug in sombre colours to go over her knees. She offered no thanks for the gifts.

For Bertha, Lucy and Isabelle had made between them a white lawn nightdress with a mass of fine tucks and crocheted lace edgings. Bertha was overjoyed at the gift but Henrietta decried it. When was her maid supposed to wear such a thing? Red flannelette was more suitable for her status.

Bertha, with some spirit, replied, 'I shall wear it on my wedding night, ma'am.'

'Wedding night?' For a moment there was a look of fear in Henrietta's eyes then she gave a 'humph!'. Who did Bertha think would marry *her*!

'Quite a few men, I should imagine,' Jonathan said in an amiable tone. 'Bertha has a most pleasant nature, she's patient, a wonderful cook and she's so attractive when she smiles.'

Henrietta's look of astonishment at this intervention had Isabelle and Lucy trying to suppress smiles. Then the old woman snapped, 'Stop making such fatuous remarks, Jonathan, just to flatter. Bertha is plain and she knows it, and she also knows her place.'

Bertha said to Sarah when she nipped into the kitchen later: 'Oh, Sarah, what a lovely man your father is. I know he didn't mean those things he said, but it made me feel I *could* get married.'

'My father doesn't say things to flatter, Bertha, he means them. And of *course* you could get married – the trouble is, you never get the chance to meet men. You should leave here.'

'I couldn't, Sarah. We need each other, you see.' The simple words moved Sarah, made her want to be kinder to her grandmother, but she doubted she ever would.

On the way home Jenny and Sarah dropped back and Jenny talked about her boss. 'He said he would take me for a run in his car one Sunday if I could manage to get away. I told him I couldn't but I wish I could, Sarah. I feel he would help me with jewellery-making. You were daft to go and work in your father's shop. If you had gone to work in a jeweller's as well we could have exchanged notes. I'm determined to have a shop some time.'

Sarah found herself talking like an old woman, telling her cousin she would be a fool to get mixed up with a married man; when Jenny declared she was sorry for her boss because his wife didn't understand him Sarah stopped and stared at her. 'You must be mad. Don't you remember your mother and mine once saying that it was the most feeble excuse any man could offer? And you said, quite cocky, that you would never believe a thing like that.'

'I know I did, but –'

'But nothing! Come on.' Sarah took Jenny by the arm.

In January there was a Zeppelin raid on East Anglia, with bombs dropped on Yarmouth, Cromer and King's Lynn. Although only four people were reported killed it made

126

everyone realise that England was no longer an island protected by the Royal Navy.

When news came of the sinking of the *Lusitania* by a German submarine with the loss of a thousand lives a smouldering resentment flared up into a ferocious burning hatred against the enemy.

Press photographs showed the corpses laid out on Irish beaches and women wept at seeing the bodies of young children – so innocent, so poignant. A cartoon bore a caption, *Why Did They Kill Us?*

Rioting crowds again began to attack shops all over the country, not only those with German names this time but also those with foreign-sounding ones. They not only looted the shops but attacked the owners.

After this, members of the London Stock Exchange, in top hats and business suits, marched on the Houses of Parliament to demand that the twenty thousand enemy aliens in Britain should be interned.

The result of this was an announcement that enemy aliens from the age of seventeen to forty-five would be interned. The elderly and women and children would be repatriated.

Isabelle said, distressed, 'Many of those people will have lived in England all their lives and it will have become home to them, but because they haven't been nationalised they're cast out. Do you wonder, Jonathan, that I worry because you wouldn't be nationalised? Can you imagine what would have happened to us if you had been German instead of Finnish?'

Jonathan pointed out gently that as he was *not* a German it was foolish of Isabelle to worry, but it made no difference, he was still an alien and that to her carried a stigma.

The newspapers did not allow the sinking of the *Lusitania* to be forgotten and the build-up of hatred had men rushing to join up, to get their revenge.

But the lists of the dead grew daily and there were so many people in mourning it was suggested that a purple armband or a white one should suffice to indicate mourning, as the poorer classes were getting into debt buying black clothes or having some dyed.

127

Many more wounded soldiers in the bright blue, red and white hospital uniforms were to be seen in the streets. Straw was spread on the roads outside hospitals to deaden the traffic and big banners were hoisted saying, *Be Quiet for the Wounded*.

There had been no word of Eddie, Chris and Joe for a long time, nor had Sarah heard from Warren Hendrix, apart from a short note, since her lovely Christmas card.

Then, at the end of November 1915, when she was alone in the shop she looked up as the doorbell tinkled and felt the colour rise in her cheeks as Warren Hendrix walked in.

'Why, hello Mr – er, Lieutenant Hendrix,' she said, trying to remove her apron. 'Are you home?'

'Not at the moment.' His smile was teasing. 'But I will be in half an hour or so. Sorry, I'm being stupid. Yes, I'm home on leave, sick leave.'

She saw then that his eyes had dark shadows under them and that his skin was pale. 'What happened? Would you like to sit down?' She brought out a stool then changed it for a chair. 'Do sit down, please.'

'It's all right, Sarah. May I call you Sarah? I never think of you really as Miss Torent, although I must say you are quite a young lady now. You've grown taller since I saw you last.'

'Yes, so they tell me. Can I make you a cup of tea?' She had managed to get her apron off and was squeezing it up between her fingers. She made an attempt to pull herself together. 'Were you wounded, or gassed, or –'

'They removed a lot of shrapnel from me then sent me home to recuperate. I'll probably be returning to the Front next week. I have already been back ten days. I was wondering if your father could repair my wristwatch, it's suddenly stopped.'

'Yes, I'm sure he will. At the moment he's at St George's Church where the clock needs adjusting.' Warren was watching her, a smile playing around his mouth and Sarah felt her colour rising again. 'I can't remember whether he said the clock was fast or slow or whether it – well, I don't

128

really know what is wrong with it. Why are you smiling? Is there a smut on my nose or something?'

'No, I'm smiling because it's so nice to see you again. I often think of the day you came to collect the debt. I was furious, I felt insulted, and yet you were right to do what you did. You had spirit. Your father is lucky to have a daughter like you who is prepared to fight for her rights.'

Sarah relaxed. 'Father was upset but he pointed out to me in his gentle way that as head of the house and boss of the business debt-collecting was his responsibility. And of course he was right, as he always is.'

Warren's eyebrows went up. 'Always? That is a bold statement.'

'It's true, nevertheless. You can ask him anything about the heavens, the stars, the planets, about science and about history and he'll give you the answer.' Sarah laughed. 'My mother gets mad at times and says that one of these days *she* will be right. But although she does read a lot she doesn't even get through a small proportion of the books that my father does.'

Warren chuckled. 'So with two clever parents you should be a walking encyclopaedia.'

The doorbell tinkled again as Jonathan returned, and after that Sarah did not have a chance to say any more.

When Warren Hendrix was ready to leave he came to speak to her. 'It was nice talking to you, Sarah. I hope to see you again when I come to collect my watch.'

After he had gone Jonathan looked thoughtful. 'He's a sensible young man. Although war is a shocking thing it's certainly shaped his character. He used to be very wild as a boy – unmanageable, his father used to say. He broke my window once, and although Mr Bentham paid to have it replaced Warren, despite a number of thrashings, refused to apologise.'

Sarah wished more than ever then that Warren Hendrix would bring in a pair of shoes for repair and her father, or Mr MacTavish, could read his character from them . . .

11

There were no more Zeppelin attacks until September 1915, when bombs were dropped on London, striking at the commercial part of the city. The Bank of England had a narrow escape but fires burst out in soft-goods warehouses, causing millions of pounds' worth of damage. The airship's last target was Liverpool Street, where a bus was blown to pieces. Thirty-eight people were reported killed and many more injured.

When they came over in October, they missed the Houses of Parliament and hit theatreland instead. Isabelle worried about her sister and suggested they ask Mary to come and live in Newcastle with them. Mary thanked them but said if she had to die, she would wherever she was.

Soldiers said that if a bullet or a shell had their name on it then that was that, and Sarah imagined Someone up above writing names and addresses on those awful instruments of war . . . '*Johnnie Jones, due to die on 5 May*' or whatever.

One late winter's day, when Sarah went in to see Mr MacTavish he raised a face ravaged with grief. Tears ran slowly down his face. Icy fingers clawed at Sarah's heart. 'It's Eddie, isn't it,' she whispered. 'He's been killed.'

'Yes, lassie, he has. His aunt came in to tell me. He was like my own lad. I'll never get over it.'

Sarah wanted to comfort him but could find no words. Dear Eddie, so quiet, so gentle. He was too young to die, he had not even begun to live. She experienced a pain that she had never known before, as though someone was tugging viciously at her innards. She dropped to her knees, and putting her arms around Mr MacTavish, laid her head against his chest. He put a gentle arm around her.

'There, there, lassie, I've made you cry, I shouldn't have done because Eddie was so proud to be able to fight for his country.' He paused then added, a catch in his voice, 'But it doesn't take away the grief, does it?'

Sarah made the old man a cup of tea then went to tell her father the sad news and he left to talk to Mr MacTavish.

A week later, when Sarah could go through a day without thinking numerous times about Eddie, her mother broke the news to her that Chris had been killed in action. Sarah stared at her, unable to take it in. Chris dead, too? It wasn't possible.

'Poor Mrs Curson,' Isabelle said, 'I grieve for her, she'll be heartbroken. She once told me that although she loved all her children Chris was special to her because he was so warm, so generous, so loving.'

Sarah began to cry then, slow painful tears and Isabelle drew her daughter into her arms and cried with her. Later when they were calmer they talked about Joe. The two boys had been inseparable: how would Joe be taking his brother's death?

During that evening Sarah kept bursting into tears and although Jonathan and Isabelle talked gently to her, pointing out that this was inevitable in war, it made no difference. Nothing could take away the awful pain of loss. She lay wide-awake in bed. going over all they had done together when the family had rented the house in Corbridge. She relived the days in the hayfield, going to the fair, Joe winning her the kewpie doll, which had a smile as roguish as his own. She remembered Joe tumbling her in the sweet-smelling grass, his touch, and felt a sudden terrible guilt as she realised it was Joe who was uppermost in her thoughts, not Chris.

Jenny had not been to work that day so Sarah was unable to tell her about Chris and in fact it was two days before she saw her, and by then a number of things had happened. First Warren Hendrix had come into the shop to collect his watch and to say goodbye before returning to the Front. Sarah, her grief still terribly raw over Eddie and Chris said earnestly, 'Oh, you *will* take care of yourself, Lieutenant Hendrix, won't you?'

'Why, yes, yes, I will,' he said, seeming surprised by her

concern. Then, obviously realising by her emotional outburst that there was more to it than her worrying over him, he looked to Jonathan for guidance. Her father explained about the two boys.

Warren was then all sympathy. 'I'm sorry, Sarah, I know how you feel. We are living in dreadful times, there is so much grief in families.' Then, in a slightly lighter vein he went on, 'I'm sure I shall be back to see you and your father again and I hope by then you'll be so proficient with your watch and clock repairs that *you'll* be able to mend my watch, should it need it, the next time.'

When he left, his grip was firm and his smile warm and caring, and Sarah felt comforted, but she was not so sure she would be any more proficient in her work by the time he returned.

Sarah had lost a little of her passionate interest in clocks recently, feeling she could be doing something more worthwhile to help the war effort. It was Jenny who had set her off, but Jenny was more interested in the money side – there were girls working as conductresses on the buses who were earning over two pounds a week, while she was still only getting five and sixpence at the jeweller's and had to pay her train fare out of it. And what was Sarah earning? Nothing. She was given a shilling a week pocket money by her mother.

Sarah thought she would like to go into a factory making shell or component parts. But there were other jobs open, like acting as a porter at a station, or as a conductress on a tram or bus. She decided she might broach the subject to her mother some time and see how she reacted.

Isabelle still gave Jenny her midday meal every weekday and the cousins would usually meet and walk home together, but on the following day Jenny said she would just have a sandwich in the shop as she had some work to catch up on. She had been doing this at odd times recently, and Sarah was getting worried. Was Jenny staying to be with her boss? However, she made no remark. Today, Sarah went in the back way as usual and was trying to think up an excuse to allay her mother's suspicions about Jenny, when Isabelle, who had been reading a letter, wailed to Jonathan, 'Oh, what do you think? Our poor Mary has had a fall and badly sprained her ankle.'

'Well, that's a pity,' he sympathised. 'She'll be laid up.'

'I know and yet I can't help,' said Isabelle. 'I couldn't leave Victor, not with this heavy cold he's got. And our Lucy is half-expecting Fred home on leave.'

'Then send Sarah,' Jonathan suggested. 'She's capable enough of looking after Mary.'

Sarah's heart leapt at the thought of going to London on her own, but her mother objected – there were all sorts of undesirable people travelling these days. Jonathan then suggested putting Sarah in the protection of the guard, but Isabelle was not ready to give in. They would have to talk it over.

Sarah prayed for another miracle to happen. It came in the form of her Aunt Lucy, who arrived at seven o'clock that evening with a red-eyed Jenny in tow. Lucy looked grim. Jenny gave Sarah a wry look and raised her shoulders.

Jonathan had not yet come home, Victor was out at his music lesson and Isabelle asked Sarah to go upstairs with Jenny.

'So what's happened?' Sarah asked her cousin when they sat on the bed.

Jenny shrugged again. 'Oh, she found out I've been seeing my boss Mr Turner. She gave me a good belting when I got home – I bear the marks on my back. I'm blooming well hurting, I can tell you.'

'So what's going to happen?'

'I don't know, I suppose she wanted to talk it over with your mother. You know what they're like, yakkety-yak. There's one thing I do know, she won't ever let me go back to the shop. That's finished. I expect she feels like beating up Mr Turner, as well. He'll be livid if she so much as goes and accuses him. He doesn't want his little love-nest at home to be disturbed. Rotten men, I don't know why I bothered with him. He's old, about forty.'

It must have been twenty minutes later when Lucy called

133

sharply for Jenny to come downstairs. Jenny gave a sudden grin. 'Now I'll know the worst.'

Sarah, impatient to know what was happening, kept going to the top of the stairs to listen, but when eventually Isabelle called to her to come down she was back in her room. Once downstairs, she found that her aunt and Jenny had gone, but before she could ask any questions Isabelle told her to sit down.

'Now then, Sarah, it's been decided that your Aunt Lucy will be going to London tomorrow.' Sarah felt a surge of disappointment then her mother went on, 'She's taking Jenny with her and *you*. I'm not altogether happy about this arrangement, but we'll see how things work out. Your aunt heard today that Uncle Fred has changed ships and will possibly arrive at the London docks. Eric will stay with us.' Isabelle went on talking, but Sarah was only partially listening. London *and* having Jenny with her!

'That's it then, Sarah. What we have to do now is to sort out which clothes you'll be taking with you.'

Packing the hamper was an excitement on its own, and even the fact that her mother was laying down laws while they were packing made no difference. She was not to go out on her own, she was to do what Aunt Lucy and Mary told her and to help in any way she could. Sarah agreed to everything, there seemed no problem.

Isabelle had a talk with Jonathan and by then she had a raging headache so went to bed. After Victor had also gone up, Sarah was alone with her father.

She said suddenly, 'Oh, Poppa, I'm letting you down, leaving you in the shop on your own and I'm going to miss you terribly.'

'I am going to miss you too, Sarah. We all are, but I'll manage the shop – you just look after Aunt Mary, she's very dear to us. We don't know exactly how things will turn out until you get there. Aunt Lucy may have to return home with Jenny, leaving you with your Aunt Mary for a while. Your mother might pay a visit, so we'll just have to wait and see the position.'

Tears had suddenly welled up in Sarah's eyes and she

wiped them away. 'I want to go, Poppa, I really do, it's just that poor Eddie and Chris came into my mind and I found myself thinking that here was I, all excited about going to London and they were dead and had never done anything in their lives, never achieved anything.'

'But they had, Sarah. They had achieved a great deal. When his father died Eddie took over the running of the house, disciplined the children and, although he was so young, they treated him as a father figure and not only respected him but loved him. That was a big achievement in itself. Then his mother married again, leaving Eddie to go and fight for his country, for he had such loyalty. He told me he was prepared to die so that the people of England could be free from aggression. Isn't that an achievement, Sarah?'

'Yes, yes, I suppose so. But Chris never achieved his ambition, he wanted to be a headmaster. He only taught for a year.'

'Sarah, let me tell you something. When Mrs Curson wrote to us she quoted a remark made by a boy in Chris's class, and I repeat it to you. "Mr Curson was the best teacher I ever had. He not only taught me about arithmetic and things, but he taught me about life and how to behave. I'll never forget him."

'Just think, Sarah, if Chris was responsible for shaping just one boy's life for the future, don't you think it was a worthwhile achievement? Every person has something to give to the world.'

Sarah looked up. 'I can't agree with that, Poppa. What about Billy Best, he's a looney, people laugh at him. He's no good to anyone, he can't even talk properly and he'll never work. Why does *he* live when so many strong young men are killed in war?'

To this her father replied gently, 'When I was young and told my mother how I, and all the class at school had laughed at a boy who had given a silly answer to a history question, my mother quoted an old Hungarian gypsy proverb to me: "Don't laugh at fools, because they may know something that you know not".'

'But Billy doesn't know *anything*. His brain's affected, people say so.'

'Billy was born five months after his father died, Sarah. He filled an empty place in Mrs Best's life. When he was a toddler and she picked him up he would throw his arms around her neck and hug her. She understands what he says and he understands her. She is his rock and he hers. They share a deep love. Billy has cared for many animals that have been badly treated by their owners or thoughtless boys, and he once stayed up two nights to feed a fledgling bird that had fallen from the nest. Such a boy should not be mocked.'

'No,' Sarah said in a small voice. She searched his face. 'Since Eddie and Chris died I feel old, as if I had lived through a lot of worlds. I feel I'll never smile again.'

Jonathan took her hands in his and said softly, 'I have felt like that many times. When I was a boy I loved my grandfather dearly and could not imagine life without him. Yet the day after his funeral I found myself laughing with other boys over something.'

Sarah remembered her father's words the following morning when she arrived with her aunt and Jenny at the Central Station. When she had said goodbye to her parents she had been all weepy, and now she was shivering with excitement – it was all the hustle and bustle, the noise of hissing steam, whistles, train doors slamming, people rushing in at the last minute.

A porter had put them in an empty carriage, but seconds before the train was due to leave three soldiers clambered in, throwing their kitbags in front of them, one apologising to Lucy, 'Sorry, missus, thought we were going to miss it.' They stacked the bags on the racks and had just finished when the guard blew his whistle; the next moment the train began to move with a huffing and puffing of steam. One of the men grinned. 'To think I wanted to be an engine driver at one time. Being a soldier is much more adventurous.'

'Adventurous?' Lucy exlaimed. 'I would have thought that that was the last word to use about war.'

This started a conversation that continued throughout

the journey. Jenny, who had visibly brightened at the arrival of the men asked them if they were going to the Front. They said they were, and were looking forward to having another go at the Huns. 'Although,' added one, 'they're not bad chaps, just like us really, having to fight for their country,'

They talked about the truce there had been between the enemy and the British last Christmas. They had exchanged chocolate and cigarettes, and had shown each other photographs of their families. But of course once Christmas Day was over they began shooting one another again. They were all so cheerful about it, Sarah found it hard to understand.

And they were equally cheerful when they talked about the rats in the trenches – vicious-looking things as big as cats, they had red eyes and ran all over you when you tried to get some sleep. One man said, 'One night I found one tucked up beside me under my overcoat,' and the others yelled with horror.

They spoke of the lice that would quickly get into every part of their clothing, and how at night they'd take a candle flame down each seam to try to get rid of the pesky things. Of course they couldn't, they were there no matter what you did; it was terrible when the body got warm.

The soldiers had to rush to catch a connection at Victoria and Lucy and the girls stood, looking about them. Mary had said that someone would meet them. Suddenly Lucy exclaimed, 'Good Lord, it's Roger!'

Roger, Aunt Mary's husband? Sarah tensed. How dare she send him! That awful man. Although she followed Lucy's gaze she was unable to make out anyone resembling the man she had imagined. Then a tall, well-dressed man emerged from the crowd milling around and Sarah stared as she realised he was coming towards them. He smiled and raised his hat and Sarah swallowed hard. *This* was Roger?

'Lucy, my dear, how good it is to see you.' He kissed her on both cheeks and Sarah saw that her aunt was smiling.

'It's been a long time, Roger.'

'Yes, indeed it has. And this must be Sarah and Jenny.' His smile was breath-catching. 'Porter!'

A big buxom girl gathered up the luggage and went striding away after him. Lucy and Sarah and Jenny exchanged glances. Jenny gave a small sigh and raised her eyes heavenwards, then her face widened into a grin as she whispered to Sarah, 'Isn't he just too gorgeous for words!

Sarah, feeling bemused, was about to agree, then she thought – no, I hated him for the way he treated Aunt Mary and I'll go on hating him, he's not going to get around me with his charm! But she had succumbed to his looks long before they reached their destination.

Roger was so beautifully groomed and quite the best-looking man she had ever seen. His hair was thick and golden, and it curled at the nape of his neck. He had a marvellous profile, just like a Greek warrior she had once seen in her history books. The interested way he listened when Lucy spoke had a certain charm. so had his smile but Sarah thought it was his voice that had enslaved her. It was low-pitched, with seductive cadences. No wonder her aunt had fallen so deeply in love with him. But Mary had sworn she would not have him back. Had she contacted him after her accident? Were they living together again?

It had not occurred to Sarah to wonder how her aunt had managed to live while Roger was in prison, but she had thought to ask the night before if Mary would have enough room to sleep the three of them. Oh, yes, Isabelle had said, she had the first two floors of a three-storeyed house – the top floor was let as a flat. This surprised Sarah, who had vaguely pictured Mary living in a two-roomed flat. And she was further surprised when they arrived at the house and Roger led the way into a large and very comfortably furnished room.

Mary, who was resting on a green velvet sofa held out her arms and said in a tearful voice, 'Oh, my dears, how lovely of you to come, I couldn't believe it when I got the telegram.' She apologised for being unable to rise.

After the first greetings were over, Roger said he would

make some tea and when he had gone to the kitchen Mary told them, 'Roger arrived soon after I had my fall. I don't know what I would have done without him. The people in the flat on the top floor have gone to visit their daughter who is having her first baby, and the neighbours on either side are out at work all day.'

After the tea was poured Roger said he would have to leave them for a while as he had a business appointment, but added he would be back in an hour.

After he had gone Lucy said to Mary, 'You haven't taken him back, have you?' The colour rose in Mary's face, emphasising the birthmark on her cheek and neck, and Lucy added quickly, 'We can talk about it later.'

They discussed all the home news then Mary told the girls that Lucy would show them to their rooms. Jenny said to her mother as they went upstairs, 'It's a queer set-up, isn't it? Is Uncle Roger living here or what?'

'I know no more than you do, Jenny.' She opened a door on the landing. 'You two can sleep in here, I'll be next door to you. You can start unpacking, I'll do mine later.'

When she had gone downstairs Jenny grumbled, 'And now the yakkety-yakking will start. *We* won't get to know anything.' She flung herself on a bed nearest the window and grinned. 'What do you think about our Uncle Roger then? Isn't he just gorgeous? I feel I want to drool over him.' She shot up. 'And I don't care what anyone says about him, I'm already half in love with the man. It doesn't matter to me that he's been in prison twice. In fact, I'm sure he wasn't wholly to blame. I bet some rotten bloke pushed those postcards of naked women into his pocket to get him into trouble.'

Although Sarah was also besotted with Roger, common-sense told her she would be deluding herself if she believed such a thing. 'No, Jenny, I can't accept this. *He* would know what he was buying. But I can understand him being desperate for money when he came out of prison, for after all, he had to live.' She paused then added, 'I heard Mother call him a conman and I think that's what he is.'

Sarah realised then how easy it would be to pass over a

man's faults if you were crazy about him, She made up her mind there and then to try not to let herself be carried away by Roger's charm ...

12

Roger did not live in the house, but Sarah thought he might as well have done for the time he spent there. He was attentive and gentle towards Mary, and although she would say he need not come so often now that Lucy and the girls were there he always answered, 'But you need to be carried, my darling, and Lucy could not do that.' Then he would add, 'Let me do these small things for you, it pleases me so much.' At these times he always seemed sincere and in fact there never was any time when he seemed what Jenny would call 'smarmy'.

Sarah thought him a most unusual man and found it difficult not to like him more than she should. He treated Jenny and herself as adults and showed a great interest in Sarah's knowledge of clocks and watches.

He explained his civilian status by the fact that although he wanted to enlist he had been turned down on medical grounds. And Mary bore this out: Roger had a heart defect. He hinted that he was involved in some war work, but that it was secret.

Roger flattered each of them, but there was never anything brash about it. For instance, he told Sarah that he admired her tremendously for becoming involved in her father's work, that many women became bored in their lives and should have some interest or hobby. Sarah did venture to point out that women with big families had no time for hobbies, but Roger seemed not to notice. He talked about Mary and her job in munitions, how worried he had been at first, thinking the work would be too heavy for her. But what was she doing? Making tiny screws. A broad smile accompanied this remark.

Mary mentioned the numerous jobs there were in connection with munitions then said to Sarah, 'I'm not sure what age girls have to be to start, but I'm sure they would snap you up, with your knowledge of lathe work and working to fine limits.'

'And the money is *very* good,' Roger announced. 'Some earn about seven pounds a week.'

'Seven pounds?' Jenny squealed. 'Lead me to it, what could *I* do?'

'Nothing,' Lucy said sharply. 'You, young lady, will be where I can keep an eye on you. At home.'

'Oh, Mother! I'm not going to stay at home for ever – I won't!'

'You can work from home. There are groups of people who do it, making small parts for machinery. I'll enquire about it when we get back.'

It was Roger who talked Lucy out of this idea, and he did it so cleverly that it never seemed like interference. He talked in a slightly poetic way about plants dying if they got no air or light. Young people were like that. Their minds must be expanded – the young needed to be with the young, to exchange ideas, to develop their brains. It was so important. Lucy listened bemused and so did Sarah. Mary sat quietly, her eyebrows raised, a smile playing around her mouth. Jenny listened, her manner demure, but Sarah knew the mischief behind the mask. And later, when the two girls were up in their bedroom Jenny went twirling around the room, hands clasped to her bosom.

'Isn't he the most fantastic man! He won Mother over. And thank the Lord he did. Just imagine what it would have been like sitting at home making fiddly parts of machinery.' She stopped and dropped to her knees in front of Sarah who was sitting on the bed. 'Do you think our mothers could be persuaded to let us both go into munitions? Just think of the money! That *might* sway them. We could live here with Aunt Mary.'

Although Sarah knew what the money could mean to her mother it was mainly the fact that she would be doing her bit for her country that appealed to her.

'I wouldn't mind doing it, but I can't see our mothers allowing it. I'm sure Aunt Lucy would never leave you here,

142

not with Roger around. He's too much of an attraction and you know how she behaved over your boss.'

'Oh, old Turner! I've forgotten about *him*.'

The two girls went over and over the idea but even Jenny had to agree it could be no more than a dream.

The following day, Roger took them all sightseeing around London, Mary included. He carried her to the car and tucked a rug around her. They saw Buckingham Palace and the Tower, drove along the Embankment, gaped at the Houses of Parliament and had lunch in an expensive restaurant, which had Sarah enraptured. This was the big Metropolis, she was really living!

That evening, Roger said he would be away all the next day and as Lucy and Jenny had planned to visit some of Fred's relatives Sarah offered to stay in with her aunt. Mary said there was no need but Sarah insisted and her aunt responded, 'Lovely! We can have a long talk.'

Sarah learned that the house belonged to Mary. 'Great Aunt Maud left it to me in her will. Your grandmother was furious – she thought the house should have been sold and the money shared between we three sisters and Harold. I would have sold it, but Roger wouldn't allow me to do so. He said it was Maud's wish that I have it and that no one should interfere. I think she left it to me because she was impressed that Roger and I had defied Mother and run away to Gretna Green to get married. She lacked romance in her life, poor soul.'

After a pause, Sarah asked timidly, 'What work does Uncle Roger do now?'

'I don't know, Sarah, and I don't want to know. I'm happier being ignorant of what he's involved in. He's here at the present time and I am glad of his help, but next week he could disappear and I might not see him again for weeks, or it could be months.'

'He's a very attractive person,' Sarah said confusedly, 'but I don't quite understand him.'

'Don't try, Sarah – he's the most complex man I've ever met. At one time I used to say I understood him and would make excuses for his behaviour but not any more. He can be kind, loving and helpful, but he's so restless. He craves adventure – he can even live on the adventures of other men. And Roger is a spendthrift. He gets into debt, but he gets out of it again, I don't know how.'

Mary was becoming agitated. When she spoke again it was in a rush of words, as though she had been bottling them up for ages and wanted to get them out of her system.

'Roger likes to be in the company of attractive women, and then he does silly things. He enjoys men's company too, people in high positions – he's a show-off, has to have admiration. He once got mixed up with a girl in high society; the father paid him money to leave her alone and he went to the races and lost the lot!'

She drew herself up on the sofa and Sarah noticed that bright spots of colour burned on her cheeks. 'And don't let Roger confuse you about wages for munitions. It's hard work – you do a twelve to fourteen-hour day, and there are night-shifts to be done. When you finish a long shift you just drop into bed and feel you could sleep for a week. Roger gets carried away, He never sees the hard work because he's never done any; he doesn't want to see pain or hardship, it upsets him. He wants only beauty in his life.'

Mary paused then said more calmly, 'I'm sorry, Sarah, I don't usually go on so much and I had no right to. You're young, and although at times you have a really beautiful look of innocence about you, there's a maturity there, you do have a lot of commonsense. I've found it easy to pour these things out to you. I can't say them to anyone else, not even to your mother or Aunt Lucy.'

Mary was silent after this and Sarah was nonplussed, not quite knowing what to say. Then, to her consternation, she saw that her aunt was crying, big tears rolling slowly down her cheeks.

Sarah laid a hand on hers. 'What is it, Aunt Mary? Tell me what's wrong.'

'You don't know the half of it, Sarah. Not even a quarter of it, and I can't tell anyone. I'm a liar, a fraud.'

She covered her face and Sarah felt more bewildered

than ever. After a few moments she said gently, 'What do you mean by being a fraud, Auntie?'

Mary took her hands from her face and turned her head and Sarah saw the sweet, pretty face ravaged with pain. 'My foot isn't sprained, there's nothing at all wrong with it. I didn't have a doctor. I bandaged it myself. I wrote the day before to Roger and told him I had sprained my ankle and was helpless and he came right away. I wanted to see him, I *had* to see him, but I don't want him back to live with me. I couldn't and that is something that I just *can't* explain.'

Sarah was getting more and more bewildered. Why should her aunt pretend to have a sprained ankle, just for attention? Mary had taken a handkerchief from under the cushion and she started pulling at the lace edge.

'I was homesick, too. I wanted to see someone from home and that is why I wrote to your mother. I knew someone would come. If I had just said I was homesick they would have invited me to come North and I wanted to stay here so I could see Roger.'

Mary began to sob and Sarah put her arms around her and held her close, still uncomprehending but feeling a lump come into her throat for her aunt who seemed to be suffering so much. 'Don't cry, Auntie. It's all right, homesickness is a dreadful thing.'

In between her sobs Mary begged Sarah not to say anything of what she had been told and Sarah, a little against her will, promised. She felt that someone, an adult, should have the chance to cope with the situation. Mary's sobs gradually died away then she whispered that her head and her eyes ached and Sarah went to find a piece of cloth that would make a cold compress.

Mary was sleeping when Lucy and Jenny returned, and Jenny went about grumbling in a whisper about her father's relatives: they were so stuffy, led such dreary lives, never went anywhere, never did anything exciting.

Lucy told her to hold her tongue, They were kind people, no matter what she thought of them. They had always been ready to help out in a crisis and that counted for a lot.

A major crisis arrived the following morning when Lucy

had a telegram to say that Fred was in hospital. Roger, who had just arrived, offered to drive her there.

They were away five hours and when they returned, Lucy was white-faced and her eyes were dark-ringed. She told them that Fred had lost his right leg and left arm. His ship had been blown up by a mine.

Sarah had thought she could never feel more grief than when Eddie and Chris were killed, but this was a different kind of pain. It was suffering deep inside her as though she had been forced to watch someone being tortured, a body desecrated, the body of a man whom she loved so much. Never once could she remember her Uncle Fred being anything other than cheerful.

A telegram was sent to Jonathan and Isabelle, and Isabelle arrived early the next morning. The two sisters clung together with Lucy sobbing, 'Poor Fred, he was actually trying to buck me up. He was saying it could have been worse, he could have lost both legs and arms as some men have done. Oh, Isabelle, I can't bear it. His naval career is ended and the sea was his life.'

'No, Lucy, it was only a part of it. He adores you and the children, and you do still have him.'

Lucy dried her eyes. 'Yes, for that I should be grateful but it's hard to accept. And yet I thank the Lord he does have his right arm. I'll make some breakfast, I must be doing something.'

Roger arrived just after the meal and his eyes widened in delight when he saw Isabelle. Sarah had to admit that no matter what faults this uncle had, he was definitely a kindly man. He could not do enough for the sisters, offering to ferry Lucy and Isabelle to the hospital to see Fred.

Jenny was upset that she was not allowed to go but Lucy said, 'Perhaps tomorrow or the next day, Jenny. At the moment we can't talk about him without you being tearful. Your father is putting on a brave face and I don't want you to greet him weeping. I managed not to cry yesterday when we met but it just about tore me apart. Be patient, love.'

When Jenny went to the front door to wave the others away Mary whispered to Sarah, 'I feel terrible, so ashamed

146

at the way I've behaved. It seems so petty, so awfully trivial, to do what I did when you hear of someone being maimed like Fred. Yet I just can't confess to the others. I can't, Sarah! I'm a coward and I hope you'll keep my secret.'

Mary looked awful, she was pale and her eyes had a haunted look.

'I'm going to get up. I'll say that the doctor came yesterday and told me I could put my foot to the ground. I'm going to have a "miracle" cure. Oh, how I hate myself, it was such a despicable thing to do.' She looked at Sarah, a plea in her eyes. 'You do understand why I did it, don't you, Sarah?'

'I think I do, but at the same time I feel it was so unnecessary. You know that Uncle Roger still loves you or he wouldn't want to come back to you.'

'I know, I know, I'm such a fool.'

Jenny came in, looking disconsolate. 'Now, more than ever I need a job, one that pays good money. Poor old Dad won't be able to go out to work. I'll just have to persuade Mother to let me try for munitions.'

Jenny went into flights of fancy after that. She would save like mad, and when she had enough money she would open a jeweller's shop, and make and sell necklaces. She reminded Sarah of their past plans. 'You can help to create them and perhaps Uncle Jonathan could make some wrist-watches. Everyone is wearing them, these days.'

Sarah gave a noncommittal answer. She was remembering Roger consoling Lucy, then Jenny over the sad news, yesterday. She longed to have his arms around her, too, comforting her. And it was so wrong, so very wrong. But how did one control emotions like that? They came unbidden.

Jenny was so preoccupied that she took little notice when Mary got off the sofa and stood up, pretending to test her ankle. 'Oh, good,' she said vaguely, and went on to ask what kind of place this Woolwich Arsenal was.

Mary said it was huge, a fantastic place, a town in itself. They were building houses there for the workers, hostels, a cinema and a church. There was a place for sports and concerts were held for the workers. Canteens offered excellent food.

'You get your overalls and caps free,' she explained. 'You can have a bath, get your hair done – all sorts of things. If you travel to a certain point, special buses will pick you up and take you on to the site. The people working there must run into thousands.'

'Oh, Aunt Mary, don't!' exclaimed Jenny. 'You're making me itch to get there. I *must* go. What an adventure! I know it will be hard work but I'll do it, I'll learn. I'm a quick learner, aren't I, Sarah?'

Sarah said yes, itching as much as Jenny now to take part in this war effort. But how would she ever persuade her father, much more her mother, to allow her to work away from home? And even if she did, how could she bear to live in a house where she would be constantly coming into contact with her aunt's husband – Roger? Well, not all the time, for if she was working long hours she might hardly ever see him. But she *wanted* to see him, and as long as there was an opportunity for them to meet her emotions would be torn. Why couldn't she convince herself that Roger was no good – he loved to be with girls, he could have dozens for all she knew. And what's more, he had criminal tendencies, had been in prison twice, for heaven's sake!

Sarah was still in this torn, emotional state when Lucy, Isabelle and Roger returned from the hospital. Lucy, to Jenny's urgent questioning, smiled and said, 'Your dad sends his love, Jenny. Yesterday I was so bitter that Fred had been injured, today I'm so thankful that he's alive. We'll cope, I know, and they'll fit him up later with artificial limbs.'

Roger excused himself and Sarah saw that he had gone pale. Mary apologised for him. 'He's so terribly sensitive, I was surprised yesterday – and today – when he said he'd take you to the hospital. He usually can't bear to see anyone in real pain.'

Lucy said, 'Oh, I'm sorry, I didn't realise. He didn't actually come right in to the hospital. It's a good job he didn't, for there were some awful sights, quite harrowing, but there . . . I'll change the subject.'

It wasn't until later in the day that Sarah had a chance to talk to her mother on their own. She was in her bedroom when Isabelle came tiredly in. 'Hello, Sarah dear. May I come in and have a quiet rest with you for a minute? It's been so upsetting hearing the news of Uncle Fred, and then all that travelling. It must have been a surprise for you to meet your Uncle Roger.' Isabelle spoke in a bright voice. A false voice, Sarah thought.

She said, yes it was, and added in a deliberate way: 'He's such a charming person, so caring, so kind.'

'Yes, he is.' Isabelle spoke a little dreamily, which surprised Sarah, considering all the whisperings and hate that had ensued when Roger had received his prison sentences. Had her mother too fallen under Roger's spell?

The next morning Isabelle woke with a headache and by midday it was so bad she had to go and lie down in the dark. She asked them all just to leave her, she would be all right. Roger sent word he was not able to take them to the hospital that day so Lucy said they would go by bus. Jenny and Sarah could come with her. If Fred felt a little better he might be pleased to see both girls.

As only two visitors at a time were allowed, Sarah sat quietly in the waiting room. She was looking around her and thinking what awful places hospitals were, with their drab-coloured walls and strong smell of disinfectant every-where, when a soldier came in. He gave her a brief smile then said in an astonished way, 'Sarah?'

Sarah's heart began a mad beating. 'Joe! What are you doing here? Who are you visiting?'

'A mate of mine in the regiment. What about you?'

She explained about her Uncle Fred and Joe said savagely, 'This rotten war! I thought it was going to be all victory, all glory, but instead it's hell, sheer hell. I wish it was over.'

They talked quietly about their families then Joe mentioned Chris and the pain in his voice made Sarah want to cry.

149

'I'll never get over it, Sarah, He didn't deserve to die. Our Chris was a good lad, one of the best.'

Sarah smiled tremulously. 'I have a lovely memory of him. Do you remember the day of the fête near Hexham, and how Chris tested his strength? You both had a go at trying to win coconuts and you won kewpie dolls for Jenny and myself. It was a wonderful day, one that shall always live in my memory. You should try and think of Chris as he was at the fête, Joe – happy and having fun.'

Joe nodded slowly, 'I'll do that, Sarah, it might help. You say that your Aunt Lucy and Jenny are here. I would like to see them. Jack's parents are with him at the moment but after I've been to see him perhaps we can all meet in here.' Sarah agreed then a middle-aged man came to tell Joe he could go and see his son. Seconds after that Lucy came for Sarah to take her to the ward.

On the way Sarah told her quickly about Joe and said that he was staying at an army hostel for the two days he had left before returning to France. Could they invite him back to Aunt Mary's for tea?

Isabelle was naturally surprised and delighted to see Joe and Mary, who enjoyed company, welcomed him. The conversation was lively as they caught up on all the news. Before Joe left to spend the evening with Jack's parents, Mary had invited him to come for the whole of the next day. Joe accepted and to Mary's urging to come as early as he liked, he grinned and said, 'I'll be here right after breakfast. No, how about ten o'clock? I'll take you all out for the day sightseeing.'

Lucy suggested he go with the girls – they would enjoy a bus ride, and this was agreed.

Sarah was especially excited at the thought of an outing. Mary had given her a coat and hat which had belonged to her when she was younger, but it had not dated. The coat was dark blue with a velvet collar and the matching hat had an upturned saucer brim with velvet streamers at the back. It was jaunty and made her look older.

When they were in bed that night, Jenny said, 'That hat

and coat of Aunt Mary's suits you, but don't you start making eyes at Joe. He's mine, remember.'

'I know he's yours, I won't be making eyes at anyone.'

But it was Joe who was making eyes at Sarah the following morning. 'You look real bonny, Sarah, the bonniest lass I've seen in a long time.'

Jenny, who had just come into the room snapped, 'And how do I look?'

'Bonny too,' he replied, but his gaze was still on Sarah.

Then Roger arrived and there was a stunned silence. He was in uniform, that of an army Major. He looked from one to the other. 'Well, come on, someone say something.'

Mary was the first to speak. 'But Roger, I don't understand. I though the army had turned you down on medical grounds.'

'Yes, they did, knowing I would be unfit for combat duties, but they did hint at a desk job. I didn't want to mention anything about it in case it didn't come off.'

Mary, Lucy and Isabelle all began talking at once. How handsome he looked . . . how well he could carry the rank . . . where was the job? . . . would he need to go abroad?

Jenny's face was one broad grin, while Sarah just felt stunned. What was it about Roger that a uniform could turn him immediately into a man of authority? He looked as if he came from an aristocratic family and had known from boyhood that he was destined for an army career.

When Joe was introduced to Roger he stood stiffly to attention and addressed him as 'Sir'. Roger immediately put him at ease. 'No need to stand on ceremony, Joe, it's good to meet you. The girls are dressed for going out. What are your plans?'

Mary explained they were going sightseeing with Joe, and Roger immediately offered to take them – he had a car outside.

Sarah, feeling that Roger would not fit in with the morning, was thinking of some excuse when Mary said in her gentle way, 'I think it might be best to let the young ones go on their own, Roger, and I'm sure that Joe would feel more comfortable.' She smiled. 'He'll feel he's on army routine with a Major in charge.'

'Yes, of course.' Roger's manner was amiable. 'See you all later. Enjoy yourselves.'

Sarah was relieved, but Jenny seemed annoyed. She said in an undertone, 'If they had let Roger come you could have been paired off with him and I would have had Joe to myself.'

13

The three of them spent a happy, carefree morning riding on buses and when they did walk, Joe linked arms with both of them and Sarah was pleased that Jenny showed no objection to this.

After a snack meal they went to Hyde Park and strolled along the paths and over the grass, mingling with families and couples, the men mostly in uniform. War seemed remote in the winter sunshine, the sky a clear blue. Then Joe stopped and stood, his head cocked as though listening. When Jenny asked him what was wrong he said, 'It's the vibrations from the guns across the Channel. Can you feel them? It's like the effect of an earthquake heard a long way off. At least, that's what I've been told.' When Jenny said he must be imagining it he replied cheerfully, 'Oh, you can believe it all right. I wish that vibrations were all I felt when I was over there. A barrage can go on non-stop for days and nights until you feel your eardrums will burst. And when it stops you go on hearing it. Some blokes go mad with the sound.'

The next moment he had raised his face to the sun and stood, eyes closed. 'That is why I want to remember this day. The sun, the sweet smell of the grass, the voices, lovers' voices . . . ,'

Sarah suddenly knew a chill of fear. Was this a premonition of death? Joe had spoken as though it was something he would never experience again.

Jenny said, a catch in her voice, 'Oh, stop it, who wants to talk about war and guns and things. Let's see if we can find somewhere to have a cup of tea.'

'A good idea, Jenny girl.' Joe linked arms with them again, but although Sarah stepped out cheerfully the fear remained, and she knew that whatever happened she would always remember these moments.

Joe did not return home with them after their day out. He said he had to go and see his friend in hospital. Sarah felt choked when they parted and Jenny made him promise to write.

That evening Isabelle told Sarah they would be going home the following day, in time for Christmas. Sarah made no plea to be allowed to stay, knowing by the tone of her mother's voice that her mind was made up.

It was a tearful parting for all of them, with Jenny begging Sarah to try and come again soon, for she would miss her terribly. Roger had said his goodbyes the previous night because he would not be able to come to the staion to see them off, yet at the last minute he came sprinting along the platform, and holding Sarah close whispered, 'You're a beautiful girl, Sarah. Keep yourself for the man you marry.' Then he kissed her with what she felt was a restrained passion. Isabelle got a quick hug and a kiss then they had to board the train. The train pulled out leaving a bravely-smiling Lucy, Jenny blowing kisses and Roger looking sad.

Sarah was glad that her mother got talking to two middle-aged women in the carriage so she could think of Roger. What had he meant by telling her to keep herself for the man she married? It seemed to suggest that he cared about her. No, no, she mustn't think like that, it was wrong. But there was no mistaking the way he had kissed her. She tried to put him out of her mind, telling herself he was a conman, a criminal, but it was impossible until her mother drew her into the conversation.

Jonathan, Victor and Eric were there to meet them at the station and Sarah felt happy to be back home and a family once more, with no dire problems such as thoughts of Roger to face.

But after a few days Sarah found herself getting more and more restless and came to realise that her uncle was responsible. She wanted to see him again, longed to see him in spite of what he was, and although she hated herself for it, the longing did not grow less.

She wanted to talk to her father about it but what could she say? 'I'm in love with Aunt Mary's husband. I know

154

he's a sham, but he's kind, nevertheless – he's a caring man, I've had proof of it. I think he's in love with me, but he's never said so. It was just the way he kissed me and told me to keep myself for the man I married. Don't you see, Father, he was trying to tell me not to fall in love with him, not to let him love me, which he knew I would have wanted had I stayed. It's dreadful, I'm tearing myself apart. I can't think of anything else. I want to go back to London. I know I'm being stupid but how can I stop? No one can help me, it's something I have to work out for myself.'

When a letter came from Jenny Sarah tore it open, hungry for news of Roger but the letter was full of a boy called Peter who had been moved into the bed next to her father. *'He's a New Zealander and has no family to visit him. Mother likes him and for once has made no complaint that Peter and I talk our heads off. I think she's glad I have someone nearer my own age to talk to. Dad is getting on fine but Mother worries all the time about him. I do miss you, Sarah, to tell you all the little special bits. Any chance of you getting to London again? Aunt Mary is always talking about you, she misses you too.'*

Sarah threw the letter down. There wasn't a mention of Roger. Where was he? Had he gone away?

Sarah not only replied immediately to Jenny but also wrote to her Aunt Lucy and Aunt Mary. In her letter to Mary she concluded, *'And how is Uncle Roger getting on in his army career? Does he like desk work?'*

Mary's reply came first. She talked about how she was 'walking' quite normally and was thinking of going back to her job in the munitions factory. *'I have to do something,'* she wrote, *'because I'm so unhappy. Your Uncle Roger has left me again, says he's sorry but gives no further explanation. I don't know where he is, he hasn't written. I think he's unhappy too, and I'm sure it's because he had set his heart on going to the Front to fight.'*

No, it isn't, Sarah thought, he would never want to fight, he's a coward. At this she sat back, wondering what had made her think such a thing. Then she remembered a time some months back, when Maggie had read her cup. She had said: 'You'll be going on a journey, quite a longish one, and you'll meet someone you like very much, but beware of him. He's no good, and also he's a coward.'

At the time a longish journey had seemed quite remote and Sarah had forgotten about the someone she was to meet. Now she knew for certain it was Roger. He only wanted to wear a uniform to appear patriotic. From then on, her obsession was eased.

She took a greater interest in lathe work, knowing if finances became any worse at home she might get the chance of working in a munitions factory. Only that morning her mother had been on to her father for spending so much time mending kettles for people instead of getting on with his own work.

Sarah had to admit she was on her mother's side in one sense, and yet she didn't really want her father to change. He liked and needed to help people, and there were very few who were unappreciative of what he did for them. Many did come in and leave coppers for a job done, even though payment had been due weeks before.

Sarah wrote regularly to Joe and in his replies he was always full of praise for her chatty letter. *'Some blokes never get letters at all and I read yours to them and they think you're quite wonderful. So do I.'*

Sarah always felt a little thrill at times like this, not only because she felt she was helping the soldiers in some way but because she felt very close to Joe.

Jenny seldom mentioned Joe, she was too taken up with Peter. He was now out of hospital, was based temporarily in London and often came to visit her at Aunt Mary's. Nothing more had been heard from Roger and Jenny wrote, good riddance to bad rubbish. She said she was still hankering after going into munitions but her mother had not yet agreed to this. However, it was sure to come as money was so tight. Her father had been out of bed and trying to use crutches but was not steady yet. Eventually he would go to another hospital to be fitted with false limbs.

A month after this Jenny wrote to say she was at last training at Woolwich and enjoying the work, the company and of course the pay packets. She wasn't earning anything like six or seven pounds a week but perhaps she would in time.

In the late spring of 1916, another scandal hit the family. Roger had been arrested for impersonating a British Officer. Sarah had never known her mother to be so furious. Isabelle went on and on about it – what a despicable liar the man was, to wear a uniform that did not belong to him, moreover an officer's, at that. He had brought the worst possible disgrace on the family. What if Henrietta got to hear about it? They would all be condemned in her eyes because they had been friendly towards him.

Lucy wrote that he was a traitor to his country and should be shot in the Tower as spies were. In olden days he would have been hung, drawn and quartered! When she thought of Fred, out of a job and mutilated for life, while Roger went swaggering about pretending to be an officer she felt she could stick a knife into her rotten brother-in-law.

Mary wrote to say she never wanted to see him ever again for this dreadful thing he had done, but God help her, she still loved him.

Sarah felt only sick and disillusioned and vowed that never again would she become obsessive over a man.

Jonathan was the only one who expressed sympathy for Roger. 'Roger always wanted to be liked, to be loved. You said he had shown you all the greatest kindness, that he was a caring man; he was at least sincere in these respects. Are not these things in his favour? He'll go to prison again, and the sentence won't be light because he already has a record. He'll mix with low types, some of them greater rogues than himself, but because they have no time for people who give themselves airs they'll crucify Roger. You can feel sorry for him, Sarah.'

'Perhaps,' she said, 'but I don't at this moment.'

In June 1916, when newsboys were shouting, 'Kitchener drowned; The *Hampshire* sunk,' Roger was sentenced to a year's imprisonment.

Isabelle wept for the tragic loss of a great military leader; Sarah wept for her Uncle Roger who would be tormented by his fellow prisoners.

The following month saw the beginning of the Battle of the Somme, a huge Franco-British effort to break the Western Front. Spirits were high. This was the battle that would end the war. People went about waving Union Jacks.

The newspapers pronounced that first day as a victory . . . Men were 'slightly wounded', losses were 'by no means excessive'.

Soldiers who returned wounded from the battle were given a hero's welcome. Women lined railway platforms to wave at the frequent ambulance trains. At Charing Cross excited crowds cheered the men being lifted from the train on stretchers. Other people lined the routes to hospitals, presenting the men with flowers and sweets.

But the truth soon came out that it had been no victory but a wholesale slaughter. Newspaper pages were black with the names of the dead.

And before long whole streets of houses had drawn blinds, and this was all over the country. In one place it was said that only seven soldiers survived out of the town's entire battalion.

Sick at heart, Sarah scanned the lists every day, praying she would not see Joe's name or that of Warren Hendrix. From time to time some of Warren's family were mentioned in the newspapers; a brother had been awarded the Distinguished Service Cross; a sister had married a Naval Commander, the son of an earl, and Mrs Bentham, his mother, was applauded for raising a large sum of money for the war effort.

The slaughter of the Somme went on week after week and people spoke of young boys being shipped to the Front as 'cannon fodder'. Despondency settled over the country; no one spoke any more of the war being over soon. Trade was bad and since married men were now conscripted, many small businesses had to close down.

Sarah was always conscious of her mother's worry about making ends meet, and one day suggested she go to London and try to get work in the munitions factory. After all, she was nearly sixteen now and no longer a child. Isabelle said no, and refused to discuss the matter further.

But then at the end of September 1916 Lucy wrote to say that she and Fred were finally coming home. He had been fitted with false limbs and had learned to use them. They were both dying to see Eric. Jenny was to stay behind as the money she earned was a godsend in the circumstances. Sarah decided to broach the subject again once her aunt and uncle were home.

On a blustery day at the beginning of October she arrived late at the shop after doing some shopping for her mother, and had closed the door hurriedly against the rain blasting in when she became aware of a man in officer's uniform getting up from a stool by the fire. Jonathan said smiling, 'We have a visitor, Sarah, a very welcome one.'

Sarah took off her knitted cap, wondering who this gaunt, hollow-eyed man could be when he spoke: 'Hello, Sarah. It's good to see you again.'

She stared. It was the cultured voice of Warren Hendrix, but – 'Well, hello,' she stuttered. 'Do please sit down again. Has Father given you a cup of tea?'

'Yes, your father very kindly made me one.' He indicated the empty brown earthenware mug on the floor.

Sarah found it impossible to associate this skeleton of a man with the attractive, virile Warren Hendrix she had known. Dear God, he looked as if he were dying. She put on a bright smile. 'Well, it *is* a surprise seeing you, Lieutenant Hendrix. How long have you been back?'

'A few days, and do call me Warren. You too, Mr Torent, *please.*'

Jonathan said, 'Warren has been wounded and was sent home to recuperate.'

'And I soon will, now that I am home.' To Sarah he added, 'Your father and I have had a most interesting discussion on astronomy.'

'Oh, that's good.' Sarah found herself studying the dull-eyed, skeleton figure with his uniform hanging on him and wondered how long ago it was that he had been wounded for the second time. She wanted to sympathise with him, say comforting things, but a lump was in her throat. A woman came in just then with a man's boot to be patched,

159

and said to Jonathan, 'Mr MacTavish must have popped out for a few minutes, can I leave this with you?'

Jonathan said certainly, then enquired after the woman's grandchild, who was ill. While they were talking, Warren was sitting straight-backed, listening.

'What is it?' Sarah whispered.

'It's the ticking of all the clocks. Doesn't it bother you?'

'No, I hardly notice it. I suppose I'm accustomed to it being here all day, but whenever I'm away from the shop for a number of days, then I become aware of the different sounds.' She laughed. 'I used to stand listening to them. There was the slow ticking that seemed to say "Don't – hurry – there's – plenty – of – time", the quick ticking like a busy bee saying "Come on, come on, there's work to be done". But I think the clocks I like best of all are the grandfathers, with their gentle tick-tock, as though they have learned so much in life and are saying "Take it easy, there is always another day."'

The woman left but she had hardly closed the door when another customer came in and Jonathan got up to attend to him. Sarah found Warren studying her.

'You're a sight for sore eyes, Sarah, as one of my men is always saying to any girl he comes into contact with. Not that you are just *any* girl – you get more lovely every time I see you.'

His expression was sombre, making the compliment seem more important than if he had been smiling. She answered him in equally serious vein.

'I don't think of myself as being attractive but it's nice if someone sees me that way. How long do you think you will be home, Warren? They won't send you back to the Front, I hope.'

'I imagine they will once I have fully recovered. They need every man they can get.' A clock on a shelf near him began to chime and he listened until the last stroke had died away. 'How time can vary in one's mind. When you are at the Front and waiting to go over the top every second seems like sixty, yet when I hadn't slept for three days, or thought I hadn't slept, time had no meaning, everything took on an air of unreality.'

The customer left and Jonathan came over. Warren looked up. 'We were talking about time, Mr Torent, or at least I was. In earliest civilization time was unimportant. Distance could mean just somewhere beyond a mountain, but now scientists speak of galaxies as being millions of light-years away. Who is to say they are right?'

'The men who assess these distances are brilliant mathematicians, Warren, and yet they have often varied in their calculations. It was decided in the past that a day and a night should be divided into twenty-four hours, the hours split into sixty minutes and the minutes into sixty seconds.'

'There's nothing wrong with that,' Sarah said.

'But if a day and a night had been split up into a hundred sections and then subdivided into minutes and seconds, an hour would have been much shorter. Time really is immeasurable.'

Sarah's brow creased in a frown. 'I don't think I quite know what you are getting at, Poppa.'

Warren nodded slowly. 'I think I know what your father means. I once read about a scientist who said if you had a bucket of sand and took out one grain it would represent our present age; the rest would represent all the ages that have gone. Is he right? How big was the bucket?'

When Sarah looked more bewildered than ever Warren went on dreamily, 'There's a line in a hymn that I think sums up time ... *"A thousand ages in Thy sight are like an evening gone."*

'It's from *Oh, God Our Help in Ages Past,*' Sarah said.

'Yes.' Warren stared into the fire. 'And it makes me feel that we are nothing. When I was wounded I lay in a shell-hole for what seemed an eternity. All hell was let loose, guns were pounding, shells screaming around me and I found myself wondering what I was doing there. Why was I living, why had I been born? At night I stared at the stars and thought – they have been there forever. What are they doing there, what purpose do they serve? What purpose did

161

I serve? Had I been born just to die on a battlefield having had only a small taste of life?'

He was silent for a moment then went on as if in a trance, 'I must have been delirious because I could hear my mother reading stories to me. They all began "Once upon a time . . ." and I began to wonder what was meant by once upon a time – did it mean a hundred years ago, a thousand . . . ?'

There was something about the flatness of Warren's voice that sent shivers up and down Sarah's back. She said gently, 'They're magical words. What wonderful images they conjure up.'

He raised his head and stared at her, as though surprised to find her there. Sarah glanced at her father and he put a finger to his lips. Warren looked back at the fire.

'They didn't conjure up any images for me. I must have lost consciousness because when I awoke I found a nurse standing beside my bed. She timed my pulse and I stated my thoughts aloud, where I had left off. What did once upon a time mean? She went to get the doctor. That was weeks and weeks ago and I still find myself thinking about time and what use we are in this world.'

He got up stiffly then and said he must go. Jonathan helped him on with his overcoat and Warren asked, a little tentatively, if he could view the heavens through Jonathan's telescope one evening. Jonathan said yes, of course, any time, he would enjoy having a talk with him. He could come that evening if he wished. Warren agreed, thanked both Jonathan and Sarah, and left.

Sarah, who watched him walking away, said worriedly, 'He has a very bad limp, he looks dreadful! I have a feeling he has no wish to live.' She felt like crying. 'I hope he doesn't do anything stupid.'

Jonathan came up to her. 'Warren won't take his own life, if that is what you are thinking, Sarah. He's too interested in life, and in time. And no man contemplating suicide would want to look at the stars. I have great hopes of a complete recovery for that young man.'

Sarah found herself looking forward to the evening. Her

mother had raised no objections to her staying later at the shop, but then of course she knew that Warren Hendrix would be there to talk about astronomy – and in her mother's eyes, Warren was class.

Isabelle led a busy life nowadays, working with a group of women rolling bandages, knitting for the troops and hospital visiting. She said that visiting wounded soldiers had taught her to control her feelings, but when she spoke of young boys, some of them who had lied about their ages to enlist, who were no more than sixteen and were maimed for life, there were tears in her eyes. She wrote letters home for those blinded, and when Isabelle told Sarah of the simple way some of them expressed themselves, Sarah was deeply moved.

One boy had dictated: *'Dear Mum, I can't see any more but I can feel the sun on my face and hear the birds singing. Aren't I lucky? Love Jim.'*

Isabelle said she always added extra lines, telling a mother more about her boy, how brave he was and assuring her he would soon be home.

The wind had died down by evening and the sky was brilliant with stars. Although Sarah's interest in astronomy had waned when she was younger, it had been revived since the talk with her father and Warren that morning. She hoped that Warren would come early.

It was half-past seven when he arrived and he said he would only be able to stay for an hour, since his parents insisted that he rest. A cousin who had driven him to the shop would call again for him at eight-thirty.

He said wryly, 'We are all bound by time, aren't we?'

They were about to go up to the room above the shop where the telescope was kept when Joseph Bell, a friend of her father, arrived. After being introduced to Warren and finding out why he had come he laughed. 'Join the club, sir, you're in good company. Jonathan and I can talk about space for hours, not that we agree on every theory put forward.'

Warren said, 'I'm a novice really, but I became interested when I met a man in hospital who believes that man will

163

go into space eventually. But he was unable to answer my question: if such a thing did happen, would it have a disruptive effect on the order in the universe?'

Joseph Bell chuckled. 'You've hit on Jonathan's pet subject. I shall let him answer it, but you had better sit down, for it will take some time.'

They sat down and Sarah was annoyed because she had hoped to be with just her father and Warren. But then Warren began talking and she became interested.

'I would like to put this theory forward, Mr Torent. We know what time the sun will rise and set, know that at certain times a comet has appeared with a regularity every seventy-five years and has done since the fifteen hundreds, so if nothing has changed in millions of years what effect could a machine have, hurtling around in space?'

'But changes do take place, Warren. Explosions are going on all the time but they are natural phenomena. It's when one interferes with nature that there is a price to be paid. With the development of industry, factories belch forth smoke, and London suffers from black, choking fog. On the other hand there has to be progress; no doubt someone in the future will find a solution to this problem.'

'But you are thinking in terms of large numbers of chimneys belching smoke. I was thinking in terms of one or two men going into space.'

'But it wouldn't stop at one or two, Warren. You can rest assured that if some men went into space the building of laboratories would follow and then the creation of space cities. *Then* there would be disruption.'

At this Joseph Bell roared with laughter. 'People living in space? Oh, come on, Jonathan, you really are letting your imagination run away with you.'

Sarah was furious. How dare this man laugh! Her father was clever, he knew about these things and, what was more, he was never wrong in any assessment. How many books had Mr Bell studied on the subject? Her father must have read heaps of them.

It was not until Warren was preparing to leave that

Jonathan suggested he have a quick look through the telescope, then call another time.

That evening was the beginning of a number of visits from Warren. Sometimes he would come in the morning and they would talk clocks, and Sarah was always pleased to be able to air her knowledge. But the thing that gave her the greatest pleasure was the fact that although Warren had only put on little weight he had lost that terrible gaunt look, and he was also learning to smile again, and to laugh.

When he did come in the evenings there were always one or more of her father's friends there and then the talk became really technical. And yet, they mentioned the names of astronomers that Sarah recalled from the times when she used to sit on the stairs listening to the men talking during the months her mother was away for her health. The names had not meant much to her then, but now she realised the impact these men had made on the world with their theories. Copernicus, Galileo, Isaac Newton . . .

Lucy and Fred's return to Newcastle was delayed because Fred needed some alterations to his artificial leg; when Lucy did write to announce their homecoming, Sarah's one regret was that Jenny would definitely not be coming with them. Her wages were still needed badly.

Sarah was astonished at how well her uncle coped with his artificial limbs. He even joked about them, but later on she realised how much both her uncle and aunt had changed. Lucy, who had always been bubbling over with life, was subdued and although Fred still joked, there was an underlying sadness in him.

'I need something to do,' he admitted. 'But what?'

Jonathan suggested that the couple move to Tynemouth with Eric and look for a house with a small garden. 'I'll do the digging,' he offered.

Fred laughed. 'I like the sound of that. I could make holes with a dibber, put plants in them and watch 'em grow. How about it, Lucy?'

She looked a little brighter. 'It is an idea. We could grow vegetables, which would be a big saving.' She hugged Eric

165

to her. 'Yes, I like it. We'll start looking around when we get home.'

There was a jollity about the evening after that, as though moving house would solve all of Lucy and Fred's problems. Even if it didn't and couldn't, Sarah thought how lovely it was to see both of them looking more like their old selves.

14

Warren was a regular visitor to the shop for another three weeks, then one morning he told Jonathan and Sarah that he was due back at his unit. Sarah felt dismayed. He was not nearly well enough to return to the Front. Although he had gained some weight, his face and body were bony, and he still limped. When she protested, he shook his head.

'I have to go back sometime and I really do feel tons better.' He smiled from Jonathan to Sarah. 'Thanks to you both for all your interest and help and our dicussions on clocks and astronomy.' His expression suddenly sobered. 'I was in a very low state when I came in that day and we talked about time.' He held out a parcel to Jonathan and then a small package to Sarah. 'Just small gestures of my regards for you both.'

Jonathan's gift was a book on astronomy he had been searching for and he glowed with pleasure as he thanked Warren. Sarah's gift was a small silver brooch with the word *Mizpah* entwined with foliage, the word meaning friendship. She had to swallow hard before thanking him. Then she said, 'Father and I must find something to give to you, as a mascot to keep you safe.'

'Your warmth and smiles will be with me always,' he said, and there was a slight catch in his voice. 'I hope I shall be able to see you before I leave, but if I don't, let me thank you once more for your kindness, and will you thank your friends too, Mr Torent. I think I've spent some of my most interesting hours with you all.' He smiled then. 'And on starry nights I shall show off my knowledge to whoever will listen.'

He shook hands with them, his clasp firm and then at the last minute, he kissed Sarah quickly on the cheek. His last words were, 'I hope it won't be long before I'm sitting beside your fire enjoying a good chat. I'll drop you a line,

167

and if either of you can spare the time, I would like to hear how things are going.'

When he left he was emotional and so was Sarah. 'Let's pray he does come back,' she said.

Warren's going left a big gap in her life; she thought about him every day, but she also thought about Joe because Mrs Curson had written to say they had not heard from him for so many months. Jonathan said that no news was good news, but this did not stop Sarah from worrying.

Then one day while she was upstairs tidying what she had come to call the telescope room, a neighbour who was home from the Front dropped in to see her father. The man was a Sergeant Major with a booming voice who talked about the horrors of war. Sarah was aware that her father had closed the door at the bottom of the stairs but she could still make out the soldier's words clearly.

'I thought I was immune to any sights of war,' he said, 'but what I saw on the Somme, Mr Torent, is burned into my brain forever. Young lads, kids really, blown to pieces – bodies without heads, torsos without legs or arms. I saw one chap, his face aflame with blue phosphorescent gas. God, to think that human beings can stoop to such atrocities as using gas. I saw men impaled on barbed wire, their guts hanging out . . .'

Sarah put her hands over her ears, but after a while she took them away. No, this was the world she was living in and she ought to know the worst – so that if ever she married and had sons she would be able to tell them of these things, warn them that there is no glory in war.

She heard about the appalling weather, the incessant deluging rain, about soldiers plodding up to their knees in mud and how some of them who had fallen had been sucked into the mud and drowned. She heard about bodies being gnawed by rats and knew she need hear no more to be able to put over her point. She went downstairs and was greeted with a glad shout.

'Why, Sarah lass! How bonny you've grown, and you're a lot taller since I saw you last.'

The man's talk after that was about the shortage of food

168

and how it would gradually become scarcer. He went on to the need for more shells, and how great numbers of workers would need to be employed to produce them. 'Women are at it now,' he said, 'and I take my hat off to them, especially those who fill the shells and see their skin and hair turn a bright yellow.'

Sarah had heard of them, women who had the nickname of 'Canaries'.

What surprised her after the Sergeant Major had gone was that he had hinted at nothing derogatory about her father, who was unable to take part in the war effort, yet he had abused other men, calling them filthy names – those slackers and dodgers who should be put up against a wall and shot.

During the next few weeks trade dropped to such an extent that even Jonathan would get his clock repairs completed as soon as possible to earn money. Isabelle began to look ill, drained, and had to give up all her voluntary work, which upset her. Recently, Lucy had been a frequent visitor. She and Fred had seen a house they liked at Tyne-mouth. It had a sitting room, living room and scullery on the ground floor, and two bedrooms upstairs. There was a small garden at the back.

The snag was that the house was up for sale, not rent. Lucy had reluctantly turned it down, when to the astonish-ment of all, Henrietta offered to lend them the two hundred pounds, saying they could pay it back in instalments. Jenny was earning good money, they could save from that. Fred was all for it, but Lucy hated to be beholden to her mother for anything. Sarah had heard her aunt talking it over with her parents several times and when Lucy came to the shop one afternoon and said she would like to have a private word with Jonathan, Sarah, presuming it was to do with the house, said she would go upstairs and tidy up.

She had started to sort things out on a number of occasions before, but there was so much stuff belonging to her father that she had not as yet made much impact. There were boxes full of his bits and pieces bought from junk-shops – springs, lengths of wire, nuts and bolts, screws, pieces of tin, metal, in fact anything that might come in handy for his inventions. Piles of newspapers lay with scientific articles underlined in red next to a heap of his *Popular Science Siftings* magazines, and there were stacks of portfolios containing drawings of his ideas. Sarah had never studied any of them properly but now she undid the string of one and pages slid over the floor. The designs were well executed and the instructions in her father's beautiful copperplate handwriting were a delight to read.

There were numerous variations of each invention: a mooring mast for a dirigible, a suction cleaner to extract dust from carpets, drawings of a turbine engine and a back-scratcher, activated by clockwork to enable a person to relieve an itch on parts they were unable to reach. Sarah laughed aloud at this. She also found drawings of a submarine with suggested attachments on the sides that would enable it to be lifted from the seabed if sunk.

She was sitting back on her heels, absorbed in the sketches of strange-looking machines for space travel when Lucy entered. Sarah glanced over her shoulder. 'So, is the buying of the house all settled?' she asked cheerfully.

Lucy gave no reply and there was something in her expression that made Sarah get to her feet. 'What is it, Auntie? What's wrong?'

'It's your mother, Sarah. We've been to the doctor's and she's ill – quite ill. She needs to go away again.'

Sarah's heart began a slow, painful beating. 'To Blanchland?'

'No. Doctor Fawcett wants her to go to Scotland, to a sanatorium.'

Sarah stared at her. 'A sanatorium? Only rich people go to places like that. We haven't got that kind of money.'

Lucy nodded. 'I know, and that is why I have suggested to your father that you go to London, live with your Aunt Mary and take a well-paid job in the munitions factory at Woolwich. You and Jenny will be together and you'll be company for one another.'

Although Sarah had hoped to return to London at some time, she had not wanted it to come about in this way. She said that she doubted whether her mother would agree, and Lucy replied sharply, 'She has no choice, Sarah! If she doesn't go to Scotland and have proper treatment, she'll die – it's as simple as that.'

When Sarah began to cry Lucy put her arm around her. 'I'm sorry, love, for sounding so brutal but it needs the truth to make an impact. Your father said he is willing to sell his own antique watches, which his father gave him, but even he admits that what they would fetch would pay for no more than your mother's fare and someone to travel with her and, possibly the first month's payment to the sanatorium.'

Sarah felt grieved, knowing how much her father treasured his watches. But then, he would not begrudge the sacrifice. She asked, 'How did Mother react to the doctor's suggestion of her going to Scotland?'

'She told him it was impossible, they were having a struggle to make ends meet as it was. He said quietly that miracles did sometimes happen, and they might find it possible to raise the money. That was when I thought about you taking the job.'

Sarah thought it a strange twist of fate that if her Aunt Mary had not 'hurt' her leg they would not have gone to London, and if Uncle Fred had not been wounded, Jenny might not have gone into munitions.

'Yes, of course I'll go to London, Aunt Lucy, and I don't care how many hours I work, if only Mother will get better.'

Lucy nodded, tears in her eyes. 'She will. Maggie told me so.'

Sarah was surprised at this because since Maggie's husband had died she had refused to make any more prophecies, not even when Sarah had begged her to say whether Warren and Joe would come back safely. 'They're in the hands of God,' she had said. 'We must accept His decision.'

When they went down into the shop Sarah ran into her father's outstretched arms and they wept together. Then, because he insisted it was impossible for her to go to London and work she said they must sit down and talk things over sensibly. The result was, as she knew it had to be, that she would go and live with her Aunt Mary.

Jonathan sold his watches and meanwhile, the doctor arranged for a very pleasant nurse to accompany Isabelle to Scotland.

The parting was made easier by Fred's presence when Isabelle and the nurse were ready to leave. He said, giving her a smacking kiss, 'Isabelle love, when I can manage to get going a little better I'll come to see you and we'll tramp up those mountains together.'

Isabelle gave a shaky laugh. 'Oh, Fred, you're marvellous, and I grumble. Bless you.'

The worst part for Sarah was the following day when she knew she would be leaving her father and brother in two days' time. How could she bear to leave them? The house was like a morgue and so was the shop. Then when the pair arrived home that evening after work there was a note from Henrietta, demanding that they go and see her.

From the moment they set foot in the house she ranted and raved at Jonathan. Her daughter was going to her death and he was responsible, but he would suffer, there was no doubt about that, for no man could get away with such cruelty. She hoped he would burn in the fires of hell!

Jonathan had told Sarah that no matter what her grandmother said she was not to answer her back, but the thought of what her father was suffering made Sarah jump up.

She accused her grandmother of being evil. 'You sit there day after day thinking of nothing else but wicked things. You haven't an ounce of kindness in you. You have no idea of the love there is between man and wife, the caring. My mother and father are deeply in love and you know it, but you won't admit it because you are jealous.'

Jonathan said, 'Sarah, Sarah – ' and made to take her by the arm but she pulled away from him. 'No, I'll have my say. Everyone has kow-towed to you, Grandmother, but I won't any more. You say you'll see Father damned in hell. Well – you are *living* in hell.'

Henrietta raised her stick. 'You get out of here, girl, and don't you ever set foot in this house again, do you hear?'

'I hear, and you need never worry I'll ever come back here because wild horses wouldn't drag me to your door-

172

step.' Sarah turned and went out of the room, stormed into the passage and opening the front door, left, slamming it behind her.

But once outside she began to shake uncontrollably, realising that her temper would react on her father, and heaven knows he had enough to contend with. She made an effort to try and force herself to go back and apologise but knew it was impossible. She wanted to be finished with her grandmother, for as far back as she could remember she had never once had a kind word from her.

It must have been fifteen minutes later before Jonathan appeared. Then from the doorway he beckoned to her. She shook her head and after a moment he came up to her.

'Sarah, I want you to apologise. Your grandmother is crying. She won't apologise to you but I want you just to go in and say you are sorry, no more than that.' When she refused Jonathan went on, 'I don't mind for myself, Sarah, it's for your mother's sake. I don't want Henrietta to write and upset her and that I shall demand of her.'

Sarah knew she had to give in, but her feet dragged as she went into the room. Henrietta was wiping her eyes. Sarah went up to her, stood a moment them said, 'I'm sorry for getting into such a temper. We've had a lot of worry. Especially Father. It hurt me that you should call him names.'

Henrietta waved her away. 'All right, I accept your apology, now leave me alone.'

Sarah then went out, leaving her father to say what he had to say. When he came out they walked along the street in silence then he glanced at her. 'Perhaps it's cleared the air, Sarah, I don't know. What I do know is that your grandmother is a terribly unhappy woman.'

'It's her own fault, Poppa, she makes her own hell.'

He was silent for a while then he said, 'Sarah, I'm going to tell you something that happened in your grandmother's life so that perhaps you will understand what made her the way she is. She made your mother promise that she would never tell anyone what happened but she did not make me promise, and I think this is the time for you to know.'

173

And so the story was told as they walked slowly back home.

'Henrietta was a gifted pianist, she loved her music and it was a joy to her to sit at the piano for hours. The trouble started when she met and fell in love with a young man who was an artist, a handsome young man who your great-grandfather denounced as a ne'er-do-well. He forbade Henrietta to see him again.'

Jonathan sighed. 'But she was wilful and disobeyed him. The couple met clandestinely. She was even planning to run away with the young man when their meeting place was discovered. She came back into the house quite unsuspecting and sat down at the piano. She was happily playing and dreaming of her lover when her father came into the room. He strode over to her, slammed the lid down on her fingers and proclaimed her a whore.'

Sarah shuddered. 'Oh, how awful, her poor fingers . . .'

'Every one was broken, but that was not the end of it. Shouting with pain she got up to run for help but her father lifted up her skirts and hit her about the legs with a stout stick and . . . broke both legs.'

'I can't believe it,' Sarah exclaimed. 'How cruel, how sadistic.'

'It was more than that,' Jonathan said grimly. 'It was diabolical that a man could treat his own daughter in this way. I gave you a graphic account, Sarah, of your great-grandfather's behaviour because I *had* to make you understand why Henrietta is so bitter. No one will ever know what she suffered, not only through her injuries but also because the man she loved left this country and she never saw or heard from him again.'

'But he probably did it for her sake, knowing she would suffer more if he tried to see her.'

'Unhappily he accepted a sum of money to leave and her father showed her a letter from the young man, saying he had no wish to marry a girl who might be crippled.'

'I feel sick!' Sarah exclaimed. 'How could *two* men stoop so low? She did marry, but was the marriage a happy one?'

A look of sadness came into Jonathan's eyes. 'I'm afraid

not. It was an an arranged marriage and your grandfather was twenty-five years older than Henrietta. He was an ambitious man and married her for the substantial dowry offered. The bones of her fingers eventually knitted together but she was never able to play the piano again. Her legs suffered compound fractures and took a long time to heal. Then rheumatism set in, making it difficult for her to get around.

'And so, Sarah,' he concluded, 'that is the tragic tale of your grandmother. Can you wonder that she broods?'

'I feel sorry for her, Poppa, but I have no affection for her, never will. I know she's had a terrible life, but so have other people yet they don't take their tragedies out on those around them. Mrs Braithwaite in Coleman Street has been beaten black and blue for years by her husband. She's had five miscarriages on account of it but she's still a kind and gentle person.'

'I understand your reasoning, Sarah, but there is capacity for love in your grandmother; she has a great affection for Victor. I don't know whether you've ever listened to them talking, but then she comes to life – they share a love of music and she helps him, he's said so many times. As you know, Sarah, when Fred was wounded she was so upset that she offered him and Lucy the money to buy the house in Tynemouth.'

'Offered to *lend* it to them, you mean. They have to pay it back and with interest, I heard Aunt Lucy say so.'

'At your aunt's insistence, Sarah. Try not to judge Henrietta too harshly. With persistent kindness she might respond.'

Sarah thought, no, never, but refrained from saying so.

Jonathan said he must go back to the shop that evening and do some more work, so Sarah went on home. Victor was busy practising his scales and she had a sudden lost feeling without her mother being there. But then Isabelle must be feeling a lot worse, for she would be among total strangers. They had had a long talk the night before. Sarah had not wanted her mother to know she was hoping to go into munitions but her father had said there must be no

175

secrets between them. He would discuss it quietly with her and point out the advantages. To Sarah's surprise her mother had been quite calm when she talked it over with her.

'It's not at all what I wanted for you, Sarah, but I won't feel badly about it if you get a job working on a lathe, rather than doing something like filling shells. I appreciate the sacrifices you are all making for me and I'm going to do my best not to get depressed.'

Then after a silence she said, 'There are certain things I have to say to you, Sarah, and I don't want you to be upset by them. As I've told you, I shall do my very best to get well. I'll do everything the doctors and nurses tell me, but we don't know what the Lord has in store for me. If –'

Sarah, her heart beating uncomfortably, put her fingers to her mother's lips. 'Don't say it, Mother, *please.*'

Isabelle took her hand away and held it tight. 'I have to, Sarah, because if it should happen there are things I want you to do and they're *terribly* important. It's to do with the care of your father, the care of Victor, and to do with you, your growing up.' Isabelle had to pause to catch her breath.

'I went to school with a girl who said after her mother had died that if only she had known her mother was so ill she would have asked her things, about looking after the house, her father, her brothers and sisters. And that is why I want to talk to you, Sarah.

'Try to be with your father as much as possible for the first year, for that is the most dreadful time. Be gentle with Victor. Let him know you love him – he's such a sensitive boy but he is young and that does help. And, of course, your Aunt Lucy and your Uncle Fred would be towers of strength.'

Her mother, hollow-eyed and with no colour in her face at all, had to pause again. Sarah begged her to say no more but Isabelle insisted. 'I must talk about you, Sarah. You are growing up so quickly. Never submit to any man other than your husband. And when you do marry, no matter what troubles you might have, always make yourself as attractive as you can for him. Also, keep your house tidy, as tidy as

176

–' here Isabelle gave a wan smile, 'as you would wish it to be, should your mother-in-law or your worst enemy drop in unexpectedly.'

'I'll remember.'

Isabelle drew herself up in the chair. 'One more thing, then. I must go to bed to get my strength back for the journey tomorrow. I want you to visit your grandmother. You might not think it, Sarah, but she needs you. She doesn't hate you as you think, but has a great respect for you – only she won't allow herself to admit it.'

Isabelle had gone to bed then and Sarah, thinking over her words now, wondered how any of them, especially her father, would cope if her mother died. She got up to fetch the scarf she was knitting for Warren, but found when she sat down again that it was impossible to concentrate. So much had happened, so much had been said in the past few days.

After a while she became aware of Victor practising his scales. She was so used to hearing them that most of the time she wasn't even really conscious of them. She had once called them 'soulless necessities' and her mother had reproached her. 'I feel so sad, Sarah, that you have no ear for music. You miss so much.'

Now, suddenly finding that the exercises her brother was playing had touched a responsive chord in her, Sarah laid down her knitting. Perhaps there was music in her soul, after all.

Every evening when Victor had finished practising his warm-ups, he would play a piece by a famous composer or two. This evening, he started with a Mazurka by Chopin; it was a piece full of gaiety and Sarah could see in her mind's eye her grandmother as a young girl, going secretly to meet her lover, running, joy in her heart, to be clasped in his arms. How many times had they met? What whispered words had been spoken, what promises made? Sarah daydreamed of meeting Warren, having him draw her closely to him, touching her cheek, kissing her, gently at first then with a rising passion. Her body began to throb

177

with longings that were becoming more frequent as she grew up.

She became aware that Victor had gone from the lovely Mazurka into Chopin's revolutionary studies and she tensed, likening the patriotic fervour of the music to the angry action of her great-grandfather, who had slammed down the piano lid so cruelly on his daughter's delicate and talented fingers.

Sarah put her hands to her face. It was as terrible an act of violence as some of the cruelties perpetrated in the so-called cause of war. Only in this case, it had been because two young people were in love.

As the time drew near for Sarah's departure to London she understood how her mother must have felt, leaving home but as it turned out, Lucy cheered them all up.

Jonathan was against Sarah travelling alone so Lucy had promised to go to the station with her niece and see that she was safely settled. But on the morning of departure, Lucy arrived all bright and breezy with a suitcase to say she was accompanying Sarah all the way to London.

'Just for a few days,' she told them. 'Fred insists. He and Eric have been invited to stay with our new neighbours, an old fisherman and his wife. And anyway, I'm longing to see Jenny and our Mary. I also wanted to see Sarah settled into a job if possible, and find out all the conditions.'

Jonathan said quietly, 'Thanks, Lucy, it means a lot to me.'

It also meant a lot to Sarah, who had not wanted to feel like a child and be put in charge of the guard, or travel with someone responsible she could possibly dislike.

The journey to London now had an air of adventure.

15

When Sarah had come to London for the first time she had thought it terribly crowded, but now it seemed busier than ever. People rushed about on the station, servicemen with kit-bags mingling with civilians, and the streets were jammed with traffic. A large proportion of it was army vehicles, with girls driving. Mary and Jenny were there to meet them, Jenny talking nonstop with a knowing air as if she had lived in London all her life.

'We're not your country cousins who you have to impress, you little town mouse,' Aunt Lucy reproached her. Jenny laughed. 'You get that way from the women you work with, toughies!

Mary smiled, refuting this. 'Jenny loves to exaggerate. We work with women and girls from all walks of life. A number in our shed are from aristocratic backgrounds, my dear, but they all mix in. Oh, here's our bus coming.' They were separated on the bus and it was not until they arrived at Mary's and were sitting down to a meal that they started any serious talk. Mary was very upset about Isabelle, but said it was good that Sarah would be able to help financially. She had spoken to her supervisor about her niece and would take her along the next day to have a talk. If the woman thought she was suitable, Sarah would go on a six weeks' training course. Mary added that they were very short of girls on lathes for the more delicate work.

Sarah wanted to know all about Jenny's current boyfriend, and although whole days could now pass without Roger ever coming into her thoughts she was keen to find out how he was coping with prison. She had an opportunity of asking these things privately when she later had her aunt, and then Jenny, on their own.

Mary's eyes filled with tears over Roger. 'I only went once to visit him, Sarah, but he didn't want to see me. I

179

thought perhaps he was too ashamed. I try to forget him, but it's not easy. I'm glad you asked after him, though, Sarah.'

It was bedtime before Sarah could ask her cousin about boyfriends. When she mentioned Peter Jenny frowned for a moment then said,'Oh, him, I had forgotten about him, he belongs to the dim ages. I've had about ten boyfriends since then.' In the next breath she added, 'Have you heard anything at all about Joe recently?' Sarah detected a forlorn note in her voice and felt her heart contract. Jenny had once said he was the only boy she would ever really love and Sarah wondered now if her cousin would always have a secret yearning for him.

She told her how long it was since she had had the last letter from Joe – and how short it had been. 'I think it was just to keep in touch with someone who would write to him occasionally.'

Jenny asked if Sarah wrote regularly and Sarah, not wanting to lie deliberately, prevaricated. 'I never seem to have a minute these days and then there was all the worry about Mother. You'll like your new house, Jenny, and it's good for your father to be near the sea. Do you miss Eric?'

They talked about different people they knew, about young men who had been killed, about families they knew who had lost husbands and sons. Then Jenny confided: 'I thought it would be exciting, living through a war and meeting lots of men. I also thought it would be fun working and earning good money. But what do I get out of it? I have to send most of it home. You'll be in the same boat, Sarah. Some girls who've left home have all their wages to themselves! By the way, that reminds me of our plan to earn a bit of extra money, something to keep to ourselves.'

Jenny explained that many of the women in the factory were big spenders; they would buy anything – jewellery, underwear, wrist-watches. She said she knew a woman who worked at home making silk camisoles. 'We'll buy from her,' Jenny said, 'sell them in the factory and earn a commission. I'll also get some beads from a warehouse here, make up necklaces as we agreed and if you can ask your father to make some watches we'll sell those too.'

Sarah shook her head at the mention of watches. 'It would be no use even asking him now, Jenny. He's so busy helping other people he would never find the time.'

'Then we'll buy them from a warehouse and sell at small profits for quick sales.' Her mouth suddenly set in a hard line. 'We'll never get another opportunity like this, Sarah. When this war's over we won't be the only ones out of a job, and the thought of going back to work for a boss in a shop, even if I got the chance, fills me with horror. I must get some money now while I have the chance. Will you do it? If we both sell it will double our output. I know the money has to be split between us but the more different items we have on the go the bigger the savings. How about it?'

Sarah felt it was too sudden to be plunged into a sideline but realised that extra money would be needed when the war was over, especially if her father had no work coming in. She said yes without even discussing the problems that might arise and hoped she would not regret it. Jenny gave her a hug. 'I felt sure I could depend on you.'

She began to talk about Sarah's interview the next day. 'You have to get this job, Sarah. Aunt Mary and I are on the same shift-times tomorrow and don't start until ten o'clock. Oh, Sarah, I'm so glad you're here. I've really missed you, missed all our talks. Boyfriends are all right but you can't talk to them about things that girls like discussing. And although Aunt Mary is kind and we are company for each other, I'm sure her thoughts are always on that awful husband of hers.'

Before Jenny settled for sleep she said quietly, 'London can be a very lonely place, do you know that?'

'Lonely?' Sarah echoed. 'With so many people and so much to see? I can't believe it.'

'Well, it is. I mix with numerous people at the factory, I eat with a group, chat to them, but when I'm back at Aunt Mary's I feel sometimes as though I'm in a prison. We never see a soul. The people in the flat upstairs haven't come back and her neighbours all go out to work.'

When a yawning Sarah asked Jenny about all her boy-friends she gave a self-conscious laugh. 'As Aunt Mary says, I do exaggerate at times. They're all fellows I meet at work. Some of them have asked me out but we always seem to be on different shifts and anyway, Aunt Mary wouldn't let me go out with any Tom, Dick or Harry. They would have to be vetted, and their antecedents known from the Stone Age. Mum has laid down the law, of course.'

Jenny suddenly brightened. 'But things could be a lot different with you here, Sarah. We'll get around. We'll go to the warehouse together. I have put money by every week for something like this, so I do have some savings to start buying.'

Sarah suddenly found herself caught up in the idea. She leaned up on her elbow. 'We could look for other things – brooches, rings, earrings. Warren Hendrix gave me a brooch with *Mizpah* engraved on it. I love it! We could buy some similar brooches wholesale, the cheaper ones.'

Jenny sat up. 'Warren Hendrix? You mentioned him in your letters but you didn't say you were all that pally with him. Come on, tell me, what happened?'

Sarah had purposely refrained from writing much about Warren, not wanting to seem boastful about his regular appearances in the shop. Now she said, 'There's not much to tell. He was home on leave after being wounded, came round to talk to Poppa about astronomy, and I think he thought it would be nice to give me something in appreci-ation of all the cups of tea I made him. After all, Mizpah does mean *friendship*, not 'I love you'.

'Yes, but – ' Jenny lay back again. 'He must think some-thing of you to make you a present of a brooch. That's more than I've ever had from any of the fellows I've known.' She sounded disgruntled.

'Anyway, a new life is beginning,' Sarah said to cheer her up. 'We'll work hard, but we'll also have fun.'

Jenny laughed and said, 'You bet we will!'

Sarah had known that there were thousands of munition

182

workers employed on the site at Woolwich, where they went the following day, but she was still astonished by the vastness of the area. It covered miles – and work was still going on, putting up yet more buildings. The sounds of hammering and drilling, and the sight of cranes and swinging girders excited her. All this must surely help to bring the war to an end. The place was black with people going on or coming off shifts, like swarms of ants. She said in awe to Mary and Jenny, 'It's like a whole town.'

Mary nodded. 'It is a town, Sarah. Workers live here – there's a church over there and they're building a picture palace, or so someone told me. There are recreation rooms where you can play tennis, there's a swimming pool, and those are the canteens over there. The food is good. Come on, we go along here. I'll take you in to the supervisor then I'll have to leave you with her. Now, do you remember how to get back home? We're only doing a ten-hour shift today so should be home with you by about nine o'clock.'

Sarah felt apprehensive about meeting the supervisor. According to what she had heard from girls who were working in factories at home in Newcastle, the women in charge were dragons – spiteful, sneering. They'd humiliate a girl in front of everyone, making her feel no bigger than a flea.

But in this case the supervisor was pleasant and welcoming. She motioned Sarah to a chair. 'Sit down, Miss Torent, or may I call you Sarah?' To Sarah's relief she was not asked her age. Miss Holland drew her out about her life at home, her work, and listened intently and made notes as Sarah described her father's trade, which she had been learning. After questioning her closely on her lathe-work, Miss Holland wrote some more notes then looked up.

'Well, Sarah, you are certainly knowledgeable about lathe-work and I feel sure we will have a place for you here. You would need some training of course, starting next Monday, but first I want to tell you about all the other aspects of the work done here.'

Sarah, who (apart from lathe-work) had thought mainly in terms of shell-filling, making cartridge-cases and small screws – which was what Mary and Jenny did – was astonished at the number of jobs that were done. Miss Holland concluded, 'You would, of course, be shown around the various sheds until you are familiar with all the different operations.'

Ten minutes later, Sarah learned she had been accepted for the job. She thanked Miss Holland who said, 'I think you'll do well here, Sarah. You seem a very sensible and well-balanced girl. Of course you'll meet all types of people here and at times hear some – ' she smiled wrily '– very "choice" language, but remember this: all the people here are dedicated, some fanatically so. They don't mind how many hours they work if it helps to beat our enemies.'

She then went on to explain the shift-work Sarah would be expected to do. While she was training she would be earning two pounds ten shillings a week, but of course this would soon rise when she was fully trained.

Mary had forewarned Sarah of the low starting wage so she was not disappointed, but longed for the time when she would be able to send greater sums home.

Her aunt had also advised her if ever she got lost in London to ask a policeman, but it was mostly women police Sarah saw. She got such explicit directions from each one that she eventually found herself getting off a bus in the East End in an area of warehouses and small shops that sold all kinds of goods at wholesale prices. She had daringly decided to use her last remaining free days to investigate stocks for the home jewellery-making project.

At first, she explained that her father was in business in the North of England and she had come to look at the stock, but she soon found there was no need to explain anything. One tough-looking middle-aged man said: 'Have a gander around, gal. See what you want and let me know and I'll give you a price, but I'll tell you this – you ain't gonna find anything cheaper elsewhere.'

In this warehouse were boxes of beads of every description: coloured glass ones, wooden ones, prettily painted ones, imitation pearls in all sizes and some china ones with delicate designs on them, although these were scarcer than

184

the others. There was a variety of clasps, coils of wire, pliers, everything to do with the making up of necklaces. Sarah was fascinated. She was spellbound too, when she went to other small warehouses and shops that sold ready-made jewellery, but when she entered a tiny, dimly-lit shop and saw the variety of clocks there, she knew instinctively they would always be her first love.

The owner was an elderly man with a shock of white hair. His voice was gentle when he asked her if she was looking for anything special. Sarah's gaze was on a grand-father clock showing the months of the year, the risings and settings of the sun, the tides and the quarters of the moon. She stood running her hand gently over the wood.

The old man came over to her. 'Ah you are a lover of time.'

She turned and smiled at him. 'Yes, I am. And I don't think I had realised it so much until now, when I'm away from my own environment.'

She explained about her father's business and the old man was greatly interested. 'A man after my own heart,' he said. 'Sit down, my dear, and tell me more.'

While they chatted, Sarah became aware of a natural rapport between them. She told the man her name and asked him to call her Sarah. He was Mr Jacobs. They looked around the clocks in the shop but then Mr Jacobs told her he would show her his special stock. They went through a back room which was piled with boxes, then upstairs to a long room which covered the length of the shop. There Sarah stood and gasped. She released her breath in a long sigh. 'Oh, Mr Jacobs, how absolutely wonderful!'

He explained that this was his showroom for his special customers, who came from all over the world. There were not only clocks of every description but watches, too. Sarah said with a breathless laugh that she didn't know which to look at first, but her attention was drawn to a metal bird in a gilded cage with a small clock on top of the cage. Mr Jacobs pressed a knob and the bird's head began to move this way and that, then it was whistling.

Sarah clasped her hands in delight. 'Oh, my father would love that!'

But she quickly came to realise there were many items that would give her father extreme pleasure. One long case-clock of marquetry was so intricately decorated that she wondered how the craftsman had managed to handle such minute pieces of wood to complete a jigsaw of artistry. Among foliage and scrolls were tiny birds and fawns, the whole a canvas of warm browns and gold.

There were other grandfathers, but Sarah's attention went to some table-clocks in gilded brass – some were square and one was six-sided. The clock-face was on the lid, which lifted to show a cavity where the owners could keep treasures, or as Mr Jacobs smilingly explained, for a man to stub out his cigar. Several of these clocks had alarms and also struck the hours.

There were other clocks in gilded brass, exquisitely engraved and some that she found much too ornate, but which apparently attracted buyers. One table-clock was so lavishly decorated, with the clock-face painted in various scenes, that it was almost impossible to read the time.

There were lantern-clocks, a Gothic domestic clock in wrought-iron (this one very rare according to Mr Jacobs), a cabinet-clock, where one had to open two doors to see the time, and one which was made in three tiers with numerous figures on each tier in enamel and gilt with the tiniest of clocks on top.

Sarah laughed. 'Crazy, isn't it, having a clock where one can hardly read the time.'

'It was a matter of prestige, Sarah. Some people thought the more a clock was embellished the greater its value would seem to other people. Come and see the watches.'

It was the ladies' watches that appealed to Sarah. They were so beautiful, some with cases in chased gold, embossed gold and silver, some diamond-studded, others adorned with pearls and precious stones set in entrancing, intricate patterns. There were round watches, oval ones, heart-shaped watches and some in the form of a cross.

There were still many more timepieces to be inspected

when a customer came into the shop and Mr Jacobs had to go downstairs. Sarah went with him and was told by the old man that she must come whenever she pleased, he would be delighted to see her. She thanked him and promised to come again, and left knowing that although she would help Jenny with her project she would never go into partnership with her. It would have to be clocks and watches. While she was in London she would learn all she could about them and when the war was over she would start up in business on her own, buying and selling them. Mr Jacobs had told her that no matter how little work there might be available after the war there would always be men with money who wanted to add to their collection of timepieces.

Sarah was surprised to note that she had been with Mr Jacobs for over an hour. Feeling hungry, she went into a little café where she devoured steak and kidney pie, a piece of treacle tart and a cup of tea – all for ninepence. She then went on a tour looking for antique shops.

It was after five when Sarah decided that she was too tired to go anywhere else. The traffic was heavy and she had to fight her way on to the two buses that would get her back to her aunt's house. And when she did arrive she was so exhausted it took her all her time to light the gas-jet and put a match to the kindling in the grate to get a fire going.

Sinking into an armchair, Sarah contemplated her future. There would be many times when she would come back from the factory to an empty house. The really bad weather would soon be starting. How would she be able to cope with the lonely hours, waiting for Mary and Jenny to come in? It was then she understood what Jenny had meant when she had said that London could be a lonely place. However, by the time the fire had caught and she had made herself some sandwiches Sarah did feel a little better, but she longed for her aunt and cousin to come in so that she could tell them about her day.

It was nearly eleven o'clock when they arrived and she was asleep in the chair. Jenny roused her with a big shake. 'Come on, lazybones, you've nearly let the fire go out.' Sarah pulled herself together.

Mary had only one thing on her mind, to get to bed, but Jenny, although pale with tiredness, wanted to know the wholesale prices of wrist-watches, earrings, brooches and beads. Sarah was given no opportunity to talk about clocks.

Jenny said, 'Aunt Mary and I are changing shifts tomorrow so you and I can go shopping in the morning, Sarah. The sooner we get some goods to sell the sooner we'll be making money.'

Although Sarah still felt exhausted the next day, she found it impossible not to get caught up in Jenny's enthusiasm for her project; she was as keen as her cousin to price the goods they went out to buy so they would make a fair profit. They had bought more beads to make up into necklaces than anything else and Sarah began right away to lay the various kinds out ready for threading. Mary and Jenny helped and by the time the two of them were ready to leave for work Jenny had ten necklaces to take with her.

'It's a start,' she said gleefully. 'I'll see what the possibilities are tonight. I hope to sell what I'm taking and get more orders, also to let them know about the other stuff on offer.'

She did, and was so exuberant the next morning that no one would ever have guessed she had just finished a night-shift. 'I've got a pile of orders,' she announced proudly. 'And I have started up another line, piercing ears at sixpence a time.'

'Piercing ears?' Sarah exclaimed.

Jenny grinned. 'The earrings have little hooks on them to go through a hole in the ears, so I've had to make 'em, haven't I? And what with? A hot darning needle, that's what, with a piece of cork behind the lobes.'

Sarah put a hand over her mouth. 'I feel sick.'

Jenny dismissed the ear-piercing with an airy wave of her hand. 'They have sore ears for a day or two, but they soon clear up. If you want to be tarted up you have to pay for it.' She tipped silver and coppers on to the table. 'How about that then, and that's only one night's takings. I'll split my ear-piercing fees with you, Sarah, because you got us organised and you'll probably have to do the buying and the bead-threading for the time being.'

For three mornings running Jenny came in to Sarah with repeat orders, but announced that the ear-piercing business had had to stop, as many of the women had suffered from badly inflamed ears. None of them had given her away, however.

Sarah threaded so many strings of beads in those few days that she felt as though she was seeing nothing but beads in front of her eyes. She told Jenny that when she started her training course she would have to stop, it was impossible to do both. Jenny agreed they would think of something else to take their place.

Sarah had written enthusiastically to her father about meeting Mr Jacobs and in his reply Jonathan said how pleased he was that things were going so well for her. There had been no word from Isabelle yet but he would let her know as soon as he heard. He and Victor were being well looked after by Maggie; then there were little snippets about customers and neighbours. Mr MacTavish was keeping so much better he was able to cope with his shoe repairs which was a relief. They all sent their love.

On the morning Sarah was due to start her training course the weather deteriorated, and a driving sleet stung her cheeks. Although the journey was not all that long she was glad when she arrived and could get into the warmth of the building.

There were thirty trainees whose ages ranged from about eighteen to forty. Some were shabbily dressed, some were neat and others wore fur coats. They were greeted by an elderly man with a limp, who after giving them a pep talk about how men's lives depended on the efficiency of the workers, told them they would be split up into small groups to be shown around the various sheds.

The sheds were huge, holding what seemed like hundreds of workers. In some the women talked and laughed above the throb of machinery but in the shed where shells were being made it was impossible to make oneself heard above the noise of the massive machinery. Before

189

they went into this shed, the various processes of shell-making were explained to them. There were so many of these processes that it was difficult to absorb them all in one go. One action made an impression on them all: as women turned the outside of shells the hot shavings curling off fell in iridescent colours around them, in all the colours of the rainbow, bathed in a silver glitter. Another impressive action was the fitting and grooving of the shells' copper bands, a process which had machines and workers half-hidden in a glow of sunset tints, as the copper scraps fell.

The work that Sarah was most interested in was in the shed called the Fuse Shop, where women sat in row after row at tables as far as the eye could see. As she watched, she hoped she would be allotted to this shop, it was so challenging. In one process, there were seventeen different gauges for the examination of the percussion end of the fuse body, and one ten-thousandth of an inch was the limit of variation allowed.

The trainees were informed that they would begin their training in earnest the following day; and the next six weeks turned out to be the busiest Sarah had ever known. The course was concentrated; she had notes to write up every evening when she got back, as well as helping with the housework and shopping when Mary and Jenny were on full-day shifts.

She had letters to write home, and to her mother in Scotland. Isabelle had sent her a long letter, singing the praises of the nurses at the sanatorium, remarking on the friendliness of the other patients, and praising the beautiful scenery.

'I had heard people speak of the beauty and of the grandeur of the Highlands, Sarah, but I had never in my wildest dreams imagined anything so awe-inspiring. The ravines, the mountains, the waterfalls, take one's breath away. My room has a balcony and from it I overlook the mountains. At times the snow-capped peaks are bathed in a golden glow and it's all so lovely it brings tears to my eyes. Most of the time I have to rest. The air is like wine. I miss you all most terribly, of course. I keep telling myself the time will pass and we shall all be together again. How one appreciates one's family when away from them! I enjoyed your letter with all your news and I am so glad you are enjoying your course and London. And how nice Mr Jacobs sounds. I'm sure that he and your father would get on very well.

'I had hoped that your father might be able to visit me, but I fear that will be impossible, not only from the expense point of view but the lengthy journey. When we left the train a car was waiting to drive us to the sanatorium, which took a very long time. For your father to attempt it he would have to come by carrier's cart, which could take days as the carrier stops to deliver and collect at all the little villages. The roads are very bad in parts, too. I'm afraid I was too exhausted to take in any of the scenery on the way. So, my dear Sarah, I shall just have to be patient until I am well again and can come back to you all.'

Isabelle then went on to describe the other patients, and mentioned three particularly interesting men: one was an artist, one an architect (such a caring man), and one a bank manager who, although a rather austere-looking man, had a lovely, infectious sense of humour.

Sarah read out the letter to her aunt and cousin. Jenny, looking thoughtful said, 'There is your mother, ill, yet able to enjoy the company of men, and what are we doing, what am *I* doing? Working my fingers to the bone making screws and then rushing around at break-time persuading people to buy wrist-watches. And what about you – making necklaces and sleeping! I must be mad.' She appealed to Sarah. 'Where is all that fun we were going to have? I haven't been out with a bloke for weeks.' She got up. 'My life has to change, starting from tomorrow. And yours too, Sarah. Also yours, Aunt Mary. We'll try and arrange to be on the same shift and book seats to go to the Victoria Palace. Let's live it up!'

They did book seats, but on the day they were due to go to the music hall, it was bombed, which shocked everyone as it was thought the bombs had been intended for Buckingham Palace, which was nearby. Although a number of people in the area were killed and injured, there was a general thankfulness that no audience had been in the hall at the time.

'We've certainly had a lucky escape,' Jenny decided. 'It makes me realise that you have to live from day to day, and enjoy yourself.'

But enjoyment was the last thing they craved at that moment and it was only the fact of Mary meeting Bill, an Army Captain she had known when she was younger that lifted them out of their gloom.

The Captain invited them to his club where they had coffee and talked. Sarah was impressed by the quiet, genteel atmosphere, the dark oak furniture and carpeted floor. Jenny was impressed by the number of young officers there were in the club.

Before they left, Mary invited Bill to come and have a meal with them some time and he accepted graciously. When they parted Mary said, 'It was lovely meeting Bill, I was in love with him once. Such a nice person. He did marry but they divorced.'

Sarah had liked Bill Rhodes on sight. A quiet, unassuming man, he wasn't good-looking but there was something about him that Sarah thought would earn him respect. Jenny remarked later that if she was not mistaken the Captain was in love with her aunt.

Although Sarah enjoyed her job she felt at times it would have been impossible to work such long hours had it not been for the breaks she had and her visits to Mr Jacobs, who had gradually opened a whole new world for her.

But there came a time when she was overwhelmed with homesickness, and would have applied for a few days' leave had it not been for the desperate need of shells at the Front. Notices were pinned up in every shed asking for a concentrated effort from the workers.

Jenny had said she was definitely going to ask for time off to go home to Tynemouth at Christmas, as she had never even seen her new home, but one day in the canteen when she mentioned this, a woman opposite said, 'You obviously don't have anyone at the Front or you wouldn't be worrying your head about going home for Christmas. It's not tinsel and baubles our men in the trenches are wanting, it's shells.'

Jenny said afterwards, 'Honestly, I felt terrible. She made me feel as if all I thought about was having a good time. Anyway, that's settled it, I won't be home for Christmas. I'll write and tell Mum and Dad.'

Sarah had already told her father she would not be home and he replied that although she would be greatly missed he quite understood how she felt.

Lucy wrote to Jenny to say that as she was not coming home they had accepted an invitation to spend Christmas with Fred's family. Jonathan and Victor had been invited too so Sarah had no need to worry that they would be on their own.

Mary and Jenny and Sarah were all due to work on Christmas Day, but as they would switch to the night-shift afterwards they decided to hold their own little party on Boxing Day. The trouble was that food was scarce; there were queues over a mile long for potatoes, sugar and flour, but although meat was scarce too, poultry was available. However, when Mary waited in a queue for over two hours everything had gone by the time it was her turn to be served.

Then two days later, a turkey was delivered. To the astonishment of Sarah and Jenny it was from the Cursons. An accompanying letter from Mrs Curson said that having heard from Sarah's father that the girls would not be home for Christmas, but working for the war effort, she thought it would be a nice surprise for them.

'A surprise!' Sarah exclaimed, 'It's heaven-sent!'

Mary and Jenny and Sarah had posted little presents home, and to Isabelle in Scotland, and parcels began to arrive for all of them. Isabelle had sent three little dolls, all in Highland dress, which she had made herself. The faces had been embroidered on and each doll had a different expression; the stitching of the clothes was so fine it was almost impossible to see the thread.

In Isabelle's letter she said she longed to be with them all for Christmas but the nursing staff were doing their best to make everything festive for them there and all the patients appreciated their work.

At this point all Sarah wanted was for Christmas to be over and done with, even though Mary had invited Bill to spend Boxing Day with them.

16

On Boxing Day morning Sarah and Jenny were up very early to prepare the turkey, insisting that Mary must have a lie-in. It was still dark when there was a ring at the front door-bell. There had been no parcel yet from Jonathan and Sarah, knowing her father was always last-minute with things shouted, 'It'll be the parcel from home, I'll get it.' She ran into the hall and opened the door, then stood, trying to make out the dim figure on the step.

'Sarah?'

For several seconds she was unable to believe she was seeing all right, then she cried, 'Warren – Warren Hendrix! I don't believe it. How did you get here?'

'By motor car. I'm on my way back to the Front again and your father asked me if I would deliver a parcel to you.'

He was still standing holding out the parcel when Jenny came running to ask who it was. When Sarah explained Jenny said, 'Well ask him in! What are you doing keeping him standing on the doorstep.'

'Oh, yes, yes,' Sarah said. 'Of course. I'm just so surprised.'

By this time Mary was down and after more explanations she suggested, 'Look, Sarah, take Lieutenant Hendrix upstairs to freshen up and Jenny and I will start cooking the breakfast.'

Sarah had managed to whip off her apron, but was very conscious that her hair must look a mess. She had not even brushed it when she got up because it was so early. 'This way, Warren,' she said and led the way upstairs.

'This *is* an unexpected pleasure, Sarah. I dropped in to see your father on Christmas Eve and he was so worried because the man who had promised to deliver the parcel to you on Christmas Day was ill and unable to come to

London. As a colleague had promised to drive me here – well, here I am.'

Sarah suddenly felt shy before the handsome, imposing figure with his lean, intense face. 'Thanks, Warren. It's good to see you and lovely to have the parcel from home. We must open it later. Come down when you're ready.'

Warren fitted in right away and when Bill Rhodes arrived later it was as though the two men had known one another for years. Bill had brought cigars and the lovely aroma mingling with the appetising smell of the roasting turkey made Sarah feel it was Christmas Day.

After the festive meal Jenny said, 'Well, are we going to get to see the presents Uncle Jonathan has sent? The suspense is killing me! Knowing Uncle, he will have made something for each of us.'

For Mary and the girls he had made musical boxes, the lids beautifully carved in intricate designs, each one unique and each one playing a different tune. For Mary it was a lively polka, for Jenny (because of her father) *Everybody Loves a Sailor* and for Sarah, Chopin's *Fantasie Impromptu*. Sarah was so moved by the thought and work her father had put into the making of the gifts she was unable to speak for a moment then all three were praising Jonathan for his beautiful handiwork.

Bill requested that all the tunes be played again and Sarah thought she would always remember these moments – the darkening room, with firelight playing on the faces of the others and showing their changing expressions, pleasure at first at the gaiety of the tunes, then when the *Impromptu* died away a feeling of stillness, as though they too wanted to store precious memories.

Mary broke the silence, saying with a catch in her voice, 'What a lovely day it has been. How lucky we are that we've been able to be together. Thank you all.' She got up and added on a bright note, 'And now, who would like a cup of tea?'

It was five o'clock when Warren said he really ought to be going. Although Sarah and he had had little chance of private conversation, she had caught him watching her several times, and each time he had given her a warm secret smile that made her feel there was a closeness between them. When he was ready to leave he put a small package into her hand.

'This is for you to open later, Sarah. I promised to write to you the last time I left for the Front and didn't, but this time I will. It's been wonderful seeing you and meeting your aunt and Jenny and Bill. You all made me feel part of a family.' For a moment his expression held a bleakness then it was gone. 'Take care of yourself and tell me all about the wonderful clocks you see. I'm becoming an addict.'

Bill then said he thought he would leave with Warren and let the 'girls' have some time to collect themselves before going on night-shift.

When the men had gone Sarah unwrapped Warren's gift and found a small, star-shaped watch in a green velvet case. The points were of chased gold, with a tiny round watch-face in the centre. Sarah guessed it was old and very expensive. A note was enclosed in which Warren said the watch had been given to him by a French soldier who was badly wounded and dying. He had bought it for his fiancée, to give her on their wedding day. A few days before they were due to be married, she had gone off with someone else.

Warren concluded, *'The officer asked me to give it to someone of my choice, someone who would appreciate it, and I knew that someone had to be you, Sarah.'*

Mary's eyes filled with tears for the poor French soldier, while Jenny retorted that she hoped the watch wouldn't bring bad luck. Sarah held it close to her and whispered, 'I shall treasure it for always.'

A week later, Sarah learned a little bit more about Warren in a letter from her father. He said that Warren had written him a note saying what a wonderful day he had spent with them all in London and how heart-warming their kindness had been.

'I'm so glad about this, Sarah. After rejoining his unit in the autumn, barely recovered from his other injury, Warren was hit by a piece of shrapnel which lay close to his spine, and caused

197

him considerable pain. He came back home to have it removed. He told me nothing about this, and in fact I learned it only today from his sister. She said that her mother and stepfather had gone away for Christmas, in spite of knowing that she too would be home on leave. She was very bitter and I don't blame her.'

'Neither do I,' Jenny said, when Sarah read out the letter. 'The rotten so and so's! What other parents would have done such a thing?'

It was from then on that Sarah had a special feeling for Warren. She wanted to hold him, to comfort him, to tell him that she cared. When she wrote to him she must try and convey this without actually saying she was in love with him. This she could not do because of Joe, who was always in the background of her mind.

January 1917 came in with bitter winds and sleet. The three women all felt utterly jaded. One evening when Sarah was alone in the house she summed up her life. Apart from Jenny she had not one friend of her own age to chat to. Not like at home, where she could pop in and see old schoolfriends at any time. It was amazing, really, considering the hundreds of girls she was with every day. There were the tough ones, the funny ones, those whose only talk was of having a good time and the quiet ones, who never responded to any effort at conversation. There were men who made up to her, but most of them were married and the young ones had a heyday with so many girls to choose from. Sarah sat huddled thoughtfully over the small fire in the grate. They had kept a decent fire going on Boxing Day, but now stocks were low. Getting fuel was becoming a worry. A friend of Mary's had promised her some wood, but so far it had not arrived. If only the three of them could all be on the same shift, it would make things easier. This had been arranged but for a few days more the three of them were on different shifts.

The night before, Jenny had said that she had had more boyfriends at *home* than she had here and was seriously thinking of changing her job. She could do portering at one of the railway stations, or be a conductress on the buses, or drive a lorry – an Army lorry.

After that she talked about Joe. His mother had said in her Christmas letter that the Cursons were half-expecting their son home on leave in the New Year and Jenny asked now if Sarah thought he might call and see them. 'If he does,' she said, 'I hope I'm home when he comes.'

But Jenny and Mary were at work when Joe arrived unexpectedly a week later. Sarah, who had been dusting, pushed the duster into her pocket when she saw him standing on the doorstep and Joe teased her.

'Well, and I thought you'd be pleased to see me after all these months.'

'Oh, Joe, I am, but you do give people surprises. Come on in. Why didn't you let us know you were coming?'

'There wasn't time. I'd only just reached home when I was ordered to return to my unit in France. But I couldn't go back without seeing you for a few minutes. By the way,' he delved into his kitbag, 'Mum sent you three a cake.'

'Oh, Joe, she shouldn't have done, she sent us so much at Christmas. She's been so kind.'

'All the Cursons are kind.' Joe gave her his cheeky grin. 'Me included. Well, are you pleased to see me?'

'Of course I am, you know I am.'

'Well then, show me. Come on, give us a kiss.'

He pulled her to him and kissed her, not just a friendly kiss but one that excited her. When she drew away she could still feel his lips warm on hers, moving sensuously. Flustered, she said she would make a cup of tea. Joe told her he didn't want anything, then he stood, studying her. 'Do you know something,' he began, 'you are–'

Sarah interrupted quickly, 'Now, don't tell me I'm bonnier than ever because I feel a mess.'

'You are – not a bit like yourself! You've gone skinny. You're hollow-eyed.'

She was taken aback and made excuses. She had been working long hours, had little sleep, but he said it was more than that. She had lost her sparkle.

Sarah was now annoyed. 'Well, thank you very much. If I thought such a thing about someone I certainly wouldn't tell them so, it's cruel.'

Joe began to laugh. 'That's my girl, fighting fit, rarin' to have a go. Oh, Sarah, fancy you believing such a thing! You're lovely, the loveliest girl I've ever met.'

'You big clot!' she snapped. 'I could slap your face, making me feel I was dying or – or something.'

He caught hold of her and swung her off her feet. When he put her down he said, 'Go on, you can make that cup of tea you talked about.'

Sarah guessed the reason for his change of mind. In spite of his fun he had been trembling and so was she. She fled to the scullery. Joe followed her. 'Sarah, I haven't much time, I would have liked to have taken you to a show but–'

She had never known him to be so serious. 'Yes, I know, Joe. Perhaps some other time.' She took cups from the hooks of the dresser and put them on a tray. As she reached for the saucers Joe came up behind her, took them from her and turned her to face him.

'I love you, Sarah, I think I must always have loved you. Your face is always before me, whatever I'm doing.' He cupped her cheeks between his palms and she searched his face. His eyes were like dark unfathomable pools. His hands were steady but as he moved closer and put his arms around her, she could feel the wild beating of his heart.

'I know it's wrong, Sarah, but I want you so desperately, I've ached to love you.'

Her body was throbbing and she knew it would be easy to give in to him, but she could hear his sister saying, 'Joe loves them and leaves them.' Commonsense took over. Easy to let him love her but easy to leave her with a child in her womb. She drew away.

'I'm sorry, Joe. I'm fond of you, but –'

'And I'm sorry, Sarah, I let myself get carried away. It was circumstances, no one here, always thinking about you.' He ran his fingers through his thick dark curly hair, a gesture that brought a sudden rush of warmth for him.

'Joe, I can understand how you feel. Lately I've felt lost, being away from those who love me. I've wanted to feel arms around me, holding me close. It's so easy to think, why not, none of us know whether we'll be here tomorrow, but if I am here and you are over there and I'm in trouble, what then?'

A slow smile spread over his face. 'Sarah, I'm sure there's no one else quite like you. My mother thinks the world of you, she says you're a lovely girl and so practical. I'm not a bit practical, but I'm glad you are and that's something I thought I never would be. I wanted you to tell me that you wanted me, that you'd thought of nothing else but me, to throw yourself into my arms and let me make wild love to you and afterwards you would be my slave.' He began to chuckle. 'That's the cinema working its charm on me. Strong silent fellow and adoring girl.'

Sarah began to laugh then. 'I never knew men could think that way. I thought it was just us lovesick girls, weaving dreams.'

Joe was suddenly serious. He edged forward in his chair. 'Dreams do come true. Sarah – would you wait for me?'

She thought of Warren and knew she could not make promises, and seeing her hesitation Joe said, 'Perhaps I'm asking too much, Sarah. Forget what I said, we'll let things take their course.'

Sarah reminded him then that although he had promised to write the last time they had met his letters were few and far between. 'Non-existent recently, in fact.'

'Typical women!' he exclaimed. 'I'm fighting a war. When I'm not fighting, I'm sleeping, or trying to. Mam is just the same, "why don't you write more?" My Aunt Jane says, "Joe, I do think you could find time to drop us a line, I never knew whether you got the parcel we sent." My sister says –'

Sarah held up a hand. 'All right, I forgive you. Now for that cup of tea.'

They talked about the war, and spoke quietly of Chris, whose death eighteen months ago was still mourned by Joe. Sarah asked him what he thought of Lloyd George who had taken over from Asquith in December and Joe said, 'I think he's a good man, but the changeover hasn't made any difference to us at the Front, not yet anyway. We're losing hundreds and hundreds of men every day, Sarah. It's wholesale slaughter and what for? We've gained perhaps a few yards of ground. I sometimes wonder how any of us manage to survive.'

There was a sudden pattering of rain on the window panes and Joe waved a hand and grinned. 'That's all I need, isn't it? But come on, tell me about your job. How many men do you go out with?'

Sarah explained about the work she did then said, 'There are thousands of women working in munitions, and although there are men working there too the women are in the majority. Sometimes I feel we're living in a world of women, children and old men.'

'That's good, so I've no need to worry that you'll rush off and get married.'

Sarah teased him. 'Don't be so cocky, it's not for the asking that I don't go out regularly with anyone. I could be married the next time you come home.'

'Don't you dare, do you hear!' Although Joe was laughing there was a sombre look in his eyes. 'You be a good girl and wait for Joe.' As the clock on the mantelpiece began to chime he got up. 'I'd better go in case there are any hold-ups anywhere.'

He drew her to him again but this time he kissed her gently. 'Bye, Sarah, think of me. Give your Aunt Mary and Jenny my regards, sorry I missed them. Don't come to the door with me. I want to think of you standing here, in a room, part of – a home.'

These words of parting left Sarah in tears. She had been mean – it would have meant so much to him if she had let him make love to her. But deep down she knew it would have been foolish. She was more than fond of him but she was too young at sixteen to contemplate marriage.

When Mary and Jenny came home and knew that Joe had visited Mary clucked her tongue. They would happen to be out, wouldn't they, what a shame. Jenny was furious. 'He should have let us know he was coming! Yes, I know you said his visit was unexpected, but you are always the one to see him.' She went off to bed in a huff.

Mary said, 'Take no notice, Sarah. She'll be sorry in the

morning, you know our Jenny. I think we're all feeling fed up. All we seem to do is work, eat and sleep. I heard from Bill that he's being moved, he doesn't yet know where. It's perhaps just as well he's going but – well, I know I shall miss him.'

Jenny was back to her old self the next morning, but the days and the weeks went by without anything exciting happening and the long hours and bad weather were beginning to take their toll of Sarah. She wondered whether she should ask for some time off.

But before she could ask for leave she heard from her father that Isabelle would not be returning to Newcastle for at least another month, despite her greatly-improved state of health. She had received an invitation from an elderly lady who had been in the sanatorium, to stay for a while at their family hunting lodge, so that Isabelle could lose that feeling of being hospitalised before returning home.

Sarah was at first dismayed, then worried. When her mother had stayed at Blanchland for her health she had ached to get home. There had been no question of having to be 'broken in' before coming back to them.

Who constituted the family at the lodge? Her mother had met interesting men at the sanatorium ... The old fear returned to Sarah; had her mother fallen in love with someone? She suddenly folded the letter and got up. No, of course not, she was being stupid, conjuring up such ideas. Her mother had never openly flirted with any man, ever.

The following day, she had a glowing letter from Isabelle about the hunting lodge; it was so luxurious and she was being completely spoilt. A hot bath was prepared for her every morning and a maid would be waiting with a warmed bathrobe when she stepped out of it. She was taken for rides in a chauffeur-driven car among scenery that was simply breathtaking.

'*You would love it, Sarah, there are huge stone fireplaces that take massive logs of wood. In every room a fire blazes merrily, and all around are mountains. The peace is something impossible to describe. I accepted this invitation, wanting to have every opportunity to be fully recovered before returning home. And yet, Sarah, my heart is with you all. I can't wait to get back and see your dear faces again . . .'*

Sarah knew this should have set her mind at rest, but she still felt uneasy.

In the weeks before spring, she had received two letters from Warren but only one from Joe. Jenny also had one from Joe. Both were quite short and were almost word for word: he said he wished the war was over so he could get back home. He had decided to start a small garage business . . .

Warren thanked Sarah in the first one of her letters and asked her to convey his gratitude to her father for the science magazines he had sent. He wrote of the articles in the magazines. In the second letter, he spoke of how the stars had come to have a greater meaning for him, and added on a lighter note how he imagined whole cities in the sky. When he mentioned this to some of his fellow officers, they had tolerantly regarded him as being 'off his head'.

Although Sarah had not expected Warren to be anything more than friendly in his letters she had anticipated that Joe, in view of what had happened between them, would at least send his love. The fact that he had not done so made her glad she had not allowed her emotions to run away with her. She was also hurt that he obviously ranked her among his 'love 'em and leave 'em' type of girls.

When March went by then April, and there was still no word of her mother's homecoming, Sarah wrote to her father asking him the reason. *'And I want the truth, Poppa. I've felt all along you've been holding something back from me. You are not being fair to me . . .'*

In Jonathan's prompt reply he said he was sorry she had been upset. Her mother had had a slight relapse, but she was not to worry. They would have her home very soon. There was more, but the word 'relapse' had Sarah worried sick. How slight a relapse? When she spoke to her aunt about it Mary said, 'It does sometimes happen, Sarah. It's often caused by excitement, the fact that the patient will be

204

going home. It was probably the best thing that could have happened to your mother, having this extra recuperation in the hunting lodge. Try not to worry.'

Sarah did try, but the build-up of longing to be home became such an obsession with her over the next three weeks that one evening she told Jenny and Mary that she was going to ask for time off. She had to, her homesickness was becoming an illness.

Jenny said that she too would ask for time off and the girls persuaded Mary to come too. Their leave was granted but it was not for another week and one evening while Sarah was in her bedroom writing a letter to her father Mary came in and said she must talk to her.

The gravity of her aunt's tone had Sarah feeling as if her body was encased in ice. 'It's Mother, isn't it? She's – dying.'

'No, Sarah, she's all right. It's just that –' Mary sat on the edge of her bed and shook her head slowly. 'I don't understand it, but according to your father she doesn't want to come home.'

The relief that her mother was not at death's door was so great that it was moments before Sarah took in the implication of her aunt's words. Then she said, 'Doesn't want to come home? Why? What about Victor? What about Dad and me?'

'I don't know Sarah. I can't think of any reason.'

Now it was Sarah who was nodding slowly. 'I know of a reason. She's fallen in love with someone else. At least, I feel sure that's the reason. Why else wouldn't she want to come back to us all? She spoke of men who were in the sanatorium, attractive men, educated. You know how Mother enjoys the company of educated men.' At this Sarah dissolved into tears and Mary got up and cuddled her.

'Don't, Sarah, don't upset yourself. I'm sure there's not another man, your mother isn't the kind of person to have affairs. Perhaps it's just that she's found such peace in Scotland that she doesn't want to face up to the normal workaday reality of life.'

Sarah dried her eyes. 'Well, if that *is* the reason she's not going to get away with it! I'll write to her today.'

The letter did bring Isabelle home and a week later Sarah was on the way up north to Newcastle with Mary and Jenny . . .

When they arrived there was quite a reunion. Lucy, Fred, Eric and Victor were there, so was Maggie. At first they were all emotional, laughing and crying. Nothing was said by her mother about the last letter but Sarah was aware of Isabelle watching her from time to time in a puzzled way. At other moments she seemed to be lost in daydreaming. Sarah thought her mother looked extremely well, and lovelier than ever.

It was not until the next day that Isabelle tackled her daughter about the letter. 'Why did you tell me I must come home at once? I thought something dreadful had happened. It made me ill. I sent a telegram to your father there and then, asking if things were all right and he wired back to say that everything was fine, but I was missed.'

'And so you came home, Mother. Don't you think it was about time? I was convinced there was another man in your life. It was the only reason I could find for you wanting to stay away from us.'

Isabelle was silent for a moment then she said, 'I wasn't having an affair, if that is what you mean, Sarah, but I had met a man whose friendship I valued. You are young and I don't expect you to understand a friendship between a married woman and a man, but I can assure you it does exist and can be a beautiful thing.'

'Beautiful?' Sarah exclaimed. 'Yes, I'm young and no, I haven't any experience of such a friendship, but I'm old enough to know that Father was fretting his heart out for you while you were away; old enough to know that your son ached for you. Did you know that Victor cried himself to sleep for nights after you had gone! No, of course you wouldn't. No one would tell you because you were *ill* and must not be upset.'

'Sarah, I –'

'I didn't mind sweating my guts out, working a twelve-

206

hour day in the factory at times so you could get treatment at the sanatorium, and I know that Poppa didn't mind working until midnight most nights so that he could keep the home going, but what I *do* object to is you, when you had recovered your health, living it up in luxury in a hunting lodge, driving round in a chauffeur-driven car with, no doubt, you and your lover in the back –'

'That's enough, Sarah! He was never in the car and we've never been lovers! You must believe me.'

'You were as good as, Mother. I had only to look at your face, see the dreaminess in your eyes. I would never stop loving you, but I hate you for the way you've treated Poppa. Do you see how he looks at you, he's glowing with love. But then I suppose you never mentioned to him about your *man* friend.'

'I didn't, Sarah, and I don't want him to know. Please, *please* don't tell him. I don't want to hurt him, I really don't.'

'Hurt him? You've already hurt him by not coming home. I don't know what his thoughts were, but you don't deserve the love he has for you. He's a truly good man. He's given you everything he possibly could, little presents, that special fob-watch, he–'

'Stop it, Sarah, please, I can't bear it.'

Sarah's anger drained away at the anguished look on her mother's face. 'I'm sorry,' she said, 'but you had to know the pain you caused. I'll leave you now, and do some shopping. I promised Poppa I would call at the shop but I won't say anything to him, not ever.' With that she left and as she walked along the path that led to the park gates she was aware of the glorious sound of birdsong all around her. A rise of tears blurred the delicate greens of buds unfolding, and she wished then she could go back to the days when she was small and knew nothing of the violence of war, or of a mother who could fall in love with a man other than her husband.

By the time she reached Mr MacTavish's shop she had her tears under control. He was hammering nails into the sole of a shoe and when she tapped on the window, indicating that she would call and see him later, he nodded and a smile lit up his old face.

Sarah then opened the door of her father's shop and stood, listening to the ticking of the clocks, the busy ticking of the little clocks, the slower measure of the larger ones, and the ponderous tick-tock of the grandfathers, and suddenly, all the months of separation were as nothing. She was home, with her father, and their beloved clocks.

17

Sarah and Jenny had been given a week's leave of absence from their work but after three days their parents tried to persuade the girls and Mary to stay, and find jobs in Newcastle. Both girls, who had been terribly homesick for the past weeks eagerly agreed, but Mary said she must go back to London. She had her house to look after and did not want to give it up.

Isabelle said she understood and added, 'In the meantime let us all enjoy being together for the next few days at least.'

Sarah thought that if her mother had not delayed her homecoming she might never have guessed there had been another man in her life; Isabelle was so loving and kindly towards them all, especially to her husband, that by the end of the week they were a close-knit family once again, discussing problems, the main one being the familiar shortage of money.

When Sarah was working in munitions she had paid her Aunt Mary her board, put a little money by for herself and sent the rest of the money home. With what she had saved, including the money from the sale of the watches and jewellery, she had over thirty pounds in the Post Office savings bank. She offered this to her parents, but they insisted she keep it – she had worked hard for that money.

Sarah told them it was there for a rainy day, and felt that the rainy day had actually arrived. Her father's trade had dropped off so much he was depending on small clock and watch repairs to keep the home going. Money was tight everywhere. One day she mentioned to her father about Mr Jacobs' trade of buying and selling antique clocks and watches and suggested using her savings to make a start, but Jonathan in turn pointed out that Mr Jacobs had made a name for himself and would have a particular customer in mind for every clock and watch he bought. Sarah saw the sense of this and although reluctant to start a new job knew she would have to get down to looking for one soon. She talked it over with Jenny and they decided they would try to get jobs as conductresses on the trams or the buses. But when they tried both depots they were told there were no vacancies; however, their names and addresses were taken, just in case.

The girls offered their services as porters at the railway station but had the same reply – no vacancies. Jenny said, 'The trouble is that so many married women are having to work, to help eke out the low pay their husbands receive in the forces.' She paused then added, 'There's a new service started for women called the WAACS, short for "Women's Army Auxiliary Corps". How about trying for that? I understand they can send you abroad.'

Sarah said, 'Yes, I thought it might be interesting too, until I met Kitty Billings yesterday. She's joined and was home on sick leave. She said that all she had done since joining was scrubbing floors and latrines, drilling, and being bossed around by hefty bullying women. She said it made her so ill she didn't want to go back.'

Jenny dismissed the girl as a weakling – Kitty Billings had never been able to stick up for herself. It would be different with them, they had been toughened by working in munitions.

Although Sarah agreed with this she was not ready to join one of the services and perhaps be sent away from home. Jenny was just the opposite, she no longer wanted to stay at home where nothing ever happened. But they did go on applying for jobs and when they drew a blank Sarah was in despair, until they both heard from the tram depot to go for an interview.

The elderly Scotsman who was to interview them eyed them belligerently, as though daring them to admit they wanted to work on the trams.

'Ye ken what ye'll have to contend with?' he demanded. 'Getting up at four in the morning for the early shift, and other times having t'deal with men who've had more than one drink.'

210

He was called away then and Jenny whispered, 'What he means is that we'll have to fight off rip-roaring drunks who want to pinch our bottoms. Well, he's not going to get rid of us as easily as that, is he?'

When the manager returned he looked from one to the other.

'Well,' Jenny said, 'we've worked in munitions, sir, so we're used to shift-working and dealing with all kinds of people.'

Sarah added, 'We only left, sir, because my mother had been very ill and my cousin's father lost an arm and leg at the Front. We are needed here at this particular time.'

He studied them. 'So ye've been in munitions, have ye? But what experience have ye had in handling money?'

When he was told of their shop experience he gave a deep sigh. 'Ye've got the jobs but–' he wagged a finger at them, 'there'll be no flirtin' wi' the men, understand? They're married for the most part and I'll no be having their lives upset.'

Jenny put on a wide-eyed innocent look. 'Oh, we'd never do that, sir, we both have boyfriends of our own.'

'Aye weel, I thought I'd better warn ye.'

He talked about shift-work and wages then took them to a middle-aged man who instructed them about the work involved. They were to start the following morning at eight o'clock and would be taken on trial runs for training.

Sarah came out jubilant, sure she would like the job, but Jenny was disgruntled at the low wages. 'Two pounds, eighteen and sixpence!' she declared. 'It's daylight robbery. I know that the men get over four pounds a week. We're being victimised, that's what – we'll be doing the same flipping work as the men.'

Sarah reminded her that if they had not been given these jobs they would have had to go back into munitions and at this Jenny cheered up. She thought after all it might be fun, as there were some quite good-looking blokes at the depot.

Sarah had assumed it would only be a question of taking fares, but found she had to learn how to change over the tram trolley at the terminus and connect it to the overhead electric cable. When she was younger she had enjoyed watching the conductors doing this, and seeing the yellow sparks shot with bright blue and green when the trolley did not connect at once.

The girls arrived together the next morning but were taken off to different trams. The trial run was mid-morning when trade was fairly slack. Sarah, done up in her serge uniform and brimmed felt hat felt uncomfortable but she knew she would have to get used to it. A young man called Alan, with a bad limp, was to show her the ropes. She was given a small machine on a leather strap with which to clip the tickets and a strapped bag for the money, both of which she hung around her neck. She was then shown how to clip the tickets and give change quickly. The problem, she found, was trying to do this competently while the tram was travelling at speed. Sarah felt sure the driver had purposely increased the speed of the tram. Twice she would have fallen, had Alan not been there to catch her. He said it was just a question of finding her balance – she would soon get used to it.

They had a route that took them through countryside to North Shields; it was quiet and pleasant and at first they had only about six or seven passengers who were all downstairs because of a rather cold wind, but then two men got on further ahead and went upstairs. As Sarah started to climb up after them, the tram driver suddenly accelerated and she had to hang on. Then she was aware of Alan behind her, his hand steadying her firmly by her waist. 'Go ahead, you're doing fine,' he told her.

The two passengers, both middle-aged, teased her. One said she would need to have the rolling gait of a sailor. The other one told her she would have to be careful she didn't trip over her skirt when she went back downstairs. Sarah smiled and balanced herself against a seat and asked them where they wanted to go. They said to the terminus, and after she had given them their correct tickets they commented on how nice it was to see a pretty face for a change.

Alan smiled at her when they came downstairs. 'You'll cope all right, you've got the temperament. I wish you luck.'

The next problem came when they arrived at the terminus, but to Sarah's utter amazement she made the trolley connect immediately with the overhead cable. Alan applauded her but the driver told her sourly that it was a sheer fluke, beginner's luck – she wouldn't do it right a second time.

Nor did she. A few older men standing around jeered at her but Sarah, having been told by her father if she met opposition just to smile in return, did so and said, 'A bit tricky, isn't it? I suppose I'll get it right in time.' At this their attitude changed.

'Of course you will, lass,' one said. 'An' I'll tell you something else, a lot of the experienced blokes have trouble with them there trolleys at times.' The other men nodded in agreement.

At the end of that first day Sarah was exhausted, but by the end of the week she was picking up her skirt, running up the stairs, clipping tickets and giving change as if she had been doing the job for years.

And after a month, despite the grim war news and her father's trade being so bad, she felt strangely happy, all of which she put down to the change in her job. While working in munitions, Sarah had been with the same people month in month out, her whole being concentrated every day on the necessity for every measurement to be precise. At times she had felt she was in a prison, and when she had finished a twelve-hour shift it was often all she could do to crawl back to her aunt's house and drop into bed.

On the trams, Sarah enjoyed the variation of the routes and meeting new people. She had that lovely feeling of the regulars treating her as a friend and telling her all their troubles. She was also getting some fresh spring air on the open platform of the tram and on the top deck.

Jenny too had settled down and was walking out regularly with a young Army Lieutenant who was stationed at Newcastle. Sarah went out now and again with Alan. He told her he had worked on the trams before enlisting and when he was discharged from the army after his leg wound, they'd taken him on again. With both of them it was more a case of companionship. Alan had a girlfriend who was a cook in the WAACS and Sarah did not want to be involved with anyone on a permanent basis.

She had not heard recently from either Joe or Warren but as her father pointed out, men at the Front who were plunged up to their knees in mud and surrounded by slaughter were not likely, when they did have time to snatch some rest, to be in the mood for writing letters.

Although Sarah still spent time at her father's shop whenever she could it was not until one bitterly cold morning, when a North East wind whipped at the spring flowers, that her interest in old clocks and watches was revived.

There had been few passengers along the route and when the tram rattled over Byker Bridge and the last two passengers alighted a black-shawled woman came running, shouting, 'Wait for me, gal!' Sarah, recognising Mrs Hetty Baker, helped her on to the tram and as the woman seemed to be hanging grimly on to a parcel tucked underneath her shawl, she made to take it from her.

'No, it's orlright, lass, I can manage. Gawd, it's a freezer, I hope you're wearing your thick bloomers this morning!' Sarah laughed as she helped her to a seat.

'Two pairs, Mrs Baker. Where are you off to this morning, for a picnic?'

'That'll be the day, gal. No, as a matter of fact I'm going to try and find a decent pawnbroker's shop. Sammy Greasley at the end of our street wouldn't even offer me tuppence for this clock, in fact he laughed his head off, said it looked like a lump of scrap metal. I know it's a bloody awful-looking thing, but at the same time I know for sure it's worth something.'

A clock, scrap metal? Sarah's interest quickened. The tram was caught in a traffic jam and although the driver kept stamping again and again on the floor-bell, no one moved; no one could. She sat down beside Mrs Baker.

'My father is a clock-maker and repairer, Mrs Baker, and I'm interested in clocks, too. Would you let me have a look?'

214

The woman brought the bulky parcel from under her shawl and began removing the sheets of newspaper. 'It belonged to my great-great-grandfather and *he* came from the gentry.' She added this last piece of information with pride. 'Me Mam told me it was valuable, but apart from the fact that I hate the thing, I need the money. I've got meself into a bit of a mess, see. I borrowed some money and I'm getting deeper and deeper in debt. The sharks have warned me if I don't pay up in a week's time they'll tell me old man, and if he knew I'd been borrowing he'd half kill me.' She removed the last piece of paper. 'Well, there it is!'

Sarah, having seen a similar one in Mr Jacobs' shop said with a small feeling of excitement, 'I think this is worth quite a few pounds, Mrs Baker.'

'It is? Well, thank Gawd for that. How much?'

'I don't know exactly, it would be a question of finding a buyer. Don't take it to a pawnship, let my father see it first and he will advise you. I'll be off-duty at four o'clock – I'll get him to come and see you.'

'Oh, no, no, I'll come to his shop. Me old man will be home about five and I'm not kidding, if he knew I had borrowed as much as a penny I'd be black and blue for weeks. He has his pride gal, and you see I owe seven quid.'

'Seven pounds? That's a lot of money.'

'It certainly is, more than my old man earns in seven weeks. He goes round the lane selling firewood for Barney Betts and nowadays there isn't all that much firewood about.'

She began putting the wrappings back on the clock. 'I only borrowed ten bob from the moneylenders in the first place and do you know, when I went to pay something off, it hadn't half growed. They were only charging me *eighty per cent* interest!'

'Eighty per cent? Oh, Mrs Baker that's terrible!'

'It is that, and it keeps on growing. I have to borrow a bit more and a bit more and now I'm really in the mire. I only borrowed the ten bob in the first place to give to me mam because her and me dad hadn't a pair of boots between them.'

215

She creaked upright. 'I'll get off at the next stop and go back home. I'll hide the clock under the bed until me old man goes out for his pint, then I'll be along. Tell me where the shop is.'

For the rest of the day Sarah found it difficult to concentrate on her work. For the first time since she had worked with her father she felt really involved in a transaction. If the clock was valuable it could be the start of her buying and selling clocks. When she came off-duty she went straight to the shop and was soon explaining to Jonathan about the clock.

'I'm sure it's a sixteenth century Chamber Clock, Poppa! It's square, with wrought-metal sides, there's a bell on top . . .'

After Jonathan had asked a lot of questions he nodded slowly. 'You could be right in your assessment, Sarah, but of course I would have to see it. And probably get someone else's opinion, too. The trouble is, I don't have the funds to buy it at the moment, what with one thing and another. Yes, I know you have your savings,' he said when she pulled her Post Office book from her bag, 'but I don't want you to touch that. I could get Mr Robinson to take a look at it, as you know he once worked in an auctioneers in London. The price will depend on the condition of the clock: what if there are parts missing?'

'If it is in working order, Poppa,' she said eager, 'how much do you think it will be worth?'

'Possibly twenty pounds.'

'Twenty pounds? Oh, that's marvellous. If we take our commission for selling it –'

Jonathan's head came up quickly. 'Commission? What are you talking about? The money will belong to Mrs Baker, all of it. I doubt whether even Mr Robinson would accept a penny for valuing it.'

Sarah stared at her father in bewilderment. 'But this is a *business* proposition, Poppa. If I am to go into the business of selling very old clocks like Mr Jacobs does, I would have to make a profit. He buys a clock and sells it to someone else, at a price.'

216

'But Mr Jacobs has the clientèle, Sarah. When he buys a clock he will already have a customer in mind who is wanting such a clock.'

'But don't you see, Poppa, this could be a start for me of going into business. We could go into partnership – I feel this is the opportunity we want.'

'It's what *you* want, Sarah,' he said gently. 'I don't want to deprive Hetty Baker of any money – she's a woman who obviously lives in dire poverty.'

'And wouldn't *we* be living in poverty at this moment if I didn't have a job on the trams?' Sarah retorted. The next moment she was looking at her father in dismay. 'Oh, Poppa, I'm sorry, truly sorry, I've let myself get carried away by imagining myself in business. And yet, I still see this as a transaction, rather than a good turn. After all, if I hadn't asked to look at her clock, Mrs Baker would not be getting it valued. She might well have sold it to someone for two or three pounds, just to keep the moneylender quiet.'

'Well, I know that Mr Robinson is a man of integrity and will be fair in his assessment.'

Sarah thought yes, and her father was a man of integrity too, but she didn't seem to have this quality. She loved clocks, but if she had a chance to make good money out of buying and selling them, then she would.

Mrs Baker arrived in a light snow blizzard, the clock this time tucked under a shabby brown serge cloak. Jonathan invited her to come in by the fire. She opened the cloak, handed him the clock and looked at him expectantly. He smiled, asked her to sit down, then explained he had an expert on clocks coming to meet her.

At first, the old woman was uncomfortable but Jonathan soon put her at ease by chatting in a friendly way as he removed the wrapping from the clock he had set on the counter.

When Sarah saw the look of pleasure on her father's face she felt a twinge of shame, knowing that money would always be the last thing he thought about when seeing something he really liked.

When Jonathan murmured, 'How beautiful,' Mrs Baker

217

grinned and said, 'Well, tastes differ as the old woman said who kissed the cow.' Then on an anxious note she asked him how much he thought the clock was worth. Did he think she could get seven pounds out of the deal, that was the most important thing.

'Possibly more,' Jonathan said. 'And here is Mr Robinson now.'

Mr Robinson examined the clock and said she might get twenty pounds for it. Mrs Baker told him she needed the money urgently, *very* urgently and he offered to take it off her hands for fifteen pounds. She accepted, thanked him, thanked Jonathan and Sarah profusely for all their help, and after joking that she would be on the lookout now for any other monstrosities, waved them goodbye and disappeared into the cold night.

Fortunately, Sarah was able to laugh about this. She said to her father and his colleague: 'There I was, waiting to have her press a pound note into my hand and what did I get? A big smile and a lot of hot air! Well, it has taught me one thing. If ever I get involved in any other such transactions I shall state at once that I expect commission.'

Jonathan chuckled. 'I'm glad you can laugh about it, Sarah, but I know this, if another Hetty Baker comes along you won't demand commission, you're too soft-hearted.'

'Oh, no, I'm not, Poppa, or I won't be if I do ever get started in business. I shall be as hard as nails.'

Mr Robinson chuckled while Jonathan just smiled at her indulgently and said that he knew differently.

18

After the incident of Mrs Baker's clock Sarah spent most of her spare time searching for clock and watch bargains in out of the way places, narrow lanes and alleyways where there were secondhand shops, but she had no luck.

Meanwhile the war dragged on. There were bombing raids in London and although the enemy met a lot of opposition Isabelle and Lucy worried about Mary. They begged her again to come and live up North. Mary wrote to say the raids had not affected her in any way, but later came to admit the reason she couldn't leave London was that she and Captain Bill Rhodes were living together.

To Sarah's surprise her mother was the one who agreed it was a good thing, saying Mary had been alone long enough. It was Lucy who talked about 'living in sin', and said she thought it was dreadful of Mary to do such a thing while her husband was still alive, albeit in prison.

'Well, I think she has every right to live her life the way she wants,' Isaballe asserted quietly.

Sarah wondered if her mother's moral attitudes had changed since her friendship with the man in Scotland, but as far as she knew there had been no exchange of letters between them.

Although neither Joe or Warren were entitled to more home leave yet, they had both started to write to Sarah more frequently. Neither mentioned the war but those men who did come home on leave were despairing that it would ever come to an end. Joe and Warren were veterans, with nearly three years' fighting behind them.

At the beginning of 1917, submarine warfare had begun in earnest. A great deal of British shipping had been lost, most of it carrying supplies to the Front; food ships from abroad were also sunk. In May, a revolution had begun in Russia, then shortly afterwards the USA declared war on

Germany, giving people hope – purpose. A month later they were celebrating the fact that Vimy Ridge had been taken by the Canadians.

There were other incidents to celebrate; the Messines Ridge was captured by the British; the first American contingents arrived in France; there was the British victory at Passchendaele Ridge and a French triumph on the river Aisne. But then came the bad news: the Italians were severely defeated by the Austrians and the Bolsheviks had seized power in Russia. There was now talk of them seeking an armistice with Germany. The name 'Bolshie' became a much-hated word by many, although to people like Sarah it was just another part of the war.

She always stored up amusing incidents to tell Joe and Warren and when she wrote, included the same story in each letter. One example was when one of Jonathan's customers offered him two seats for the music hall, as his wife was ill and unable to go. Jonathan and Isabelle had not been to the music hall for ages through lack of funds; now even Isabelle, who had always gone to please Jonathan, looked happy. It would be such a welcome change.

The tickets were for the first house so that Sarah was still up when they arrived home. Victor, who had been practising all evening, had gone to bed. 'Well, and how did you enjoy it?' she asked eagerly.

Isabelle drew off her gloves. 'I really loved it, Sarah. It was all so bright, made one forget the world's troubles. Gertie Gitana was a bit saucy but she had the most beautiful pink feather in her hat – huge.'

Jonathan said, 'It was a lovely feather, dear, but it wasn't pink, it was lavender.'

Isabelle protested. 'Oh, come on now, Jonathan, I know you are usually right but in this case you are definitely wrong. You can't tell a woman anything about colours. That feather was *pink*!'

They began to argue, or as Jonathan would put it, 'discuss the matter', but when neither would give in he announced he would write to Gertie Gitana, to settle things; he would not mention any particular colour, to make it fair.

220

By return of post came an amused note from the actress herself, saying that she hoped the lady was right but the feather she had worn in her hat on that particular performance was pale blue.

'Well!' exclaimed Isabelle. 'At least for once, Jonathan, *you* were wrong, too.' They both laughed about it and this was one snippet Sarah knew she would repeat to Joe and Warren.

Another incident Sarah wanted to include in her letters was when her mother had been cross with her father for not raising his hat to the Lord Mayor as he passed in his car. Jonathan had said, 'I raise my hat to the dustmen, Isabelle, the milkman and the paper boy but I don't know the mayor, I've never met him.'

When she pointed out that as he was a man of high office he should be shown some deference Jonathan sighed.

'Isabelle, I was brought up to believe that all men are born equal. If you were to put four men in a row naked, their hands behind their backs, men you had never met before, a labourer, a school-teacher, a clock-maker and a king, would you know which one was the king?'

Isabelle declared at first that yes, she would, then suddenly she began to laugh and said, 'If the clock-maker looked like you, Jonathan, I would have picked you as king.'

What surprised Sarah was Joe's and Warren's different reaction to her little bits of humour. Joe wrote that his pals all had a good laugh at her letter and heaven knows they needed something to laugh about. They thought the incident of the feather was really funny, and the bit about the men all standing in a line naked funnier still.

'Your father is a great man, Sarah, such a philosopher. I wish I could have a chat with him right now, he talks such common-sense. All my pals thought your father a character too and they liked your mother because she could laugh at herself. One said that his mam would have hit his father on the head with a frying pan.' There were bits of news about Joe's own family and then he said, 'Keep the funny pieces coming, Sarah,' and this time he signed it, 'Love, Joe.'

Warren was more inclined to dissect the incidents thus.

221

Had Sarah realised that the different colours seen by her parents were due to the multi-coloured spotlight being on the feather at different times? Sarah said aloud when she read it, 'Of course I did, you daft happ'orth. Do you think I'm a complete nitwit?' And when he commented on the different men standing in a row naked he pointed out that there *would* be differences, quite noticeable ones: the labourer, for instance, would have much more developed muscles, because of the heavy work he did. The clock-maker would be inclined to have a stoop because of his work. At this point Sarah sat back.

Warren had become very pedantic. Was it because he didn't mix with other men, as Joe did? Or was it because of his elevated position in life? As Sarah came from the working class, he might assume she was not very intelligent. But then he did appreciate her father's knowledge.

The next time she wrote to both men, Sarah mentioned the incident with Mrs Hetty Baker and awaited their reaction with interest. Joe was on her side; he said that she and her father had gone to a lot of bother and should have been paid something. MrsBaker was a 'right meanie'. All the men agreed with him.

Warren again reasoned the incident out. The woman had not asked for the clock to be valued; Sarah had suggested it, therefore she should not have expected any reward.

As this was more or less her father's opinion, Sarah did not so readily condemn Warren this time for his seeming pedantry. How she longed for both men to have some leave, so that she could have a talk with each.

But this did not take place until the beginning of 1918, when people everywhere were becoming war-weary after three and a half years of continual conflict.

Joe was the first to arrive home. Sarah had been on the early-morning shift and was coming off-duty at two o'clock when she noticed a soldier standing at the depot gates. There was something familiar about him, but she failed to recognize Joe until he spoke. 'Sarah?'

She had been talking to some of the drivers and she stopped suddenly and stared. 'Joe! Well, for heaven's sake.'

222

She said to the other men, 'See you tomorrow,' and turned back to Joe, smiling. 'So when did *you* arrive?'

'I've been back at Corbridge for a few days now. I called at the shop this morning and your dad told me where to find you. You look very businesslike.'

He was lean, battle-hardened, and although he wore the familiar grin there was a seriousness about his eyes she had not seen before. 'Mother's out but she'll be back at teatime,' Sarah said. 'Come on home and I'll get you something to eat.'

'All I want to eat is *you*.' Sarah gave a shaky laugh and said it might be best if they went back to the shop, but Joe suggested they had a walk, adding, 'I can't get enough clean, fresh air.'

Knowing what was in his mind she tried to keep her voice light. 'We'll walk to St Margaret's Park and you'll get enough fresh air up there to freeze your ears off. When I left the house at half-past four this morning I was like a kid stamping on the frozen pools to hear the ice crack. We've had a lot of fun on the park lake over the years, especially in the winter. Father is an excellent skater. I learned to ice-skate when I was five years old. Oh, Joe, I'm talking far too much, but I'm just so pleased to see you.'

He gripped her elbow. 'And no one is more pleased to see *you* than I am. When I knew I was getting some leave I could hardly wait to see you and the family, of course, I wouldn't be human if I didn't, but you've been on my mind all the time. Your letters were the one thing that kept me sane. You're a good letter-writer, Sarah. All the ones I get from home are about the pigs, the cows and the sheep! He laughed softly. 'But the family have at least made the effort to write. There are blokes over there who never ever receive a letter and do you know why? Because their parents can't read or write. Tragic, isn't it? But there, *I'm* talking too much now. I reckon we'll both simmer down in a minute. But there are so many things I want to say, many of them about the war. Mam says I ought not to talk about it. Dad tells me I'm a country lad, born and bred, and I should always keep that in mind when I'm away.'

223

When he fell silent Sarah urged him to talk, said she understood. 'It's like having a grudge against someone, Joe, and unless you talk it out it gets worse and worse.'

He nodded, 'That's it exactly. Sometimes I think I'll never get the smell of war out of my nostrils. Dad says I should think happy things about the farm, the countryside, but then he's never seen huge areas of fields, good arable land desecrated, whole villages wiped out, trees that are full of blossom one day, blackened the next. There were others, beautiful oaks, chestnuts with great thick, glorious trunks that ended up being stumps . . . like men.' His voice was bitter.

Joe paused then went on, 'One day, I found a lad who was very badly wounded. I raised him up because he wanted to tell me something, and do you know how old he was, Sarah? Fourteen – *fourteen*! He was a kid, had run away to enlist. He asked me to write to his parents and tell them he loved them. With his dying breath he said he'd always wanted to and never could. I bawled, Sarah, I couldn't help it. An hour later, I was told that the Germans had started to use liquid fire.'

Joe was silent for quite a while, then he stopped suddenly and with his eyes closed took a deep breath.

'Lovely, and now –' he linked his arm through Sarah's, 'no more talk of war. So come on, tell me about your job.' He glanced at her, his eyes now teasing. 'I noticed you had plenty of men around, as usual.'

'What do you mean by "as usual"?' she demanded. 'Those men are all married and treat me like one of them. I can tell you this, I was up against some opposition at first, they hated having to work with women. I had a real go at them one day and told them that if there was an invasion they'd be glad enough for women to take up guns to protect them; they were just miserable old men, and weak. That got them, I had no more trouble after that.'

'Good for you, Sarah.' After a pause Joe said, in a casual tone, 'By the way, do you ever hear from that Hendrix chap?'

Sarah told him yes and to tease him added, 'I think he should be coming home on leave soon.'

'Oh, should he? And how does he rate with you in the opinion stakes? He is one of the nobs and a Lieutenant, to boot.'

Sarah pretended to be angry. 'That's a fine thing to say, suggesting that I would prefer Warren Hendrix because he comes from a wealthy family.'

Joe was quick to refute this, it wasn't what he had meant at all. Then he said, 'Oh, heck, you know what I'm getting at, don't you? I'm in love with you.' He grinned suddenly, ' I'll show you how much when we get to the park.'

Sarah felt a thrill go through her, but all she said was, 'Oh, will you? You'd better behave yourself, Joe Curson, or you might have the park-keeper after you.'

'Park-keepers!' he exclaimed. 'I eat them for breakfast.'

Sarah laughed and they stepped out, a happiness between them. When they crossed the road to where the long slope led up to the park Joe stopped and looked about them. 'What's happened? This used to be all fields.'

'And now they're allotments. There was an order to "Dig for Victory", and people everywhere have given over gardens, tennis courts and what have you to plant vegetables. Even the royal palaces have planted potatoes where there were once rose gardens. And why not? Everybody has to do their bit.'

At the top of the incline the wind was strong and Joe put his arm about Sarah's waist as they walked towards the park. There was a big lake in the centre with tree and shrub-lined paths leading from it. The wind ruffled the water and the feathers of the four swans. Several women with children strolled at the lake's edge and Joe said, 'Poor swans, there's no one feeding them. When I was a nipper you threw them bits of stale bread.'

Sarah explained there was now a law forbidding anyone to feed birds or wild animals. Wheat was desperately short with so many ships having been sunk. Then she quoted a piece to him by heart from a public leaflet:

'I am a slice of bread . . .
I am wasted once a day by 48,000,000 people of Britain.
I am "the bit left over", the slice eaten absent-mindedly,
When really I wasn't needed; I am the waste crust.

If you collected me and my companions for a whole week you
would find that we amounted to 9,380 tons of good bread.
WASTED!

SAVE ME AND I WILL SAVE YOU!

'Well,' said Joe, 'that's a tale of woe, isn't it?'

'But it's true, after all.'

He agreed then he pulled her to him and said in a low voice, 'At the moment I'm hungry for *you*. Oh, Sarah, we've got to be alone.' Her body was one big throb but she drew away and Joe took her hand and led her towards one of the paths. At the end of it she saw a wooden seat among a group of trees.

Joe just sat there for a while before putting an arm around her and drawing her head against his shoulder.

'I've dreamed of this moment so many times, Sarah,' he said softly. 'Just holding you close. Have you ever thought the same thing?'

'I've thought of you many times, Joe, and wondered how you were. I looked forward to hearing from you, but – '

He tilted her face. 'But not my making love to you?' When she made no reply he put his lips to hers in a gentle way and the mere touch set her heart racing. He had both arms around her, and his face was buried against her throat when a voice said: 'Now then, what's all this, soldier? You'll have to move from here. We don't have any funny goings-on in this park.'

The sharp-faced elderly man glared at them and thumped his walking stick on the ground. 'Up, the pair of you, and you, young lady, ought to be ashamed of yourself.'

'For what?' Sarah asked quietly. 'For allowing my boyfriend to hold me? But then you wouldn't understand,

226

would you? You're old and no doubt have forgotten what it's like to be young and in love.'

'It's because I do remember and know all the trouble it can cause that I'm moving you on,' he snapped. 'Now go on, get moving.'

Sarah, seeing Joe's fists clench linked her arm though his. 'Come on, don't argue, he's only doing his job.'

'His job!' Joe grumbled. 'We weren't doing any harm.'

Not then, Sarah thought, but what might it have led to? Not that they could have got themselves into a compromising situation in a public park, but with emotions running high they might have found an opportunity for making love. Would she have been willing?

They walked along the paths with Joe's arm around her waist in silence for a few moments then he said, 'Sarah, I want to suggest something to you. I have an aunt who has a cottage where there are no near neighbours – she lives about a mile away from the farm in Corbridge. The first day I was at home, when everyone was talking and people kept dropping in to see me I wanted to get away from them all, just for a while. Our Beth, sensing this, suggested I went to see Aunt Florrie, saying she wouldn't pester me with questions. And she didn't. I remember sitting back in the armchair in front of the fire with my eyes closed and just listening to the gentle sounds of the country and thinking how peaceful it all was.' Joe paused and Sarah waited.

'During the few days I was home I kept slipping off to the cottage, then my Aunt told me she was going away for a week to stay with a sick friend. She asked me if I would like to have the key to her place. I took it and kissed her.'

When Joe fell silent after this Sarah said, 'And you want us to spend some time there. I couldn't Joe, I have no excuse for going away and I doubt whether I could get time off anyway.'

He turned eagerly and gripped her by the shoulders. 'But you *would* go if you could manage it. You would, Sarah, I know it. You want me as much as I want you.'

She was aching for him to love her; she had experienced

227

sensual feelings before at various times, but never anything like this.

'It's impossible, Joe, and you know it. What excuse could I possibly make to go to Corbridge?'

'I'll think of something,' he said grimly. 'I must, I don't want to make love to you like a raw farmhand on a bundle of straw. I want us to make love properly, in bed, all night.'

Sarah gave a low moan. 'Oh, Joe, don't please, you're not being fair.'

He became agitated. 'Could you go and stay with your Aunt Mary for a weekend, or say you were going there and we could stay at a hotel?' He shook his head. 'No, no, that sounds cheap. I want to make love to you at the cottage. I've dreamt about you being there for the past few nights, and I'm so tormented. I need to take the memory back with me when I return to France. I have to have something to dream on, Sarah, I must or I think I'll go mad.'

Although Sarah had not the faintest idea how she could arrange to go to Corbridge she said she would try and think of something and Joe said, a break in his voice, 'Thanks, Sarah, I knew you would.' He gave her a quick hug and then released her.

And from that moment he talked about food as if it was the only thing that had been on his mind for days. Sarah appreciated this but wasn't able to forget the pressing problem of getting to Corbridge, so that Joe could make love to her.

In the end it was Joe who arranged everything, and did it so effortlessly that Sarah was left speechless. When they went home, Isabelle made a great fuss of Joe, but was alarmed by his thinness. 'But then,' she went on, 'your mother will see that you put on some weight. I expect she'll feed you up with all her lovely country cooking.'

Then Joe said, 'I was thinking how peaky Sarah looked when I met her. I think she's been working too hard.' He laughed. 'She could do with some of our fresh Corbridge air.' To Sarah he added, 'How about packing a bag and coming back with me?'

He was treating it as a joke and she answered lightly:

228

'There's nothing I would enjoy more, but it's impossible. I'd never be able to get time off work.'

'Why not?' This came from her mother who was eyeing her thoughtfully. Sarah held her breath as Isabelle went on, 'You've done extra shifts for a lot of the staff, Sarah, I think you could do with a rest and a change. I'm sure your father would agree, even if it was just for two or three days. You could ask.'

Sarah, whose mouth had gone dry felt it was all too easy. She managed to say yes she could, then Joe got up. 'Well, let's go and see them now. If the boss agrees you could go back with me tonight.'

'Tonight?' Sarah's voice had a squeak in it. 'I couldn't, I would have to pack and – '

'All you need is one bag – you wouldn't be packing to go to the Arabian desert.' He turned to Isabelle. 'Would that be all right with you, Mrs Torent?'

She said yes, why not, and told them to run along, she would get the tea ready.

Once they were outside Sarah gave a gasp. 'I just don't believe it? I know it's not going to work out, it couldn't. I won't be granted any time off, I know it. Something has to stop us. Do you realise that my mother hasn't queried a thing? She hasn't even asked how we are going to get from the station to the farm.'

'We must go, Sarah. You'll just have to tell your boss a tale, that you feel exhausted and don't want to end up going to the doctor's and having him put you on the sick for a week. That might do it – make it sound true. Ask for the next three days off, then you can come back in the train with me. Please, please, make it sound true about you being exhausted.'

She laughed. 'I'm worn out now just thinking about getting away. By the way, how will we get from the station to the farm?'

'We won't be going to the farm, not tonight. We'll be going to the cottage.'

Tremors of excitement began to run through Sarah's

229

body, delicious sensations that made her decide she would get time off even if she had to take it without permission.

She left Joe waiting for her in a little alleyway some distance from the depot, and when she came back about ten minutes later she looked around the corner and shook her head at him. 'It's no good, Joe, they couldn't let me away, not now.' The next moment she came running and flung her arms around him. 'I've got it, I've got it! Three whole days' leave.'

He swung her off her feet but when he set her down and made to kiss her she pushed him away. 'No, not here, we might be seen. I'll walk on ahead and you catch me up.'

In the few moments before he did catch her up she had thought of all sorts of reasons why their plan was not going to work. Her father would suggest her mother went with them; someone that Joe knew would be on the train; some relative of Joe's was going to be on the station ready to board the train . . .

Joe said if any of these things did happen, they would just have to accept them. If her mother came with them, it wouldn't stop the two of them going for a walk and ending up at his aunt's cottage. Then he added, 'And now we must try to calm down, Sarah, otherwise we'll give the whole thing away.'

Jonathan did suggest Isabelle accompanying them, but to the great relief of Sarah and Joe she said she would rather go when the weather was warmer. Sarah marvelled, sure that her mother was wanting to give the two of them an opportunity of being together. At the same time, she was also sure it would never enter her mother's mind what they were planning.

The one person that Sarah grieved over deceiving was her father, but much as she hated this part of it she knew she would not willingly sacrifice the time she was to spend with Joe.

Because they were leaving in such a rush it added an extra excitement and also there was no time for any last-minute change of plan. Goodbyes were said. Jonathan told

230

Sarah to make the most of the fresh air, and Isabelle said, for the fiftieth time, 'Give my love to them all at the farm.'

On the train, there were two elderly men and a soldier in the compartment with them, and the talk between the men was all of the war situation. Sarah was glad of this opportunity to think things over in a more rational way. She had become very enlightened about sexual matters since her job in the munitions factory. She knew that soldiers who went to the Front were issued with something called French Letters to wear if they went with a girl; this was to prevent her having a baby, but she had never seen one. She hoped that Joe was sensible enough to have this kind of thing with him. She dare not take the risk of becoming pregnant. What she was planning to do was bad enough, it was a sin in the sight of God, but she could not help wondering why nature gave one these emotional feelings *before* a couple married if it was so wrong of them to make love while they were single.

According to what she had been told by the factory girls, every courting couple made love before marriage, and although Jenny had not said outright that she and her boyfriend did so, she had once or twice hinted at it. Sarah wondered what her cousin would say if she ever found out what she and Joe had planned to do.

Isabelle had asked Joe how they would get to the farm from the station and he had said it was no problem, there was plenty of traffic in war-time and they would have no difficulty in getting a lift in a van or a lorry as they went past the door all the time. But then they were not going to the farm. Where was the cottage? Joe had said a mile away from the farm, and had given the impression it was isolated.

When they arrived at Corbridge it was like stepping into nowhere in the blackness. Pin-points of light could be seen, but they were widely scattered. Joe said, 'I know I told your mother we would have no difficulty in getting a lift, but I think it would be wise if we walked, Sarah, as we don't want anyone seeing us. We can cut across the fields and through the woods, it's not far. And I noticed in the train that you were wearing sensible shoes.'

It was the first time that the word 'sensible' had cropped

231

up in their conversation and Sarah wondered now if they had not been too hasty in regard to their planning. As Joe had said, if they had to go to the farm they could always slip away the next day and make for the cottage. In this way they could have done away with all the subterfuge and not had to tramp over rutted paths in fields.

Before they had gone very far it began to rain. 'Just a shower,' Joe said cheerfully, but before long it had become a deluge. Sarah had put on a knitted cap and one of the lighter-weight coats and could feel her shoulders getting damp. She stumbled and Joe caught hold of her. 'I know it's pretty miserable but it's not far.'

There was ice in the rain and a rising wind drove it against Sarah's face so that her cheeks felt numb. She gasped out, 'I think we're mad. We should have gone to the farm, Joe. If ever my mother and your mother meet and start talking it'll come out that we didn't stay there tonight.'

'Of course it won't. You're just making problems where there aren't any, Sarah. We'll go home tomorrow night. I can't see the pair of them checking up on the dates.' Joe stopped suddenly and turned her to face him. 'Sarah, will you promise me one thing? When we get to the cottage don't change your mind about – about us making love, will you? I don't think I could bear it.'

It was strange, she thought, but all her excitement had gone. When she pictured them making love she felt nothing. Even when Joe drew her to him and kissed her, it aroused no emotion whatsoever. He pulled away and said, his tone accusing, 'You've already changed your mind, haven't you?'

She was silent a moment then touched his arm. 'No, Joe. I suppose it's just that guilt is hitting me now, deceiving everyone, but I haven't changed my mind. We'll make love, I promise you that.'

He put his arm around her waist. 'It'll be something for us to remember, Sarah. Oh, my love, I can hardly wait.'

They walked on and with every stumbling step she was getting colder and colder and increasingly miserable. Joe kept asking her if she was cold and when she told him no he would say, 'It's not far now,' and it got to the pitch where she thought she would scream if he said it once more.

Pathways that led from one field to the other seemed to go on endlessly but at last some trees loomed up. They had reached the woods, which did at least get them out of the wind. But then there were other setbacks, like the exposed roots of trees to trip you. Once when she stumbled, Joe stopped and putting his arms around her held her close. 'Poor Sarah, I'm sorry it had to be weather like this.' He pulled out his handkerchief and wiped the rain gently from her face. 'I suppose there had to be some snags, but why did they have to happen on our honeymoon night?'

There was such sadness in his voice that she said sincerely, 'It *will* be all right, Joe, I promise.'

They walked on and had come out into a narrow clearing with a thick group of trees beyond when Joe stopped abruptly. 'Oh, Lord,' he breathed. 'My aunt must be home.'

Sarah, who had been walking with her shoulders hunched, straightened up. 'What do you mean. How do you know?'

He pointed ahead. 'I can see the glow of the fire through the trees. There's no light on, she could be in bed. You wait here and I'll go and take a look.' He was about to move away when she grabbed at his jacket.

'If she is back you'll have to tell her about us. I'm not going any further, I could *not* go on to the farm tonight.'

'There's only one bed in the cottage. You would have to sleep with my aunt and I would have to sleep on the sofa.' In the blackness his face was just a blur, but in spite of the circumstances there was a teasing in his voice.

'Then I'll sleep with your aunt!' she said.

He cupped her face between his palms. 'But before you do I shall take you right here under a tree, Sarah Torent, so help me. I'll be back in a minute and tell you your fate.'

She called after him, 'Oh, no you won't, Joe Curson, I won't be seduced under this waterfall.' She could hear him laughing softly and she kicked at the ground. Why, oh why,

233

did this have to happen? Was it a punishment for the lies she had told?

She moved back to the shelter of the trees, but the rain-sodden branches dripped water down the back of her neck and her teeth began to chatter. Joe was away for ages and Sarah had just made up her mind to barge into the cottage, no matter what, when she saw a light through the trees. An oil-lamp? She waited another few moments then crossed the clearing and went through the belt of trees, which brought her out into a small cobbled courtyard – and there was the cottage.

The glow from an oil-lamp standing on a table in front of the window turned the slanting needles of rain into a golden curtain. The front door opened and Joe came out. She called, 'I'm here,' and he came to her.

'It's all right, Sarah, the cottage is empty. My aunt left a note.' He took hold of her arm. 'Come inside out of this wretched rain. I've put some wood on the fire, it'll soon catch hold, but the room is warm.'

It was and to Sarah in her partially-paralysed state it was like coming into a haven. 'Look,' Joe held out a piece of paper. 'My aunt left this note. She's been here today to light a fire in case I wanted to be on my own. She's gone back to be with her friend and won't return until the weekend. She says she'll see me before I leave. Oh, Sarah, you're shivering. Come to the fire and get these wet things off.'

The wood had ignited and sparks were flying up the chimney. Joe pulled off her hat and helped her off with her coat. 'I can't have you catching cold or your parents would never forgive me. I think you should get into a hot bath. There's one that hangs on the wall outside, I'll bring it in. There's plenty of hot water in the boiler. Put this around you for the moment.' It was a sofa blanket but although it was large and all-wool nothing would stop the shivering or the chattering of her teeth.

Sarah suddenly felt a bubble of hysteria rising. Joe was worrying what her parents would think if she caught cold but was not worrying what they would think if they knew

234

that their only daughter was about to be seduced. She dropped to her knees on the rag rug and sneezed. A seduction which she had thought would be so wonderful now looked like being the fiasco of the century.

19

A few minutes after Joe had gone outside to get the big tin bath Sarah heard a clatter on the cobblestones as if he had dropped it, and when he came into the scullery there was another clatter like pans being dropped. He came into the living room with a broad grin on his face.

Sarah said: 'What are you trying to do – send a message to the whole countryside to say that Joe Curson and Sarah Torent are spending the night alone at his aunt's cottage?'

'Well, not being in an Indian reservation I didn't have any drums to beat out the message. Out of the way, girl, while I get this bath filled.'

'The tender lover,' she retorted and got up. 'I must be out of my mind to have agreed to come.'

He came over to her and touched her cheek. 'You'll have no regrets, my darling, when I start washing your back.'

She drew away in alarm. 'Oh, no you won't. I can wash my own back.'

'You will never want to again,' he said softly, 'not after I have washed it for you. I can guarantee that a thousand drums will be beating in every part of your body.'

Sarah stifled a sneeze, but could not stifle the one that followed, and she thought that nothing Joe Curson did now would raise even the tiniest flicker of desire in her. He went into the scullery and came back with a metal scoop with which to fill the bath.

The black-leaded kitchen range gleamed and when Joe raised the lid of the boiler at the side of the fire the steam from the water cast a film over the polish. 'Lovely and hot,' he noted with satisfaction as he started scooping the water into the bath. 'Start getting undressed.' Sarah wrapped the blanket tighter around her.

'I'll start getting undressed when you're out of this room and not before.' Joe made no answer. When the bath was a quarter full he went to get some cold water to put into it and after feeling the temperature with his hand he straightened. 'That's it then, madam. I shall bring you towels, soap and a flannel, then leave you to your ablutions.' When these were brought he bowed himself out into the scullery. The next moment he threw in a big sponge, saying he had just seen it. There was laughter in his voice. When the door closed Sarah removed the blanket, but she waited for a few moments before starting to undo her blouse.

When at last she was sitting in the hot water she drew a quick breath of pleasure. What bliss after the misery of the walk. She had turned down the lamp and the firelight cast shadowy shapes on the wall . . . and for the first time since leaving the train she felt the first little stirrings of sensuousness. She wanted to linger over the bath and it was only the fact of Joe being in the icy-cold scullery that made her grope for the soap in the water, then the sponge, and start to wash her shoulders. She knew a longing then to have Joe come in and wash her back.

Moments later she heard the door-handle turn and she tensed. She was sitting with her back to the door and when Joe came up behind her he took the sponge from her hand, soaped it and drew it gently across her back. She clasped her hands tightly as emotions flooded over her, and when he started to trickle water down her back she closed her eyes, feeling pulses beat in the sensitive parts of her body.

'Stand up, Sarah,' he said in a low voice. She felt unable to move. 'Sarah, stand up and face me.' There was a raggedness in his voice. She gripped the sides of the bath, got to her knees then levered herself to her feet; but it was seconds before she could bring herself to face him. When she did she saw that he was stripped to the waist; she also saw that although he had seemed to have lost weight he was still well-built.

Without a word he dipped the sponge into the water and began to draw it over her breasts and underneath, pausing once to kiss each nipple. Her body was now on fire. He brushed the sponge lightly across her stomach and her muscles contracted with delight, but when after dipping the

237

sponge into the water he drew it between her legs she gave a moan, 'Oh, Joe, don't, don't . . .'

He quickly wrapped the towel around her, lifted her out of the bath, moved it aside then divested himself of the rest of his clothes. He stood without any sign of embarrassment, a rather proud tilt to his head.

Sarah, for all the knowledge she had gained about a couple mating, had never seen a man undressed and realised now she had never allowed for the growth from childhood to manhood. She began to tremble and Joe drew her to him and buried his face against her neck. 'Sarah, Sarah, I want you now.'

She wanted to feel his flesh against hers and she let the towel fall away. He laid her down on the blanket and turning away brought something from his trouser pocket. Although she guessed what it was and knew it was sensible she had to restrain herself from shouting, 'Take me now, Joe, I can't wait.'

There was none of the loveplay with Joe that girls had talked about but it mattered little to Sarah then. All she wanted was something to happen to ease the torment of the agonising ecstasy that was building up inside her.

Then Joe was over her saying, 'I'll try not to hurt you, Sarah.'

She put her arms around him and ran her fingers over his back. His skin felt surprisingly silky, which for some reason added to her strange excitement. She dug her nails into his flesh and told him she didn't mind if he hurt her, she wanted him so much.

At this he gave a gasp and she could feel the wild beating of his heart. There was pain when he entered her but overriding it was the exquisite torment of feeling him swell inside her and his thrusts quickening.

Her blood began to pound and when Joe suddenly put the tip of his tongue in her ear a frenzy of pleasure rose from the source of their coupling, spiralling until she was in a delirium of ecstasy. The throbbing went on and on until slowly it began to subside, then they lay spent.

When Joe rolled away from her he put his arm under her

head and drew her to him. 'Oh, Sarah, that was wonderful, unbelievably wonderful. I'm sorry it was so quick but I just couldn't wait. Did I satisfy you?'

When she didn't answer he drew his arm away and sat up. She lay smiling at him and he gave a joyous shout. 'I did! You look like a smug little kitten that's had the cream of the milk.'

'You're kidding yourself,' she teased. Then she touched his cheek and added more seriously, 'I had never imagined it would be like that, Joe. Will it always be the same?'

'With me it will, of course,' he said with a roguish grin, 'but I can't say the same for other blokes.'

'Bighead,' she said and he chuckled. Then he lay down beside her again and drew her to him.

'You don't have any regrets, Sarah, do you?'

'No. I might feel guilty later, but I'll try not to let it worry me because neither of us knows what the future has in store. I only know that I'm glad we have this one whole night together.'

'And tomorrow,' he reminded her.

'Yes, tomorrow,' she repeated softly. She closed her eyes and Joe tapped her on the cheek.

'Here, don't you dare go to sleep on me! The night is still young and we have a lot of loving to do.'

'I wasn't going to sleep, I was just feeling – slumberous, is that the right word? No, no, it's langourous, what a lovely word. Lang-our-ous. It's sexy . . .'

'Come here, wench.' Joe's breathing was harsh. He cupped her breast then his mouth came down over hers. The next moment they were locked in an embrace, passion mounting between then.

Sarah's last recollection was of seeming to have made love all night in front of the kitchen fire, but when she roused it was to find herself in bed, cocooned between soft cushions and a plump feather eiderdown. Whose bed? she thought sleepily. Then suddenly she was wide-awake and not in a proper bed at all but one made up on the floor. It was daylight, the wind was howling round the eaves, rain lashed against the window panes and logs were crackling in the kitchen grate. Then she became aware of the pungent smell of burnt toast and of someone whistling. Joe . . . she sat up. When had he made up the bed?

The whistling came nearer. She sank back, pulling the eiderdown over her to cover her nakedness.

'Come on, lazybones, I know you're awake, I saw you move. Do you know the time? It's after eleven.'

'Eleven?' Sarah sat up again, the eiderdown pulled up to her chin. 'I can't believe it, and I couldn't believe it when I woke either. I thought I was in bed.'

'Well, when Mohammed won't go to the mountain the mountain has to come to Mohammed. And it's only the eiderdown from my aunt's bed. The blankets I found in a chest and the cushions came from the sofa and the chairs. Satisfied, madam?'

'More than satisfied,' she said, with a cheeky grin.

'Oh, like that, is it? We shall soon have to rectify that fault.' Joe leaned over and tried to wrest the eiderdown from her but she clung to it, laughing.

'No, Joe, not now. I'm famished. For *food*. You're a good bedmaker, but a rotten toastmaker. You've burnt it!'

'Soon put that right.' He brought over some slices and started scraping off the burnt parts. 'Musn't waste bread – as you said, it's considered a sin these days.'

'Well, that wouldn't be the only sin committed here,' Sarah countered.

'That was not a sin, my love, it was sheer unadulterated pleasure.'

'Joe, just how many times did we make love last night?'

He shrugged. 'What would you say – ten, twelve, fourteen? Could have been sixteen times. My middle name is Samson.' Then he was laughing and Sarah was laughing with him, calling him the biggest bighead she had ever met.

The weather remained wild but they were content to stay indoors. They laughed a lot and made love, but they talked quite a lot, too. Joe told her of his plans about starting a garage. 'I know Dad will want me back on the farm, Sarah, but I'm interested in the mechanical side of things. I'll enjoy tinkering with cars and lorries and could repair tractors.

You should know how I feel because you are interested in clocks. But mind you, when we're married you will have to look after the house and kids, do you hear?'

'I hear,' she said airily, 'but we'll have to have a shop beside the garage because I want to have a business, too. I can always pop the baby into the garage for Daddy to look after.'

'Oh, you can, can you? Well, let me tell you this . . .'

She put a finger to his lips and said, 'Argue with me later. I want you to hold me, just hold me, not to make love.'

But it was difficult for Joe to take her into his arms without making love.

Once after one of their sessions, she told him how ignorant she had been about sex as a girl of twelve until his sister Beth had enlightened her. 'And Jenny too – neither of us really had a clue until we first went to Corbridge of what was meant by taking the bull to the cow. And I still don't know whether animals too get pleasure when they mate. Do they?'

Joe grinned. 'If so it's too good for them!'

'Shame on you, why shouldn't they get pleasure. And do you know, Joe, at that time I thought that couples behaved the same way as - well, the bull and the cow.'

'You didn't!' Joe spluttered into laughter, then he was falling about. 'You thought –' the tears began rolling down his cheeks. 'That's the best thing I've heard in a long time. My sweet lovely Sarah, I love you, love you, love you.' He hugged her and rocked her to and fro, then suddenly he sobered and tipping up her chin looked into her eyes. 'Promise you will always love me, Sarah.'

'I promise,' she whispered. She nearly added, 'Until death do us part' and stopped herself in time.

When at last the time came for them to go to the farm and they closed the cottage door behind them, Sarah had her first little twinge of guilt. This place had been their haven and she felt that she had betrayed a trust, not only to the cottage but to Joe's aunt. But for his sake she tried to throw off the guilt.

241

'I bet all the family's there,' Joe said. 'I have an uncle and a cousin who's home on leave too, they'll be off tomorrow morning so they're sure to call.'

It was the joyous welcome from the family that deepened Sarah's guilt. Everyone seemed to be talking at once, Mrs Curson saying how lovely it was to have Sarah there too, after such a long time, but what a night! Why hadn't they let them know and someone would have met them. The uncle was there and the cousin and two aunts and there was a rushing around to get a meal on the table. And how were Sarah's parents and her aunt and uncle and Jenny?

Sarah never did get all the questions answered because of the cross-talk. Joe put his arm around her at one stage and said, 'You couldn't have a better family to marry into, Sarah girl, they all love you.' He laughed. 'You'll have no mother-in-law trouble and neither will I. Your mam's a lovely woman, so understanding.'

'Yes,' she said, feeling she wanted to cry.

After the meal the men got together discussing the war and Sarah caught snatches of conversation that gave her insights into things Joe had never fully described.

'I'll tell you this, Adam: you stand up to your ankles in water in the trenches; if you get the chance to snatch forty winks you bed down in water, then you wake up in it and crawl on your belly in it. Water and mud, a no-man's-land, never knowing which minute is going to be your last.'

The cousin said grimly, 'I've often wished it would be when I've crawled over limbless dead men, men with their entrails hanging out . . .'

Sarah wanted to close her mind to the conversation but she forced herself to listen as though accepting punishment for her sins.

It was Mrs Curson who cut the men's talk short. 'War, that's all we hear. Let's talk about something more pleasant. Joe, did I tell you that your cousin Frances is getting married soon? To a chap who lives at Alston. He's in a reserved occupation, thank goodness . . .'

It was late morning on the day they were due to leave before Sarah and Joe had a chance of being alone. The wind had dropped, it had stopped raining and a feeble sun had broken through the early clouds. They were walking up to the top fields when Joe stopped and turned her to face him.

'We have time to go to the cottage, love. It'll be our last chance.'

She drew away. 'I can't, Joe, not after having been with your family. They wouldn't expect it of us. I would feel I was betraying their trust.'

'Oh, so it was all right betraying *your* parents' trust but not mine.' Joe's half-angry, half-disappointed tone had Sarah bursting into tears. Then he was gentle with her, tender, he wouldn't ask any more of her, but he did beg that she would not regret what they had done.

At this she dried her tears. Joe would be going to France that evening and she could not let him leave feeling she was unhappy. She managed a smile.

'No, Joe, no regrets. It was beautiful, a memory that will be with me always.'

'Me too,' he murmured and held her close.

They travelled to Newcastle together that evening and although they had not made love again she felt there was a bond between them that was strong, strong enough to keep them together in spirit and for both of them to relive their time in the cottage over and over again.

Their parting at the station was made easier by the fact that Joe met up with a number of men from his regiment and there was a lot of back-slapping and laughter, also they seemed to be caught up in such a crowd; there were servicemen everywhere, some arriving, some ready to depart.

Sweethearts, wives, mothers and families were there to see them off but the men were determinedly cheerful. 'We'll be back before you know it . . . Get the cake made, Jessie, we'll get hitched on my next leave . . . Be sure and let me know when the kid arrives, Susie, and don't you dare call it after your ma or da . . . Send us some comics, Mam, we always get a laugh . . .'

One man began to play on a harmonica *Pack Up Your*

243

Troubles In Your Old Kit Bag . . . and within seconds it seemed the station roof would lift off with all the voices.

Then the guard called 'All aboard!' and hasty last-minute goodbyes were said. Joe's last words to Sarah were: 'Think of me, Sarah love.'

'I will, always. Take care of yourself.' She was unable to say more for the constriction in her throat but she did manage a smile.

The guard blew his whistle and the train began to move. Those men who had managed to get to lowered windows were frantically waving and shouting out messages.

One woman, who was dabbing at her eyes said, 'To hear them you would think they were off for the holiday of a lifetime. But then I wouldn't want it to be any other way, bless them.' A cloud of steam from the engine enveloped them and when it cleared the train was rounding a bend. Sarah waited until it was out of sight then walked slowly away, a chill feeling around her heart. Would she ever see Joe again? Although the cottage had seemed such a haven at the time, now she realised it was something that had passed as though in a dream. And wasn't life just like a sequence of dreams, some good, some bad?

It was not until she was home and caught up in the love of her parents, that she felt secure again. Pray heaven that she would always have her home to return to.

Isabelle held her daughter away from her. 'I think you do look better for the change, love, but of course it would be a sad time seeing Joe off at the station. How are Mr and Mrs Curson and the family? They must have been surprised when you arrived with Joe.'

Sarah suddenly found that she no longer had a feeling of guilt, for having deceived the Cursons and her parents. Men like Joe needed something to dream about in all the appalling conditions of the trenches. What had happened between Joe and herself was as sacred to them both as if they had been married, even if everyone else considered it a sin. And it was this that sustained Sarah while she waited to hear from Joe. She wrote a few lines to him every day,

244

pouring out her love, and how much it had meant to her to have those few days together.

It was nearly three weeks before she heard from him and it was the most loving letter she had ever received. The trouble was, she had to be careful where she kept it. She knew her father would never read a letter belonging to her, but she was not so sure about her mother. Mothers were known to find out about their daughters' love lives. Not, she knew, out of sheer curiosity, but from concern for their welfare.

Her father had asked about the Cursons and the conditions of farming and at odd times she had a feeling that he knew what had happened, but she felt if she were ever to tell him he would understand.

Although Sarah knew she would never confide in Jenny about her new relationship with Joe she realised that she would have to 'come clean' about the visit to Corbridge. She had expected Jenny to be annoyed but all her cousin said was, 'Oh, yes,' then went on to tell her she was definitely thinking of joining the WAACS.

Sarah felt dismayed. 'The WAACS – that means you'll probably have to go away. I'll miss you, Jenny, I really will. I know we haven't seen so much of each other since you started going out with Roy, but I always knew you were there to have a chat to, to share our little secrets.'

'Secrets, did you say?' At this Jenny burst into tears. 'God, I wish I was dead. I've really got myself into a mess.'

Alarmed, Sarah went over to her. 'What is it, Jenny, what's wrong?'

Jenny looked up, her eyes brimming over with tears. 'I'm pregnant, Sarah. What am I going to do? Roy assured me he would take care of that side of it, but he obviously missed taking precautions once, or it could have been more often. I've kept telling everyone I was thinking of joining the WAACS because I wanted an excuse to go away somewhere where I could get rid of this baby. Roy said he would marry me but I don't want to get married and settle down to looking after kids. I still want some fun!'

Beating in Sarah's mind were the words that Roy had

obviously missed taking care once, or it could have been more often . . . Joe was supposed to have taken precautions, but supposing he had not done so every single time? Their love-making at times had been wild, really wild. She felt an iciness steal over her. There were another five days to go before she would know. Although she loved Joe she knew she did not want to have his baby under these circumstances. Yet she tried to persuade Jenny to keep hers.

'You can't get rid of it, Jenny. Girls have been known to bleed to death from these back-street abortionists. Their treatment is crude, they'll use a knitting needle or a crochet hook. Oh, please think again! You just can't risk it.'

Jenny flung out her hands. 'But don't you see, I'll *have* to take the risk. It's Dad, more than Mam, I'm thinking of. He's had enough to put up with without having an illegitimate grandchild on his hands, because I just won't marry Roy, I won't. I like him all right, he's a decent bloke but I'm not in love with him, never have been.'

Sarah stared at her. 'I can't understand how you could let him – how you and he could – without loving him.'

'Oh, grow up, Sarah, come out of your fairy tale world of knights in shining armour. It's done and I've got to get rid of it and that's that!'

'I don't believe in a fairy tale world,' Sarah said quietly, 'and haven't done so for a long time. I can only ask that you don't go to one of these back-street women. Is there something you can take? I've heard women say that – '

'I've tried everything – I've soaked in hot baths. I've jumped off the table and down eight stairs and all I got for my trouble was a bump the size of an egg on my head and arm and bruises from shoulder to elbow. I had to say I had tripped and fallen down the tram stairs.'

Sarah shook her head. 'I still say you shouldn't go to one of those awful women, you could die.'

'I'd be better off dead.' Jenny gave a deep sigh. 'The only alternative is to say I want to go back into munitions for the money, stay with Aunt Mary and when the baby's born have it adopted.'

Sarah dismissed this as stupid. 'Supposing your mother

or mine came to spend a few days with Mary – you couldn't very well say about your big bump that you were "blown up with wind" as old Mrs Smith always says.'

They both laughed but it was laughter close to tears.

After talking a while longer Jenny came to the conclusion that there was no other way, she would have to take the risk. She threatened Sarah that if she so much as breathed a word of it to either of their parents, she would never speak to her again.

Sarah offered to accompany her and it was agreed they would try and arrange to do an early shift together. They would supposedly be going out shopping and when they came back, Jenny would not be feeling too well; she would have started her period.

The abortionist lived on the second floor of a slum tenement. As the girls went up the filthy wooden stairs Sarah and Jenny exchanged glances. There were children squalling, a man and woman yelling obscenities at one another and overall was the smell of cabbage water and stale urine. When they reached the first landing Sarah laid a detaining hand on her cousin's arm but Jenny shrugged it off and started to climb the next flight.

To Sarah's relief the woman who answered the door looked clean and was quietly-spoken. She invited them in. The room was tidy but sparsely furnished. 'No names, no pack drill,' she said. 'Which of you is –?' Jenny held up her hand and the woman said, 'Come with me. Now don't worry, I sterilise what I use.' They went into a room off the kitchen and the door closed. Sarah sat, her heart beating madly. If anything happened she would be partially responsible.

Once she heard Jenny cry out but otherwise there was silence. Not even a murmur of voices. She had been prepared for Jenny to look a little washed-out, but was horrified by the drained-looking face, paper white against the flame of her cousin's red hair as Jenny limped out of the room half an hour later.

The woman said briskly, 'See she goes to bed when she gets home. She'll be all right.' Sarah could only nod.

They went down the stairs slowly with Sarah supporting her cousin. Jenny whispered, 'Don't say anything. It's done and finished with. She was careful. She used to be a nurse before she was married.'

Two people on the tram asked Jenny if she was all right and Sarah said, 'She's been sick. It was something she's eaten, but she's over the worst now.' Once they were off the tram she blurted out, 'Oh, Jenny, I think we ought to call the doctor.'

Jenny gripped her arm. 'Don't you dare. All I need is a night's rest. For God's sake look as if it was just my period I was suffering from.'

Fortunately Isabelle was out visiting a neighbour when they arrived back. Sarah crumpled up the note and said, 'Thank heavens for that! I'll fill a hot-water bottle. Go on up to bed, Jenny, I'll be up in a minute.'

It all went as they hoped it would. Isabelle accepted the story, went up to see Jenny who was curled under the bedclothes, and said to Sarah, 'She'll feel better in the morning. Why do women have to suffer from the wretched thing?'

And it was Isabelle who insisted that Jenny stay in bed the next day, saying she didn't look fit enough to go to work. Jenny made no argument.

The following day she did go back to work and the day after that was laughing and joking once more with the men at the depot. Sarah, who had been really worried about her cousin and was also apprehensive about the uncertainty of her own condition, was angry.

'I think your behaviour is terrible, Jenny. You're absolutely heartless.'

To this Jenny replied quietly, 'If I didn't laugh and joke, Sarah, I would throw myself off the Tyne Bridge for what I lost.' She gave her a quick hug. 'Thanks for all you did for me, kiddo. I promise I'll never let myself get in such a situation again.'

When, five hours later, Sarah gratefully felt the familiar monthly pains she vowed she would never again run the risk of becoming pregnant until she was safely married, no matter how high passions ran between Joe and herself.

With so much going on she had not thought about Warren Hendrix at all, but when her father came in one evening a few weeks later and told her he was home, Sarah was surprised at how excited she felt.

'Warren? On leave? How is he?'

'He looks very well,' Jonathan smiled. 'He has invited you to a party next Saturday. It's being held at a friend's house. No doubt he'll be in touch with you later.'

'A party?' Sarah stood hesitant. Should she go? It was hardly fair to Joe. And yet –

Isabelle said laughing, 'I can read your mind, Sarah. I know you are wondering what you can wear. Well, that's no problem – we shall go through Aunt Maud's chest, find some nice material and I shall make it up for you.'

This settled it for Sarah. It was ages since she had been to a party of any kind, and it would really be good to have a long talk with Warren. It wasn't as if he had ever hinted at anything more than friendship between them.

They chose the material for the dress that same evening, with Isabelle saying it must be simple but classy. The choice was a pale cream silk for the main part of the dress, with a sleeveless tunic of cream silk broderie anglaise. Isabelle suggested that the tunic should have a point at front and back and be encircled by a narrow girdle of pearls. Sarah approved, knowing that her mother had a flair for design. Skirt lengths had shortened as the war progressed and although they had not yet reached mid-calf, you could show off a pair of shapely ankles.

She would have liked the dress to be off the shoulders, but although Isabelle did demur at this she cut the neckline reasonably low.

Warren had not been back to the shop to confirm about the party and Sarah was thinking about him and worrying a little as she came off-duty late one afternoon, when she came face to face with him. Colour rushed to her face. Why had she not stopped to freshen up and tidy herself?

'Hello, Sarah,' he said softly.

'Warren, how good it is to see you. Father told me you had called at the shop.'

'Yes, and I'm sorry I couldn't get back. I was staying with my great-aunt and she just about wet-nursed me, saying, "You must rest, my boy, you must have plenty of rest." Well, I've had all the rest I want – now I'm ready for partying, having some fun.' He put his hand under her elbow. 'Shall we go, Sarah? You will come to the party with me, please say yes.'

'I'd love to, Warren.'

'Good.' He went on to talk about his great-aunt and what a wonderful person she was, but Sarah was only partially listening. She found herself comparing Warren with Joe. Joe never changed. He was the same earthy, happy-go-lucky Joe, making her laugh, that she had first met, but Warren seemed to change every time they met. His face was much leaner but this only seemed to add to his attraction. He turned his head and smiled at her. 'It's so good to see you again, Sarah. No matter where I am or what I'm doing, you always seem to be there with me.'

Sarah was astonished to find she was trembling at his nearness. And yet there had been no seductive hints in his voice: it was more a statement than anything else.

She felt she ought to tell him about Joe, but instead asked who was giving the party.

'A friend of mine, he's in the air force, just been given a gong. The party is to celebrate it.'

'A gong? Oh, yes, of course, a medal. I'm not wholly conversant with service jargon. Had he shot down a lot of planes?'

'Yes he had, and while he was wounded. He's a great person.' Warren laughed softly. 'I had better warn you that the guests will be mostly army types, letting their hair down. There will be plenty to drink, it will be noisy, brash, but I think we can all do with living it up for a change.'

'I agree,' Sarah said stoutly. 'I run up and down tram stairs so many times in a day that I'm still doing it in my sleep. In the rush hour it's bedlam, I find myself crushed to death.'

250

'So how do you manage to look so beautiful?' he teased.

'Flatterer, I look a mess.'

'Not to me you don't.' He stopped suddenly and taking hold of her hands said earnestly, 'I just can't express how really good it is to see you again, Sarah.'

In the gathering dusk his sombre expression made a big impact on her. She was afraid of his being so serious, yet at the same time she knew she wanted to feel his arms around her. It was wrong, wrong. She drew her hands away.

'I've often thought about you, Warren, wondering how you were, what was happening.'

'Sarah, is there someone else in your life?'

'I do have . . . friends.'

Warren was now smiling. 'Then that's alright. As long as they're just friends I stand a chance with you.'

They walked on and Sarah thought, Oh, God, why did I lie, why didn't I tell him that I'm madly in love with a man called Joe and that we made love for a whole night and a day recently?

Warren drew Sarah's arm through his. 'We're going to enjoy this party on Saturday, Sarah, I know we will, but please don't make any more *friends*, will you? I don't want any more competition.'

'I won't,' she said, and wondered what Joe would have to say if he could have overheard this conversation.

20

After Sarah had left Warren Hendrix she came to her senses. A mutual attraction between a couple did not mean that they were in love. It was wartime, when people were living unnatural lives. She doubted very much whether she would have stooped to deception to be at the cottage with Joe had he not come back from the trenches. The times they were living in heightened emotions. She was missing Joe, missing love. Warren had stepped into the breach. He had invited her to the party, she would accompany him and enjoy it – but it must go no further than that.

She knew the dress was going to be a success by the glowing comments from neighbours who had popped in while she was having fittings; this was certainly confirmed when Warren called for her on the Saturday evening. His admiration was unmistakeable when he saw her, then he said warmly to Isabelle: 'You've done your daughter proud, Mrs Torent. I understand you made the dress: an exquisite dress for a very beautiful girl.'

Isabelle said quietly, 'It's a pleasure to make for Sarah, she's so appreciative. My husband hasn't arrived home yet but he will be here when you return.' She smiled. 'He is a night bird but don't be too late back.'

Warren promised, then they prepared to leave. He had arrived in a taxi and it was waiting. Petrol had become so scarce the allowance was minimal for private cars. The house where the party was being held was in Benton and stood in its own grounds.

'A big advantage,' Warren said with a laugh. 'There'll be no complaints from neighbours at the noise.'

There were only chinks of light showing in the house from outside but once the front door was opened the hall was ablaze with the lights from a crystal chandelier.

Everyone seemed to have congregated in the large hall and above the hubbub of voices were bursts of laughter.

Although some men wore mufti the majority were in khaki, with one or two of the officers showing wings above their pockets. Sarah knew that Warren's Air Force friend was named David, but when a cheery-faced, sandy-haired man hailed them and came up, Warren said, 'Sarah, this is our host, Socks, the recently decorated –'

Socks held up his hand. 'There will be no mention of gongs.' His face was one broad grin. He held Sarah at arms' length. 'So . . . this is the beautiful gal that old Warren has been raving about. How are you, Sal? I want every dance with you, but I'll settle for six. Musn't be greedy, even though it is *my* party.'

Warren laughed and took Sarah by the hand. 'Come along, I had better take possession before the mad-hatters take over. See you later, Socks.'

Mad-hatters was right. Sarah was introduced to men with names like Toecap, Elbow, Pants, Shoelace, Joppy: and to girls who were called Dawn, Dody, Puss, Yolande, Titania. Yolande took Sarah to 'powder her nose'. Everywhere was elegance – thick carpets, beautiful paintings, lovely vases . . .

Yolande said, 'I love your dress, Sal. Who designed it?'

'My mother, and she made it.'

'Your mother?' The girl's eyes went wide. 'She's a genius.'

'Yolande, why do all the men have funny names like Socks and Shoelace?'

'Oh, it's just a crazy thing, Sweetie. They have to be crazy to be flying kites. They're here today and gone tomorrow. Ready? Come along then, let's go and join in the fun.'

Sarah found she had entered a completely new world. Champagne flowed. She had one glass and drank it quickly, and it went to her head. After that she was cautious and sipped the next. Maids handed round plates of tit-bits, succulent beef rolled up in wafer-thin brown bread, tiny chicken patties, pieces of puff pastry containing seafood.

253

For the first time she tasted smoked salmon. There were anchovy and ham and pork sandwiches in various shapes – diamonds, hearts, rounds. Mouth-watering gâteaux tempted her, with their fillings of fruit and cream. Sarah wished she could take some of the goodies home.

Never at any time was there any serious conversation. These people talked a different language. Things were 'whacko, bang-on, bung ho or wizard'. A man would address a girl affectionately as Pie-face, or Podge. Men who spoke to Sarah called her Duckie or Sweetie; one told her she was a 'spiffing gal'. They all wanted to date her. She referred them laughingly to Warren for permission and they would groan and say they might have known she was snapped up.

And Sarah loved every minute of it. Everyday life seemed drab in comparison: sometimes up at four o'clock in the morning, going to work half-asleep, clicking tickets, pushing among the tightly-packed passengers in the rush-hour collecting fares, being almost crushed to death.

At about ten o'clock Socks held up his hand for silence. He had an announcement to make. The phonograph had 'conked out', but an American friend was supplying the music, he had just arrived. 'Meet Butch, who has brought a pianola. And rolls!'

A fair-haired giant, an American officer, came in pushing the pianola. There was a burst of applause and he acknowledged it with a friendly grin and a wave.

'Thanks, folks, glad to be of service. I've brought the latest roll from the States, *Steeplechase Rag*, but first I'll get you all going with *Alexander's Ragtime Band*'.

Within a minute of setting the roll going on the pianola, everyone's feet were tapping. To Sarah's surprise the American came up to her. 'Can I have this dance, ma'am? And in the next breath asked if she could do the Turkey Trot.

She smiled and nodded. 'Yes, I can, but it's a little old-fashioned now.'

'So we'll be old fashioned.'

He placed his hands on her shoulders and away they went, their shoulders going up and down to the music.

Within seconds ten or twelve other couples had joined them on the floor. Sarah felt excited. This man was different, she loved his voice, the slow drawl. Warren, who was dancing with Yolande called as they passed, 'You take good care of my girl, do you hear?'

The American grinned broadly. 'Sure will. Want to fight for her? Swords or pistols?'

'Pistols, every time.' Warren was laughing, too.

At the end of the dance Butch relinquished her saying, 'That's only until I have some pistol practice. Save me another dance.' She promised and as Butch went to change the roll Warren came up.

He wagged an admonishing finger at her. 'You beware of these Americans.' Although his tone was teasing Sarah had a feeling he was jealous. 'Yes, sir,' she answered meekly.

She did dance with Warren, but found herself in demand. A tall, thin man with a serious expression claimed her, saying, 'So, you are the dreamboat in Hendrix's life! No wonder he's kept you hidden. How about meeting me in the conservatory at midnight?'

'What, and lose my glass slipper?'

He guffawed. 'What a gal, snap bang with the answer, eh? I like you, Sal.'

Sarah was allowed no time for sitting out, but she didn't want to. She two-stepped with some, went back to the old one-step with another and did the Bunny Hug with Butch. With others she simply followed what steps they decided to do.

Once Socks seized her, saying to her partner, 'Sorry, Hats, this should have been my jig with Sal. Hello, Sal, can't have you besieged by these army Johnnies, can we?'

This was all heady stuff to Sarah and she tried to think up something to reply that would fit in with the jargon.

'No, we can't. It's the fliers who hit the target every time!'

'Good girl, good girl.' In the next breath he added with a groan, 'Oh, here's old Warren coming in to attack.'

Warren laughed. 'Sorry, Socks, this lovely girl and I have an assignation in the conservatory.' He took Sarah by the

255

hand and led her between the dancing couples to the conservatory.

As he opened the door the humid air met them. Warren said, 'I thought it was time we had a few minutes alone together.'

From a corner a gruff voice said, 'We thought the same, chum, but no hope in here, it's becoming overcrowded.'

When Warren asked how overcrowded, heads kept popping up from among the large potted plants and foliage. A dark-haired girl called, 'Why not try the rose arbour, duckie? It's a bit draughty, but it was vacant five minutes ago.'

Sarah and Warren burst out laughing and left. In the hall he took an overcoat at random from a pile on an ottoman and draped it around Sarah's shoulders. 'We'll find somewhere.'

What they found was a summerhouse with a mingled smell of earthiness and creosoted wood. Warren flashed a pocket torch round and they saw there was a cane sofa. 'Just the job. Sit down.' The cane creaked and Sarah said, 'I don't feel exactly safe.'

Warren, misinterpreting her words, put an arm around her and gave her a quick hug. 'You are safe with me, Sarah, I promise. I just wanted for us to have a talk.' After a moment's pause he went on earnestly, 'I was attracted to you from the first moment we met, although you were only a child then. I felt I had to give you time to get to know me, but time is not on our side. One never knows what is going to happen from one day to the next.'

Sarah gave a shiver. 'Please don't say that.'

'But it's true. "I'm in love with you, Sarah. I feel sure you like me or you would not have agreed to come here this evening, but do you think you could love me? I'm crazy about you. I – well, I want to marry you, Sarah.'

'Marry?' She turned to him startled, but in the darkness of the summerhouse his face was just a pale blur. 'I like you, enjoy your company, Warren, but marriage . . .'

'Don't give a definite no,' he pleaded. 'Think it over.'

'But Warren, I'm not interested in marrying anyone at

256

the moment. When the war is over I'm hoping to go into the clock and watch business, just buying and selling, not on the repair side. It's become a sort of dream of mine.'

He turned her face towards him, kissed her lightly on the lips and said, laughing, 'You can have your business and we can still get married.'

Now that she was used to the darkness she could see him more clearly. He looked so serious she said, 'Usually a man wants his wife to stay at home and have children.'

'I must admit I would prefer it, Sarah, but I don't want to think of the future, I want to live for now. I want you, I want you to be there to meet me when I get leave. A man needs something to dream about in all this horror of war.'

Sarah felt a quick pang. Joe had used similar words. Why did she not tell him about Joe – now? She said instead, 'I would like to keep on seeing you, Warren, but I don't want marriage to be discussed.'

'Fair enough, I accept.' Warren kissed her again, this time more lingeringly, but not with any real passion. He drew away and said softly, 'I think we had better go before I find it too difficult to keep my promise to you.' He got up, drew Sarah to her feet then wrapping his arms around her held her close, and kissed her with much more passion. He released her, saying with a tremor in his voice, 'I do wish I hadn't made any promises to myself.'

Sarah's thought's were in a turmoil. She could not deny to herself that she had wanted to respond to his touch. She tried to force herself to concentrate on the party and enjoy it all, for there would be time enough for some serious thinking later. And when two of the men started doing a tango, everyone, including Sarah, was helpless with laughter at their antics.

Afterwards, Sarah threw herself once more into the dancing, and became the most sought-after girl there. Although she felt light-headed, she was not too hazy to know when men tried to fondle her breasts. She would push a hand firmly away and say, 'Behave yourself, or else . . .' And it was enough to make them desist.

By one o'clock some of the men were maudlin drunk and

told her all their troubles, and Sarah, by then feeling a little drunk herself, commiserated with them. Once or twice Warren came up and said in a forlorn voice, 'Will you listen to *my* troubles?' and she would make room for him on the settee, or the floor, wherever she was sitting and say, 'You tell me everything.' But he never said a word and would just get up and wander away again.

Then, at about half-past one, he came up again and said, 'I don't think I'll take you to any more parties. I think I'll keep you locked up in a tower.'

'Good idea,' said one man. 'Which tower?'

'Any old tower, where you can keep a beautiful girl all to yourself.'

'Thass greedy,' said Socks, and laid his head on Sarah's shoulder. 'I wanna take care of you. I'm a good take-carer of people, aren't I, Warren old boy?'

Warren nodded then he began to laugh and couldn't stop laughing and that was when Sarah began to cry and said she wanted to go home. Then Butch appeared and took charge. He would take Sarah and Warren home.

In the doorway Warren stopped to call, 'Thanks for a spiffing party, you must all come to – to mine on my next leave,' and they said that would be whacko or wizard.

Sarah was aware of Butch seating her in the back of a car with Warren and of Warren putting an arm around her and saying, 'Sorry, Sarah, about messing things up,' and she leaned against him and closed her eyes.

'You didn't. It was lovely, I shall always remember it. It was sort of different, wasn't it? I've never, *ever*, *ever*, been to a party quite like it before.'

Warren kissed the top of her head. 'We have a few more lined up, and I'll take you to them – all of them!'

After that Sarah remembered no more until Butch was shaking her and saying, 'You're home, Sarah. Warren will walk you to your front door.' To Warren he gave instructions. 'Now remember to say you've brought Sarah home safe and sound. Come along, Sarah, walk straight.'

When the front door opened Warren repeated what he

had been told and added, 'I'll see you tomorrow, Mr Torent, sir.'

'Yes, Warren, good night and thank you.'

Jonathan put his arm around Sarah and said softly, 'I think you had better go straight up to bed, pet. Don't make a noise, don't want to wake your mother, do we?'

'No.' Sarah put her finger to her lips.

She remembered going up the stairs, but no more after that.

It was daylight when she awoke and saw by her bedside clock it was after ten o'clock. For a moment she panicked, thinking she had overslept and should be at work, then she remembered the party and the fact that she was on late-shift and she lay back again. The party . . . *what* a party. She was surprised she did not have a hangover. Had her father realised she was drunk? Warren seemed to have behaved all right when he brought her to the door . . . thanks to Butch.

She thought of all the dancing, all the people she had met, the fuss the men had made of her. Although Sarah suffered no headache her mouth was dry and she had made up her mind to get dressed and make a cup of tea when Maggie brought one up.

'I was bringing your ma one and thought you might be glad of one too.' Her eyes twinkled. 'I hear, from all accounts, that it was a good party. Your ma will want to hear all about it, so go and have your tea with her. She had a migraine last night but she's over it now. She's anxious to hear how you got on.'

Sarah jumped out of bed and pulled on a dressing gown, wondering if her father had said anything about the state she had come home in. If he had, her mother showed no signs of it. She patted the bed, smiling. 'Come along, tell me all about the party.'

Sarah talked her mother to death, about the house, about the food and the people, but played down the fact that champagne had been flowing and omitted Warren's proposal of marriage.

It was not until later that Sarah had a chance of getting

down to some serious thinking and then she found herself comparing Warren with Joe.

Jenny had once said about Joe that he had an animal attraction and that was how Sarah saw him. There was no love-play as far as Joe was concerned. It was all rush, get it over with and rarin' to go again. Warren, she felt, would be more of a gentleman. There *would* be love-play with him, she was sure. He could keep a rein on his feelings. He had done so last night.

And yet, would she have wanted Joe to be different? She had enjoyed every minute they had been together. She loved him, of course she did, otherwise she would not have done what she had, would not have deceived her parents and his. Oh, Joe, she wailed inwardly, I'm such a turncoat. Why should I even consider such a thing as having Warren Hendrix make love to me, and yet I did, I really did.

The thought of Warren caressing her had Sarah's blood on fire. Was this a normal thing – did every woman feel like this? Did her mother have these feelings towards the man she had met at the sanatorium in Scotland? Had they made love? Sarah did not want to think of her mother doing such a thing, in spite of her own actions. *She* was young, nature made her blood run hot. Her mother was married, had children. A mother did *not* do that sort of thing. And yet Sarah could understand her having longings for another man apart from Jonathan, just as she had with Joe and Warren. Why couldn't these urgent feelings wait until the moment a man and woman were married? And yet, what a lot would be lost. Those three days she had spent with Joe had been utter heaven. Of course it was Joe she loved. What she had felt for Warren was just a sensuality. Men had made a fuss of her, made her feel important, so had Warren by asking her to marry him. Her mother, if she knew this, would consider it an honour for her daughter to be married into the Bentham family, even though Warren was a stepson.

Jenny, who was on the same shift as Sarah, called to walk with her to the depot. She had not shown much interest when Sarah told her about the party invitation, nor did she when Sarah mentioned it as they left the house; but as soon

260

as Sarah told her about Warren's proposal Jenny became nasty.

'You know what that's leading up to, don't you? The next thing you know, you'll find yourself in the same position that I was in. Toffs like Warren Hendrix don't marry girls like us, it's just a tale to get you to give in to him.'

Sarah said quietly, 'Don't, Jenny. Don't get into the habit of condemning every man because of what happened to you. Warren has already asked me to marry him, but I've said no. And there's been nothing more than a kiss between us. I don't want to get married, I want to have a business, as you know. And I will have one, after the war.'

'I wanted a business, didn't I?' There was a forlorn note in Jenny's voice. 'You were going to be my partner. What happened?'

'War,' said Sarah. 'War going on and on. It's taken so much out of people, young as well as the older ones.'

Jenny touched her arm and now there were tears in her eyes. 'I didn't mean it when I said I didn't want to get married and have kids. I do, but not to Roy. The right man hasn't come along – at least, he did, as far as I was concerned, but he didn't want *me*. Joe.'

Sarah's heart began an uncomfortable beating. She was trying to think up something to say when Jenny went on, 'It's you he likes, isn't it? I've seen the way he looks at you. How do you feel about him?'

'I – like him, but I am not thinking about going steady with anyone, it's useless. I want to go into business and nothing will stop me. Jenny, look, why don't you make plans to go into the jewellery business again, you were so keen. Don't let anyone or anything put you off. It helps to have a goal in life, it's something to look forward to.'

A bitter look came over Jenny's face. 'At our age we should be thinking of enjoying ourselves, dating men, having fun, going to parties and hoping to meet a man we could settle down with. We'll become a nation of spinsters . . . or unmarried mothers. Betty Sherriff's had a baby, did you know? She's gone to live with her grandmother. What sort of life will she have with that old miserable skinflint? I don't

261

know who got her into trouble, she's not telling. Who would have thought that *any* bloke would want to make love to her, she's no oil painting.'

'Poor Betty,' Sarah said.

'Yes, and you could have been saying it about me. Do you know what, Sarah, I think I *will* start thinking about going back into business. I wonder if I could get a line to sell, like we did when we were in munitions. I'll think about it. Just forget what I said about Warren Hendrix. See you later – don't work too hard!'

Usually when the girls were on the late-shift together Jenny stayed overnight at Sarah's house, but this time before they parted she said, 'I'm going straight home tonight. I think Dad misses having me around when I stay, because it means I don't see him for a few days. If I hurry I'll catch the last train. I'll run on, see you tomorrow.'

Sarah thought that her cousin had either changed and was very concerned about Fred, or that she was up to something, probably meeting someone at the station. There had been a look of excitement about her cousin. It could be a man she had met on the trams.

Jonathan had cocoa and a snack waiting for the two girls when Sarah came home and when she explained that Jenny had decided to go back to be with her father he said, 'I know how she feels, know how Fred feels about Jenny. So, give me your coat, Sarah, and sit by the fire and tell me about the party last night.'

'I wasn't drunk, Poppa. I did have some champagne, but I was more merry then anything, and very sleepy. Did Warren call and see you this morning?'

'Yes he did.' Jonathan smiled. 'He looked a little rough, but he did bring you home safely and that was the important thing.' He eyed Sarah, a thoughtful look in his eyes. 'He tells me that he asked you to marry him. He also told me that you had refused him. I think that was wise, Sarah. You're too young to settle down and the times are so uncertain.'

Sarah said gently, 'Poppa, if I had really been in love with him, I would have begged you to let me marry him . . .'

21

At the first party Sarah had gone to with Warren the gaiety
had been fresh and spontaneous, but at the second, given
by Titania, it was forced. Word had arrived that day that
two of the men, a young Lieutenant and Hats, who was a
pilot, had been killed. 'We must enjoy ourselves,' was the
cry. 'Jimmy and Hats would have wanted it that way!' but
despite the drinks and dancing to a phonograph, Sarah
could not get in the right mood. She found herself thinking
of Joe, fighting, while she was here doing her best to have
a good time and in the company of another man. Soon
Warren himself would be going back to the Front.

They did not go to another party because by then Socks
and his friend Toecap had been killed. Warren's pleas that
one must not dwell on this kind of thing brought a response
from Sarah that it would be like dancing at a funeral.

'I wouldn't enjoy it, Warren, I couldn't.'

They decided to go to the cinema instead. The Pathè
News showed the slaughter of the soldiers on the battle-
fields, on both sides. At one time it had been all glory for
the British and defeat of the enemy, but people were sick
of being fed lies and now demanded the truth. Everywhere
there were changes. The troops no longer sang as they
marched to the station to be packed off to France. There
was talk of getting brass bands to accompany them, but
nothing came of it. After sitting through the news Sarah
told Warren she wanted to go. He did not try to persuade
her to stay.

Outside he said quietly, 'We can't get away from it, can
we?'

They had gone to the first house at the cinema and he
went on, 'The night is still young, Sarah, and my parents
are out for the evening. Would you like to come back to

Bentham House? We can sit and talk.' She agreed, but hoped that Warren would not become amorous in any way.

He didn't, not at first. They sat in front of the drawing room fire and drank coffee that Warren had made. Sarah made an effort to pull herself together and teased him. 'Nice to know you are domesticated.'

He smiled wrily. 'I'm afraid that is as far as it goes. But would you want it any other way? You surely wouldn't want a namby-pamby husband who did all the housework and the shopping and –' He ran a finger down her nose. 'Speaking of husbands – have you given any more thought to what I asked you?'

Sarah gave a quick nod. 'Yes, I have, Warren, and I just don't want to get married now. I should like to think we can remain friends but I will understand if you don't want to see me again.'

'Of course I will want to see you.' He laughed softly. 'Don't think you are going to get rid of me as easily as that.' He slipped an arm around her waist and Sarah did not draw away. 'I always imagined myself remaining a bachelor until I was thirty or so, then perhaps deciding it was time to settle down. I didn't bargain for falling in love with a lovely young girl who would reject me out of hand. It has not done much for my ego.'

'I should hope not! I thought you very arrogant when we first met. Oh, you were really on your high horse.'

He tucked her hair behind her ear and said softly, 'And now you've found out what a warm-hearted, loving and kind person I am.' He ran his lips over her cheek, cupped her face between his palms, then his mouth covered hers . . . and Sarah felt pulses beating. She made to pull away but his arms tightened around her. 'Sarah, Sarah, let me love you, just once, that's all I ask. I ache for you.'

Although there was not the wildness in her she had known with Joe she was very much aware of her own need as well as Warren's, but it was wrong, so wrong. She could not go about letting every man love her who wanted to. But then it was not every man, it was only Joe and now

Warren . . . She responded to the kiss and Warren began to undo the buttons on the bodice of her dress.

It was when he had cupped her bared breast that she heard the voice of a woman she had met in munitions: 'It's all right if you stick to one bloke, love, but if you let another, then it will be a third and a fourth and before you know where you are you're a whore.'

Sarah drew away hastily and began to button up her blouse.

'Sarah, you can't do this,' Warren said in an anguished voice. 'You can't leave me in this state.'

'I can,' she said in a shaky voice. 'Before you leave *me* in a different kind of state.'

'I won't, I promise, I'll be careful.'

'I know how you feel, Warren, know how *I* feel, but it just can't be. I'm sorry.'

He sighed. 'If you had just given me a little more time you would have wanted me as much as I want you.'

Sarah's fingers fumbled over the last button. 'The difference between a man and a woman is that a man doesn't have anything to worry about afterwards, but a woman does. And probably suffers for the rest of her life.'

'But Sarah, if anything had happened, which it wouldn't have done, you know I would have married you.'

'You couldn't if you were –' She stopped abruptly and got up.

Warren finished the sentence. 'Killed?' He held out a hand and when Sarah took it he drew her down on to the settee again. 'Don't worry, I too have come to my senses. Let's just talk.'

The talk was rewarding in many ways. Warren spoke about his life and that of his mother and stepfather, and how he had learned not to rely too much on people, not to put them into categories, such as good and bad, because there were so many facets to a person's character. As they talked Sarah thought it was a discussion her father would have enjoyed. It was a talk she could not imagine having with Joe.

Joe and Warren . . . Joe and Warren . . . their names

265

went over and over in Sarah's mind that night when she was in bed, as she tried to balance the good and the bad points of both. There would always be that toughness with Joe, that earthiness, yet she had revelled in it during their love-making. But a woman also needed a man to be tender, to be caring. Warren had been so gentle after their first small onslaught. He had spoken loving words, apologised for the way he had behaved, and assured her he would never try to seduce her like that again.

Then she thought – but if you really love someone, you would not be weighing up their good and bad points.

She had promised Warren she would spend as much time as possible with him during his leave, but the next morning he called to say he had to go and visit an aunt in Leeds who was ill, and that afterwards he would have to join his unit.

Sarah felt emotional as they parted and thought then that she could love Warren, but in a different way from Joe.

At home, as 1918 crept onwards, food became more scarce, at least for the working people – the wealthy could still live well. In top-flight places like the Ritz in London there was no shortage of luxury; at a traditional Lord Mayor's Banquet it was reported there was such a demand for roast beef that the carvers were kept busy all night, cutting the huge barons of beef into slices. Ordinary restaurants, meanwhile, were ordered to have meatless and potato-less days.

Posters were put up everywhere. *Save Your Food, Save Your Country*; *England's Dread Enemy, Not Wilhelm, But Waste* . . . It was forbidden to throw rice at weddings, to use icing sugar or to mix starch for shirts.

If word got around that a certain shop was awaiting a new stock of tea, within ten minutes there would be hundreds of people queueing. It was said that in London more than a thousand people could be in a queue, and yet very often, the news of certain goods arriving turned out to be only unfounded rumour.

There was also an acute shortage of fuel. Men, women and children queued at railway coal sidings with bags, sacks, prams or wheelbarrows, while others beachcombed along the shores and river banks.

Then food rationing was introduced and it ended the queues. If you registered with your butcher and your grocer you could have fifteen ounces of meat a week per person, five ounces of bacon and four ounces of butter or margarine.

In July 1918, ration cards were withdrawn and replaced by ration books with coupons for all rationed food. Only tea, cheese and bread remained unrestricted, but this did not mean they were readily available. You had to depend on your regular shopkeeper allowing you some of these items.

The battlefront news was far from good. Now that the Germans had concluded peace negotiations with the Russians they had more troops to bring to France for a major offensive. The Allied armies were forced to retreat, losing all their hard-won ground, with all its tragic loss of life.

Then the German armies threatened Paris and even the Channel ports. The British Commander-in-Chief, Haig, issued an order: *'With our backs to the wall and believing in the justice of our cause, each one of us must fight on to the end.'*

People were bitter. 'Fighting to the end' could mean sacrificing husbands, fathers, sons or sweethearts, and yet not one person, deep down, wanted it any other way. The enemy *had* to be beaten.

More and more casualties arrived at Charing Cross station. And greater numbers of men were despatched to France to fill the gaps.

A new song, intended to cheer the soldiers, conveyed a melancholy:

> *Goodbye-ee! Don't sigh-ee!*
> *Wipe the tear, baby dear,*
> *From your eye-ee.*
> *Though it's hard to part I know,*
> *I'll be tickled to death to go,*
> *Don't sigh-ee! Don't cry-ee!*
> *There's a silver lining in the sky-ee!*

Bon soir old thing! Cheerio chin-chin!
Napoo! Toodle-oo! Goodbye-ee!

When invasion seemed imminent, officials formed a militia, a 'home guard', drawn from men up to the age of sixty years old. This only brought the comment that things had to be drastic to enlist grandfathers!

Fear of invasion brought hysteria to many places and there were demands for all aliens to be interned. Isabelle was ill with nerves, something she had managed to control since her six months in the sanatorium. 'The people will want all the aliens shot!' was her anguished cry. Did Jonathan realise *now* what he was responsible for, by not having been naturalised? Although Jonathan pointed out that many naturalised men had lost their sons she ignored him.

It was perhaps the huge counter-offensive now launched by the Allied Armies, that helped to reduce public hysteria. Every small victory was a reason for celebration, in spite of the fact that these small triumphs were costly in lives and money. The army was still short of men. There was a campaign by the newspapers to worm out the fit from 'funk-holes' in government and industry. Munition workers were reviewed and a hundred and four thousand of them were released for the services. Even the reluctant miners' unions released over fifty thousand young men from the pits. Military police rounded up men attending football matches, theatres and music halls, ordering them to produce evidence of exemption.

The age of conscription had been raised to fifty-one, but none of these men were sent to the Front.

Large-scale efforts were made to raise desperately-needed money. The Government sold war bonds, and war savings certificates, offering a generous five per cent on money invested.

Individual cities could help to buy a submarine, aircraft or a warship. If a city raised enough money it could have its name on a tank, to be proudly displayed at the Front.

A notice was issued that it took four months to build a warship and four minutes to sink it.

Schoolchildren were encouraged to save; they were also asked to collect rags, metal – anything that would help the war effort. Victor and Eric particularly enjoyed this. They were avid collectors and were hardly ever in the house.

Towns and cities began to look tatty, and there was a sombreness among the people. Many, of course, were in mourning and the shops stocked little else but black and grey material.

Travel was difficult and much more expensive. Rail fares had gone up by fifty per cent. In a number of districts, railway lines had been pulled up and sent to France to help get supplies to the troops. The petrol shortage affected public transport, buses and taxis, and in consequence those that did run were full to overflowing, so were the trams, in the rush hours.

Sarah, describing the journeys to her father said, 'They're becoming a daily nightmare. Men have lost all courtesy – they use their strength to shove and punch their way on and women get their umbrellas broken, hats knocked off and suffer bruised shins, as well as other knocks.'

'But this shouldn't be allowed, Sarah!' Jonathan protested. 'You shouldn't have to cope with this sort of behaviour.'

'Oh, I cope,' she said, '*with* some help from the passengers.' Sarah smiled to herself at this point, but did not explain exactly what happened. On every journey during the rush hours people were not only packed like sardines inside the tram and on top, but they were jammed on the stairs and on the platform; and the tram even travelled with men hanging onto the outside of the platform. It was impossible even to attempt to get upstairs to take fares but she did her best not to let anyone off the tram without paying.

This, at times, failed, until she found herself with a number of helpers – black-shawled and cloth-capped women who made a half-circle and brandished sticks. One woman shouted, 'Money is needed everywhere to fight this war and I ain't gonna have my man and my lads fighting for you bleedin' lot. So pay up or else!'

269

As all were regulars, it came about in time that everyone had their fare ready and paid up meekly. Some of the vicious shoving stopped, too, when the offenders were warned off by Sarah's 'brigade'.

Despite this, the strain began to tell on Sarah. She had no appetite and was losing quite a lot of weight. Isabelle, after complaining one evening that Sarah looked like a ghost, went to the depot, asked for the manager and demanded that her daughter be given some time off.

The manager said, 'Sorry, Mrs Torent, we haven't got anyone to replace Sarah, and she is one of our best conductresses.'

'You would have to replace her if she dropped dead,' Isabelle retorted, 'and that is what *will* happen if she doesn't get some leave. Have you looked at her recently? She's skin and bone, and falls asleep over a meal she doesn't even have the strength to eat. Now make your mind up. She either gets leave or I take her off the job, which I know she doesn't want to do. The trouble is, she's too conscientious.'

A bewildered Sarah came home off the late-shift that evening and said, 'I have two weeks' leave, I can't believe it. I didn't want to take it but the manager insisted.' She fell asleep over the cup of tea that Isabelle had poured.

She slept for most of the next three days then announced she was ready to go back to work. 'Oh, no, you're not,' Isabelle said. 'You and Aunt Lucy and I are going to London for a few days. We're getting a ride in Mr Peterson's van. Your father has arranged it all. Mary is so excited at the thought of seeing us all. It's months since we've all been together.'

Isabelle then went on to explain that Maggie would look after Jonathan and Victor, and Jenny, who was quite happy to stay in Tynemouth, would be taking care of Fred and Eric.

Jonathan said to Sarah, 'Give my warmest regards to Mr Jacobs when you see him. And do try to rest, pet. You must come back looking a lot better than you do now, otherwise there will be no more working on the trams.'

'And you take care, Poppa. I'll sit and talk to Mr Jacobs

270

and I know I shall come back with a lot more knowledge of clocks.'

The journey was not the most comfortable one they had ever made but as Lucy said, it helped to know they had no train fares to pay, just a gift of money to Mr Peterson for his kindness. He received a petrol allowance for his business.

Although Mary was still living with Bill Rhodes, who was working at Army HQ, they did not see him during the first two days. Sarah thought he was being discreet and allowing the women to have plenty of time for talking. Which they did: the first day, they talked non-stop, catching up on all the news. Sarah learned that her aunt had not seen or heard anything from Roger since June 1916, when he had been sentenced to a year's imprisonment. When she spoke of him there was a rather forlorn note in her voice.

The next morning, Sarah announced that she wanted to go and see Mr Jacobs. 'Don't worry, Mother,' she said. 'I won't be rushing around anywhere.'

Mr Jacobs' pleasure at seeing her brought a lump to Sarah's throat. 'Such a surprise,' he said, taking her hands in his. 'A wonderful surprise. Come and sit down, my dear, and tell me all you have been doing. But first, let me make you a cup of tea.' He chatted happily as he filled the small tin kettle and put it on the primus stove. 'I so enjoy your letters! Oh, that Mrs Baker and her clock on the tram . . . I have so many things to tell you myself, and something special to show you. I bought it a week ago. But there, I am talking too much, far too much. You must tell me about your family and what you are doing. You look very thin, dear Sarah, I think you must have been working too hard.'

Sarah told her old friend of the little happenings in her life. He kept nodding and smiling when she told him about the young men at the party, but looked sad when she mentioned those who had been killed. He put his palms to his cheeks and shook his head. 'So many young men lost, it's a tragedy.'

After they had drunk a second cup of tea each, he took her into the back section of the shop and whipped a cover

271

from a bulky object, like a magician doing a disappearing act. Then he looked at her to see her expression.

'A water clock!' she exclaimed. 'But what a size!' She walked around the large stone bowl then stopped to examine the inside, which had engravings of Egyptian figures in between the lines which indicated the hours. Sarah looked up. 'But surely it would take the water more than an hour to run out with the circumference being so large.'

'No.' Mr Jacobs pointed to a number of holes that were not easily discernible because they were incorporated into the pattern of the carved stone.

They talked about water clocks and about Egypt, which Mr Jacobs had visited several times, then Sarah told him about wanting to start a clock and watch business. He looked at her for a long time before replying.

'I know of only two women who are in this business, Sarah, but they are people whose families were clock-makers and they learned the art from childhood. They are both elderly ladies now. It will take years of experience to know what to buy – and who will you deal with? The men who collect clocks and watches as a hobby also have years of experience behind them, and I'm not sure that they would take kindly to dealing with a young girl. You would have to offer them something unusual, something *most* unusual, for them to be interested.'

Sarah gave a disappointed 'Oh,' and waited.

'Your father has a lot of experience, Sarah; he also seems to be a most interesting man. Other men would enjoy talking to him, but a girl on her own –' Mr Jacobs' shoulders raised in an expressive shrug.

Sarah said she wouldn't mind going into business with her father but she would like to do the transactions herself.

'It's a challenge, Mr Jacobs,' she said earnestly. 'Women are being accepted into commerce much more now. The war has changed everything.'

'It has,' he said grimly. 'But there are some men who, I feel, will never want to deal with a woman. Please don't think that I am pressing you to abandon your idea, Sarah, but you need to be warned of several things. If we win the

272

war there will be jubilation and trade will boom – for a time. Men who made money out of the war will want to invest, and believe me they will run into thousands. They will also want to spend, have holidays abroad after the grim, weary years of conflict. There are those who have been in reserved occupations and whose wives also worked - they were able to save and will also want holidays. It will be spend, spend, spend. But then will come the aftermath, a slump. It comes in time after every war. What then, Sarah? You might have a collection that could be useless, clocks that could become what you call . . . white elephants?'

Sarah was silent for a while then she said, 'I think you are right in all you say, and I have often heard my father say the same. However, if I waited for a depression to be over and trade to pick up again I could be middle-aged, and then I wouldn't be wanting to buy and sell clocks.'

Mr Jacobs threw up his hands and chuckled. 'I knew I was wasting my time. Of course you will buy timepieces and I hope you will find customers for them.'

They moved into another room and there Sarah saw several clocks arranged on a long table. Mr Jacobs jokingly referred to them as his 'active acquisitions'.

They were all brass, all ornate and all, she was told, had moving figures or animals and birds which appeared on the stroke of the hour. As Mr Jacobs set them all to strike at different intervals, Sarah had time to observe the scene of each one . . . and was completely captivated.

In the first, three robed men came out of doors, took turns to strike a bell, then went back in again and the doors closed. Following this a window above opened and a woman leaned out and with a long stick hit the bell. When she withdrew, three small boys banging drums appeared on a platform under the dome. This whole procedure was repeated twice and then the clock next to it began to strike.

On the first stroke a bird spread its wings and warbled a song; while it was warbling two shepherds on either side began to play pipes. On this clock numerous figures appeared, each one playing an instrument of some kind.

On the third clock, while a dog balanced a ball on its

head and did a dance, metal roses began to unfold their petals. The petals on the inside were enamelled in various shades of pink. Sarah laughed at the dog because it looked so happy.

The dial of the fourth clock showed a stormy sea scene. At the first stroke a sailing ship came into view with sailors seen to be lowering the sails. The ship rose to the crest of the waves then dropped into the troughs and in the background were the sounds of the storm. This clock really fascinated Sarah and she said to Mr Jacobs, 'I like this one the best – the storm seems so real.'

'It was made by a craftsman, Sarah, but then, of course, they all were. I must show you now a very beautiful watch I've just bought. It was made by a Dutchman in the seventeen hundreds.'

The watch was silver, the case repoussé work showing a biblical scene. Sarah had seen her father doing this work, beating the metal into relief from the reverse side, but he had never been successful with the figures he wanted to portray.

'It's beautiful,' she said admiringly. 'There are so many exquisite watches, they must have taken months and months to make.'

'Some took years,' Mr Jacobs assured her.

'Were many watches made all those years ago?'

'Thousands.' When Sarah looked up surprised he smiled. 'Many thousands. The Swiss trade developed from one man who took a watch from England home with him. He spent a year in creating the requisite tools for making a watch, and then another six months to make his first one. His sons learned the trade from him and from then on more and more people turned to watch-making. The number of Swiss watches imported from Switzerland to this country in 1858 was over three hundred thousand.'

Sarah stared at him. 'I can hardly believe it. It must have done a great deal of harm to the English trade.'

'It did because the Swiss watches were cheaper, but at that time the quality was not so good. Our American cousins still preferred English watches.'

Mr Jacobs went on to tell her about the smallest watch ever made: it measured about half an inch in diameter. Sarah's head spun with all the wonderful things she had to write home about.

22

Sarah had gained so much new knowledge from Mr Jacobs that she was itching to start her own business. Her mind was full of the names of famous clock-makers, of dates, of different methods and the improvements that had been made over the years. On her last visit, Isabelle had come with her and was as charmed by Mr Jacobs as he was with her.

Before they left, Isabelle invited the old man to come and stay with them if he was ever up North and he said he would be delighted to accept. Isabelle said later, 'Mr Jacobs reminds me of your father, Sarah, with his courtesy and his general philosophy.'

Sarah was looking forward to getting home to talk to her father and to see Jenny, but Isabelle warned her she was not to talk 'clocks' the moment they got home, as there was other news that Victor and Jonathan would want to hear.

They were late arriving on the Saturday evening, and it was not until Sunday morning that Jenny came over with her family and the two girls had the chance of a talk.

'So,' Jenny said, 'how was London, meet anyone interesting?' Before Sarah could reply she went on, 'I've met a lovely chap, a Naval Lieutenant, home-based. His name's Andy, he – ' Jenny paused. 'Who's that peering in at the window?'

Sarah looked up. 'It's Maggie. That's funny – she isn't expected today. Why isn't she coming in?' Maggie was frantically beckoning her and Sarah went to the front door.

The gypsy-woman came hurrying up to her. *'Where are the boys?'*

The urgency in Maggie's voice had Sarah frightened. 'They're out. I should imagine they've gone to the park, but why?'

Then there was the sound of running feet and a woman shouting, 'There's been as accident! Two boys –'

A man who had followed her said, 'Is this the right house? I'm afraid both boys are badly hurt. Are your parents there?'

By this time Isabelle and Lucy had come running out. The man explained, 'It was a runaway horse, missus. Your lads tried to stop it and got knocked down. They've been taken off to the Infirmary.'

The colour drained from Isabelle's face, and Lucy put an arm around her. 'One of the boys is mine,' she stammered. 'How badly hurt are they?'

'One's had his hand crushed and the other his foot.'

A cold chill crept over Sarah. A crushed hand. Victor?

The man said, 'I saw it all. I was in my car, it's up the street. I'll fetch it and take you to the Infirmary.'

Isabelle, now calm said, 'We would be deeply grateful, my husband and brother-in-law are visiting a friend in the next street: could we collect them on the way?'

Maggie offered, 'I'll stay here with the girls, Mrs T.'

Sarah felt she was in a nightmare. One minute she and Jenny had been chatting, her mother and aunt had been in the kitchen preparing the dinner and laughing over something and now . . .

People were coming out of their houses in Berkeley Avenue, wanting to know what was wrong. Maggie dealt with them all: could they come later, as the girls were still shocked. She got Sarah and Jenny inside, made them sit down and put on the kettle.

Sarah said, 'Tell us, Maggie, how did you know that something was going to happen?'

'I had a vision: I saw the boys grab the reins of a horse pulling a dray and I knew they were going to be hurt. I ran all the way here, but I think I knew I would be too late.

Jenny asked in a shaky voice which boy had the crushed hand, and which the crushed foot, but Maggie said, 'Only God knows that.'

They got the full story two hours later when Jonathan and Fred returned, not to stay, just to tell them what had happened. Some small children had been in the path of the runaway horse and would have surely been killed had the older boys not intervened. Victor seized the reins on one side and Eric the other. Victor had his hand crushed and Eric, his foot.

'The surgeons will be operating on the boys shortly,' Jonathan said. 'We're going back to be with your mothers, but will let you know the result as soon as we can.' The girls wept in their fathers' arms then the men left. After that every minute dragged.

Sarah was suddenly aware of music coming from somewhere, a piano being played. It was the Telfers across the road. They had a daughter-in-law who sometimes played their piano when she came with her husband on a Sunday. The tune was a Mazurka, by Chopin. Sarah suddenly went cold. It was the one she had associated with her grandmother's love affair – a happy, light tune, as she ran to meet her lover. But then it had ended in tragedy . . . her father had brought the lid of the piano crashing down on to her fingers . . . breaking them. Sarah's blood ran cold. Was history repeating itself? Her grandmother unable to play her beloved music any more . . . Victor's fingers crushed. Oh, God. She looked up. 'Our grandmother should be told.' Maggie suggested they wait for further news and this was agreed.

It was midnight when Jonathan and Fred finally reappeared. They both looked pale and drained. Jonathan said, 'We wanted to wait until both boys came out of the operating room. They've managed to save Eric's foot, thank God. He'll limp, but he will be able to walk again.'

'And Victor?' Sarah looked at her father with a desperate appeal in her eyes for good news.

'He won't ever be able to play again, Sarah, but he will be able to use his hand – in a limited way.'

Sarah felt her throat tighten as she saw the look of desolation in Fred's eyes. This mutilation of his son was a painful blow. He said to Jenny, 'Your mother and your Aunt Isabelle wanted to be there when the boys come out of the anaesthetic, in case they ask for them.'

'How are Mother and Aunt Isabelle coping?' Jenny asked him.

'Amazingly well. I think that the Lord made women better equipped to cope with things like this. But I must say I take my hat off to the surgeons who fought for hours to get the blood flowing through Eric's foot, and to repair Victor's hand. Although war is a terrible thing a lot of valuable knowledge has been gained through the injuries that men like myself have suffered.'

Maggie, who had made tea, said piously, 'God works in mysterious ways. Drink your tea, everyone, then I think it would be sensible if you all went to bed and got some sleep. I'll stay on here till things have settled.' They all said they preferred to wait up with her until Isabelle and Lucy returned.

Dawn was breaking when they arrived. One of the doctors, who was coming off-duty, had driven them home. Although both women looked exhausted there was a calm acceptance in their bearing that allayed Sarah's fears that her mother might collapse with all the worry. One day, Isabelle had dreamed, Victor would be a famous concert pianist.

Afterwards Sarah came to think of the following day as one of the worst in her whole life. Isabelle and Lucy, looking like ghosts, dealt with a reporter from the local newspaper and made tea for people who called – and it seemed that they came from every street. Then Sarah and Jenny had to leave for work without knowing how the boys were. The adults were going to the hospital later. At the depot she was greeted with commiserations on all sides. How on earth did news travel so fast and cover such a wide area? It was the women passengers who had lost sons in the war and who cried as they talked about the accident that upset Sarah the most, and she felt utterly wretched as she came off-duty with Jenny. When they were walking towards the gates they saw their fathers waiting for them. They stopped and Sarah gripped Jenny's hand.

The men came forward. 'It's all right, girls,' Jonathan said, 'It's not bad news. Both your mothers suggested we met you, thinking that you'd be wanting to know how Victor and Eric are. They are out of danger and although sedated are able to talk. They are really much better than had been anticipated, thank God.'

Fred added:'We've been to see the manager and he's letting you both have the afternoon off work tomorrow so you can go to the Infirmary and visit the boys.'

It was not until they were nearly home that Jonathan told Sarah privately that Victor had asked to see her. It had seemed important to him. When Sarah asked her father why especially her, he shook his head.

'I have no idea, Sarah, except that he did say you would understand. He'll explain tomorrow no doubt.'

When Sarah walked with Jenny into the ward the following afternoon and saw both Victor and Eric anxiously eyeing the people coming in, she felt tearful, and when she reached the beds saw with a shock that her brother and Eric were no longer children, but on the verge of manhood.

She kissed each boy in turn, told Eric she would have a word with him in a few minutes, then drew a chair closer to Victor's bed. 'Well, and here's a fine how-do-ye-do and no mistake!' Victor gave a wan smile, knowing it was one of Maggie's favourite expressions when anything out of the ordinary happened. Then his smile faded.

'I'm glad you came, Sis.' He reached out his right hand and touched her arm and Sarah had to swallow hard as she noticed the long slender fingers compared with the bulkily bandaged left hand.

'I wanted to come before, Victor, but Mother thought it would be better to wait until you were – well, over the operation.'

'I needed to talk to you because I felt you would be the only one who would understand what I have to tell you. I love my music, as you know, but I was always worried that one day I would be expected to play in front of a big audience, that is, if I ever had become a concert pianist. Mother wanted it so much, and so did Grandma, perhaps Grandma even more than Mother. Now I won't ever have to do it and I'm glad. I want you to tell them, to make them understand.'

His gaze went to his bandaged hand and after a moment's silence he said, 'It hurts that I won't ever be able to play properly again, but I can still use my right hand, and perhaps use my left a little bit some time in the future.'

'You can compose,' she said earnestly, 'you've always been making up little pieces of your own. You can write down the music.'

'Yes, I suppose so.'

Sarah realised by the flatness of his tone that it was too soon to suggest this. 'I mean in the future,' she said. 'At the moment you have to concentrate on getting well.'

Victor asked Sarah about her visit to London and she told him all the amusing little things she could remember, pleased to watch him giggle, and repeating them to Eric when she and Jenny changed places. As she sat, looking from her dark-haired, good-looking brother to her fair-haired, equally attractive cousin, she could not help but wonder what the future held for each boy.

When they got up to leave Victor took Sarah's hand and made her promise again to tell their mother and their grandmother how he felt about his music. He begged her please to come again.

Sarah promised, but wished she did not have the task of telling her grandmother, because she guessed it would take something away from the sour old woman's life. Henrietta had always counted on Victor's success to compensate for her own unfulfilled life.

Sarah and Jenny kept looking back and waving as they moved slowly with the other visitors towards the exit. Sarah felt depressed as she saw how forlorn the two boys were. They had bravely done their best to accept the tragedy but they were still so young and vulnerable that she wanted to cry.

Jenny was emotional, too. After they had given a final wave to their brothers, she said, 'Bravery isn't just doing exceptional deeds, is it? It's trying to accept a situation that's

281

devastated a person. Our brothers are brave. Pray heaven they'll soon be over the worst.'

Sarah said yes, but wondered what the worst would entail.

Isabelle refused to believe that Victor had never really wanted to be a concert pianist. She said it was his way of trying to lessen the blow for them. Henrietta was of the same opinion and in fact accused Sarah of enlarging on the story. Sarah did not pursue it. Perhaps in time Victor might be able to convince them of the way he felt. The important thing now was to get the boys on the road to recovery. And this turned out to be slow. The doctor said that both were suffering from severe shock to their nervous systems, and there could be depression to cope with.

It was when the boys were allowed home that the depression set in. Victor would start crying for no particular reason and it was Sarah he wanted with him at these times, which upset Isabelle. Lucy complained that Eric went into deep silences and refused to talk to anyone. Jonathan suggested that the boys might do better together. So it ended up with Victor going to Tynemouth for a week and Eric coming to Berkeley Avenue for the next week.

Mrs Curson, a regular correspondent of Isabelle's, heard how depressed the boys were and wrote to Isabelle, *'You and your sister Lucy must bring the boys here, your old house is waiting for you all. The fresh air will do them the world of good and you know how those lads love to be with the animals.'*

And so the four of them went off to Corbridge. The following weekend, after Jonathan and Fred had been there on a quick visit, they came back with a glowing report. Jonathan said, 'You wouldn't know the lads. There's Victor using a shovel, balancing it on the back of his left wrist, and Eric hobbling all over the place on his crutches. It's wonderful to see them.'

During the weekend that her father and uncle were away, Sarah made up her mind to start a clock and watch business with no more delay. She wrote to Mr Jacobs, letting him know of this. *'You said you started in a small way, Mr Jacobs; what advice could you offer?'*

A letter by return advised her to get some small cards

282

printed, saying that the firm of Torent were in the market to purchase antique clocks in good repair. She should deliver them to houses in the better-class districts.

'In these houses, Sarah, live different types of people. There are those who live beyond their income and are always looking around for something they can sell, but might not look at advertisements in newspapers. If, however, they found a card on their doormat . . .

'There are other people who have made money out of the war, from armaments or food – people who have risen from nothing, who have little culture but who like to own something as a talking point when entertaining, such as an unusual clock or watch. You will, I feel sure, get results from your advertising. Spread the word as far as you can. Buy as much as you can – buy, buy, buy and at first keep your prices down. When you have a stock all sorts of people will come in looking for bargains: give them just that, aim to sell at small profits and quick returns. When you get established you can increase your prices. And always remember, you must have a reasonable stock and keep changing it.

'Now then, Sarah, I know that you need money to buy and I am going to finance you. You can pay me back when you become successful. Talk it over with your father. I do not want any interest on the loan, my rewards will be in seeing your enthusiasm and your dedication come to fruition. My very best wishes to you and to your family . . .'

'Finance me?' Sarah gasped. 'Oh, I couldn't accept anything. I'd be worried to death in case I was unable to pay it back.'

'Mr Jacobs has faith in you, Sarah, or he would not have offered a loan. I suggest you take it,' Jonathan said surprisingly. 'You will be able to pay it back, I'm sure.'

Sarah did not have the same faith in herself, and when a registered package arrived containing three hundred pounds she stared at it aghast. 'It's too much, Poppa, it really is.'

Jonathan talked to her, explained that few people were given such a chance in life. It would be ungrateful, an insult to Mr Jacobs if she returned the money. He would feel his faith had been misplaced. Sarah said surely her mother would prevent her from accepting the loan and Jonathan suggested that for just this once it would be something between the two of them. 'No use worrying your mother, Sarah, she has enough problems to cope with. The time to tell her will be when you start selling.' It was then Sarah began to get excited. She was finally on her way!

They had some cards printed and gave a number of young boys a few coppers each to deliver them. They were mostly boys who had paper rounds and knew the districts.

Sarah was on late-shift the following week and spent the Monday morning and lunchtime at the shop. And she was glad she had. There was not exactly a rush of people wanting to have timepieces valued, but there were enough enquiries to keep her father and herself busy. Sarah was surprised that a proportion of the people who came in were from a working class background, and learned that servants who had picked up the cards remembered a relative having an unusual clock or watch.

Those from the higher bracket invariably asked that someone come to the house to value a timepiece, and the ones who did bring in a clock or a watch assumed a casual air. They were curious to know the value, it had been in the family for generations. 'An interesting piece, wouldn't you say?'

Some of them were very interesting indeed and Sarah had to control her excitement as she and her father conferred over values. The ones who did the most haggling were invariably those from the better-class districts. When they demanded more than Jonathan had offered he would say quietly, 'I regret, sir, that is all I can offer. Perhaps you would care to get a second opinion.' In every case the offer was accepted.

By the time trade had eased off Sarah was due to go in to work. She said, 'I don't want to go, Poppa, I want to study all we've bought. Do you realise we've paid out nearly two hundred pounds! It's staggering. Oh, I'm sure I'll give all the passengers the wrong tickets and the wrong change.'

'Now calm down,' Jonathan said, amused, 'or you'll be falling down the stairs. I'll meet you coming off-duty this evening and we'll pop back here, have a bite of supper, and then we can go over everything.'

And when she came off-duty it was the anticipation of studying all they had bought earlier that gave Sarah the strength to run to meet her father.

'Well, Poppa,' she greeted him eagerly. 'Are you satisfied with our purchases?'

'More than satisfied, Sarah, and so will you be when you see them again. There are some beautiful pieces. I bought another two clocks this afternoon and six watches.'

'You didn't!'

'Yes, and believe it or not, I've already had offers from collectors for several items. I told them they must come back tomorrow and that nothing had yet been catalogued.'

Sarah gave a gleeful laugh. 'Catalogued? Our clocks and watches! We really are in business, aren't we? How did these collectors know we had so much for sale? Probably had cards in their doors and were waiting to see what came in, I expect. Poppa, I must give up my job. I can't let you do all the work, which you would have to do if I stayed on at the depot. You have the repairs to do, after all. But I must say, I did notice that I was ignored if I offered a price. It was you they looked to for guidance.'

Jonathan, who had drawn Sarah's arm through his, patted her hand. 'Leave things as they are at the moment, pet. I can cope for the time being. There won't be another rush like the one we had this morning, believe me. Perhaps there'll be another few people coming in who have thought the matter over carefully before deciding to sell.'

Although Sarah knew this was sensible, she was itching to be at the shop day in and day out.

When they went in and she saw all the new stock she drew in a quick breath. It was unbelievable that the cards had produced so much. Jonathan had placed all the watches and smaller clocks on the counter and arranged the long case-clocks around the shop. 'Quite impressive, madam, wouldn't you say?'

Sarah let out a long sigh. 'Oh, yes, very impressive, Poppa, very impressive indeed.' She walked towards the two clocks that Jonathan had bought that afternoon then looked enquiringly at him.

He smiled. 'A seventeenth century night-clock that would once have had a candle to illuminate the dial. A little the worse for wear but certainly collectable. As for the other . . .'

A clock was balanced on the backs of two horses which were side by side. Sarah laughed. 'It's quite ridiculous really, horses carrying a clock between them and supposedly galloping along. But it's different. It will probably appeal to someone.'

For a while she concentrated on some of the watches, most of which had been sold by the owners without any seeming sense of loss. She gently fingered a pinwork case-watch, the name stemming from the method of driving in gold and silver pins on leather to form a pattern. A Turkish watch, with four cases, all gaudily coloured, was brought in by a girl whose father had gone to sea. She said it had been kept in a drawer since he brought it home and that her mother would rather have the money. A remembrance watch, where the name of a person replaced the numbers on the dial, bore the name 'Prudence Hart'. Sarah felt tempted to keep it. Who was Prudence Hart? The woman who brought it in said it had been given to her mother when she was a girl.

The next one Sarah picked up gave her a feeling of excitement. It was one of those she classed as a 'find'. It was what is known as a rock crystal watch, but whereas they were mostly made out of clear stone this was a smoky crystal, and considered to be rare. This much she had learned from Mr Jacobs. She held it out to Jonathan. 'How much do you think we shall get for this?'

He shook his head. 'I don't know, Sarah, I had never seen one before. And that is going to be our trouble. *You* told me that the smoky ones were rare and I keep wondering if we paid the woman enough. What is its real value?'

Sarah said she thought they had been fair; they would sell most of them at a small profit for quick sales and learn as theywere going along, like most antique dealers had done in the past.

Although the collectors did call the next day and bought, it was not before there had been some fierce bargaining. Unfortunately, nothing else moved and eventually they resorted to sending cards out again, in different districts, advertising unusual clocks for sale.

This tactic brought in one or two more customers but certainly not enough to make Sarah feel she was on her way. Jonathan said one evening, 'I know how you feel, Sarah. When I first opened my shop my one big worry was that I would be so busy selling clocks and watches that I would not have time for doing repairs. Yes, I did,' he added when she smiled in a disbelieving way. 'I think it must be true of most people when they start up in business, apart from those selling necessities, such as food. I'm sure there must be days when Mr Jacobs does not sell a thing. And he is in London and has a clientèle. If the worst comes to the worst all the clocks and watches could be put in an auction sale.'

'No, Poppa, definitely not. I must try to be patient. I could put advertisements in newspapers further afield – it might help to draw dealers and collectors. In the meantime I think, if you don't mind, that I should like to go to Corbridge this weekend. Perhaps Jenny might come, too.'

But Sarah never got to Corbridge. Isabelle and Lucy came home, leaving the boys there. The Cursons had had bad news. *Joe was missing . . . believed killed . . .*

Sarah stared at her mother, stunned, unwilling to accept it. Not Joe, with his cheeky grin, his rushing into love . . . dripping the water from the sponge down her back . . . *Oh, no, not Joe!*

Jonathan pointed out gently that although the telegram from the War Office had said *'Believed killed'*, it didn't mean they had proof Joe was dead. He could have been taken prisoner of war, could have got separated from his regiment and they had no trace of him. Many men had turned up after their families had received such a telegram. One must never give up hope,

Sarah had already given up hope. She felt withered inside and was sure that Joe was dead. She also knew that she had loved him, really loved him, and that all the most beautiful clocks and watches in the world could not make up for his loss.

23

It was, unhappily, a different kind of tragedy that now put the news about Joe temporarily from Sarah's mind . . . the Spanish Influenza epidemic. It swept across the whole of Europe and travelled swiftly with every army. It was said that under-nourishment caused the deadly virus to take such a hold, but the rich and well-fed were as vulnerable as the poor.

No one knew its source. Some blamed the slums of India, others pointed to the rat and lice-infested trenches, but because the press in Spain were the first to announce the scourge it became known as the Spanish 'Flu . . . and was the worst epidemic since the cholera outbreak of 1840.

Lucy was the first to go down with the infection. She and Fred and Eric had come for the weekend and Lucy was taken so ill that Jonathan went straight for the doctor. He was told they might have to wait for a visit, as the doctor was rushed off his feet. By the time Jonathan got back to the house, Isabelle, Eric and Victor were already suffering the first symptoms. And the next morning, Fred succumbed. That was when a very flustered doctor arrived, gave a cursory examination to each patient and subscribed medicine, saying, 'I've never experienced anything like this before, Mr Torent. People are going down like nine-pins.'

People died so suddenly from the pneumonia which developed with the influenza that it was frightening for those attending the sick. And when Jonathan collapsed, he who had never had a day's illness in his whole life, Sarah was terrified. 'Oh, God,' she prayed, 'don't let Poppa die. Don't let any of them die.'

Jenny took a more philosophical view. 'All our family are survivors, they'll pull through.' Sarah wished she could share her cousin's optimism.

There was no question of either of them going to work,

for the patients needed twenty-four hour nursing. The obituary columns of civilian and war dead filled several pages of the newspapers. Sarah scanned them every night and Jenny called her morbid. She was looking for the names of people she knew, and found many. There were two or three funerals in a street at a time. Whole families were wiped out; undertakers were almost unable to cope.

Business was at a standstill and if people did manage to get to work they wore masks over their noses and mouths. Streets, trams, buses and trains were sprayed with disinfectant; schools, cinemas, music halls and theatres closed down.

Bertha reported that she and Henrietta had escaped the 'flu so far; and although Maggie had escaped it too, she was busy nursing a number of relatives. Jenny and Sarah did four-hour shifts looking after the patients during the night. One evening when Sarah tiptoed into each room she heard her father talking in a rambling way. 'I'm the last on the heap I think . . . There was a man over there, but he seems to have gone . . . I'm the last one on earth . . . Don't grieve, Isabelle dear . . .'

Sarah's heart began a mad thumping. She had turned the gas-jet low and now she turned it up again. Isabelle, her face shiny with perspiration, was still. Jonathan's cheekbones burned and his eyes, wide open and staring, held a feverish light. Sarah gripped his shoulders and called to him, 'Poppa, come back from wherever you are. You must live! I won't let you die, I *won't!*'

Victor came wandering in looking like a ghost. 'What is it, Sarah? Why did you call me? Where are we going?' He waved his useless hand in the air. His nightshirt was soaked with perspiration.

'Oh, God,' Sarah said, and turning him guided him back to bed.

She shouted downstairs for Jenny to come and help her and went into the bathroom to fill a basin with cold water. She came out as Jenny climbed upstairs, rubbing her eyes.

'Jenny, I need your help, urgently. I want you to hold

290

Poppa up while I splash cold water in his face. I want to give him a shock.'

'A shock? You'll kill him!'

'If I don't do something he'll die anyway. Maggie once did this to an aunt who she said was slipping away to the Other Side. I can only pray it will work – if it kills him I'll kill myself. Come on, *hurry!*'

She could feel the heat coming off her father's body. She put a towel around him and splashed the water in his face over and over again. He showed no reaction for some time, then he gave a sigh and murmured, 'Oh, my goodness, I feel so tired.'

In a panic, Sarah glanced at Jenny, then Jonathan gave a wide yawn and her body went slack. It had worked, she knew it. Jenny laid him down. Sarah took the towel away, gently wiped his hair and chest and covered him up. Within a few minutes he was breathing easily and regularly in sleep. Jenny said, 'Thank heavens for that. It's a start. Come along, I'll do the round of the wards with you then we'll have a cup of tea.'

At eight o'clock the next morning Jonathan was still sleeping and the other patients were also asleep. At nine o'clock when a locum called he said, 'Let them sleep, it's nature's way of healing. They're on the mend.' He gave the girls his congratulations on their excellent nursing, along with some instructions on diet. He told them he would call again in two days' time, unless needed.

Both girls gave sighs of relief that it was finally almost over, then Jenny said she would go out shopping. When she came back she took off her mask and blurted out, 'Oh, Sarah, this 'flu is still raging. In every street more and more crosses are being chalked on the doors. Poor Mr MacTavish has died and his wife is near the end.'

'Oh, no! Poppa will be so upset.' Tears rolled down Sarah's face.

'Mr and Mrs Hudson and their twin babies are being buried this morning. When I saw those two tiny white coffins in the hearse on top of their parents' coffins – ' Jenny drew a finger across each eye and broke down. 'It's awful, awful.' She sobbed her heart out.

Worse news was to follow. In the local paper that evening was an article about Warren's family: Mr Bentham, his wife, two stepsons and their daughter had all died that day. Lieutenant Warren Hendrix, Mr Bentham's stepson who was serving at the Front, had been informed, the report said.

Sarah read it out to Jenny and then sat staring at her in a state of shock. 'Nearly the whole family – in *one* day. Oh, God help us, what is happening? Poor Warren. What a tragedy.'

During the following few days, with the family improving, Sarah had time to think about Warren and about Joe. She had been told that Warren was home on compassionate leave and that many people had attended his family's funeral. She had written a note of sympathy on behalf of the Torents but had heard nothing. She had also written to Mrs Curson, and had a reply saying the farmer's wife was pleased to hear from her but sorry to learn that the family had been so ill. They had all escaped the 'flu so far, at the farm at least. Then she mentioned Joe. They were over the first shock and were hopeful they would hear that he was alive; she felt sure he was . . . If any of the Torent family wanted to come on a visit to recuperate they would be more than welcome . . .

The day Maggie came back Jonathan said he would like a bit of fresh air and would walk to the shop. Maggie suggested that Sarah go with him, to put a bit of colour in her cheeks. And Maggie, who never minced her words, added, 'A skinny ghost, that's what she looks like. Now off you go, I'll see to the family.'

Although the weather had been hot recently there was a cool morning breeze and Sarah, feeling the freshness on her face, realised just how long she had been cooped up in the house. Jenny was the one who had done the shopping every day. Jonathan smiled at her. 'It's good to be out, isn't it? How one appreciates the simple things in life. Not having ever been ill before I began to understand how your mother must feel when she has one of her headaches.'

Sarah noticed that several front doors were smudged where chalked crosses had been rubbed off, but there were still many deaths in the obituary columns, showing that the epidemic was still taking its toll.

It was an emotional moment when they reached Mr MacTavish's shop and Jonathan said, a catch in his voice, 'I can't believe that we shall never see our dear old friend again. He coloured my life, Sarah, and I think yours too.'

'Yes, he did.' Jonathan unlocked the shop door and when he opened it Sarah was aware of a change. Most of the clocks were silent. 'I should have come to wind them,' she said slowly.

'I think you had plenty to do, pet. I'll soon get them attended to.'

What surprised Sarah during the next half hour was how detached she felt towards the timepieces. But then Death had hovered over her home making everything else seem unimportant. She had put the kettle on the primus stove to make some tea when the doorbell pealed. The next moment she felt a great weakness in her limbs as she saw Warren come in.

'Hello, Mr Torent, hello Sarah,' he greeted them quietly. 'I heard you had illness in the family and - '

Jonathan went forward. 'Warren, we were so sorry to hear your sad news. Come and have a cup of tea.' Sarah pulled up a chair. 'We were all thinking about you. It's been a terrible time.'

Several times Sarah had imagined meeting Warren again and she had always anticipated a certain embarrassment; however before long they were all sitting discussing the epidemic, its effect and the tragedies, with Warren talking about his family as though it was an everyday happening. Then Sarah realised that death *was* an everyday occurrence for him at the Front. Probably, men became immune to it.

The two men talked about the war, with Warren saying the end was in sight, at long last. The German advances had spent themselves, Allied counterstrokes in the second

Battle of the Marne had pushed them back, then a massive British attack using several hundred tanks had the enemy retreating fast.

He suddenly turned to Sarah. 'Forgive me, Sarah, I'm neglecting you. You know what men are like when they get talking about war.' He looked about him. 'I noticed when I came in that you had a larger stock of clocks and watches. Are you extending the business?' This last remark was addressed to Jonathan.

'It was Sarah's idea. We did some advertising and had a good response.'

'From people wanting to sell,' Sarah put in. 'I was terribly enthusiastic, but at the moment my enthusiasm has gone. Perhaps in a few weeks' time . . .'

The door opened and an elderly man came in. 'Oh, Mr Torent, I'm glad to see you back, I've brought my clock. It needs to be looked at.'

Jonathan excused himself and Warren sat looking at Sarah. There was such desolation in his eyes that she held out a hand to him. He took it, holding it firmly and said in a low voice: 'You've no idea how much I've longed to see you, Sarah. It seems an age since we parted together. I'm not in a celebrating mood, naturally, but I would be so pleased if you would have dinner with me. I leave again for the Front in three days' time. I feel I have been fighting all my life.'

Sarah said she would like that and it was arranged he would call for her the following evening. When he did arrive, in a taxi, Warren said he hoped she wouldn't mind but friends had invited them both for dinner.

'No, of course not,' she said, but wished they could have been on their own.

As things turned out, it looked as if they would be on their own. When they arrived at the house they found an envelope pinned to the door, a key inside it and a note explaining that the couple had been called away as the man's sister was dangerously ill. The rest of the note went on, *'I'm terribly sorry about this, Warren, but I know you will understand. The meal is in the oven, so do you think your nice*

Sarah could manage to dish it up? We won't be back this evening, but Richard and I will call to say goodbye before you leave for France. Love from both of us, Barbara.'

'Well!' Warren said, 'and does my *nice* Sarah think she can dish up the meal?'

'I don't think it would be any problem, but –'

Warren put the key in the lock. 'No buts.'

There was a rabbit pie in the oven, with a golden crust, new potatoes and garden peas, and apple tart and custard to follow.

'Looks delicious,' Sarah enthused. 'I'm sure we'll enjoy it. I'm only sorry that your friends had to leave because of bad news.'

'So am I, Sarah, but there comes a time when you can't absorb any more tragedy and you have to concentrate on something brighter or you would go mad. Do you know what I mean?'

His expression held that awful bleakness again and she forced herself to say lightly: 'In other words – eat, drink and be merry! Unforunately, we don't have anything to drink.'

His smile banished the bleakness. 'I don't need any. You are heady enough for me, darling Sarah. Let's eat.'

It had been sultry all day and while they were eating the sky darkened and raindrops spattered the window-panes. Warren glanced outside. 'A storm has been brewing for hours. It must break sooner or later and then we shall probably have a deluge.'

Sarah felt a sudden chill as the situation reminded her of Joe and the cottage. It had poured with rain then. Warren began to talk of one of his men, a sturdily-built fellow with a roguish grin, who was so good for the morale of the regiment. 'Always joking – he'll even crack jokes when we are ready to go over the top.'

Sturdily built . . . a roguish grin . . . always joking . . . Joe?

Warren laughed. 'What makes this Irishman even more funny is the fact that he has a lisp and he trades on it. I should think in fifty years' time, if I'm alive, I'll still remember old Paddy.'

Sarah relaxed. She must put Joe from her mind. Warren had suffered a tragedy that warranted him getting her whole attention.

The storm broke after they had finished the meal and were washing up. The first heavy rattle made Sarah jump and she nearly dropped a plate. 'Whoops!' Warren said. 'Break that and it will have to come off your wages.'

'What wages? I gave my notice in at the depot today, so did Jenny. Parents' orders. Fortunately they had a waiting list of women to replace us. But when the war is over the men will be taking up their jobs again and women will have to be looking for other work to do.'

'But will they? I should imagine men will expect their wives to stay at home and look after them and the children.'

'Typical male attitude. Times have changed, sir! Women have discovered independence, and they want to keep it.'

Warren teased her. 'Since when did you join the Suffragette Movement? No, don't let us discuss the Suffragettes. I did say you could run your clock and watch business when we married and I stick by it.' Warren put the last plate back on the kitchen dresser. 'There, that is the washing up finished. I've become very domesticated during this war.' He grinned. 'I might even learn to bath the baby.'

Sarah turned away, remembering how she and Joe had talked about getting married and how she had teased him, saying she would bring the baby into his garage for him to look after. She wrung out the dishcloth and spread it over the draining board. Then as lightning flashed, followed almost immediately by another heavy explosion of thunder she let out a small cry. Warren came up behind her and put his arms around her. 'It's all right, darling. The storm will soon die away. Come along, let's go into the other room.'

The house was detached but rather somberly furnished. Sarah, wanting to get her mind away from Joe, asked about Warren's friends, what sort of people they were. He said they were kind, always willing to do a good turn for people, but added that he felt they had missed out on life. They were rather prim and proper.

'For instance,' he said, 'I can't ever imagine them making love.'

'But how can you tell? I don't think that one can judge by a person's outward manner. They could be very passionate but keep their passion, naturally, for the bedroom.'

'Are you an authority on the subject then?'

At Warren's teasing smile Sarah picked up a cushion and threw it at him. 'Thought you were being clever, didn't you? Well, end of subject. And no, I am not an authority on it. I only know that appearances are deceptive. When I was about thirteen and at a party, a boy asked me out in Postman's Knock. I had always found him painfully shy, but believe me there was nothing shy about him when he got me in the passage. And *that* is definitely end of subject.'

'But I want to know what happened,' Warren protested. 'It would be like seeing the first episode of a Pearl White serial then to be told that no more episodes will be shown.'

'There will be no more episodes of this particular story.'

Warren's smile, the slumberous look in his eyes and Sarah's own feelings had her regretting pursuing the subject. At the mention of the word passion familiar tremors had run through her body. She got up. 'Shall we go for a walk?'

Warren's eyebrows went up. 'In this weather?'

It was still pouring with rain. Lightning was flashing and although the sound of thunder was more distant it was certainly not weather to go out in. Realising that her foolish remark must have made Warren aware she was disturbed, Sarah felt the colour rise to her cheeks. She made the excuse that because the thunderstorm was no longer overhead she was thinking that the rain had eased.

Warren said softly, 'Or could it be that your mind was on other things, Sarah, more interesting things? Such as people making love and the wild passion in a boy.'

She held up a hand and said, 'Now, Warren, I told you that the subject was closed.' Then she rushed on, 'Did I tell you that my cousin Jenny is going steady with a young Naval Lieutenant?'

Warren came over and sat beside her. 'I'm not interested in your cousin, I want to talk about you, about us.' He laid an arm across her shoulders and turned a strand of her hair over his finger, which sent a delicious thrill running up and down her spine. She wanted to move away but was held there by emotion, a need to be loved. Warren now had a finger under the collar of her dress and was caressing her skin. She drew in a quick breath, and this had him drawing her to him.

'We need each other. Why deny ourselves when there is so little time?'

If the sky had not darkened then, bringing the intimacy of night, Sarah might not have succumbed to Warren's urgent kisses, but she responded and put her arms around his neck.

'Sarah, Sarah darling,' he murmured. 'It has to be now, I'm going crazy, please, please.'

Commonsense was temporarily forgotten in the desperation of his plea and her own sexual needs. Without fully undressing they sank to the floor; and it was not until he had partially penetrated her that Sarah realised he had not taken any precautions. She tried to push him away, saying, 'No, Warren, no, I could have a baby.' But it was too late.

When he rolled away from her he apologised. 'Forgive me, Sarah, I didn't bring anything because I had no intention of anything happening, and that is the truth.'

She lay motionless, chilled, as he went on, 'It'll be all right, I know it will, it wasn't as if I had – well, gone the whole way.'

Sarah knew different, knew that many women had baby after baby because a husband depended on withdrawal; knew that the seed could travel to the womb from partial penetration. She got up and picking up her underwear went to the bathroom.

She had thought that Warren would be different, that there would have been love-play, she had been so sure he would take care. But then she had no right to condemn him. She had been as much to blame for their love-making, letting her emotions run away with her. There was no excuse – heaven knows she had been told often enough by other girls how easy it was for women to become pregnant.

Pregnant? She felt sick. What would her parents think? There was a gentle knock on the bathroom door. 'Sarah, we must talk, please.'

She came out and brushing past him went into the sitting room. It was moments before he followed. She went over to the window. The sky had lightened, the rain had eased and the thunder was just a faint rumble in the distance.

Warren came up behind her and put his arms around her waist. She tensed. 'Sarah, I'm sorry, so terribly sorry. Please don't reject me.' The pain in his voice made her turn to him.

'I was as much at fault. I can only pray that everything will be all right.'

'If it isn't you must let me know and we'll get married. Oh, Sarah, I'll never forgive myself for having given you this worry, especially after all the anxiety you've suffered, nursing your family. If only I didn't have to go away.'

The awful desolation was back in his voice again and when she saw a glint of tears in his eyes she said gently, 'I'm sorry, Warren, everything might turn out right. Don't go away worrying about what might never happen.'

They sat down and talked of dates, with Warren asking when she would know for sure. She told him in four days' time, and thought of how she had been worrying herself sick after being with Joe, wondering if he had taken precautions every time. He obviously had . . . or, she had just been lucky.

Warren wanted to make arrangements for the following evening, but Sarah said she thought her mother might object. And so they said their goodbyes in the house, with both of them emotional and Sarah feeling a deep tenderness for Warren. It had been an awful home-coming for him and now he was returning to the Front with a different problem on his mind.

The biggest trouble Sarah had during the next few days was in keeping her worry from the family and at times she felt she was overdoing her bright manner. But no one passed any remark until the day after her period was due when Jenny, after studying her for a few moments said: 'You're not pregnant, are you?'

Sarah, who had been brushing her hair in front of the dressing table mirror, laid down the brush and stood tense.

'What made you ask such a thing?'

'Because of the way you've been acting and also the way you've been studying your face every morning in the mirror, as I did, when I thought I might be pregnant. Lord knows why I did it, it didn't give me any answers.' When Sarah made no reply she said, 'Well – are you?'

Sarah stared into the mirror. 'I could be. I'm a day overdue.'

'I suppose it's the dashing Lieutenant who's responsible.' Jenny patted the bed. 'Want to talk about it?'

Sarah sat down, and was glad to. Her limbs felt weak now she had confessed.

She explained the time and the circumstances that had led up to the seduction and Jenny said, 'Well, if the worst comes to the worst you know where to go to get rid of it.'

'No! I could never do that.' Sarah got up and walked around the room. 'Warren said he would marry me. I don't want to get married, but I would for the baby's sake.'

'You're mad to talk like that – marriage is for life! You could meet someone else. After all, you said you weren't in love with Warren.'

'I'm fond of him, perhaps more than fond. The important thing is that if I am pregnant the baby would have a father.'

Jenny shrugged. 'Well, it's your life. And anyway, you might not need to get married.' Her expression softened, 'I'm glad you told me, Sarah. You see I know how you feel, about keeping the baby, I mean. I wish I had kept mine. But there, I didn't want to get married then. Come on, time for bed.'

There was one thing Sarah did know: if nothing happened by tomorrow her mother would want to know why. She had the date marked on the calendar every month.

When nothing did happen Isabelle made no remark but the following evening she said, 'All right, Sarah, what have you been up to? And don't make any excuses, the guilt is there in your face. I was only praying that I wouldn't need to be told. It's Warren, isn't it?' When Sarah, miserable, nodded, her mother went on, 'Mind you, your period *could* be delayed. You had a lot of worry and strain when you were helping to nurse us all through the 'flu, but if you haven't started by the end of next week then you'll have to write to Warren. He'll have to marry you. I'll tell your father.'

Sarah was so taken aback by her mother's reaction, the cut and dried way in which she had dealt with the problem that she was unable to answer. Was it that she was pleased Warren might be coming into the family? The next moment she knew by the hurt in her mother's eyes that she had wronged her.

She pleaded, 'Don't tell Poppa yet. If he has to know I would rather tell him myself.' Isabelle agreed.

When Sarah started with morning sickness she wrote to Warren then went to the shop to see her father; and to the sound of the ticking of the various clocks she told him about the baby. He put his arms around her and held her close, but it was several moments before he spoke.

'I'm sorry it had to be this way, Sarah, but you know that your mother and I will stand by you. Come and sit down, pet.'

She could almost feel the waves of his love and concern reaching out to her and for the first time she gave way to tears. She whispered that she was sorry for bringing shame on the family and he stroked her hair, soothing her.

'You were both so vulnerable, Warren needing love and someone to care about him after his dreadful loss, and you wanting to comfort him. It's circumstances, overcharged emotions. Warren does love you, he told me so, and he does want to marry you. Do you want to marry him, Sarah? That is the important thing.'

She said yes, because she did for the baby's sake. It was true that emotions had been heightened because of circumstances, finding themselves alone, but it had been a sexual need in her that made her submit; yet she knew that

301

nothing would be gained by making this confession, it would only cause more pain.

'There could come a time, Sarah, when you feel resentment at having a rushed marriage and could turn against Warren. Try to stifle this. A child thrives on love from both parents, from a happy background. But there, I don't want to lecture you.'

'You've never lectured me, Poppa, nor Victor. Thanks for understanding. It helps tremendously. I'll do my best to make Warren happy.' She managed a smile. 'You'll make a lovely grandad.' She leaned over and kissed him then got up.

Isabelle had been so calm that Sarah was sure there would be an outburst of reproach at some time, but her mother dealt with the situation in a businesslike way. As soon as they heard from Warren they would see the registrar and fix a date for the wedding. She added that there would be no comments from neighbours about a hasty marriage because so many couples were arranging marriages when their boyfriends came home on leave. She discussed then where Sarah would live.

'I know Warren will be taking over his parents' house when the war is ended but in the meantime you can go on living with us.' For the first time Isabelle showed some emotion. 'We want you to, Sarah. We want you with us while you are carrying the baby, to care for you.' Isabelle broke down then and it was some time before she could control her tears.

'I'm sorry, love, I've tried not to upset you, tried to be understanding, but it's not easy. When you are a mother yourself you'll understand. I've bottled up my feelings for your sake and your father's. We'll have to send a letter to Warren.'

Letters and telegrams were exchanged and the final wire from Warren said, *'Will meet you at the Register Office in Newcastle, 10 am on the 24th. All my love, darling, Warren.'*

Sarah wore a silver-grey marocain dress and coat and a pale blue hat and gloves. When she saw Warren waiting, a look of love in his eyes, she felt a lump come into her throat.

And although the ceremony took place in the Register Office she thought afterwards it could not have been more sacred to her had it been held in a church.

24

On looking back over the day when they set off to spend their honeymoon night in the Station Hotel in Newcastle, Sarah thought how wonderfully happy it had been. There were no miserable faces or disapproving looks, such as she had once seen at the wedding of a friend who had been married under similar circumstances.

What had surprised Sarah was the number of people waiting outside the Register Office to wish them well; neighbours, a number of conductresses and drivers from the depot and many friends of Warren. His two stepsisters who would have come were abroad.

In the taxi Warren took her hand and said softly, 'You look simply beautiful, Mrs Hendrix, a most radiant bride. Thank you, my darling.'

Sarah could suddenly hear Joe calling her 'darling'. He had come into her thoughts many times, but from the moment she knew about the baby she had determinedly dismissed him; and she did so now, for this was Warren's night.

The hotel was busy with a coming and going of Service personnel. It was not a place they would have chosen under different circumstances but Warren had to catch a train at seven o'clock the following morning to return to France. 'And I have to be on it,' he said, 'they will not accept any excuses. The army is no respecter of couples on honeymoon. There's a war to be fought.'

He had spoken lightly but Sarah gave a sudden shiver. She had forgotten the war that day . . . Neither of them were hungry, as they seemed to have been having snacks all day so they decided to go straight up to their room. The strange thing was, that although they had made love and she was carrying Warren's child, she felt shy.

She pottered about the room, took her nightdress out of

her bag, spread it on the bed then folded it up again. She went over to the window, came back, got out her toothbrush and flannel and was standing with them in her hand when Warren took her by the shoulders.

'What is it, Sarah? You don't have any regrets, do you'

'No, no, of course not. It's just that, well, I suppose it's daft, but I feel shy. After all, it's not as if it was the -' she paused and Warren finished the sentence.

'– the first time. Would it surprise you to know that I feel the same?'

Her eyes rounded in surprise. 'I couldn't imagine a man being shy.'

'Why? Do you think they make love to every woman they meet?'

'I hope *you* don't!'

'Of course not!' A twinkle came into his eyes. 'Only every other one.'

She gave him a playful punch. 'Oh, you –' The next moment he became serious.

'I haven't had a chance to say much today, Sarah, with so many people there and everyone wanting to talk to us. I'm glad you told me about the baby and didn't want to – well, do something about it. I can't think of anything more wonderful than being a father.'

Sarah hesitated a moment then knew she would have to ask him. 'Warren, did you get me pregnant deliberately so that I would marry you? And please, I want the truth.'

He looked at her, shocked. 'No, I didn't. I'm sorry you had to ask, I told you the truth when I said I had not carried anything because I had had no intention of making love to you. It was circumstances – atmosphere, a build-up of things. You must believe me, Sarah.'

She met his gaze squarely. 'I do. I had to ask, otherwise it would have been something there in my mind all the time. I've always loved babies, and used to think how wonderful it would be if I could have one, but that was when I was much younger. Now I can't believe I'm pregnant. Oh, Warren, I want this to be a good marriage! I've had so much love from my parents – I want our baby to know that same kind of love.'

'It will, Sarah.' He drew her to him and ran his hand over her hair. 'I hate to be leaving you. I want to be with you all the time, see that you take care of yourself and don't work too hard.' His lips moved over her cheek. 'We have so little time.'

'We have the whole night,' she whispered.

'I want a whole week of nights with you.'

She should have been thrilled at the desire in his voice, the way his hands were exploring her body, but she felt nothing. He began to undo the buttons at the back of her dress and she waited, not making any attempt to undo the buttons on his shirt. It was all done leisurely, with no hint of the haste he had shown when they had made love before.

He picked her up and carried her to the bed, caressing her with the love-play she had anticipated when mentally comparing him with Joe, and yet it did not even arouse a flicker in her. Was she consciously holding back because the image of Joe had surfaced? Or did she need a wildness in love-making to arouse her? For Warren's sake she made a pretence of enjoying it . . . and she must have been successful because afterwards Warren murmured, 'That was wonderful, darling, really wonderful.' He lay, his arm around her, enjoying the slumberous aftermath, while she remained wide-awake, conscious of every sound – of people talking in the corridor, noises outside the window, taxi and bus horns blaring, the rumbling of wheels, the clatter of trams . . . And then she saw that Warren had fallen asleep. She leaned over and kissed him on the brow. No wonder – he had travelled overnight, with many delays, and had arrived with barely an hour to spare before getting to the Register Office.

Sarah found herself remembering all the people who had come to Berkeley Avenue for the reception. How thrilled Bertha had been for her. 'You know something,' she had confided, 'your grandma might be all uppity about you getting married in such a rush and her not able to come because of her rheumatism, but I know when I get back

306

she'll demand to know every little detail. She's lonely, Sarah, and I think she must hate herself at times that she can't be pleasant to people.'

The wedding took place so quickly that there were few presents as yet, they were to come later, but Henrietta had sent with Bertha a beautiful handmade linen and lace tablecloth with twelve napkins. The card enclosed said, *'Best wishes to you both.'* There was no signature. Bertha commented, 'You should feel honoured, Sarah, she treasured that cloth. It was given to her on *her* wedding day by a titled lady.'

Although Sarah did not visit her grandmother regularly she had been to see her many times over the years, but they still did not see eye to eye and she was sure if Henrietta found out the reason for the hasty wedding she would never want to see her again.

Warren went on sleeping but Sarah was still wide-awake when the traffic began to ease. It seemed she had gone over a hundred and one things, the lovely speech her father had made; her Uncle Fred strumming on the piano with his one good hand and singing his comic songs; Jenny's tears as he played. She had wanted to cry when Victor said, his voice now breaking as he reached into manhood, 'I hope you'll be very happy, Sarah. We don't talk a lot like we used to but I want you to know that I – well, that I love you.' She had hugged him until, embarrassed, he had pulled away.

Then there was Maggie, who had presented her with a beautiful ivory fan that she had been given by an aunt to take to her first dance. Maggie had said with that raucous laugh, 'I bet you can't imagine me going to a dance, can you, but I was as light as a feather!' And there had been tears in Maggie's eyes, too.

Yes, there had been some tears, yet overall there had been happiness: her parents had seen to that. They had kept bright the whole time, determined that nothing should mar her wedding day. Isabelle had said afterwards, 'I think everything went very well, Sarah. You looked lovely and Warren is so proud of you. He's a thoughtful, caring person, I feel sure he'll make a good husband and father.'

Her father had said, in a still-bright voice to cover his emotion, 'Now don't worry about the clocks and watches – I shall take care of them.'

She had been going to remind him that she would only be away overnight but had kept up the illusion of a longer honeymoon by replying lightly, 'I hope you sell out.'

Yes, there would be no unhappy memories to look back on.

Sarah eventually drifted into sleep and did not rouse until they had their early-morning call. Warren was in a terrible state. How could he possibly have fallen asleep on their wedding night? It was unforgivable. Sarah begged him not to upset himself, he must have been so terribly tired. She learned then he had not been to bed for forty-eight hours before that night. Sarah said no wonder he had fallen asleep.

Warren would not allow his wife to get up and see him off, she was to rest. He talked to her while he shaved and washed. She would receive army pay, but he would arrange with the bank to deposit some money in her account so she would be able to buy what she needed.

'I hate leaving you, Sarah, and I can only pray it won't be for too long. The war should end soon, everyone is saying so. Thank goodness you have such marvellous parents. I've never known people like them – never a word of reproach to me, just a plea that I would care for you and love you.' He looked at his watch. 'Heavens, is that the time! I must have some breakfast...'

Sarah reflected that if it had been Joe he would have foregone food to make love to her before leaving. Then she felt ashamed at her thoughts. She had no right to compare the two men, one of whom was dead and gone. She wanted to get up and say goodbye properly to Warren but knew as soon as she put her feet to the floor the nausea would start and then there would be her usual bout of morning sickness. So it was a very brief goodbye, with Warren kissing her from the side of the bed.

'Forgive me for spoiling our wedding night, Sarah darling,' he murmured. 'I promise to make it up to you on my next leave. Take care of yourself.'

308

'And you.' She felt a sudden rise of tears. 'God bless. Come back to me, Warren, to us.'

He smiled then. 'You bet. And when you talk to junior in the quiet of the night tell him that his daddy loves him. I'm sure it will be a boy.'

He blew her a kiss then he was gone ... gone to the pounding of guns, the screaming of shells and the slaughter. For the next few minutes Sarah thought of all the things she could have said to him to make him long to be back with her. She would have to say them in a letter ...

Because Sarah was living at home and life went on in the normal way she could not get used to the idea that she was a married woman, nor had she yet really accepted that she was carrying a baby. In fact, it was not until the morning sickness mercifully stopped that she began to have some feeling for the life in her womb. She wondered now how she would take to married life, living in Warren's home, Bentham House, where most of his close family had died in one day, and caring for the baby, bathing it, feeding it. Would Warren keep his word and allow her to run a business? She still went to the shop every day and although that first fulsome enthusiasm had diminished a little she was still sufficiently interested to go on working with clocks and watches. The trouble was, that although they had a rush of people bringing in their timepieces to sell, Jonathan and Sarah were not finding suitable buyers for them quickly enough for Sarah to feel she was really on her way. She worried about the money Mr Jacobs had lent her. She had sent some back to him, but he had asked her not to send any more; he had made the loan for the sole purpose of helping her to get established in a business. *And that takes time, Sarah*, he had written. *'Be patient.'*

She had written to the old man, telling him about her wedding, but had heard nothing from him since and hoped he was all right. She had written at the same time to Mrs Curson and had a lovely letter of congratulations back, saying how delighted they all were and how she hoped to come up soon and see them all. *'Yes, Sarah, I'm really going to venture to have a look around Newcastle. I've only been once...'*

Sarah appreciated the warmth of the letter, knowing that Joe's mother had understood how she and Joe had felt about one another.

She wote long letters to Warren; his to her were full of love and hope that they would soon be together. In each letter, Warren repeated his belief that the war would definitely soon be over. News of conditions at the Front was certainly favourable, but there had been so many half-truths printed in the press for so long, that the public were disinclined to take much notice.

But as the weeks went by there was positive news that the German allies, Bulgaria and Turkey and then Austria, had surrendered. The German generals, despairing because of near-revolution at home and of mutiny in their Navy, began negotiations for an Armistice.

At this there was a lightening of spirits; people talked excitedly of the latest developments – perhaps the end was truly in sight at last.

One morning at the beginning of November 1918, when Sarah got out of bed she felt her baby quicken and stood transfixed at the wonder of it. She put her hands on her abdomen and feeling the movement again wished that Warren had been there to share her joy. Wanting to tell someone, she hurried to her parents' bedroom where Isabelle was still in bed. In her haste, Sarah tripped over the small slip-mat in the doorway and went headlong into the room. Isabelle cried, 'Oh, Sarah!' and flung back the bedclothes, then ran on to the landing and shouted for Jonathan to come quickly.

Sarah was aware of her father and Maggie pounding up the stairs and of them getting her back into bed. She kept saying she was all right, it was just her nose that hurt, but Jonathan said he would go for the doctor.

The doctor examined her, said that everything seemed to be all right, but added that it might be wise for her to stay in bed for two or three days. Sarah was glad to follow his advice. Although she had no pain and the baby was still moving she felt she had no strength. She stayed in bed for five days then feeling stronger got up. But she had been up and about for no more than an hour when agonising pains began in her back.

An hour and a half after that she miscarried. The midwife tried to console her, saying there would be other 'babbies', for wasn't she young and strong, but Sarah refused to be consoled.

She was paying for the 'sin' of letting Joe and then Warren make love to her. But the pain of thinking how a tiny life had been sacrificed in payment, just when the baby had begun its first explorative movements, was more agonising than the actual miscarriage. How could the church talk about a just God, who could do such a thing?

The following day the Armistice was signed and Sarah lay listening to the sounds of revelry in the street, the shouting and singing, feeling nothing.

What would Warren be coming home to? A wife who wished herself dead and no baby to love.

She longed to be at rest with Joe, knowing now he was the only man she had ever loved, the only one she would ever love, and for the first time since losing the baby she wept . . .

25

Sarah's recovery was slow, simply because she had made up her mind she was not going to recover. Isabelle and Jonathan talked encouragingly to her and so did Lucy and Fred. Jenny tried to coax her into joining the celebrations, the street parties, and got mad when Sarah just shook her head listlessly.

'You're being stupid! You have a husband who will be home soon and what is he going to find? A wife who is determined to make herself an invalid. He's been fighting a war, he deserves better than that.' When Sarah made no response Jenny went on, 'You're becoming like your mother used to be, enjoying her illnesses.'

This roused Sarah. 'That isn't true, she had consumption.'

'But didn't she love the fuss, just as you do. Well, you can get on with it! I'm not going to kiss your backside just because you lost a baby.' With that she stormed out.

It was this last remark that got Sarah out of bed, but even then she would not join in anything, or hold any conversations. She stayed withdrawn until Isabelle persuaded her one morning to go and see her grandmother and seemed surprised when she agreed. 'Oh, Sarah, I'm so glad, she's been asking after you constantly. Wrap up well, it's cold, and perhaps you could call and see your father on the way back. It might get you interested in your clocks again.'

Sarah was surprised herself that she had agreed to go and see her grandmother, for normally Henrietta was the last person on earth she wanted to visit. It was weeks since she had seen her. Perhaps she had agreed to go and see her now because the old lady too had a grudge against mankind.

Bertha greeted Sarah with a glad cry, but warned her

that 'madame' was not in a good mood this morning. To this Sarah replied in flat tones, 'Is she ever?'

'Hmm!' Henrietta said with a sniff. 'So you've finally deigned to come and see me. And about time. Anyone would think we are not even remotely related.'

Sarah unwound the white scarf from her throat. 'I came because I didn't care whether I came or not. And to be honest I don't care about a thing.'

'Well, it's time you started caring,' the old lady snapped. 'I see no reason why you should think you're so special because you've lost a child. A woman in Coppen Street lost her husband and all three sons. And do you know what she did – she took in two orphaned children to stop them being sent to the poorhouse. She goes out charring to clothe and feed them.'

Sarah got up. 'If you're going to start preaching to me . . . and anyway you are not the one to do so, you've been miserable and bad-tempered ever since I can remember.'

'I know and I've just realised what a fool I've been. Not that I'll change now, I'm too old, but you are young with a life before you.'

'What sort of life?' Sarah was stung to retort. 'It's all right for you to sit here and condemn me, you don't know how I feel.'

'I know how you look – you're pathetic, pasty-faced and drooping like a wilting flower as though you were a badly-treated heroine from a melodrama. Get your back up!'

Sarah moved away. 'I don't have to stand here and listen to your tirade.'

'You'd better wait to hear a bit more. You filled your father's shop with clocks and watches, hoping to set yourself up in a business and what happens? You leave him to sell them. He tramps all over the place trying to find customers, thinking that if he could sell them you might take an interest in it all again. Oh, *he* didn't tell me, he's too much of a gentleman for that. It was a nosy neighbour who likes to ferret things out.'

'I didn't know what Father was doing,' Sarah said in a low voice. 'He didn't say.'

313

'No, of course he wouldn't – and you didn't bother to ask, did you? He's neglecting his own business trying to help you. I don't give a tinker's cuss what happens to *you*, but I care about my daughter and my grandson. You're taking food out of their mouths by your stupid actions. Grow up for heaven's sake. Now get out, get out of my sight!'

Sarah turned away, but not before she had seen a glint of tears in her grandmother's eyes, and realised for the first time that the old lady did care.

Bertha was waiting to open the door. She whispered, 'She doesn't really mean it, Sarah love.'

Sarah nodded, 'Yes, I know.'

She walked along the street, her head lowered against the cold North East wind, then suddenly she straightened up. It was time she faced up to life, accepted that she had responsibilities.

The change did not take place overnight but she did go to the shop the next morning and took an inventory of all the clocks and watches she had bought. She said to her father, 'Do you know, Poppa, I think I've been wrong in my buying. I've been buying what *I* wanted, not perhaps what the public wants, or should I say the collectors, for they are the ones I should have been considering. I think I'll start going to the auction sales as Mr Jacobs suggested some time ago.'

Jonathan said quietly, 'I'm so glad you are taking an interest again, Sarah. Your mother and I have been very worried about you.'

'I know and I'm sorry. I've been thoroughly selfish. It was Grandmother who brought me to my senses. She read me the riot act. She had quite a flow of descriptive abuse! But it did me good. And do you know something, she considers *you* a gentleman.'

'She does? My, I am going up in the world.'

They were back on their lovely close footing again and Sarah knew it was a turning point for her.

When they got home that evening Isabelle said, 'Why, Sarah, you look tons better. I met Mrs Ingram this afternoon

314

and she tells me her husband is home from the Front. Apparently the soldiers are being demobbed in their thousands. Warren might be lucky enough to be home soon. Oh, by the way, Mrs Curson writes to say she'll be coming to see us in a few days' time.'

It was the following morning when the farmer's wife turned up. Sarah, who was ready to go to the shop exclaimed, 'Why, Mrs Curson, we weren't expecting you yet. Mother is out shopping with Aunt Lucy but they'll soon be back. Come on in; how lovely to see you.'

Mrs Curson explained that a neighbour who was going to Newcastle had offered her a lift in his van. 'He brought me almost to your door, Sarah. It was an opportunity I couldn't refuse.'

'Of course not. Here, give me your coat, then I'll make a cup of tea.'

After Sarah had put the kettle on the fire Mrs Curson said, 'I was so sorry to hear about the baby, Sarah. I know what it is, I lost my first child. But then look how I made up for it!' Her attempt at brightness did not come off . . . Those babies were Chris and Joe, who were no longer with them.

Sarah longed to ask about Joe but felt she would have to wait. Then Mrs Curson mentioned him. She thanked Sarah for sending her son such long and newsy letters. 'He used to tell me about them, Sarah, how you always wrote something funny that he could tell the other men in the trenches to make them laugh. I remember one particular verse, to do with a man called Mr Mears. Does it ring a bell?'

'Yes. It was one of the first verses my father ever told me. I loved it and was never tired of hearing it repeated:

'There was a man he had a clock, his name was Mr Mears,
And every night he wound that clock for five and forty years,
And when at last that clock turned out an eight-day clock to be,
A madder man than Mr Mears I never hope to see.'

They both laughed and Mrs Curson gave Sarah a hug. 'It means so much to me, Sarah, to –' there was suddenly a

315

catch in her voice, 'to know that Joe and his fellow soldiers could have something to laugh about.'

'I don't suppose you've heard any more about –'

'No, not yet, Sarah, but we're all still hopeful. I heard of a son coming home after being missing for six months. One *must* hope.'

Sarah made the tea and by then Isabelle and Lucy were back. From then on the women exchanged family news, but although Sarah was the listener she felt better for seeing Mrs Curson.

It was not until after Christmas 1918 that Warren returned from France and he came straight to Sarah's home. He looked so ill that Isabelle insisted he went straight to bed and called the doctor. Warren had apparently had a bout of 'flu, and was also suffering pain where pieces of shrapnel had been removed from his body. He ran a fever for several days but even when it came down he seemed distressed. It was Jonathan who told Sarah the cause.

'He's had a bad shock, Sarah. First, it was the loss of the baby, then he learned that his stepfather had not left him the family house or any money; everything has gone to Mr Bentham's brother.'

Isabelle said, 'It's so unfair, because from what I hear Mr Bentham had all of Warren's mother's assets made over to him. Warren does have some money left him by his maternal grandparents, but it's not enough to keep you both in the style he hoped. This is what is upsetting him.'

'It doesn't matter about the money,' Sarah exclaimed. 'We'll get by. I have been to one or two auction sales recently and I'm beginning to get the feel of the market. We can rent a small house.'

'Well, don't worry about that at this stage,' her mother advised. 'All we want at the moment is for Warren to get well. We have enough room here.' Isabelle paused then added gently, 'Give him plenty of love, Sarah, he needs it.'

Sarah had no need to be told. She ached with sympathy for Warren, for his grief over the loss of the baby and the fact that his stepfather had cut him out of his will. When she went upstairs she put her arms around her husband.

316

'Everything's going to be all right, Warren. We have each other and that is the most important thing. But in future tell me if you have any worries, we *must* share everything.'

'I will. I just feel so awful – there was so much I wanted to give you.'

She put a finger to his lips. 'We'll rent a little house, it doesn't need to be big for us to be happy. And when you are better you can come to the auction sales with me for a while until you feel ready to look round for a job. But the important thing at the moment is to get well. Warren – you've been fighting and taking punishment for four whole years! We all have so much love to give you.'

He gave a faint smile, but there was a glint of tears in his eyes as he said, 'I wouldn't dare do anything else after all that encouragement.'

Warren certainly didn't want for company. Eric and Victor were often sitting with him and plaguing him for war stories; sometimes they had to be turned out because they were tiring him. Lucy and Fred and Jenny were frequent visitors and Maggie was always popping in and out saying, 'And how are you feeling now, sir? I'll just tell you a little tit-bit that might cheer you up.' and it would be some piece of gossip that made Warren smile. He and Jonathan would have long discussions. Isabelle, having known what it was to be alone and sick, shared quiet talks with him. His own friends called round but only Yolande and Titania stayed for any length of time, reminding him of all the parties he and Sarah would be going to when he was up and about again.

The visitors did at least give Sarah the chance to pop out to the shops for a while and attend the occasional sales. Although she had bought several more timepieces that she had managed to sell advantageously, she still did not have the thriving business that was her dream.

But she was able to talk to Warren about her sales, about the people she met, and they grew very close.

One evening he said quietly, 'Do you realise, Sarah, I've been home five weeks and we've never made love.'

She teased him. 'Ah, but tomorrow you can get up for

317

half an hour, and increase the time every day and then,' she dropped a kiss on his brow, 'and then, sir, we shall make up for lost time.'

This brought a smile. 'I hope so. I've nearly forgotten how.'

'Not you!'

Once Warren was up and moving around his recovery took rapid strides and one evening he said to Sarah when they went up to bed, 'I think the time has come to make up for lost time! What do you say?' She felt excited when Warren began an exploration of her body, but then he wanted her urgently and he was so quick Sarah got no satisfaction. He apologised. It had been so long, it was impossible to wait. Next time it would be much better.

On the next occasion, he was able to control his feelings for longer, but Sarah still did not get any satisfaction, nor did she on subsequent occasions although she made a pretence of enjoying the act. At first she blamed the lack of wildness in her husband's love-making, then came to realise it was being in too close proximity to her parents' room.

The next morning Warren said he thought it was high time he started looking for a job and Sarah said fine, she would try to find a small house to rent. Unfortunately, neither were successful. In spite of Warren having connections through his step-father in commerce he kept getting the same reply: 'Sorry, Warren. I'm duty-bound to give jobs to former staff who have been through the war.'

And Sarah found that all the 'To Let' signs had been taken down. Although hundreds of thousands of men had been killed, there were similar numbers being demobbed. Many of them were young, and with their fiancées would have courted for a few years, and saved up – before the war. When they had enlisted, however, they had rushed headlong into marriage and now they wanted to set up homes.

Weeks went by and Sarah was in despair of finding anything when Maggie told her of a young couple who were going to Essex where the husband had found a job as groom on an estate. 'A furnished cottage goes with the job,' Maggie said, 'so they would like whoever takes their house to make an offer for the contents. They would sell it cheap – it's good stuff, not rubbish.'

Sarah went at once. It was a terraced house, two rooms up, two down. The windows were sparkling and the front step sandstoned, which Sarah thought a good sign. The woman who answered the door was neatly dressed and pleasant. She invited Sarah in, saying how delighted she would be to keep everything where it was. An aunt had lived in the house and they couldn't take the furniture with them.

Sarah was impressed with the living room, and although the furniture was dark it was not the heavily-carved Victorian kind. Doors and skirting-boards had been painted cream and there were red velvet curtains at the window. There was lino on the floor but Sarah thought with a carpet it would be really cosy. The furniture in the front bedroom and bedrooms was walnut. In the main bedroom a narrow table with carved legs held a delicately-carved swivel mirror which was used as a dressing-table.

'It's all lovely,' she said. 'I do want the house, so perhaps we can come to an agreement about the contents?'

They did and Sarah left to see the landlord. It was settled that they would move into the house in two weeks' time. She rushed to the shop to tell her father – and met Warren in the doorway. Before she could open her mouth to speak he told her he had found a job with a firm of insurance brokers. Then they were both hugging each other and Sarah was shouting for joy when Jonathan finally opened the door to see what was going on.

When they had all calmed down they went to tell Isabelle the news. She was equally delighted and said she was looking forward to seeing the house. Sarah felt she could hardly wait to move in and when they did it was the first time since their marriage that she felt able to relax when Warren made love to her. Although it was not the perfect experience it had been with Joe, she felt sure it could be, now they were in their own home.

And it might have been, in time . . . had Sarah not heard a week after their move that Joe was alive – and had come home.

26

Sarah thought if she lived to be a hundred she would never forget the moment she learned that Joe was alive; and she would always associate it with daffodils because she had been arranging some in a bowl when her mother arrived almost breathless and announced the news.

'I'm on my way to the station, Sarah, to spend the day with Lucy and Fred, but just as I was coming out I picked up this letter from Mrs Curson with the most wonderful news that Joe is home! I simply had to call and tell you. I don't know any details yet, but no doubt Mrs Curson will be telling us the whole story later, or Joe might even come to see us.'

Sarah nearly blurted out, 'Oh, no!' but said instead, 'That really is wonderful news. Don't miss your train, Mother. I'll call in this evening and see you – what time will you be back?'

Isabelle pulled on a glove. 'I feel I'm half-dressed. Lucy's letter came by the first post saying she had some news to tell me. I suspect that Jenny and Andy will be getting engaged. I should be back in time for your father coming home. See you later, Sarah, 'bye . . .'

Sarah sank on to a chair. What would Jenny say when she knew about Joe? Only a week ago she said she would never love Andy in the way she loved Joe . . . yet Joe had never made love to her.

Memories came flooding back to Sarah of those first days at Corbridge so long ago; riding on the hay wagon, being tumbled in the sweet-smelling grass, going to the fête, Joe winning the kewpie dolls . . . How innocent she had been that summer. Then there was all the guilty subterfuge of going to the cottage with Joe, drowned in excitement, sexual delirium, the wild love-making. What dreams she had had, then. Where were those dreams now? Where were Jenny's dreams? She had been the first one to fall in love with Joe. And what about the business that she and Jenny had been going to share? That had gone to the wall. Jenny was currently working in a newsagent's at Tynemouth – and said she hated it. Sarah sighed and got up.

She *did* have a business to run but wanted more sales, wanted to make it a flourishing concern, and this eluded her.

Sarah picked a daffodil from the bowl and replaced it in a different position. As she did so, she thought that life was like a chess-game – you made different moves that so often lost you the game. She had lost Joe forever by making the wrong move with Warren. Believing her first love to be dead, she had not stopped to think of the risks and the possible outcome, but had just rushed into an affair with Warren. She did love her husband, but he would always be second-best, no matter how hard she tried to believe otherwise.

Sarah was getting ready to go to the shop when Jenny arrived. Like Isabelle, she was breathless.

'I came to tell you my news and met your mother at the station. She told me all about Joe. You know the way I felt about him once, well, I think it was because he was my first love. Andy's my love now. I'll probably forget Joe altogether – in time.'

A verse Mr Jacobs had once quoted to Sarah came into her mind:

> *Time is:*
> *Too slow for the aged,*
> *Too swift for those who fear,*
> *Too long for those who grieve,*
> *Too short for the joyful ones,*
> *But for those who love,*
> *Time is eternal.*

Eternal? Would she go on loving Joe forever, as she was sure her Aunt Mary would do with Roger?

Then she thought no, it would be wrong to crucify herself

322

with thoughts of Joe. Carrying a cross could put a heavy burden on her marriage. She would never forget Joe but Warren must be the important man in her life. Sarah straightened her shoulders.

Although she told Warren about Joe's unexpected return the news was lost in his excitement about his job. It was all he could talk about. He had plans for buying a house. 'It will be the best I can afford, Sarah.' She loved the little house they were in but let him talk, knowing it would be wrong to deprive him of the pleasure of giving her something he thought she wanted.

A letter from Mrs Curson eventually brought more news of Joe. He was changed, withdrawn and had lost a lot of weight. It was understandable, of course, the poor boy had suffered so much. He had been taken prisoner with ten more of the men, and they were on their way to a camp when the lorry in front of them exploded, giving Joe and two more men a chance to escape. The other two men were shot and Joe was on the run for four days before he collapsed. A farmer found him and took him to his home, where he and his wife had hidden him until the war ended. Joe would need time to get over his experiences...

Sarah had more details of Joe when Beth came one Saturday on a flying visit.

'It must have been hell for him, Sarah. The only people he ever saw were the farmer and his wife and their daughter Monette. According to Joe Monette is a gentle girl; she taught him French and he taught her English. She had never been out with a boy. The farm is very isolated, you see. Joe is talking about going back to France, but whether he will or not I don't know.'

Sarah felt a sudden pang. Was Joe going back with the intention of marrying Monette? If he did she had no cause for complaint. She had not waited to see if he would ever return, despite his mother's certainty. Beth's parting words were, 'You must come and see us all, Sarah. You might be able to cheer him up, because we certainly can't. You and Joe always got on so well together.'

Yes, Sarah thought, they had got on splendidly together. But what did Joe think about her having married Warren?

A sudden big spending boom helped Sarah to put Joe temporarily from her mind. She went to sales frequently and bought clocks and watches, selling most of them soon afterwards. Although her profits were not enormous she felt able to repay her debt to Mr Jacobs, leaving a surplus in the bank. When she wrote to him telling him she was sending the money, he replied, asking her to keep it for the time being. He was thinking of coming up North soon on business: he would let her know the date.

An invitation to stay at Berkeley Avenue was issued immediately, and Mr Jacobs accepted. Jonathan was especially looking forward to meeting the old man at last, having heard so much about him from Sarah and Isabelle. When Sarah and her father went to the station to met Mr Jacobs and she saw her friend getting off the train, a slightly stooped figure in his black Homburg hat and long black overcoat, she felt a rush of affection for him. She ran to give him a hug. Jonathan was introduced and it was then the talking started. They were still talking when they arrived home. Isabelle introduced Victor and by the end of the evening Mr Jacobs was absorbed into the family.

He was a veritable mine of information. He talked to Victor about his music and when he found the boy was interested in composing he said he had a friend in London – a well-known composer who, he was sure, would be pleased to help him. Victor's eyes shone with pleasure. Later, when Sarah tried again to repay the loan, Mr Jacobs told her to use it now for expanding her business.

He talked to Jonathan about his inventions, told Isabelle she had a very clever husband and suggested the couple should emigrate to America, where Jonathan's genius would be recognised. His own son had had no success with his ideas until he went to America and now he was doing exceedingly well, and was working in his own laboratory. He suggested that Jonathan write to Henry Ford with his ideas.

Mr Jacobs then began talking about Victor's injury. 'I

324

understand that the doctors here can do no more for him. Now, my son's father-in-law is an eminent surgeon in America and he specialises in industrial injuries. I could ask his advice. If he feels he can do something for your son's damaged hand, it might be worth saving towards that end.' Mr Jacobs smiled. 'Then you can kill two birds with one stone.' He turned to Sarah. 'But emigrating to another country is not achieved in a few weeks, let us talk about your business, my dear. Why not go in for antiques, other than clocks and watches. One side helps the other. And if you did get to America you would have more scope for starting a business.'

Isabelle said with a laugh, 'I can see why you are so successful in business, Mr Jacobs. Emigrating is mentioned in one breath and already you have us all there.'

He eyed her solemnly over the top of his spectacles. 'Anything is possible, Mrs Torent. I bought my first watch when I was twelve years old. It cost two shillings, each one of those twenty-four pennies hard-earned. I sold it and made a profit. I bought two more watches and made a profit on those. Big businesses are built from small transactions.'

Jonathan said, 'But it does depend on what a person wants to achieve.'

'Of course, and I feel sure that you and your wife long for your son to be able to use his injured hand.' When Jonathan said in reply that no sacrifice would be too great to achieve this, Mr Jacobs spread his hands and beamed at them. 'So, you emigrate.'

Warren, who had been working late, arrived at that moment. He also took to Mr Jacobs but when they were home and Sarah mentioned that she was thinking of expanding the business and going in for antiques, he was against it.

'You do enough already, Sarah. If I had my way you would stay at home – which is where a woman's place should be.'

Sarah flared up. 'Oh, is that so! Then how do you think this country would have fared during the war had it not been for the thousands of women taking over men's jobs at home?'

'I accept that in wartime, Sarah, but the war is over. Anyway,' he smiled and drew her to him. 'we are not going to quarrel, my darling. I've been thinking about you all day, wanting you.' He began to undress her and she let him although she was still smarting from his remarks and was unable to respond.'

'Sulking?' he teased her, as he lifted her on to the bed.

'No – just a bit mad that you won't see me as a businesswoman.'

His mouth covered hers, putting an end to the conversation but although Sarah did try then to give herself wholeheartedly to his love-making, a picture of Joe being passionate with Monette suddenly intruded.

Mr Jacobs stayed for four days in Newcastle but most of the time he was out meeting business acquaintances. On the evening before he was due to return to London he promised Isabelle and Jonathan that he would write to his son about Victor. He also told them he would contact his composer friend to see if he would help the boy. 'I feel sure he will,' he said. 'Joseph and his wife lost their only son at fifteen and both have done a great deal for young musicians with talent.'

His leave-taking was a touching moment because Isabelle and Jonathan were so overwhelmed with their gratitude. Mr Jacobs, emotional himself, said it would be the least he could do, he had never before encountered such wonderful hospitality. He then turned to Sarah.

'And you, young lady, learn all you can about antiques. Go to sales, note prices, read books on the subject and try to find yourself a part-time job in a showroom. There you would learn a great deal.'

After Mr Jacobs had gone Isabelle was all set to talk about the family emigrating, but Jonathan said to wait until they heard from Mr Jacobs about the possibility of an operation on Victor's hand. Then he added, in a gentle way, 'And we must think, Isabelle, of the snags of taking such a step. You would be leaving Lucy and Mary and your mother,

326

and we would need sponsors in America to vouch for us: we would not be allowed in unless we were sponsored. We would also need sufficient money to keep us while I was looking for work.'

Isabelle urged, 'Do as Mr Jacobs suggested and write to Henry Ford with your ideas. Please, Jonathan, I don't want to emigrate any more than you do, but if it means getting your ideas recognised and having Victor's fingers straightened . . .'

Jonathan promised and he did write, but he said to Sarah later: 'You know, my dear, there are other snags. Because I haven't been naturalised I will have to apply to Finland for a visa. Suppose that you all had yours and I was turned down?'

Sarah looked up. 'I couldn't go in any case, Poppa. There's Warren's job, he's wrapped up in it. He wouldn't leave England. I think the best thing would be to let Mother take Victor to America, if the operation could be done. I can sell my clocks and watches to finance it.'

'No, no, Sarah, I won't have you doing that, you've worked so hard to get what you have. But anyway, let us leave it for the time being until we hear from Mr Jacobs. Are you interested in going in for antiques?'

'Yes, I am, but where could I display them? Do you think there would be room in the shop?'

'Plenty, if we move things around, it just needs organising. Should we start now, no time like the present.'

Sarah laughed at her father's sudden change of policy but she felt excited.

To her surprise, she became absorbed with antiques – china, small pieces of furniture, and even bric-a-brac, which she came to think of as the bread and butter lines. She bought warily at first to get the feel of the market and never made a big outlay. Then one day, Yolande called, all bright and breezy and announced she had a load of small stuff in the car – would Sarah be interested?

Sarah was pleased to see her and they chatted for ages before Yolande brought the 'small stuff' in. She said they were mostly pieces belonging to friends who needed some ready cash, but some of them were her own. There was a small inlaid walnut corner cabinet; a late Regency rosewood 'teapoy' with mother-of-pearl; an apothecary box; a camphor wood writing slope; a brass-bound toilet box; a silver vase, a plated brandy warmer, grape scissors, sugar nips, several snuff-boxes . . .

Yolande named a price, saying amiably, 'Take it or leave it, darling.' Sarah accepted, knowing she could make a profit.

Yolande became a regular visitor and Sarah discovered that she knew a great deal about antiques. They went to sales together and although Sarah was still cautious in her spending, she did take Yolande's advice at times and got a bargain.

Warren began to complain that Sarah was never at home. She retaliated by saying that when she *was* at home he was always working on his books.

'But this is all for you, Sarah. It's important that I make a success of my job. I want to go up in the world, to be able to buy you a house.'

She put her arms around him. 'Warren, it doesn't matter. I'm happy with you in this one. It's foolish to work so hard.'

'And foolish that you do, darling. Your mother gives me lovely meals, but I want *you* there when I come home.'

Sarah promised that in future she would be, but there was always some sale to attend. One day Yolande said, 'There's a big house sale at Ryton. Why don't we go and stay overnight?' Sarah said she would have to think about it, but Warren created such a fuss that she told Yolande she could only go for the day.

Then at the last minute Warren relented. He was being selfish, she could go, but he teased her, saying there must be no talking to strange men.

Sarah laughed. 'I never get the chance! It's all work.' She felt excited, for it was like going on a little holiday.

On the first day she made no bids but tried for a number of items on the second day, and got most of them. Elated, the girls came back to their lodgings when Sarah stopped, seeing a telegraph boy outside the door. He held out the telegram. 'It's for Hendrix.'

Sarah's mouth went dry as she took it. It was from her father, saying that Warren was ill and could she return home at once. Yolande said she would take her in the car.

But by the time they arrived Warren was dead. A piece of shrapnel in his body had pierced his lung.

For a week after Warren's sudden death Sarah felt icy cold. Her mother said it was shock, but Sarah felt it was mainly remorse, a regret that she had not given her husband more attention. She should have been aware that he was not himself. Apparently he had been to the doctor's, but had told no one. If only she had been at home instead of constantly rushing off to sales, she would have known Warren was ill.

Her father told her not to reproach herself – the doctor himself had not known the shrapnel was so close to Warren's lung. 'Warren loved you, Sarah. It was the last thing he said before he died – "Tell Sarah I love her dearly".'

Her mother said, 'If only you could cry, Sarah, you would get relief,' but her tears seemed to be frozen.

Mrs Curson and Beth came for the funeral. Beth told Sarah that Joe had married Monette, but as the French girl did not want to come to England he was going to work on her father's farm. Mrs Curson said, a sadness in her voice, 'Joe's dream was to have a garage of his own.'

Sarah wept then, and wondered if her tears were for lost dreams – Joe's, her own and Warren's.

Isabelle wanted Sarah to come back home to live but Sarah said she would keep the house on for the time being at any rate. Yolande had promised to stay with her for a while.

Yolande was lively, with plenty of little anecdotes to tell about people she knew, but although Sarah was glad to have her in the house to take her mind from dwelling in a morbid

329

way about Warren, there were times when she would slip away to her father's shop in the evenings for a quiet talk.

One evening he said: 'Take solace, Sarah, in the fact that Warren loved you and would be the last person to want you to grieve. You are really belittling his memory if you think otherwise.'

'Yes,' she said, 'You are right.' Her acceptance of this did not lessen the grief, but helped her to cope with it.

Jenny came at times and stayed overnight but it was mainly *her* future she talked about, when she and Andy would be married. Only once did she mention Warren and then it was to say, 'It's frightening, isn't it, that anyone so young can die so suddenly? It wasn't until Warren died that I realised how much I cared for Andy. Do you remember how crazy I was about Joe? I still think of him at times, and I'm sure when I'm old I shall say to my grandchildren. "I remember my first love was Joe Curson," then I'll say how he came back from the dead and married a French girl whose parents hid him in their farmhouse during the war. And my grandchildren will say, "how romantic." '

Tears suddenly filled Jenny's eyes. 'And you know, Sarah, I don't think it's romantic at all. I don't think Joe loves this Monette. But there, we can't change anything, can we?'

Mr Jacobs had been away at the time of Warren's death but he sent his condolences and said he would write again. The next letter brought good news. The composer and his wife had offered to have Victor in their home for a few weeks so he could have some concentrated tuition. Perhaps Isabelle could bring him.

There was also news from his son's relative, the surgeon, saying he felt sure that something could be done for Victor, but that of course he would have to see the boy.

These two things in themselves were enough to send waves of excitement through the Torent household, but by the second post more good news was to follow. Jonathan had a reply to his letter to Henry Ford; the great man wrote that Jonathan was obviously a man of vision, the type of person needed in America, and he offered him a job and

330

accommodation for himself and his family. The letter was signed by Henry Ford himself.

Sarah had never seen her father so emotional. Isabelle wept as she put her arms around him. 'Oh, Jonathan, to think that your work will be recognised at last.' She smiled through her tears. 'And I have scolded you so often about your inventions. We really must see now about our passage to America.'

Jonathan said, 'First things first, Isabelle. You must take Victor to London. And while you are away Sarah and I will set the wheels in motion about emigrating. There will be numerous forms to fill in.'

This was when Isabelle began to worry. It *would* be terrible to leave Lucy and Mary and her mother. And would she be able to cope with all that needed to be done? Jonathan would have to sell the business, and the house and furniture would have to go. They would need every penny they could get. After all, anything could happen. They could arrive and find that Henry Ford had died and there would be no job. Or supposing they were turned back when they reached Ellis Island? She *had* had consumption . . . It was useless to tell Isabelle that the doctor would give her a certificate to say she was cured.

And what about Victor's hand? They might not allow him into the country. Yes, she knew they could say he was going to have an operation and the surgeon would give them a letter verifying this, but . . .

They did manage to get Isabelle and Victor packed off to London, but to everyone's astonishment Isabelle was back in three days. Oh, yes, Victor had settled in fine, she said, the Meggestrones were such lovely people, so warm-hearted and they had a beautiful house. Isabelle's face suddenly crumpled.

'But, Jonathan, I'm so sorry, we won't be able to emigrate to America.' Tearfully, she explained that Mr Jacobs had taken her to the Finnish Embassy to see about Jonathan applying for a visa and they were told that the quota of people going from Finland to America had been filled for that year.

Jonathan drew her to him. 'Well, it's not the end of the world, Isabelle. Don't cry, dear, we can apply next year.'

'But Mr Ford might not be interested in your ideas in a year's time, anything could happen. And what about getting the operation done on Victor's hand? I feel the longer we wait the worse it will be. His fingers are getting more claw-like every day, curling in.' Isabelle paused then went on, 'Mr Jacobs suggested that I take Victor to America and offered me the money for our fares, but I couldn't take it.'

'No, no, of course not. You did right, Isabelle.'

Sarah said, 'I accepted money from Mr Jacobs to start a business. I still have it in the bank. He told me to keep it for the time being to extend the business. Well, I've been buying, now I'm going to sell my stock.'

There were protests from her parents. Jonathan suggested they could sell the house and move into a rented one, but Sarah said no, her mind was made up. Victor's future was more important than mere goods. She would get a job and move back home as her parents had wanted. After further discussion both Jonathan and Isabelle accepted the decision.

The following day, Sarah put an advertisement in the paper, announcing there was to be a big sale of clocks, watches and antiques and that there would be many bargains.

She sold at little above cost-price and within two weeks her stock was nearly cleared. From then on letters went to Mr Jacobs and from him to America. And the result of this, was Mr Jacob's son and daughter-in-law offering hospitality to Isabelle and Victor and the old man deciding he would go with them for a holiday. He had wanted to see his son and daughter-in-law for some time and what better time than now?

But even arranging the permit for this visit took time. The surgeon had to write and verify that he would be operating on Victor's hand. There was so much red tape, wailed Isabelle. Would they ever get away?

Victor was thriving down in London with the composer

and his wife, and they sent back glowing accounts of his talent: Victor would go far.

Sarah in the meantime had been seeking a job, but without success. The boom-time was beginning to peter out and the predicted slump came insidiously creeping in. Men were finding it difficult to get employment. Many families were emigrating. Big posters everywhere proclaimed America as the Land of Opportunity. There were similar ones praising South Africa. Although whole families were emigrating there were others who had no hope of going.

Men in uniform were reduced to begging in the streets and the number grew daily: men minus an arm or a leg, blinded men being led by a small child. Some men played a harmonica, others a tin whistle or a trumpet. The tune most played was *'Roses of Picardy'*. When it first came out it had seemed to speak of romance. Now there was something sadly haunting about the melody.

Other men would display placards, such as: *'Help me, I have no job and a wife and six children to support'*. Another would state: *'I've suffered four years of hell on the Western Front and now I'm bound for the rubbish heap, unless you help. Give a penny, please.'*

And it was not only ordinary soldiers who were seen begging – there were officers selling bootlaces and matches from cardboard trays slung round their necks by a piece of string.

One day Sarah came in lamenting, 'Oh, those poor men having to beg!' then stopped as she saw her mother holding a letter, her eyes tear-filled. Sarah's heart missed a beat. 'Mother – bad news?'

'Sad news, Sarah, but only to me.'

Sarah waited and her mother went on in a low voice, 'You knew that I met a man when I was in the sanatorium in Scotland. You were worried because you thought I was having an affair with him. He's just died, Sarah. His wife wrote to tell me. She knew about our friendship and appreciated that Franklyn and I had helped each other over a very lonely period in our lives. Our friendship was sweet and good, Sarah. The only time we kissed was when we said goodbye. I told your father at the time and he understood. I will tell him tomorrow that Franklyn has died, but I want this day to myself to mourn him. Then I shall mourn him no more.'

'Would you have married him if you had both been free?'

'Yes, Sarah, I would, although I loved him in a totally different way from the way I love your father. I think with Franklyn it would have been a marriage of minds; we had so much in common, we both loved music and could discuss it for hours. I think we would have led a quiet life. With your father –'

Isabelle smiled but her eyes were still brimming with tears. 'With your father it's been stimulating, exciting; there have been quarrels, or should I say "discussions" – your father's word. I've been angry, hysterical at times, as you know, but we've never sulked and making up our differences afterwards has been . . . I ought not to say this to you, Sarah, but I want you to know the differences in the ways of loving different people. With your father, making up a quarrel was a wonderful experience, and I do not regret a single moment of our lives together. Do you understand what I mean?'

'Yes, I think I do.'

It was evening before Sarah sat down to think over the talk with her mother, and then she compared her marriage to Warren with her mother's feelings for Franklyn, even though they were two different types of men.

Franklyn's mind had been attuned to music, while Warren had been absorbed in learning all the aspects of business, and she felt he would always have been this way. Also, Warren had none of the wild primitiveness in his love-making that Joe had. And yet Joe could be gentle, too. They would have quarrelled, Sarah was sure of that, but then there would have been the ecstasy of making-up. Although Isabelle had not been so explicit, Sarah felt sure that this was the point she had been trying to put over.

What a mess she had made of her life. If she had not experienced Joe's love-making she might never have known a desperate sexual urge for Warren to take her. But then she did not regret one minute of the time she had spent with Joe at the cottage. It was a wonderful experience that would be with her until the end of her days.

A week or so later Isabelle came running into Sarah's bedroom waving a letter. 'It's all settled! We have a sailing date for America. Oh, Sarah, at last. Mr Jacobs will bring Victor up and he's going to hire a car to take us to Liverpool. Isn't it wonderful? And do you know what? He's paid the extra for us to travel first class. What on earth will I wear? I must go to Tynemouth to tell Lucy and Fred, then when I come back I'll call and let Mother know.'

Sarah laughed. 'Mother, calm down for heaven's sake!'

'I can't. Your father's gone to the shop. Maggie's here, she's making the breakfast. I couldn't eat a thing. Oh, Sarah, let your father know, will you?'

Before Sarah had finished dressing she heard the front door slam. When she went downstairs Maggie threw up her hands. 'If your ma gets to America without a nervous breakdown I'll eat my hat.'

Sarah poured herself a cup of tea. 'I can only pray that the operation on Victor's hand will be a success. If not –'

'Oh, it will be.' Maggie gave a knowing nod. 'I've had several visions lately. I can see him grown up, conducting an orchestra – the hall is crowded and people are wildly clapping.'

'Why, Maggie, that's wonderful. You haven't been seeing visions for a long time. What do you see for me in the future? No, don't tell me, it might be bad news.'

'I can tell you this, lovey, it's possible you could be working in an antique shop soon.'

'You've *seen* this?' Sarah's eyes were wide.

Maggie grinned. 'No, but I met Mrs Dorking on my way here. She told me about a man who's just opened an antique shop in Jesmond. He's on the lookout for a young lady assistant with some experience of clocks and other antiques.'

Sarah jumped up and Maggie waved a hand at her. 'Sit down and have your breakfast, there's no rush. You'll get the job. I'll write down the address for you.'

Sarah was not aware of eating her breakfast. When she

did set out she felt like running all the way, but she took
the tram. It was no use arriving all hot and flustered. She
must try to give a businesslike impression.

27

The shop, set between two large office blocks, was big and well-stocked. The name John Farquarson Ltd., Antiquities, was painted in old English lettering in black on a white background.

A tall, well-groomed man who was standing opening letters at a desk looked up as Sarah came in. He came forward smiling. 'Good morning.'

He was well-spoken, his manner courteous, but she was aware of blue eyes weighing her up – rather sharp eyes. Was she a prospective customer, or just someone who wanted to browse around? Sarah gave her name and stated her business. He motioned her to a seat beside the desk.

'Please sit down, Mrs Hendrix. I do want someone rather urgently, someone with some experience of the trade. My name is Julian Clayton.'

When she told Mr Clayton of her father's interest in clocks, about his business and her own and her reason for selling her stock, his eyes were full of interest.

'You sound perfect for the job, Mrs Hendrix.' He explained that the main showroom was down in London, but the company had opened shops and showrooms in several major towns and were planning to open more. He was sure that this one would be a success. The advantage, he went on, of having a number of outlets was that you could move items that were 'sticking' in various showrooms. He mentioned a wage of one pound fifteen shillings a week, but quickly added that Sarah would receive commission on every item she sold. They opened at nine o'clock and closed at seven. There would be an hour's break at midday and she would have Wednesday afternoons off. He told her the job was hers if she wanted it and she accepted without hesitation.

She arrived home breathless, having run nearly all the

way. Her father was there, having come back for a tool he had forgotten. He wanted to know all the business side of things while Maggie questioned her about her boss. Sarah answered her father's questions first, then turned to Maggie. 'He's tall, has very blue eyes and as *you* would say, "knows how many beans make five". I think I like him, I'm not sure yet, but I know I'll like the job. Mr Clayton has some beautiful things. He's letting me start next Monday on account of having to help Mother get ready for her trip.'

For the next week the Torent household was in a turmoil, what with friends and neighbours dropping in, wanting to know all about the trip and asking Isabelle to find out about job possibilities for them if they decided to emigrate.

Sarah concentrated on getting not only her mother's things properly packed, but Victor's as well. Lucy saw to small last-minute sewing jobs and to keeping Isabelle calm.

Everything was more or less under control when Sarah started her job. She loved it, and soon learned why Julian Clayton was so successful. He not only had a vast knowledge of antiques, but his charm and eloquence had the most stubborn of customers buying. Many women came in, some just to talk and make eyes at him, but everyone went out with some item, no matter how small.

Sarah was intrigued by the beautiful furniture, the exquisite porcelain, the oil-paintings and, of course, had a lively interest in all the clocks. One that she particularly liked played English airs on twelve bells. The clock itself was set between two columns and below, on a shelf, were a young couple embracing. Julian played three of the tunes for her – *The Easter Hymn, The Cornriggs Are Bonny* and *The White Cockade*, which had Sarah entranced. 'How sweet the bells sound. My father would love this.'

Julian smiled. 'I'll give you a good discount. You can have it for a hundred and fifty pounds.'

'Oh, is that all? In that case I'll take the Viennese enamelled one, too. Mother would so appreciate its gentle tick.'

Sarah was glad that Julian had a lighter side because at first he had seemed such a serious, dedicated man.

Mr Jacobs arrived with Victor, two days before they were

due to sail. They were to travel to Liverpool the next morning and stay overnight at an hotel. Everything had to be done leisurely. They arrived in the evening and there was a joyful reunion, with Victor brimming over with all that Signor Meggestrone had taught him and very excited about the forthcoming voyage.

When the three left the next morning it seemed that the whole of Berkeley Avenue was there for the send-off. Isabelle was pale, but quite calm. Maggie, wiping her eyes, declared she looked like a duchess. Isabelle did look elegant. She was wearing a honey-coloured velvet costume which she kept for special occasions, and a musquash fur coat, a last-minute gift from Henrietta and delivered by Bertha. Isabelle had been touched by it, seeing it as a peace offering. Henrietta had been dead against her going to America, insisting that the operation could have been done in England.

Mr Jacobs had hired a limousine to take them to the docks and after Isabelle had called out her last instructions, already given about ten times, they were away, with much waving and a few cheers.

Sarah said, a catch in her voice, 'Well, Poppa, we'll have to get on with life. I must go to work. See you later, 'bye!'

As the days went past Sarah found herself attracted towards Julian but was determined not to succumb to his charm. She did accept a luncheon date but it was to discuss business. Julian explained that there would be times when he had to go to certain sales. Occasionally, he would need to go to Head Office for a day – did Sarah feel capable of taking over the shop? 'Definitely,' she said firmly. 'Perfectly capable.' They discussed a number of other matters and Sarah talked with confidence about the stock. Julian seemed pleased with her.

A few days after this they rearranged all the stock more attractively in the shop and at the end of it Julian asked her if she would have dinner with him to show his thanks. She refused, made an excuse, which Julian said he knew was an excuse and asked why.

'Because I don't want any involvements,' she said.

339

'Neither do I.' His terse reply had the colour rushing to Sarah's cheeks. 'I simply suggested dinner because you had worked so hard.'

Sarah felt a complete fool. For several days Julian was cool towards her, then one morning while she was lost in thought studying a painting of a Roman soldier who reminded her of Joe, Julian came up behind her.

'And is this man your type, Sarah?'

She said quietly, 'He reminds me of someone I was once in love with, *am* still in love with. He's married.'

'I'm sorry.' There was a compassion in Julian's voice she had never heard before. 'I know how you feel. I was once in love with someone, who is also married.'

After that there was a new understanding between them and when he asked her for another date Sarah accepted.

It was the first of several pleasant evenings they spent together but although Sarah longed at times to feel a man's arms around her, she was pleased that Julian made no advances. He talked to her about his life, and his travels abroad. His parents were dead, victims of the 1918 'flu epidemic. In turn, he drew Sarah out about her own life. When she had letters from her mother she told him about them: what a wonderful voyage they had had . . . how Mr Jacobs' son and his wife were kindness itself. The surgeon was going to operate on Victor's hand soon. Meanwhile, they had been taken to classical concerts and Isabelle and Victor had been in a seventh heaven of delight . . .

One evening, Sarah went home feeling terribly restless, and finding the house in darkness went on to her father's shop. The place was also in darkness but there was a light in the room above. She rattled the door-handle and Jonathan came down.

'Sarah! Oh, I'm so sorry – I forgot the time. I intended to have a meal ready for you at home.'

'It's all right, Poppa,' she said. 'I wanted to talk.'

'Of course. Come upstairs, I'll tidy away. One of Mr MacTavish's customers asked me if I would make him a surgical boot. This is something I would like to do. My own trade is so dead at the moment.'

'And why not, Poppa? It's not as if you would be taking any trade from Mr Davies.'

Mr Davies, a young ex-soldier who had bought all Mr MacTavish's stock, had set up business near his own home. He had repaired boots in the army but was unable to make them.

The tangy smell of the leather brought the old cobbler and Eddie vividly back to Sarah's mind. It seemed ages and ages since they had died. 'There now,' Jonathan said at last, putting his patterns into a box. 'Pull up a chair, Sarah, and tell me what's troubling you.'

'I don't know, Poppa, I just feel so restless.'

'You are missing your mother and Victor, pet, and no doubt Yolande.'

Yolande had gone abroad with her parents for three months. Sarah did miss her but she was sure this was not the reason for her mood, and said so.

'Is trade bad at the shop? Perhaps you are missing talking to people.'

Sarah shook her head. 'On the contrary, we're very busy. It astonishes me, the number of people who are ready to pay big prices for antiques yet there are so many thousands of others on the poverty line.'

'That's life, Sarah. Shall we go home now and have something to eat? We can talk on the way.'

She chatted to her father about some new clocks that had come in recently and found that by the time they arrived home her restlessness had gone.

On the first day Julian went off to London on business, Sarah realised just how much knowledge she had gained from him and how she could discuss certain items with a new expertise. She also discovered that she could sell to men, but not to women. They would come again to see Julian.

When Julian learned how much Sarah had sold he was full of praise.

'You've done splendidly, Sarah, especially to sell the Chinese vase to Bertram Eccles. I usually have to use all

341

my powers of persuasion to get him to part with his money. We must celebrate . . .'

Then there came a time when Julian, who had been to a big house sale in Dunbar said, after singing her praises, 'I think we ought to go into partnership, Sarah. I'm sure we would do well.'

He had spoken lightly and she answered in like vein: 'I agree.'

But then Julian took her by the shoulders and added quietly, 'I think I mean a double partnership, Sarah – business *and* marriage.'

Although Julian had always kissed her when he brought her home after a date his kisses had been brief, and she found herself saying with surprise, 'But you haven't even met my father.'

He laughed. 'It's not your father I want to marry.'

'No, I know but–' Sarah gave a rueful smile. 'I suppose it was a stupid remark to make but usually there's some involvement with families if a couple intends marriage.'

'I'll meet your father if you wish but surely you can make a decision without his approval.'

'Yes, of course.'

'So?' He held her at arms' length. 'I'm in love with you, Sarah, very much in love. I didn't realise I could feel this way about anyone again, not after Carol. But one can't carry a banner for one person forever. Carol has a happy marriage and the man you are in love with probably has, too. How much do you love him? There's a life out there to be lived.'

Sarah drew away. 'I like you, Julian, enjoy working with you, but marriage was never in my mind. You certainly never hinted at it. I couldn't give you any sort of answer at the moment.'

Julian raised his shoulders. 'Understandable, I suppose. I have rushed things a bit.' He paused and added softly, 'It was just seeing you standing there, your eyes alight with excitement at making such good sales, and I suddenly thought how flat my life had been without you. I realised, or rather had it confirmed, how much I love you. I'll wait,

342

Sarah and–' a gleam of mischief came into his eyes, 'and come and meet your father.'

The next moment his manner was brisk. 'Think it over. In the meantime come to the office and let me show you some Egyptian bracelets I brought back with me.'

The fact that they had business to discuss eased the situation but Sarah was glad when it was time to go home and she could think over Julian's proposal alone.

Although she knew it was foolish to go on loving a man who was out of reach, how did one stop loving that person? Her Aunt Mary still loved Roger, and would no doubt go on dreaming about him until the end of her days, and yet Roger, by his behaviour, did not deserve such loyalty or love. It was true Mary was talking of marrying Bill when the time came, but then would it be fair to marry Bill while she was still bound in that way to Roger?

Sarah's thoughts drifted this way and that. She longed for her own man, her own home, longed to have a family. She liked Julian, enjoyed working with him, but could she ever really love him – and would there always be Carol between them . . . and Joe? It would not be easy to forget him. And yet how foolish it would be, as Julian said, to go on carrying banners. There *was* a life to be lived.

When her father came home she told him her problem and he was silent for a long time before answering. 'It's difficult to advise, Sarah. Love can grow out of a mutual respect, it can grow out of friendship, but it depends entirely on the couple in question. If you were to go on thinking of Joe and Julian was to go on thinking of Carol, there could be discord. A row could easily erupt if, for instance, you could not let your husband make love to you because you were thinking of another man. Or vice versa. Julian could find himself so obsessed by this girl that he could see faults in you that he had never found in Carol. Discord can evolve so easily and build up into huge proportions. One has to work hard at marriage, even when two people are deeply in love. A couple have to work doubly hard if there are problems right at the beginning.'

Jonathan laid a hand gently over Sarah's. 'I'm not trying

to create problems but trying to prevent them. If you and Julian can have a long talk and come to an understanding–'

'Yes,' Sarah said, but was still not sure of herself. And when Jonathan pointed out that she was still young enough to wait, to make sure she was doing the right thing, she said yes again.

Julian was busy all the next morning with special customers and it was not until the midday break, when he suggested to Sarah they go and have lunch together, that they had a chance to talk. She told him what her father had said and at first Julian seemed annoyed, telling Sarah she was old enough to know her own mind, but by the time they were ready to leave he said he had to admit that her father was right. He added that he would really like to meet Jonathan and Sarah said she would arrange it.

Two evenings later Julian came to supper and as Sarah had guessed, the two men cottoned on to one another right away. Julian pronounced Jonathan to be one of the most interesting men he had ever met and Jonathan said that he thought Sarah would never be dull if she married her 'boss'.

Sarah was glad that the two men got on so well, but it did not make her want to rush into marriage. 'Give me time to get to know you better, Julian,' she said.

He not only agreed but made a promise that he would not in any way make it difficult for her; he would not make any advances towards her. This seemed fine at the time to Sarah, but later became a problem. She had learned through knowing Joe that she had a passionate nature and because Julian continued to give her only a brief kiss each evening when he brought her home she had no way of knowing whether his passion could match her own. Some men put business above everything else. And yet she could not very well make advances towards Julian . . . he would take it that she wanted him to make love to her there and then.

Sarah found herself watching Julian talking to various women and felt a twinge of jealousy if he smiled at one or if a woman and he laughed together. And yet, in all honesty, she had to admit he was not really flirting.

The next time they had a night out she responded to his

kiss and immediately it was like unleashing a volcano. She could feel Julian trembling and thrills went running through her as he kissed her eyelids, her throat. 'Oh, God, Sarah,' he breathed, his voice ragged, 'how I've wanted you. We'll have to go to my flat.'

They were outside her own front door at the time and although Sarah knew she would be courting danger she had started to walk away with him when her father hailed them from down the street.

'Hello, have you forgotten your key, Sarah?'

She managed to pull herself together. 'Yes, I must have left it in my other bag.'

Jonathan said he was glad he had arrived at that moment. He brushed past them, unlocked the door and held it open for them. Julian gave Sarah an anguished look, then with an air of defeat he followed her inside.

Then Jonathan said, with a smile, 'I have news for you, Sarah. A second operation on Victor's fingers has been completely successful. A letter from your mother came by the late post.'

And with this everything else, as far as Sarah was concerned, was forgotten.

Julian's first words to Sarah the next morning were, 'Sarah, we can't go on like this. This waiting is killing me. You must give me an answer.'

And because Julian had proved to be a passionate man and because she felt so happy, Sarah said with a smile, 'It's yes, Julian.' He took her by the hand and drew her into the office, where he pulled her roughly to him.

When she surfaced she gave a shaky laugh. 'I don't know what a customer would have said at seeing us.'

'Who cares! Oh, Sarah, you've made me so happy. We shall have champagne this evening.'

Jonathan showed a quiet pleasure at the news but Sarah knew his whole being was wrapped up in the thought that Isabelle and Victor would soon be home. Isabelle had said in her letter that although they had had the most fantastic time she was now unbearably homesick and just longing to see her husband and daughter again.

On the day that Isabelle and Victor were due to arrive, Sarah had a letter from her old friend Mrs Curson containing news that took her breath away. Joe's wife had died, and he would eventually be coming home.

Sarah found herself trembling all over, her feelings in a turmoil. She felt grief for Joe's loss but an overwhelming rush of love and longing for him – and knew then that marriage with Julian was out of the question. Of course, Joe might not want her but it would be unfair to marry any man with this indestructible love she felt for Joe.

When she told Julian, his reaction was one of anger. 'You can't do this to me, Sarah, you promised. I've bought the ring! And anyway, how do you know that Joe would want you?'

'I don't. He probably won't but it would be foolhardy going into marriage the way I feel about him. As my father said, marriage has to be worked at and we would be working against all odds. You say you are over Carol, but are you, Julian? Are you?'

He told her that he was, but his voice lacked conviction. He spread his arms. 'Yesterday I felt positive I was. Now – well, I'm full of indecision again. I can't tell, I just don't know any more!'

There was such despair in his voice that she reached out a hand to him. 'Forgive me, Julian. I'll leave, of course. I'll write out my resignation now.'

'Oh, no, you won't. I'm not going to be punished yet further by losing a damned good assistant.' There was a slight catch in his voice that made Sarah feel like weeping. And she might have done so, had he not given her a smile. 'Look – I know you're right, Sarah. I think I've been aware for some time that your thoughts were elsewhere, but I didn't want to accept that you were thinking of Joe. Now, shall we get down to checking those lists?'

In spite of Julian telling her not to worry, Sarah still felt guilty and mourned for Joe's loss. But then there was the wonderful homecoming of her mother and Victor, and seeing her parents' tearful but happy reunion. Oh, the joy on Victor's face when he held up his left hand, the fingers

346

straight and strong. 'Look, Sarah, look! I can move them a little! The doctor says they'll become more flexible in time – aren't I lucky?'

Sarah hugged him. 'Oh, Victor, I'm so delighted for you. I'm sure you'll do big things in time.'

Mr Jacobs had stayed in America with his son and daughter-in-law for a time but planned to come back to London, sell up his business and emigrate permanently to America. Isabelle said he was one of the most wonderful men she had ever met.

There was so much to tell about the trip that Sarah hurried home every evening to hear more. It kept her from dwelling too much on thoughts of Joe. She had written to Mrs Curson to say that when her mother was settled in they would all be coming over to Corbridge, if that was all right. It would be so lovely to meet again.

Although Isabelle said she was sorry to hear about Joe's wife she added that it was perhaps for the best, as the girl had been seriously ailing for some time. This was something that Sarah had not been told. Perhaps she would get to know the full story when they went to Corbridge.

28

Isabelle and Victor went to visit Henrietta but Isabelle said afterwards that although her mother had wept with pleasure over the success of Victor's operation, the old lady had practically ignored her. 'Not that I care any more,' she said. 'I know now that Mother will never change, not until the day she dies. She's determined to be miserable.'

Jonathan was more tolerant. He said that Henrietta was embittered because of what had happened in her life and that actually she looked forward to company. Sarah felt a little ashamed then for not having made time to visit her grandmother while Isabelle and Victor had been away.

When Sarah told her mother about Julian, Isabelle said she thought she had been foolish to turn down his proposal. 'He loves you, Sarah, and is in a good position, which is very important in these hard times.'

'But I didn't love him enough, Mother. I know people say that love can grow, but I had doubts and in all fairness I had to be honest with him.'

'I know you *think* you are in love with Joe,' her mother went on, 'but –'

Sarah interrupted, annoyed. 'Did you *think* that you were in love with Father, *think* you were in love with Franklyn?'

Isabelle flushed. 'No, Sarah, I didn't. I'm sorry. But go carefully when we visit Corbridge. Joe will be vulnerable after losing his wife. He'll be aching for love.'

Sarah said she would be careful, but knew if Joe needed love she would not deny him.

Jenny said she would not accompany them to the Cursons' farm. She wanted to spend every minute looking for a house for when she and Andy were married.

It was a lovely spring day when Sarah, her mother and her aunt went to Corbridge. Although there was a nip in the early-morning air the sun was bright. The mild weather

348

of the previous week had brought everything forward and from the train window Sarah found pleasure in the passing scene; the lovely greens of foliage unfolding; the groups of golden daffodils, the drifts of purple and yellow crocuses. In the hedges, downy catkins were swinging in the breeze like the tails of tiny kittens.

It was a resurgence of life – the yearly cycle. Lambs were frolicking, leaping and skipping; men were harrowing the wheat.

The day before, Sarah's mind had been in a turmoil. One part of her longed to see Joe again and the other wished they could have had more time before meeting, after his wife's recent death. But once they all arrived at Corbridge she was calm again. She must stop thinking of herself – it was Joe and his family who were suffering the immediate sorrow.

Mr Curson was there with a horse-drawn wagon to meet them. Beth jumped down, her face beaming. 'Come along, the family are waiting.' She laughed. 'Mum has been baking since dawn.'

Mr Curson helped Isabelle onto the front seat and the girls sat in the back. 'Joe's changed,' Beth told them sadly. 'You know how full of fun he used to be, well, all that's gone. I know he can't be all laughy-daffy when he's lost his wife, but Joe could always come up with something to take your mind off any trouble.'

'It takes time,' Sarah said gently. 'A lot of time, as I well know, and we must remember he was more or less a prisoner for months with only Monette near his own age for company.'

Beth sighed. 'I know, I think I would have gone mad. I have to be outdoors, have space. Tell me, Sarah, what's happening in your life? It must have been a terrible disappointment to all of you when you found you couldn't get to America.'

They talked until the farmhouse came into view and then Sarah was transported back to the time of their first ever holiday in Corbridge. Those days seemed aeons away.

The family came out to greet them, and there were so

many people that it was some time before Sarah realised that Joe was not among them. Nor was he in the kitchen when they went into the house. Mrs Curson whispered to her that she would see him later.

They were all seated for a meal when he finally entered. He acknowledged Sarah, her mother and her aunt briefly and took a seat at the opposite end of the table. Sarah's heart began a slow, painful beating. Was he going to deny her the chance of having a word?

The chatter was lively so that Joe's silence passed unnoticed. Although she kept glancing in his direction he never once looked up. He was leaner in the face but still had the same strong, sturdy build. What she missed was the lovely roguish grin. He was so terribly solemn.

When they had finished the main course Joe excused himself and left. Sarah felt so choked for his unhappiness that she had a job swallowing the apple tart and cream that followed.

Amidst all the talk and bustling around as the dishes were cleared away Mrs Curson said quietly to Sarah, 'Joe has gone to his Aunt Flo's cottage. He's more or less living there. Flo has a job up at the big house now and sleeps in. I think Joe will be waiting for you, Sarah. Go and see him.'

Sarah slipped away but once more her mind raced with conflicting thoughts. Would he want to see her? He might reject her and that would be hard to bear. Had she the right to intrude on his grief? She had not even waited for him in the hope that he might come back alive from the war.

When the cottage came into sight Sarah stopped dead. Joe was in the garden digging, not vigorously as she would have expected, but leisurely, turning over the soil in a corner. The garden was neat, but without colour.

She found herself thinking back to their 'honeymoon' in the cottage, when their love-making had been as wild as the weather. Did Joe ever think about that time, or had he put her completely out of his life? It was quiet everywhere, not even a bird sang. She walked on and as a twig snapped under her feet Joe looked up. He made no move until she reached the gate then he thrust the spade into the soil. But

350

he waited. Sarah stayed at the gate. 'I wanted to see you, Joe, to have a talk.'

'Come in.' He made no move, not even when she fumbled with the catch on the gate. She opened it, walked a few steps along the path then stopped again. Joe wiped his hands on a piece of rag then offered her a cup of tea. She accepted and followed him into the living room.

Sarah was surprised at the overwhelming emotion the scene evoked, of her first visit to the cottage. The clatter of the tin bath as Joe had brought it in, his subdued laughter as he threw in the sponge, their passionate love-making . . .

He pulled up a chair. 'Sit down, I'll make you a cup of tea but then you'll have to go.' His manner was brusque. 'You must have known I wanted to be alone.'

Sarah swallowed hard. 'But your mother said – Look, I felt I couldn't go home without having talked to you alone.' He turned his back on her and the sun glinting through the window brought a gleam to his dark curly hair, making the ache she felt for his sorrow a physical thing. 'Sometimes it's good to talk,' she said quietly.

'I don't want anyone pitying me,' he retorted.

'It's not pity, it's caring.'

'*You* care?' His look was scathing. 'You married someone else, didn't you? Just leave me alone with my misery.'

Sarah began to plead. 'Joe, self-pity is a killer. You can't shut yourself away from people. And remember, my husband died, too.'

'I'm not full of self-pity!' He was shouting now. 'My misery is for someone else's suffering. You know nothing about it, you wouldn't understand. No one understands. Monette was a lovely gentle girl. She came to love me and I to love her. She would have let me make love to her but she couldn't.'

The lid of the kettle on the fire began to rattle and Joe snatched it up with such anger that the water spilling from the spout sizzled on the hot coals. He rinsed the teapot, spooned tea into it and poured on the boiling water. Sarah wished to say she didn't want any tea, it would choke her but Joe went on, 'And do you know why Monette couldn't?'

The teapot lid was put on with such force Sarah was sure he must have cracked it. 'It was because she had been brutally assaulted.'

'Oh, Joe –'

'She was working in the fields when a soldier tried to rape her.' His voice had dropped but it rose again. 'Monette fought, she hit him with a piece of wood and in revenge he violated her body with the broken branch of a tree!'

'Oh, God.'

Joe sank on to a chair and covered his face. After a while he raised his head and Sarah thought she had never seen a face so ravaged with grief and pain. 'She had been ill a long time. I don't think she ever got over it, or her parents. They were inarticulate people, unable to show their affection for their daughter. When the war was over Monette begged me to go back to England. I went because I had to see my family, show them I was alive, but I knew I would return to France and marry Monette. Her parents, I think, died of grief and weariness, then Monette died.'

Sarah went to him but made no attempt to touch him. 'Joe, I'm sorry, more sorry than I can say and I mean this.'

'I believe you.' He looked up. 'But go now, will you? Perhaps some time in the future we can meet again. I don't know, I just don't know what my plans are.'

She turned and walked slowly away, praying he would call her back, but there was a silence that hurt.

Whenever Sarah recalled that day she wondered how she had got through it without anyone guessing at her torment. To Mrs Curson's query as to what Joe had had to say she glossed over the meeting, said it would take him time to recover from Monette's death. She said she would like to come again.

But it was four months before she and Joe met again, and then it was at his request. She received a short letter from him, saying he wished to apologise for his appalling behaviour in the spring. He was going away and wanted to see her before he left: would she come straight to the cottage?

Going away? To France? After a meeting to apologise

she would be left with painful memories that caused her such anguish she wondered at times how she could bear it.

Isabelle asked her what was wrong and for the first time she unbared her soul to her mother instead of her father.

Isabelle was gentle with her. 'At one time I might have said you were being a fool, Sarah, that no man was worth such suffering but I do understand how you feel. I can only tell you that time does heal. You can't go on longing for someone who doesn't want you.' Isabelle added quietly, 'You do know that Julian still loves you.'

Sarah nodded. She had remained very fond of her boss and at times had thought she could love him, had it not been for Joe.

She wrote to Joe, telling him she would come over to the cottage on the following Saturday.

It was a glorious late summer morning when she set out to walk to the cottage from the station and although she would have enjoyed the walk under normal circumstances she went through the torment of reliving again their last meeting, his rejection of her.

On her last visit there had been no colour in the cottage garden, but now it was ablaze with the crimson of rambling roses, the lavender of wistaria, the gold of sunflowers and marigolds and the lovely blue of lupins . . .

Joe opened the gate as she approached. 'Hello, Sarah.' He had lost his gaunt look and his skin was deeply tanned.

She said hello, what a beautiful morning it was and how much she had enjoyed the walk across the fields . . . and thought how trite were their remarks, coming from two people who had been so passionately in love.

Joe had tea ready and when it was poured they sat opposite one another discussing the crops, like two farmers. She said at last, 'So you are going away, Joe. Your mother never mentioned it in her letters.'

'No, I just made up my mind before I wrote to you. I knew I had to apologise to you for my behaviour last time. My only excuse is that I was not myself that day.'

'I understood that. Where are you going – France?'

'No. I thought of emigrating to Australia. I know I shall

353

miss the family, but I need a complete change of environment. I need something to distract me, to stop me going over and over everything that has happened.'

'Distance won't make it any easier,' Sarah said gently. 'In fact, you could feel worse being among strangers.'

Joe's mouth set in a stubborn line. 'I have to get away from thoughts of Monette, and of you. I want to be thousands of miles away from you.'

'Oh, Joe, do you really hate me as much as that?'

'I don't hate you, I wish I did, then I could put you right out of my mind. I still want you and I hate myself for it.' He waved a hand at her. 'It's all right, I know you no longer care for me. You proved that all right when you didn't even wait to see if I came back alive.'

Her heart began a slow pounding. 'And it's eating into you. Is that why you went back to France, to marry Monette?'

'No, of course not, it was something I knew I had to do. She had never been shown any affection in her life.'

'So,' said Sarah quietly, 'if I had waited for you *I* would have been left without love.'

'But you didn't wait, did you? You married someone else – Warren Hendrix!'

'Yes, I did, Joe, but Warren is dead and so is Monette, God rest their souls. Oh, Joe, don't you see, we're torturing ourselves with what is past! Someone once told me it was wrong to go on loving a person who was married and out of reach, but I went on loving you . . . I can see now that I was full of self-pity. You have been through a great deal more than I have. How I grieve for poor Monette. No girl should have suffered so much. I can only hope in time, Joe, that your pain will ease. Perhaps you're right, perhaps it would be better to make a new life for yourself in Australia.' Sarah got up and going over to him, kissed him on the brow. 'Goodbye, Joe.'

In the sunlight the flowers merged into a blur. She was at the gate when Joe called to her. She stopped and he came up behind her.

'Sarah, I loved Monette for her gentleness and because

she needed me, but I always thought of you as "my woman". Yes, I would have returned to France to see Monette, but I don't honestly know whether I would have married her, had you not already been married to Warren.'

Sarah turned to face him and when she saw the anguish on his face, she touched his cheek. 'When I married Warren I was pregnant. I tried to make it a loving marriage, but I know I would have gone on loving you, in a different way, to the end of my days.'

Joe drew her to him and held her close; it was a precious moment to savour.

'I don't want to go to Australia,' he whispered. 'I want to run a garage, work with cars and tractors.' He pulled away and held her at arms' length. 'I know a place I could turn into a garage.' There was a sudden eagerness in his voice. 'I have plenty of ideas – I know I could make it a success. I want to experiment.'

Sarah sighed. 'Ideas, experiments, you are my father all over again. You'll be working all hours. I'll never see you.'

'Oh, yes, you will. I can always pop home for a cup of tea. And a little bit of loving.'

The lovely roguish glint she had missed was back in his eyes.

'Just a little bit?' she teased.

'You know how much, don't you.' His expression at that moment was tender.

'Yes,' she said softly, and offered no resistance when Joe led her back to the cottage.